Acknowledgments

I want to thank the many pastors' wives, lay-leadership workers, servants, church builders, teachers, and firestorm survivors who shared their painful, often very private, experiences with me. Many of you bear scars from "building a church." Many of you are deeply wounded and still serving in the midst of persecution. Keep the faith! Be encouraged! Man plans, but the Lord prevails.

I would like to offer my deepest appreciation to Kathy Olson, my outstanding editor, and the Tyndale team for their continued support. Also, I would like to thank Bob Coibion for sharing his expertise on building projects.

Brothers and sisters, we are one in the body and Spirit of our Lord Jesus Christ, the *only* cornerstone on which to build that which lasts forever: a relationship with our Creator, Savior, and Lord.

Francine Rivers
PSALM 127:1

and the
Shofar Blew

—— ❖ ——

FRANCINE
RIVERS

Tyndale House Publishers, Inc.
Carol Stream, Illinois

Visit Tyndale online at www.tyndale.com.

Check out the latest about Francine Rivers at www.francinerivers.com.

TYNDALE and Tyndale's quill logo are registered trademarks of Tyndale House Publishers, Inc.

And the Shofar Blew

And the Shofar Blew is a work of fiction. Where real people, events, establishments, organizations, or locales appear, they are used fictitiously. All other elements of the novel are drawn from the author's imagination.

Library of Congress Cataloging-in-Publication Data

Rivers, Francine, date.
  And the shofar blew / Francine Rivers.
    p. cm.
  ISBN 978-0-8423-6582-6 (hc)—ISBN 978-0-8423-6583-3 (sc)
    1. Church buildings—Design and construction—Fiction. 2. Architects—Fiction. 3. Clergy—Fiction. I. Title.
  PS3568.I83165 A84 2003
  813'.54—dc21   2002156552

Second repackage published in 2013 under ISBN 978-1-4143-7067-5.

Printed in the United States of America

19	18	17	16	15	14	13
7	6	5	4	3	2	1

To Rick and Sue Hahn
Faithful servants of Jesus Christ

PART I

THE CALL

CHAPTER I

———— ❦ ————

1987

Samuel Mason sat parked in his white DeSoto across the street from Centerville Christian Church. The old place was like him; it had seen better days. Half a dozen shingles were still missing from the steeple, blown off in a windstorm three years ago. The paint was chipped, revealing aging gray clapboards. One of the high, arched windows was cracked. The lawn was dying, the roses overgrown, and the birch tree in the courtyard between the church, fellowship hall, and small parsonage had some kind of beetle killing it.

If a decision wasn't made soon, Samuel was afraid he would live long enough to see a For Sale sign posted on the church property and a Realtor's lockbox on the front door. Reaching over, he picked up the worn black leather Bible lying on the passenger seat. *I'm trying to keep the faith, Lord. I'm trying to trust.*

"Samuel!" Hollis Sawyer limped along the sidewalk of First Street. They met at the front steps. Hollis gripped the rusted iron railing with his left hand, planted his cane, and hitched his hip, lifting his prosthetic leg to the second step. "Otis called. He said he'd be late."

3

"Trouble?"

"Didn't say, but I heard Mabel talking at him in the background. He sounded pretty frustrated."

Samuel unlocked the front door of the church and looked in at the once-mauve, now sun-bleached gray carpet in the narthex. Hollis winced as he limped across the threshold. Samuel left the door ajar for Otis.

Nothing had changed inside the foyer in years. Faded tracts remained stacked in perfect piles. The frayed edge of the carpet was still pulled back from the door to the small ministerial office. The dusty leaves of the silk ficus tree in the corner continued to host a spider. Another web was in the corner of a high window; someone would have to get the ladder out and swipe it down. But who would be willing to climb a ladder when a fall might land their old bones in a convalescent hospital? And calling in a professional to clean was out of the question. There was no money.

Hollis hobbled down the aisle. "It's as cold in here as a Minnesota winter."

The sanctuary smelled as musty as a house closed up all season. "I can turn on the heat."

"Don't bother. By the time the place warms up, our meeting will be over." Hollis stepped into the second pew, and hung his cane on the back of the one in front of him, as he eased himself down. "So who's preaching this Sunday?"

Samuel took the pew across from him and set his Bible beside him. "Sunday is the least of our problems, Hollis." Resting his wrists on the back of the front pew, he clasped his hands and looked up. At least the brass cross and two candlesticks on the altar were polished. They seemed the only things to have received any attention. The carpet needed to be cleaned, the pulpit painted, the pipe organ repaired. Unfortunately, the workers were fewer each year, and the financial gifts dwindled despite the generous spirits of the parishioners, all of whom were living on fixed incomes, some only on Social Security.

Lord . . . Samuel's mind went blank as he fought tears. Swallowing the lump in his throat, he looked at the empty choir loft. He remembered a time when it had been full of singers, all robed in red and gold. Now there was only his wife, Abby, who sang every few Sundays, accompanied by Susanna Porter on the piano. As much as he loved the old gal, Samuel had to admit Abby's voice just wasn't what it used to be.

One by one, the programs of the church had dried up and blown away like dust. Children grew up and moved away. The middle-aged became elderly, and the elderly died. The pastor's voice echoed with no live bodies to absorb his sage words.

Oh, Lord, don't let me live long enough to see the doors of this church locked on Sunday morning.

For nearly forty years, he and Abby had been part of this church. Their children had gone through Sunday school and been baptized here. Pastor Hank had performed their daughter Alice's wedding ceremony, then conducted the memorial service when the body of their son, Donny, had been brought home from Vietnam. He couldn't remember the last baptism, but memorial services were coming all too often. For all he knew, the baptismal had dried up.

Samuel felt dried up, too. Old, dry bones. He was tired, depressed, defeated. And now, a new tragedy had befallen them. He didn't know what they were going to do to keep the church functioning. If they couldn't find a way, what would happen to the small body of believers who still came every Sunday to worship together? Most were too old to drive, and others too shy to travel the twenty miles down the road to worship with strangers.

Are we all going to be relegated to watching TV evangelists who spend three-quarters of their time asking for money? God, help us.

The front door of the church banged shut, and the floorboards creaked under approaching footsteps. "Sorry I'm late!" Otis Harrison came down the aisle and sat in a front pew.

Samuel unclenched his hands and rose to greet him. "How's Mabel feeling?"

"Poorly. Doctor put her back on oxygen. She gets downright crabby dragging that tank around the house. You'd think she could sit a while. But no. I have to keep a sharp eye on her. Caught her yesterday in the kitchen. We had a shouting match. I told her one of these days she's going to turn on that gas burner, light a match, and blow us both to kingdom come. She said she couldn't stand eating any more frozen dinners."

"Why don't you call Meals on Wheels?" Hollis said.

"I did. That's why I'm late."

"They didn't show up?"

"Came right on time, or you'd still be waiting for me. Problem is,

I have to be there to open the door because Mabel flatly refuses to do it." The front pew creaked as Otis settled his weight.

Over the years, Samuel and Abby had spent numerous pleasant evenings at the Harrison house. Mabel had always prepared a feast: stuffed game hens, homemade angel food cakes, and roasted or steamed vegetables from Mabel's backyard garden. Otis's wife loved to cook. It wasn't a hobby; it was a calling. Mabel and Otis had welcomed new families to the church with a dinner invitation. Italian, German, French, even Chinese cuisine—she was game to try anything, to the delight of everyone who sat at their table. People used to stampede to whatever casserole or pie Mabel set on the long, vinyl-covered potluck tables. She'd sent cookies to Donny when he was stationed in Hue, Vietnam. Otis used to complain that he never knew what to expect for dinner, but no one ever felt sorry for him.

"She's still watching those cooking shows and writing out recipes. Drives herself crazy with frustration! Drives me crazy right along with her. I suggested she take up needlepoint. Or tole painting. Or crossword puzzles. Something. *Anything!* I won't repeat what she said."

"What about an electric stove?" Hollis said. "Or a microwave?"

"Mabel will have nothing to do with an electric stove. And as for a microwave, our son gave us one a couple of Christmases ago. Neither one of us can figure out how it works, except to set it for one minute and warm coffee." Otis shook his head. "I miss the good old days when I never knew what she'd have on the table when I came home from work. She can't stand long enough to make salad these days. I've tried to do the cooking, but that's been a complete disaster." Grimacing, he waved his hand impatiently. "But enough of my troubles. We've got other things to talk about, I hear. What's the news on Hank?"

"Not good," Samuel said. "Abby and I were at the hospital last night with Susanna. She wants Hank to retire."

Hollis stretched out his bad leg. "We should wait and see what Hank says."

Samuel knew they didn't want to face facts. "He's had a heart attack, Hollis. He can't say anything with a tube down his throat." Did they really think Henry Porter could go on forever? Poor Hank was way past pretending to be the Energizer Bunny.

Otis frowned. "That bad?"

"He was doing visitation at the hospital yesterday afternoon, and he collapsed in the corridor just down the hall from the emergency room. Otherwise, we'd be sitting here planning his memorial service."

"God was looking out for him," Hollis said. "Always has."

"It's time *we* looked out for his best interests, too."

Otis stiffened. "What's that supposed to mean?"

"Samuel's just had a long night." Hollis sounded hopeful.

"That's part of it," Samuel conceded. A long night, indeed, of facing the future. "The truth is, this is just one more crisis in a long series of crises we've faced. And I don't want to see this one put us under. We have to make some decisions."

Hollis shifted uneasily. "What time did you and Abby get to the hospital?"

Anytime the discussion turned toward unpleasant things, Hollis leapfrogged to another subject. "Half an hour after Susanna called us. Hank hasn't been feeling well for a long time."

Otis frowned. "He's never said anything."

"His hair has gone completely white in the last two years. Didn't you notice?"

"So's mine," Hollis said.

"And he's lost weight."

"Wish I could," Otis said with a chuckle.

Samuel strove for patience. If he weren't careful, this meeting would turn into another gab session on the miserable state of the world and the country. "About a week ago, Hank told me about a friend from his college days who's dean at a Christian university in the Midwest. He spoke very highly of him and of the school." Samuel looked between his two oldest friends. "I think he was trying to tell me where we should start looking for his successor."

"Now, wait a minute!" Hollis said. "This isn't the time to retire him, Samuel. What kind of blow would that be for a man flat on his back?" He snorted. "How would you like it if someone came into your hospital room, stood over you, and said, 'Sorry you had a heart attack, old friend, but your useful days are over'?"

Otis's face was red and tight. "Hank's been the driving force of this church for the past thirty-odd years. He's been the steadying hand at the helm. We can't do without him."

Samuel had known it wouldn't be easy. There was a time to be gentle, and a time to be direct. "I'm telling you, Hank isn't coming back. And if we want this church to survive, we'd better do something about finding someone else to stand at the helm. We're about to drift onto the rocks."

Hollis waved his hand. "Hank was in the hospital five years ago having bypass surgery. He came back. We'll just invite some guest speakers until Hank's back on his feet. Like we did the last time. The Gideons, Salvation Army, someone from that soup kitchen on the other side of town. Ask them to come and talk about their ministries. They'll fill the pulpit for a few Sundays." He gave a nervous laugh. "If push comes to shove, we can always have Otis show his Holy Land slides again."

Samuel's heel came off the floor, moving up and down silently as it always did when he was tense. What would it take to get through to his old friends? Did the Lord Himself have to blast the ram's horn in order to get them to move on? "Susanna said their oldest granddaughter is expecting a baby this spring. She said it would be nice to see Hank with a great-grandchild on his knee. They'd like to be part of their children's lives again, to sit together in the same church, in the same pew. Which one of you wants to tell Hank he hasn't earned the right to do those things? Which one of you wants to tell him we expect him to stand in that pulpit until he drops dead?" His voice broke.

Hollis frowned and then looked away, but not before Samuel saw the moisture in his eyes.

Samuel leaned his arm on the pew. "Hank needs to know we understand. He needs our thanks for all his years of faithful service to this congregation. He needs our blessing. And he needs the pension fund we set up years ago so he and Susanna have something more to live on than a monthly check from the government and the charity of their children!" He could barely see their faces through the blur of tears.

Otis stood and paced the aisle, one hand shoved in his pocket, while he scratched his brow with the other. "The market's been down, Samuel. That fund is worth about half what it was a year ago."

"Half is better than nothing."

"Maybe if I'd pulled out of tech stock earlier . . . As it is, he's going to receive about two hundred and fifty a month for forty years of service."

Samuel shut his eyes. "At least we've been able to keep up their long-term health-care policy."

"Good thing he applied in his midthirties, or we wouldn't have enough for premiums." Otis sank heavily onto the end of a pew. He looked straight at Samuel, who nodded, knowing he and Abby would have to come up with the money, as they had whenever there wasn't enough in the offering plate to meet expenses.

Hollis sighed. "Five years ago, we had six elders. First we lost Frank Bunker to prostate cancer, and then Jim Popoff goes to sleep in his recliner and doesn't wake up. Last year, Ed Frost has a stroke. His children arrive, rent a U-Haul, stick a For Sale sign in their front lawn, and move them to some residential-care facility down south. And now Hank . . ." Hollis's voice hitched. He shifted his hip again.

"So," Otis drawled. "What do we do without a pastor?"

"Give up!" Hollis said.

"Or start over."

Both men stared at Samuel. Otis snorted. "You're a dreamer, Samuel. You've always been a dreamer. This church has been dying for the past ten years. When Hank heads north, it'll be dead."

"Do you really want to close the doors, lock them, and walk away?"

"It's not what we want! It's what has to be!"

"I don't agree," Samuel said, determined. "Why don't we pray about it?"

Otis looked dismal. "What good is praying going to do at this point?"

Hollis stood. "My leg's seizing up on me. Got to move." He took his cane from the back of the pew and limped to the front of the church. "I don't know what's happening in our country these days." He pounded his cane on the floor. "I brought up all four of my children to be Christians, and not one of them attends church anymore. Only time they ever go is on Christmas and Easter."

"Probably commuting to work all week," Otis said. "It takes two people working to pay for a house these days, and then they have to replace the car every few years because they're driving so much. My son puts 140 miles on his car every day, five days a week, and his wife about half that. And then they have to pay for child care. Plus insurance, and . . ."

Yada, yada, yada. Samuel had heard it all before. The world stinks. The new generation has no respect for the older. The environmentalists are all hippies from the sixties, and the politicians are all crooks, adulterers, and worse. "We know the problems. Let's work on solutions."

"Solutions!" Otis shook his head. "What solutions? Look, Samuel. It's over. We have a congregation of what?"

"Fifty-nine," Hollis said dismally. "On the membership roster. Thirty-three made it to church last Sunday."

Otis looked at Samuel. "There. You see how it is. We haven't got the money to pay the bills. We haven't got a pastor to preach. The only child we have in the congregation is Brady and Frieda's grandson, and he's only visiting. Unless you want to take over, Samuel, I say we walk away gracefully."

"*Gracefully?* How do you shut down a church *gracefully?*"

Otis reddened. "It's finished. When are you going to get it through your thick head, my friend? The party was fun while it lasted, but it's over. It's time to go home."

Samuel felt the heat well up from deep inside him as though someone were blowing softly over the dying embers in his heart. "What happened to the fire we all felt when we came to Christ?"

"We got old," Hollis said.

"We got tired," Otis said. "It's always the same people working while the rest sit in the pews and expect everything to run smoothly."

Samuel stood. "Abraham was a hundred when he fathered Isaac! Moses was eighty when God called him out of the desert! Caleb was eighty-five when he took the hill country surrounding Hebron!"

Otis harrumphed. "Eighty must've been a whole lot younger back in Bible times than it is now."

"We came together in this place because we believe in Jesus Christ, didn't we?" Samuel clung stubbornly to his faith. "Has that changed?"

"Not one iota," Hollis said.

"We're talking about closing down the church, not giving up our faith," Otis said hotly.

Samuel looked at him. "Can you do one without the other?"

Otis puffed up his cheeks and scratched his brow. His face was getting red again. Always a bad sign.

"We're still here," Samuel said. "This church isn't dead yet." He wasn't backing down, no matter how much Otis huffed and puffed.

"There was $102.65 in the offering plate this past week." Otis scowled. "Not even enough to pay the utility bill. It's past due, by the way."

"The Lord will provide," Samuel said.

"The Lord, my foot. We're the ones paying all the time. Are you going to pay the property taxes again, Samuel?" Otis said. "How long can this go on? There's no way we can keep this church going now, especially without a pastor!"

"Precisely."

"And where are you going to get one?" Otis glowered. "Last I heard, they didn't grow on trees."

"Even with a new pastor, we haven't got the money to pay the bills. We'd need more people." Hollis sat down and stretched out his leg, kneading his thigh with arthritic fingers. "I can't drive a bus anymore, and I'm not up to going door-to-door like we did in the old days."

Otis skewered him with a look. "We haven't got a bus, Hollis. And now that we haven't got a pastor, we haven't got a service to invite them to." He waved his arm. "All we've got now is this building. And an earthquake would probably bring it down on our heads."

Hollis laughed bleakly. "At least then we'd have insurance money to send Hank off in style."

"I've got an idea." Otis's tone dripped sarcasm. "Why don't we turn this old place into a haunted house on Halloween? Charge ten bucks a head. We could pay off all our bills and have enough to give Hank a love offering."

"Very funny," Samuel said dryly.

Otis scowled. "I'm only half-kidding."

Samuel looked back and forth between the two men solemnly. "We still have thirty-three people who need fellowship."

Hollis's shoulders dropped. "All of us with one foot in the grave and another on a banana peel."

Samuel stood his ground. "I vote we call that dean."

"Okay." Otis raised his hands. "*Okay!* If that's what you're after, you've got my vote. Call that dean. See what he can do for us. Nothing, I'm betting. Call whomever you want. Call God, if He's bothering to listen anymore. Call the president of the United States for all I care. I'm going home and make sure my wife hasn't set the kitchen or herself on fire." Shoulders slumped, Otis walked up the aisle.

For all Otis's bluster and protestations, Samuel knew his old friend didn't want to give up any more than he did. "Thanks, Otis."

"Just don't go getting some hotshot who'll bring drums and an electric guitar!" Otis called over his shoulder.

Samuel laughed. "That might be just what we need, old buddy."

"Over my dead body!" The front door of the church banged shut.

Hollis hauled himself to his feet, took his cane from the back of the pew, and sighed deeply. He looked around for a long moment. "You know . . ." His eyes went shiny. His mouth worked. Pressing his trembling lips together, he shook his head. Raising his cane in a faint salute, he limped up the aisle.

"Keep the faith, brother."

"Night," Hollis said hoarsely. The door opened again and closed firmly.

Silence filled the church.

Samuel put his hand on his Bible, but didn't pick it up. He prayed, tears running down his cheeks.

———— ❧ ————

Samuel drove up the narrow driveway, passed under the carport, and pulled into his garage. The back door of his small American bungalow opened, and Abby stood in the light waiting for him. She kissed him as he crossed the threshold. "How did the meeting go?"

He touched her cheek tenderly. "I'm going to call Hank's friend tomorrow."

"Thank God." She crossed the kitchen. "Sit down, honey. I'll have your supper warmed up in a few minutes."

Samuel put his Bible on the white Formica table, pulled back a chrome chair, and sat on the red vinyl seat. "We've got our work cut out for us."

"At least they'll listen to you."

"Only because they're getting too tired to argue anymore."

Abby smiled over her shoulder. "Don't get cynical this late in the game. Something like this can make us feel young again." She punched in numbers on the microwave.

"Otis says I'm a dreamer." He watched Abby put silverware and a napkin on the table in front of him. She was as beautiful to him now at seventy-four as she had been at eighteen, when he married her. He took her hand. "I still love you, you know."

"You'd better. You're stuck with me." The microwave pinged. "Your supper's ready."

"Otis was fit to be tied when he got to the church. Mabel is having a hard time of it again. Back on oxygen."

"So I heard." She set the plate before him. Meat loaf, mashed potatoes, green beans. "I called her this evening. We had a long chat." She took the chair opposite him.

He picked up his fork. "Was she behaving herself?"

Abby laughed. "I could hear someone talking about layered salads in the background; then Mabel turned the television down."

"Poor old soul."

"Oh, stuff and nonsense. Half her fun is frustrating Otis. She knows exactly which buttons to push to make him jump."

"She doesn't miss cooking?"

"Not as much as he wishes she did."

"Women. You can't live with them and you can't live without them."

She left her chair and opened the old refrigerator. She poured a tall glass of milk, set it down in front of him, and sat again. She could never sit for long. It was against her nature. She tented her fingers and watched him. Despite his lack of appetite, he ate, slowly, so she wouldn't worry.

"Susanna will be relieved, Samuel. She's wanted Hank to retire since he had bypass surgery."

"They won't have much to live on. It's not as though they have a place to sell."

"I think Susanna will miss that old parsonage. She told me they have about ten thousand in savings. Thank God we have a retirement fund to give them. Otherwise, they'd be depending on their children to help support them."

Samuel told her the bad news. Abby bowed her head, saying nothing. He set his fork down and waited, knowing she was sending up one of her desperate prayers again. When she raised her head, her face was pale, her eyes moist. He shared her shame. "I wish I'd been born rich instead of handsome." The old joke fell flat. Abby reached over and put her hand on his. He shook his head, unable to speak.

"I wonder what the Lord is doing this time," she said wistfully.

"You're not the only one."

———— ❧ ————

Paul Hudson could hear the racket the moment he opened the front door of his rental house. He shrugged off his jacket and hung it in the hall closet. He laughed when he saw his three-year-old son, Timothy, on the kitchen floor, banging on the bottom of a pot with a wooden spoon while Eunice sang, "Genesis, Exodus, Leviticus, Numbers . . ."

Grinning, Paul leaned against the doorjamb and watched them. Timothy spotted him. "Daddy!" He dropped the spoon and jumped up. Paul scooped him up, kissed him, and swung him around and up onto his shoulder.

Smiling, Eunice put a handful of wet silverware into the drain rack and reached for a towel. "How was your day?"

"Great! The class went well. Lots of questions. Good discussion. I love seeing how on fire people can get." He came over and kissed her. "Hmmm. Mommy smells good."

"We made cookies today."

"Can I have a horseback ride, Daddy?"

"If you go easy on your old man." Paul got down on all fours. Timmy swung on and clamped his skinny legs against Paul's rib cage. Paul reared up and made a whinnying sound. Timmy held on, shrieking with laughter. He kicked his heels twice into Paul's ribs. "Easy, cowboy!" Paul glanced up at Eunice laughing at them, his heart swelling. How could any man be so blessed? "Good thing he doesn't have spurs!" He allowed Timmy to ride him around the living room three times before he rolled over, spilling Timmy onto the rug. The child clambered quickly onto Paul's stomach, bouncing none too gently. "Uh! Uh!" Paul grunted.

"There's a call from Dean Whittier on the answering machine," Eunice said.

"I haven't talked with him in a while. What time is it?"

"Four thirty."

"Airplane ride, Daddy. Please!"

Paul took him by one arm and one leg and swung him around while Timmy made roaring sounds. "He never leaves the office before six." He landed his son gently on the sofa. "Let's play soccer, Timmy." He kissed Eunice before heading into the backyard. "Give me a whistle at five thirty, okay? I don't want to leave the dean hanging."

Outside, Timmy kicked the ball to him and he nudged it back. When Timmy tired of the game, Paul pushed him on the swing. When Eunice came to the door, he swung Timmy up on his shoulders and came back inside. She took him. "Time to wash up for supper, munchkin."

Paul headed for the telephone. He pushed the button on the answering machine. "This is Dean Whittier. I've had a call and I think it concerns you."

The cryptic message left Paul uneasy. He punched in the dean's number. Dean Whittier had encouraged him through his college years. Paul had tried to keep in touch, but it had been six months since he last talked with him. He was grateful for the dean's support at Midwest Christian College, especially when he had felt the pressure of everyone's expectations. Because he was the son of a well-known pastor, some people thought he must have inherited a special kind of anointing. It would've surprised everyone to know he'd never been privy to the workings of his father's church, other than understanding his dad held the reins. Paul had listened and watched parishioners stand in awe of David Hudson and jump to do his bidding.

Paul had worked hard to earn top standing in his classes. It hadn't been easy, but he hadn't dared do less from the time he was old enough to enter school. Anything less than excellence had earned his father's contempt. His father expected perfection. "Anything less than your best dishonors God." Paul had struggled to measure up, and had often fallen short of his father's expectations.

Dean Whittier had recommended Paul for the position of associate pastor at Mountain High Church, one of the biggest churches in the country. Sometimes Paul felt lost in the masses on Sunday mornings, but as soon as he entered a classroom, he felt at home. He loved to teach, especially small groups, where people could open up and talk about their lives and be encouraged in faith.

"Dean Whittier's office. This is Mrs. MacPherson. How may I help you?"

"Hi, Evelyn. How're you doing?"

"Paul! How are you? How's Eunice?"

"She's as gorgeous as ever." He winked at Eunice.

"And Timmy?"

He laughed. "He was just playing drums in the kitchen. Future music minister."

Evelyn chuckled. "Well, that's no surprise, considering Eunice's talents. The dean has someone in his office, but I know he wants to talk with you. Can you hold? I'll slip him a note and let him know you're on the line."

"Sure. No problem." He flipped through the mail while he waited. Eunice had already opened the bills. Ouch. The gas bill had gone up. So had the telephone and utilities bills. He set them aside, sifted through the junk mail from various charities pleading for money, and then flipped through the CBD pastors' catalog.

"Paul," Dean Whittier said, "sorry to keep you waiting." They exchanged greetings and pleasantries. "I talked to Pastor Riley the other day. He gave me a glowing report on your progress. He said your classes are always full and have waiting lists."

Paul felt uncomfortable beneath the praise. "There are a lot of people hungry for the Word."

"And areas that are dying for lack of good teaching. Which brings me to the reason for my call. An elder from a small church in Centerville, California, called me this morning. Their pastor's an old friend of mine. He had a heart attack and isn't up to coming back. The elder said the church will fold without someone in the pulpit. The congregation is down to about fifty members, most over sixty-five. They have some assets. They own a hundred-year-old sanctuary, a fellowship hall built in the sixties, and a small parsonage, where the pastor can live rent-free. The Lord immediately put you on my mind."

Paul didn't know what to say.

"The town is somewhere in the Central Valley between Sacramento and Bakersfield. You'd be closer to your parents."

The Central Valley. Paul was familiar with the area. He'd been reared in Southern California. Every summer, his mother had driven him north to visit his aunt and uncle in Modesto. Some of his best memories from childhood involved those weeks with his cousins. His father had never come along, always claiming work at the church that demanded his attention. When Paul had gotten up the courage to ask him why he avoided his aunt and uncle, his father had said, "They're nice people,

Paul, if all you want to do is play. But I don't have time for people who have no interest in building up the Kingdom."

The summer after that, Paul's mother had headed north without him, and Paul had gone to a Christian camp on Catalina Island instead.

Sometimes Paul wondered about those cousins who had long since grown up and moved away. They were the few relatives he had on his mother's side. His father was an only child. Grandma Hudson had died long before Paul was born, and Paul could remember very little about Grandpa Ezra, who had spent his last years in a convalescent hospital. The old man died when Paul was eight. Paul remembered feeling relieved that he would never have to go back to that foul-smelling place, or see the tears running down his mother's face every time they walked out of the depressing facility.

Odd how the mention of an area of the country could bring such a flood of memories washing over him in the space of a few seconds. He could almost smell the hot sand, vineyards, and orchards and hear the laughter of his cousins as they plotted another prank.

"You'd be a staff of one," Dean Whittier said. "And you'd be stepping into the shoes of a pastor who shepherded that church for nearly forty years."

"Forty years is a long time." Paul knew a loss like that could cause a firestorm in a church, enough of one to incinerate the congregation before he even got there. Or incinerate him if he did feel called to head west.

"I know; I know. Losing a long-standing pastor can kill a church quicker than anything else. But I think you may be the man God is calling there. You have all the qualifications."

"I'll have to pray about it, Dean Whittier. They may be looking for someone much older and far more experienced than I am."

"Age didn't come into the conversation. And this is no time to be fainthearted. The elder wasn't looking for anything in particular. He called for advice more than anything. But it struck me after ten minutes of talking to this gentleman that he wants to do more than keep the doors open."

Paul wanted to say yes on the spot, but he held back. "You know I've dreamed of pastoring a church, Dean Whittier, but I'd better do some serious praying first. I don't want to run ahead of what the Lord wants me to do." He knew emotions could be deceiving.

"Take all the time you need. But let Samuel Mason know you're thinking about it. Here's the number so you can talk things over with him." He rattled the numbers off quickly, but Paul was ready with paper and pencil. "Talk it over with Pastor Riley and Eunice and anyone else you trust."

"I will."

"And let me know what happens."

"I'll call you for a lunch date when it's all settled, sir."

"Do that. God bless you, Paul. And say hello to that pretty wife of yours." He hung up.

Euny came into the kitchen with Timmy.

"Dean Whittier says hello."

"You look excited about something."

"You could say that." He took Timmy and settled him into his booster seat while Eunice took the casserole out of the oven. "He got a call from the elder of a small church in California. They need a pastor."

She straightened, eyes bright. "And you're being called!"

"Maybe. Maybe not. Let's not run ahead of the Lord, Euny. We need to pray about it."

"We pray every morning and evening that the Lord will lead us where He wants us to go, Paul."

"I know. I don't think Dean Whittier's call is a coincidence. Nothing happens by coincidence. I'd love to jump in and say yes, Euny. You know how much I've dreamed of having my own church. But I'm in the middle of teaching two classes. I can't just quit and walk away."

"If this is the Lord's will, it will be very clear."

"Dean Whittier gave me the name of the elder who called from Centerville Christian. Samuel Mason."

"Maybe you should call him. The term is ending in less than a month."

"A month might be too long. Their pastor had a heart attack. They need someone as soon as possible."

"Do they have an interim pastor?"

"I don't know. Their pastor has served their congregation for almost forty years, Euny." That was as long as his father had pastored his Southern California church. "It would be hard to step into that pastor's shoes."

"It would be hard."

"Dean Whittier suggested I call Mr. Mason. I suppose it wouldn't hurt. I can go over my background and experience, and explain my responsibilities here. If Mr. Mason says they can't wait, that will be the answer from the Lord. No go."

"When do you think you'll make the call?"

"Not for a few days. I want to fast and pray about it first."

Samuel was dozing in his chair when the telephone rang. Abby set aside her crossword puzzle and answered it. Samuel still dozed. The drone of television always served to put him to sleep. He would start out on ESPN, fall asleep, and wake up to Turner Classic Movies, the remote firmly in Abby's possession.

"Just a minute, please. Samuel. *Pssst. Samuel!*"

Samuel raised his head.

"Paul Hudson is calling for you," Abby said.

"Who's Paul Hudson?"

"A pastor from Mountain High Church in Illinois. He's calling in regard to your conversation with Dean Whittier."

Samuel came fully awake. "I'll take it in the kitchen." He slammed his recliner down and pushed himself up, giving a cursory glance at the television. He gave her a mock scowl. "Pulled another fast one, did you? Since the Dodgers game would be over by now, you can finish watching *The Sound of Music* with my blessing."

She gave him a smirk as she lifted the telephone. "My husband will be with you in just a moment, Pastor Hudson."

Samuel picked up the telephone in the kitchen. "I've got it, Abigail." His wife hung up. "This is Samuel Mason speaking."

"My name is Paul Hudson, sir. Dean Whittier called me last week and said you're looking for a pastor. He thought I should give you a call."

Samuel rubbed his chin. How did one go about this? "What do you think we should know about you?"

"What are you looking for?"

"Someone like Jesus."

"Well . . . I can tell you straight up that I'm a long way from that, sir."

Paul Hudson sounded young. Samuel took a pad and pen. "Why don't we start with your qualifications?"

"I graduated from Midwest Christian College." He hesitated. "It might be best if you spoke with Dean Whittier about my work there. Since graduating, I've been on staff at Mountain High Church."

"Youth?"

"New Christians. All ages."

Sounds good. "How long have you been there?"

"Five years. I just completed my master's in family counseling."

A jack-of-all-trades. "Are you married?"

"Yes, sir." Samuel could hear the smile in Hudson's voice. "My wife's name is Eunice. I met her in college and married her two weeks after I graduated. She was a music major. She plays piano and she sings. I don't mean to brag, but Eunice is very gifted."

Two ministers for the price of one. "Any children?"

"Yes, sir. We have a very active three-year-old son named Timothy."

"Children are a blessing from the Lord." Samuel was about to launch into stories about his daughter and son, but he pulled himself up short as the pain of Donny's loss struck him again. He cleared his throat. "Tell me about your relationship with the Lord."

He leaned back against the kitchen counter as Paul dove enthusiastically into his personal testimony. Born into a Christian family. Father, a pastor of a church in Southern California. *Hudson?* The name was ringing bells in Samuel's head, but he wasn't certain if they were fire alarms or chimes.

Paul went on talking. He accepted Christ at the age of ten, active in youth groups, counselor at church camps, worked summers for Habitat for Humanity. Between college classes, he volunteered at a senior-citizens center near the college. He worked with disadvantaged youth and tutored students in reading at an inner-city high school.

Paul Hudson sounded like a gift from heaven.

There was a long pause.

"Mr. Mason?"

"I'm still here." *Just flabbergasted at the energy of the young.*

"Should I e-mail my résumé?" Paul sounded embarrassed.

Samuel was drawn to his youthful zeal. "We haven't got a computer."

"Fax machine?"

"Nope." Samuel rubbed his chin again. "Tell you what. Send your résumé to me FedEx." Since there wasn't anyone on staff at the church, Samuel gave Paul his home address. "What's your situation? I'm assuming you have responsibilities at Mountain High Church."

"I work in a number of areas, but my primary responsibility right now is teaching two foundational classes."

"How long is the course?"

"Both classes will finish in three weeks. We have a covenant ceremony the week after for those who have made a decision for Christ."

"So you wouldn't be available for four to five weeks."

"That's right, sir. And if I was called, I'd need time to pack and move and settle my family."

"That would be no problem. But we don't want to move too fast. I'll notify the other elders. We all need to pray about this. Considering all your qualifications, this may not be the best place for you. We're a small church, Paul. Fewer than sixty people."

"It could grow."

It would have to grow or they couldn't afford to pay a new pastor. "Send your résumé. I'll talk with Dean Whittier again." Samuel wanted to make sure Paul Hudson was the young man the dean meant. "I'll get back to you in a week or so. How does that sound to you?"

"Wise, sir."

"I'd hire you right now, Paul, but we'd better slow down and see if this is where the Lord wants you."

"I can tend to run on overdrive, Mr. Mason. I've been praying that the Lord would call me to pastor a church."

Samuel liked the sound of his voice. "Nothing you've said to me will work against you."

They exchanged a few pleasantries and Samuel hung up. He went back into the living room.

"'Do, a deer, a female deer,'" Julie Andrews sang from the screen.

"You know this movie by heart, Abby," Samuel said. "How many times have you seen it?"

"About as many times as you've fallen asleep to *Monday Night Football*." She picked up the remote and turned the volume down, then put it back on her side table.

He sat in his recliner, tipped it back, and waited. He knew it wouldn't be long.

"So . . . ?"

"Give me the remote and I'll tell you."

"You know I'll get it back again when you fall asleep." She gave up the remote.

"He's twenty-eight, happily married, and has a three-year-old son."

"That's all you learned about him in thirty minutes?"

"Master's degree. Zealous."

"That's wonderful." She waited while he considered. "Isn't it?"

"Depends." Fire from on high could raise a church from the ashes. Misplaced zeal could burn it down.

"You could mentor him."

He looked at her over the rim of his glasses.

"Well, who else would you suggest? Otis? Hollis?"

Samuel pushed his recliner back. "We might see if we can find someone older, more experienced."

"You aren't that fainthearted, Samuel."

"I'm not exactly a mover and shaker anymore, my dear."

"You know what they say: 'Youth and skill are no match for old age and treachery.'"

"A bowl of Rocky Road would taste good right about now."

She sighed and got up. Samuel caught her hand as she came near his chair. "Give me a kiss, old woman."

"You don't deserve a kiss."

He smiled up at her. "But you'll give me one anyway."

She leaned down and planted a kiss on his mouth. "You're an old codger." Her eyes twinkled.

"You can have the remote when you get back."

He began praying over Paul Hudson the moment Abby left the room. He prayed while he ate the ice cream. He prayed while his wife watched *The Sound of Music*. When they went to bed, he prayed with her, then lay awake praying long after she went to sleep. He prayed the next day while mowing the lawn and oiling the garage door hinges and springs. He was still praying while he added motor oil to his DeSoto, rubbed a few bugs off the car's grille, and went out to trim the hedge.

Abby came out to the garage with a FedEx envelope. Paul Hudson's résumé. No moss would grow on this kid. Samuel opened the packet, read the résumé, took it inside, and put it on the table. "See what you think." He headed for the door.

"What about lunch?"

He took a banana from the bowl on the nook table and went back outside to talk some more with the Lord. He didn't come in until she called that lunch was ready. The résumé was on the table. "Well?"

Abby let out a soft whistle.

"Precisely."

He called Dean Whittier that afternoon. "He had to work to prove himself when he came here."

Samuel frowned. "Why would he have to do that?"

"His father is David Hudson. It would be hard for any man to live up to that kind of reputation."

Before Samuel had an opportunity to ask who David Hudson was, the dean charged on with the various projects Paul had started and finished while in college. The dean's secretary spoke in the background. "I'm sorry, Samuel, but I have another call. Let me just say this: Paul Hudson has the potential of becoming a *great* pastor, maybe even greater than his father. You'd better grab him while you can."

Samuel went looking for his wife. "Ever heard of David Hudson?"

"He's pastor of one of those megachurches down south. His sermons are televised. Pat Sawyer loves him." Her eyes lit up. "Oh, my goodness! You don't mean to tell me Paul Hudson is related to him, do you?"

"You could say that. He's David Hudson's son."

"Oh, this is more than we ever dreamed . . ."

"Don't start doing cartwheels yet, Abby." He headed for the door.

"Where are you going now, Samuel?"

"Out for a walk." He needed time alone to think and pray before he called the other two elders.

CHAPTER 2

—— ❧ ——

SAMUEL WENT TO THE HOSPITAL the next day and spoke to Hank and Susanna Porter about Paul Hudson. Hank said he was relieved that the church was moving ahead and looking for someone to replace him. Their son would be in Centerville on Saturday. "He's not taking no for an answer this time. He's moving us to Oregon."

When Hank's mouth trembled, Susanna put her hand over his and squeezed tenderly. "We've been talking about this for the last few years, dear. It's time."

Hank nodded. "I'll leave my library of books with the church."

Susanna looked at Samuel. "Most of the furniture will stay. We can't use much. We'll be moving into Robert's granny unit. It's one room with a kitchenette and a bathroom. Just our bedroom set, the nook table and chairs." Susanna dabbed tears from her eyes. "How soon do we have to be out of the parsonage?"

Samuel swallowed hard. "You stay as long as you need, Susanna."

Hank looked at Susanna. "I'm sorry to leave you alone to do it, but the sooner you can have things ready, my dear, the better." He looked Samuel in the eye. "If you call this young man to Centerville, he and his wife are going to need a place to live."

24

A nurse came to the doorway. "It's time for my patient to rest."

Samuel rose reluctantly, put his hand on Hank's shoulder, stepped away, and bent to kiss Susanna's cheek. He couldn't speak past the lump in his throat.

Samuel left the hospital, sat in his old DeSoto in the parking lot, and wept. Then he drove home and telephoned Otis Harrison and Hollis Sawyer.

They met at the church on Wednesday night, and he presented them with copies of Paul Hudson's résumé. They were impressed. After a long prayer, they talked for two hours about the good old days of the church and what this young man might do. Samuel suggested they pray more before they decided. Otis said they would, and then he and Hollis discussed football, aches and pains, and the idiosyncrasies of their wives. Samuel suggested they adjourn and meet again in a few days.

By the following week, they were convinced that Paul Hudson was the answer to their prayers and voted unanimously to call him and offer him the pulpit—providing the congregation agreed.

The members of the church were notified by telephone of an important congregational meeting following the worship service Sunday morning. Thirty-seven people sat through Otis Harrison's slides of the Holy Land. Twenty-one were still awake when he finished.

Abby served coffee in the fellowship hall. Samuel read Paul Hudson's résumé. Someone said it was a pity there were no cookies to go with the coffee. It was suggested the congregation hear Paul Hudson preach before they made a decision. Otis announced the church didn't have the money to send a round-trip airline ticket for an audition, and it was going to take a miracle to scrape together enough money to move the Hudsons, if they were lucky enough to get them. Which led to a discussion of Hank and Susanna and the parsonage and how they felt about someone being called to take Hank's place.

Someone asked why Hank wasn't preaching and Susanna wasn't in church. The news of Hank's heart attack was repeated—louder. Someone said Susanna had been at Hank's bedside from dawn to dark every day since the Tuesday Hank had collapsed in the corridor of the hospital.

A member noticed a water stain on the ceiling and said the roof must need fixing, which led to another discussion about the repairs needed in the sanctuary, fellowship hall, and parsonage, which in turn led to a discussion of the lawn, the hedge, and the beetle or blight killing the tree on the corner. That led someone to the medfly, past governors, the sharpshooter attacking California grapevines, droughts, blackouts, floods, and the downturn in the market, which led to rambling conversations about the Great Depression and World War II.

It was two hours past Otis's lunchtime, and his patience was thinner than flatbread. He called, loudly, for a vote. Hollis seconded. Someone asked what they were voting about. "All those in favor!" Otis shouted, face red. Two people were startled awake. Twenty-eight voted yes. Ten voted no. One was told she couldn't vote twice, so she crossed her arms and refused to vote at all.

Otis assigned Samuel Mason to call Paul Hudson and offer him the pulpit of Centerville Christian Church. "Since you were the one to call him in the first place."

Paul Hudson spoke with the senior pastor of Mountain High.

"Actually, Paul, I'm surprised you've been here as long as you have," Pastor Riley said and encouraged him to step out in faith and accept the call to California.

After speaking with Eunice, Paul called Samuel Mason with the good news. During his remaining few weeks at Mountain High, Paul finished the foundational classes, rejoiced in welcoming ten new Christians to the fold, and wrote an inspiring piece for the church newsletter about accepting the call of God to go out into the world with the gospel. He had the family car serviced, washed, waxed, and the tires rotated.

A bon voyage party was thrown for the Hudson family. The love offering was generous.

"There's more than enough for our moving expenses." Paul and Eunice both saw the gift as a reaffirmation from the Lord that Paul had made the right decision. They would even have extra to put in savings for whatever they might need when they arrived in Centerville.

On moving day, Paul rose before Eunice and packed the last few things before he awakened her. While she made coffee and put doughnuts on a tray, a crew of friends loaded the U-Haul truck.

By eight, the rental house was empty, thanks expressed, prayers offered, and good-byes said. Paul climbed into the driver's seat of the U-Haul and started off for California, Eunice following in their red Toyota, Timmy strapped into his safety harness in the backseat.

Paul had prepared two maps, with the shortest route between two points marked on both. The mileage was divided by three, and each overnight stop circled in red. Late-arrival reservations had been made, confirmation numbers recorded. Paul and Eunice wanted to waste no time in getting to California and beginning their new life.

When word spread through the church that Hank and Susanna Porter were leaving for Oregon, the entire congregation showed up to bless them, hug and kiss them, and promise to stay in touch. Even Mabel came, dragging her portable oxygen tank behind her, Otis beside her with a picnic basket of goodies his wife had cooked up for the trip north.

Tears flowed freely. Hank reminded everyone to love the Lord and love one another. He told them to embrace the young pastor coming, for Paul Hudson was the answer to many prayers. Hank told his friends to keep the faith, and then could say no more. He shook hands with some, hugged others. He finally gave in to his son's urgings and was helped into the Suburban, where a bed had been prepared in the back.

Abby embraced Susanna again before she got into the car. "We'll miss you, Susie," she said through tears.

"I'm so sorry to leave the house in such a mess, Abby." She pressed the key into Abby's hand. Leaning close again, she whispered, "I've put names on a few things in the house. Whatever's left can go to the Salvation Army."

Abby hugged her dear friend again. "Write as soon as you and Hank are settled. Tell us how you're doing."

"We'd better go, Mom," Robert Porter said.

Abby stepped back as Susanna's son helped his mother into the car and closed the door firmly. Samuel stood beside Abby and put his arm around her shoulders as the Suburban and trailer pulled away from the curb. No one moved until the trailer disappeared around the turn onto the main street. No one said a word as they walked away. Some were close enough to walk home. Several came together. One was wheeled back inside the courtesy van from a residential-care facility.

"The only one who didn't make it was Fergus Oslander," Abby said sadly.

Samuel smiled. "They said their good-byes at the hospital. Hank told me the nurse caught Fergus trying to put his pants on and ordered him back to bed."

She gave a teary laugh and blew her nose. "Well, I guess we'd better get started."

They spent the rest of the day washing out cabinets, scrubbing floors and bathrooms, and vacuuming the worn rugs. The Salvation Army truck came and took what furniture was left. Samuel and Abby loaded the few things marked for friends into the old DeSoto and dropped them off on the way home, keeping the two small boxes marked for themselves unopened until the following morning.

Abby cried as she lifted a Blue Willow teapot out of its nest of tissue paper. "She loved this set." Susanna had also given her the matching creamer, sugar bowl, and two cups and saucers.

Hank had given Samuel an olivewood carving of St. George and the dragon.

———— ❦ ————

Paul called Samuel Mason from a motel in Lovelock, Nevada, to let him know they would be arriving in Centerville by midafternoon the following day. "It's been a good trip. No problems."

"We'll be ready for you."

Paul hit traffic coming through the Sacramento area, but after nine years in the Chicago area, he was not undone by it. He kept a watchful eye on Eunice in the side mirrors so he would not lose her. Once through the jam of cars, it was easy going down Highway 99 to the Centerville turnoff.

There were only two main streets in town. Paul spotted the landmarks Samuel Mason had given him: an old courthouse that had been turned into the town library, four palm trees in front of a Mexican restaurant, and a big hardware store. Two blocks down, he turned right and drove three blocks east. The steeple towered above a line of maple trees.

Paul drove slowly past the quaint New England–style church, made a U-turn at the residential intersection, pulled up behind an old DeSoto parked in front of the small corner house, and got out of the truck. Eunice drove by, made a U-turn at the corner, and pulled up behind the U-Haul.

Standing arms akimbo, Paul looked at the church and felt joy flood him. This was his church.

Eunice came to stand beside him as Timmy headed for the courtyard. "It's beautiful, isn't it? Like something you'd see on a New England postcard."

"Yes, it's beautiful." He looked up. "It needs a lot of work."

"Pastor Hudson?"

Paul turned and faced a tall, thin, whited-haired, bespectacled gentleman walking toward him. The man was neatly dressed in tan slacks, a white button-down shirt open at the collar, and a brown alpaca cardigan sweater. "I'm Samuel Mason." He had a firm grip for an old man.

Paul introduced Eunice and Timmy. "Could we look around, Samuel?"

"Oh, there's plenty of time for that later." He extended his arm toward the small house on the corner. "My wife has dinner ready for us."

Paul was too excited to be hungry, but Eunice was quick to thank Samuel, call Timmy, and fall into step beside the elder as they walked along the unkempt hedge to the narrow cement walkway leading to the parsonage. The house was a simple rectangle without any adornment, probably a prefab added to the property.

Paul smelled the tantalizing aroma of beef stew as soon as he walked in the door. Samuel Mason ushered them through the empty, dingy living room into a lit kitchen, where Mason introduced his wife, Abigail.

"Please, sit down." She gestured to the small table with five place settings. "Make yourselves comfortable." She ladled stew into bowls. "We found that booster seat in the fellowship hall storage room."

"It hasn't been used in years," Samuel said ruefully.

Abigail put a pitcher of milk and a basket of French bread seasoned with garlic and cheese on the table. When everyone had a bowl of stew, Abigail took her seat and took her husband's right hand. When the circle was formed, it was Samuel who thanked God for traveling mercies and for sending a new pastor to the church. He asked the Lord's blessing on the food, conversation, and Paul's ministry. "Amen," said Timmy and they all laughed.

Paul was eager to ask questions about the congregation, but Abigail was quicker with questions about their cross-country journey. Eunice talked about the beautiful spaces and historical places they had seen. Paul was thankful she didn't mention they had merely driven by them all due to his eagerness to reach California.

Samuel apologized for the condition of the parsonage. "Every room could use a fresh coat of paint, but we didn't have time."

"Or the money," his wife added apologetically.

"We have some money set by," Paul said. "And Eunice is a terrific decorator." He took her hand and squeezed it.

Abigail told them how hard the Porters had worked for the church. "His health has been failing for a number of years." She told them about his collapse. "We were so sorry to see them go." She blinked, blushed, and quickly added, "Not that we aren't delighted to have you three come to us."

Eunice put her hand over the older woman's. "We understand." She told them how she had grown up in a small coal-mining town, where her father was a miner and pastor. He had served his congregation until he died of black lung disease. "The congregation never really recovered."

Paul was taken aback by Euny's comment, and prayed the same wouldn't happen here. "That was a different situation, Eunice. The mines were closing, the town dying. Centerville is small, but it's going to grow. God willing. It's within commuting distance of Sacramento."

While decaf coffee burbled in the percolator, Abigail served warm peach cobbler with vanilla ice cream. Timmy finished and fussed. "He's been a good traveler," Eunice said. "But I think he's had enough of sitting." She excused herself and went out to the car to get his box of toys.

Paul helped clear the dishes.

Samuel pushed his chair in. "Would you like to take a look at the sanctuary and fellowship hall?"

"Very much."

The church had been built in 1858 and was considered a Centerville historical landmark. "The citizens built the church before they built the courthouse you passed on Main Street," Samuel said. Over the years, the church had housed several denominations, the last of which had been Baptist. "That was in the early fifties." When word spread that the church was going to be sold, a group of ten families bought it.

"We hired Henry Porter and built the fellowship hall and the parsonage on the corner." The church enjoyed growth for two decades and then began a slow decline in membership. Children grew up and moved away. The town fell on hard times when the highway bypassed it. Local farms were purchased by corporations; almond orchards pulled out in favor of the more lucrative vineyards.

Samuel Mason unlocked the front door of the church and gave Paul a set of keys. The responsibility they represented weighed heavily in Paul's hand. Was he up to the job of reviving this church? Paul looked around the narthex, seeing the dust and cobwebs. Samuel opened a door into a small office off the narthex. There was an old oak desk, shelves still lined with books—some so worn Paul couldn't read the titles—and a large, black, rotary dial telephone. Euny would love that antique! "Hank left the books for you," Samuel said.

"That was kind of him." Paul hoped he wouldn't be expected to keep them. Most were years behind the times, and he had been building up his own personal library.

The sanctuary was cold and smelled musty. A dozen things needed fixing, painting, replacing. Some of the work he knew he could do himself. His mother had told him long ago that a pastor had to be a jack-of-all-trades. Though his father had laughed at the idea, Paul had enrolled in carpentry and plumbing classes. His skills would come in handy here.

The high, octagon-shaped pulpit was the most impressive thing in the sanctuary. It was to the left of the altar area and high enough that his voice would carry even without a sound system. He was tempted to stand in it now and try it out. Samuel opened a door to the left and led him into a wide hallway. At the back were two single-stall bathrooms and a door that led into a room that had been added behind the church. The air was cold and still. "This was the nursery," Mason told him. "It hasn't been used in ten years."

When they came back out into the corridor outside the side door of the sanctuary, Samuel opened double doors. Paul's spirits lifted as he walked into the fellowship hall. He could see the possibilities! "We used to hold cantatas every Christmas on that stage," Samuel said. There were three classrooms along one side of the hall, and a large kitchen with a functioning stove and refrigerator.

They exited through the kitchen and went down brick steps into a courtyard dominated by a towering evergreen. The lawn was patchy, but reseeding and some fertilizer would solve that. Six picnic tables with benches sat in no particular pattern. The handicap access ramp ran from the sidewalk along the west side of the church in through the back door to the corridor off the side of the sanctuary.

"So, there you have it," Samuel said, the afterglow of sunset behind his back. "There's a lot to do."

Paul smiled broadly. "I'm eager to push up my sleeves and get busy."

Eunice dried dishes while Abigail washed. "How long have you been a member of the church, Mrs. Mason?"

"Oh, call me Abby, dear."

Eunice liked Abigail Mason's warmth, and thought she was the loveliest old lady she had ever seen, with her bright, sparkling blue eyes and her white hair pulled up into a Gibson girl bun. She wore navy-blue pants and a red tunic with a wide collar. Her only jewelry was a single strand of imitation pearls and clip earrings. Some people could wear polyester and still look elegant.

"Samuel and I were young when we joined this church. Let's see now . . ." She paused, leaving her hands in the warm, sudsy water. "Our son, Donny, was about Timmy's age. Our daughter, Alice, was six. About forty years ago. Yes, I think it was forty years."

"Do your children still live in the area?"

Abby retrieved some silverware from the sudsy water. "Donny was killed in Vietnam. He was a Marine, stationed outside of Da Nang." She scrubbed the forks and put them in the rack. "And Alice moved away when she married." She scooped up more silverware and scrubbed. "She and her husband, Jim, live in Louisville, Kentucky. We don't see them as often as we'd like. They would love to fly out here for a visit, but, with three children, it's far too expensive. They offered to buy us airline tickets last year, but we didn't go." She put the last of the silverware into the drain rack.

"Why not?" Euny picked out the knives and began rubbing them dry.

"Samuel likes to keep both feet on the ground." She pulled the drain plug. "I've tried to talk him into taking a tranquilizer as soon as we get on the plane, but he won't have it. Flying brings back memories he would rather forget. The last time we flew back east, he had nightmares for days afterward." She dried her hands. "Samuel served in Europe during World War II. He was a belly gunner on a B-17." She put the towel aside. "Why don't I show you your new home?"

Seeing Timmy was content playing with his cars and trucks in the living room, Eunice followed Abby through the house. Other than the kitchen with its nook, there was a living room with a fireplace and two bedrooms with a bathroom between.

"I'm so sorry we didn't get more done," Abby said. "We only had enough time to steam-clean the carpets and wash cabinets. The tile needs regrouting and every room needs a fresh coat of paint and . . ."

"It's a wonderful house, Abby, and we're grateful to have it. Give me a few weeks and we'll have you and Samuel over for dinner again, and you'll see what we do with it." She and Paul had paid four hundred dollars a month for a two-bedroom house near Mountain High. This house was a gift from God. They would be living right next door to the church—rent-free. Though Paul's salary was very low, they might be able to meet expenses without her having to take a part-time job.

"Oh, dear," Abby said in dismay. "I hadn't even thought about what you would sleep on tonight."

"We have sleeping bags. We can begin moving things in tomorrow." She could go to the local hardware store to buy paint and rollers, and Walmart for sheets to make curtains.

"It's so good to have you here," Abby said. "There are so few of us left, but what we lack in strength, we make up for in love."

"How many do we have in our congregation?"

"Oh, not more than sixty. There are the Harrisons and Hollis Sawyer, the other two elders. And then there are the Bransons, Kings, Carlsons, Knoxes." They returned to the kitchen and sat talking. Eunice soaked up everything she could about the families who had been faithful over the years. "Oh, and Fergus. How could I forget Fergie? Hank was visiting Fergus Oslander in the hospital when he collapsed. Poor dear. Fergus has been moved from the community hospital to Vine Hill Convalescent Hospital. We have several members there now."

"If you'll give me their names, I'll take Timmy for a visit."

Abby's eyes lit up. "Of course! Let me know when, so that I can go with you and make introductions. They've all been told about Hank and Susanna's retirement, but they won't be expecting you. Oh, they will love Timmy. There's nothing like a child to lift spirits."

The men returned from their tour of the church and fellowship hall. "Can I help you carry in some boxes?" Samuel said.

"Oh no, sir; I'll take care of that."

Eunice saw the look in Samuel Mason's eyes and wished Paul had accepted his offer of help.

Samuel slipped his hand to Abby's elbow. "Well, I guess we'd better be going, so these young folks can get settled for the night."

Eunice hugged Abby. "Thank you so much for your wonderful welcome."

Paul thanked them as well and walked them to the polished DeSoto parked out front. When he came back inside, he caught Eunice up in his arms and swung her around. "What do you think?"

"If everyone is as wonderful as the Masons, it couldn't be more perfect."

He kissed her. "My thoughts exactly."

"I think Samuel Mason would've liked to carry in a box or two."

"I know, but the last thing I want to do is give one of our elders a hernia on our first night here. He's got to be over seventy, Euny."

"I know you didn't mean to do it, Paul, but I think you may have made that dear man feel useless."

"I hope not. I just didn't want to impose on him anymore. His wife fixed us dinner, and he gave me a full tour of the church. I wasn't about to ask him to move us in."

"What are we going to do about the piano and refrigerator?"

"I'll go by the high school tomorrow and find out where the local hangout is. Then I'll go there and hire a couple of teenagers. It would be good to find a crew of workers. There's a lot to be done on the church and fellowship hall." He looked around. "And this place as well."

Eunice knew it wasn't just moving or working on the church facility that Paul was considering. She knew how excited he could get when put in charge of a project or program. No doubt, he was already thinking of ways to attract young people into this dying church. Which was exactly what Abby had said Samuel had been praying for over the years. Still, Eunice wanted to caution her husband. "Don't move too fast, Paul. Wait and see the flock the Lord has given you."

Telephones were busy all over Centerville as word spread among the congregation that the new pastor and his wife and son had arrived safely. Over the next two days, half a dozen ladies came by with offerings of homemade goods to ease the Hudsons' burdens as they moved in and settled in the parsonage. Even Mabel rallied and sent a disgruntled Otis with a tray of lasagna fit for the mayor. There was hardly room for it on the counter already laden with other welcome dishes of fruit salad, apple pie and peach cobbler, meat loaf, chili, pork and beans, and carrot-and-raisin salad.

When Sunday morning rolled around, Samuel and Abigail Mason were first to arrive. Samuel offered to pass out the bulletins Paul had printed off the computer he'd set up in Hank's old office. Abby took charge of Timmy, eager to return to her old post as Sunday school teacher. A large arrangement of flowers had been sent by Paul's parents and placed on the altar, and candles were lit on each side.

Eunice came down the side aisle of the sanctuary and took her seat at the piano.

Hollis sat beside Samuel and read the bulletin. He leaned over. "Says here we should pray for our youth group." He snorted. "What youth group?"

"Paul hired four students from Centerville High to help him move into the parsonage. They're all coming back Tuesday evening for a Bible study on the book of Daniel."

Hollis's eyebrows shot up. "You don't say!"

Otis leaned forward from the pew behind. "He's wearing a suit! Why isn't he wearing a robe like Hank always did?"

"You can ask him when we have coffee and cookies after the service," Mabel wheezed testily. "In the meanwhile, stop your bellyaching."

Otis harrumphed, sat back, and crossed his arms.

Samuel looked around. Every church member who wasn't in a hospital or convalescent home was in attendance. Some whispered, nodded, smiled, their eyes alight with hope for the first time in years. Others, like Otis, sat alert and searched for anything out of order, anything that might press the boundaries of tradition.

"Well, I can say one thing for sure," Hollis said out of the corner of his mouth, gazing at young Eunice Hudson at the piano. "She is a sight for sore eyes."

"And ears," Durbin Huxley said on the other side of him.

Elmira Huxley leaned forward. "I hear she's already been out to visit Mitzi Pike at Vine Hill."

"She took roses with her," Samuel told them softly. Abby had told Eunice that Fergus had been a high school English teacher and Mitzi won prizes at the fair for her roses. When Eunice came by the house the next morning to pick up Abby, she had a bouquet of yellow roses for Mitzi and several audiobooks of classic novels for Fergus.

"Oh, you should've seen Mitzi's face, Samuel." Abby had dabbed tears. "And Fergus . . . Eunice won their hearts before I even had a chance to introduce them."

Within moments, Eunice's piano playing silenced everyone in the sanctuary. They all sat moist-eyed, listening to a beautiful medley of familiar hymns.

Paul Hudson came up the center aisle, went up the steps, and sat in the pastor's chair against the wall. Closing his eyes, he bowed his head while his young wife continued to play.

Samuel studied Paul Hudson. How strange it was to see such a young man sitting in Hank Porter's place. He prayed for the old friends scattered around the sanctuary, knowing some would see Paul Hudson as a boy to be coddled and cajoled, or controlled and commanded. A new pastor was bound to bring new ways. *Lord, only one thing is important. You are Lord, our Lord. Keep us united in Spirit and in love.*

Trust wouldn't come overnight. He hoped Paul was up there praying for wisdom as he sat in Hank's old chair. Hank might not have lit fires in the hearts of his parishioners, but he had kept them safe in the sheepfold through four long decades. Samuel hoped when Paul Hudson looked out over his small flock that he wouldn't see just age and infirmities, but hearts needing to be built up in the Spirit of the Lord.

Eunice's prelude ended with a melodious cascade of notes and a delicate chord. She rose gracefully, came down the steps, and took a seat in the front pew. A waiting silence fell over the congregation. Samuel doubted he was the only one holding his breath when Paul rose and stepped up to the pulpit.

Paul hoped those looking up at him couldn't tell how nervous he was. His palms were sweating, his heart pounding, his throat dry. He took a deep breath and slowly exhaled through his nose as he looked out over his small flock of elderly parishioners.

Samuel Mason was sitting in the second row, flanked by an older man with a cane and another elderly couple. Paul smiled at him, thankful for his presence. Old couples were scattered around the sanctuary, probably sitting in seats they had occupied for the past forty-plus years, the empty spaces between vacated by those who had gone to be with the Lord. He looked at Eunice in the front row, relieved at the love shining in her eyes. She smiled, and his heart ached with love for her. He wanted to make her proud.

Oh, Father, give me Your words to speak to these people. I'm like a frightened child. I don't want to fail You. I want to build Your church so that Your light will shine in their hearts. They look so old and frail.

"I am humbled to be called here to serve you." Paul made eye contact with as many as he could. He acknowledged his youth and inexperience and talked about youth and passion, using the apostle John and disciple Timothy as examples. He talked about how the Lord measured success, and how God chose farmers and shepherds to do His work. He spoke of the few faithful who had stood at the cross, and the frightened disciples who had hidden themselves behind locked doors until the risen Jesus had appeared to them. He spoke of the small number of faithful disciples who returned from witnessing Jesus' ascension and waited in the upper room, of one mind and heart, continually devoting themselves to prayer as they waited for the fulfillment of God's promise of the Holy Spirit.

"And when the Lord Himself indwelled them, those few faithful saints carried the gospel of salvation out into a dying world and brought new life to thousands." Paul held his hands out, palms up. "From a small handful of people, the Lord spread His Word to the world." He looked into the faces of the people God had given him to shepherd and felt a welling love for them. Some listened intently. Some dozed. "Yes, we are only a few. But God only needs a few to accomplish much. On the Day of Pentecost, the Holy Spirit filled the disciples. They ran into the streets of Jerusalem, and proclaimed God's message of redemption and salvation! Three thousand souls were saved that day. And from those three thousand came thousands more as they carried the message back to their homes in Crete, Mesopotamia, Asia, Cappadocia, Greece, Rome." He smiled tenderly at the elderly men and women. *Lord, revive them.* "We are few in number, but strong in faith. Let us pray."

Eunice returned to the piano and led the congregation in several hymns. Paul stood before the altar, a plate of crackers in one hand and a tray of small glasses of grape juice in the other. "'The Lord Jesus the same night in which he was betrayed took bread: And when he had given thanks, he broke it, and said, Take, eat: this is my body, which is broken for you: this do in remembrance of me. After the same manner also he took the cup, when he had supped, saying, This cup is the new testament in my blood: this do ye, as oft as ye drink it, in remembrance of me. For as often as ye eat this bread, and drink this cup, ye do show the Lord's death till he come.'"

Eunice played and sang another medley of hymns as Paul served Communion to each member of the congregation. "May the Lord renew your strength and bless you," he said softly to each member of his congregation.

He spoke briefly about the blessings God promised to pour upon a cheerful giver and gave the brass offering plates to Samuel and Otis. After collecting the gifts, Samuel stacked the plates and brought them forward, placing them on the altar before returning to his seat.

Paul stood on the platform before the altar and prayed for the congregation. He prayed for open hearts and passion for the Lord. He prayed for the power of the Holy Spirit to renew their strength so that each could carry the message of salvation out into the world. And he asked for the Lord's blessing on each individual who had come to the service that morning. Then he and Eunice walked up the aisle to the front door of the church and shook hands as the parishioners filed out, inviting each to stay for coffee, tea, and cookies in the fellowship hall.

"I hope he doesn't expect us to go into the mission field," one old man said, taking his wife's arm before hobbling down the steps.

"Why would we be going to a missile field?"

"Mission field, I said. *Mission* field!"

His wife tapped her hearing aid. "I think my battery is dead."

Paul's shoulders drooped. His sermon had been received by deaf ears.

Samuel Mason was the last one out of the church. His eyes were moist, his handshake firm. "Good sermon."

Eunice put her arm around Paul's waist as the last couple went down the steps. "Your sermon brought tears to my eyes and a song in my heart."

Paul wished everyone else was as easy to please.

Samuel took Abby to Denny's for lunch. "Timmy was good as gold." She sang the boy's praises for fifteen minutes before she asked about Paul and Eunice.

"He has passion, and she plays piano and sings like an angel." He smiled wryly. "You told Mabel about Eunice's visit to Vine Hill the other day, didn't you?"

Her eyes sparkled with mischief. "I knew it was the best way to get the word out to everyone else about what a wonderful young lady Eunice is. What about Paul's sermon?"

Samuel told her, "He's trying to raise the dead."

"Good!" She sipped her decaf laced with cream and sugar. "You're pleased, aren't you?"

"Yep."

"What about the others?"

"He shook 'em up."

"We all need a little shaking up now and then."

Samuel chuckled. "I don't think it's going to be a matter of now and then, Abby, but a matter of *from now on*."

Paul retreated to his church office and spent the rest of the day planning out a schedule for the week. He started up his computer, made a full list of the church members—elders first—with addresses and telephone numbers, and made lines and columns to keep track of future visits. He was going to meet every member of the church and find out how best to serve them. But he needed to meet others outside the congregation as well. The church would need younger people if it was going to survive.

He started another list. He'd call the chamber of commerce and see if there was a newcomers club. He'd drop by the high school hangout, get to know the proprietor, meet some more kids. He would make a point of meeting some of the merchants on Main Street. He would attend city council meetings and see what was going on in town. He needed to get involved in the community and let people know that the doors of Centerville Christian Church were wide open to everyone.

It wasn't until Eunice called him at five and said dinner was ready that Paul remembered he hadn't eaten all day. He'd been too excited before the service, and a little queasy before he entered the fellowship hall. He locked up the church and went home.

The kitchen counter was lined and stacked with crockery, pots, Tupperware containers, and Pyrex dishes. The mountain of food that had arrived over the last three days was gone. Euny saw his look and grinned. With a flourish of her hand, she opened the freezer so he could see the neatly packaged, family-size portions in freezer bags sardine-packed on the shelves. "I won't have to shop or cook for weeks."

"You can put the dishes in the fellowship hall and ask everyone to pick them up next Sunday."

She closed the freezer door. "I'd rather hand deliver everything. It'll give me the opportunity to get to know members of our little flock. And talk up my husband."

He sat at the table. "I could use a public-relations representative right now." She had put a nice tablecloth out, and a small bouquet of roses stood beside a single red candle. He wished he felt more like celebrating. Instead, he felt as though he had failed.

"It's your first Sunday, Paul." She stood behind him, kneading his shoulders. Leaning down, she kissed his cheek. "People need time to get to know *you*, Paul, not just what you want to do for the church."

"Where's Timmy?"

"Asleep. I fed him earlier, gave him his bath, and put him to bed." She laughed. "Abby wore him out. Bless her heart."

Paul turned his chair and drew her onto his lap. He kissed her long and hard. She tasted like heaven. What would he do without her? "I'm going to start visitations tomorrow."

She ran her fingers through the hair on the back of his neck. "They'll love you."

"It didn't feel like love."

"They're still mourning the loss of Henry Porter, Paul. But these people are eager to get to know you. Ask them a few questions; encourage them to talk about their lives. You'll be amazed."

"You were born with people skills, Euny. I had to take classes."

She kissed him again. "You're very good with people."

Five years of marriage and she still stirred him as much as she had when he first met her.

"Abby called a while ago and said Samuel was tickled with your sermon."

"Tickled." He wanted to stir them, light them up, get them off their pews and out into the community, not *tickle* them.

Euny ran her fingers through his hair again. "Samuel has been praying for revival in this church for the past ten years."

"Did he tell you that?"

"Abby told me, right after she said Samuel felt some hope after hearing you speak today."

His worries seemed smaller as her hand glided down his neck and across his shoulder. She whispered a laugh in his ear. "Paul, your stomach is growling."

"I didn't eat this morning."

"Or in the fellowship hall." She rose and went to the stove.

He followed her. "I am hungry." Smiling, he put his hands on her hips and kissed the side of her neck as she ladled thick beef stew into a bowl. He inhaled her scent, loving it. His stomach growled again.

She laughed. "You have a wolf in your belly." She nudged him aside and set two bowls on the table. She took a book of matches from her apron pocket and lit the candle. He took his seat again and watched her turn off the kitchen light. When she sat, he stared at her. She raised her brows in question.

"I love you, Eunice." So much it hurt sometimes, and scared him.

Her eyes softened and glowed. "I love you, too."

She was sweet and wise, beautiful and so strong in faith; he was sometimes in awe of her. *Lord, I never thought I'd marry an angel.* His throat closed as gratitude overwhelmed him.

Euny leaned toward him, her hands outstretched. "It took you more than one day to win my heart, Paul Hudson. It may take them a little time, too. Be patient. You'll win their hearts just as you did mine. Give them time."

He took her hands, kissed her palms, and gave humble thanks to the Lord for His blessings.

4:20 P.n.
1/9/16

CHAPTER 3

———— ❧ ————

AT SIX THIRTY, Stephen Decker entered Charlie's Diner and took a seat at the counter with the other early risers. He put his *Wall Street Journal* down as the waitress turned from the cook's counter with two breakfast plates in her hands. She gave him a double take and smiled before turning her attention to two customers several stools away. She set an omelet in front of a man in oil-stained coveralls and eggs Benedict in front of a man in a brown UPS uniform. In a fluid motion, she turned, picked up the coffeepot from its hot plate, refilled their cups, picked up another cup, and walked the length of the counter. She smiled. "Coffee?"

"Please."

She set the cup down and filled it to the brim. "Cream? Sugar?"

"Black is fine, thanks."

"I don't think I've seen you before. I'm sure I'd remember if I had."

Lifting his cup, he smiled back over the brim and took a sip of the scalding brew.

"My name's Sally Wentworth, by the way. And yours?"

"Stephen Decker."

She looked from the *Wall Street Journal* to his work shirt. Stephen wondered if she was trying to get a fix on who and what he was. "Anyone ever tell you that you look like Tom Selleck?"

"Once or twice." He smiled. "He's older."

She laughed. "Well, aren't we all? What sort of work do you do?"

"Construction."

"Carpenter?"

"A little of everything."

"You're not exactly an open book, are you?"

The cook slapped the bell twice. "Hey, Sally, quit pestering the customers. Pancakes and a Denver omelet up."

"One of these days I'm going to take that bell away from you, Charlie!" She looked back at Stephen and jerked her head. "My husband."

"I like to see you jump!" Charlie hollered from the back.

"Yeah, yeah." Laughing, she put the coffeepot on the burner and picked up the two plates. She carried them out to an elderly couple sitting in a booth by the front windows. Stephen could hear her talking to her customers. Apparently, they were regulars because she told them to say hello to their daughter and asked about their grandchildren by name.

"Hey, you there at the counter!" Charlie peered at him. "If Sally asks too many questions, just tell her to mind her own business!"

Stephen laughed. "This is quite a place you have here."

Sally sauntered back behind the counter. "We like to treat our customers like family." She pulled her tablet out of her apron pocket and her pencil from the blonde bun on her head. "Now, what can Charlie fix you for breakfast? Something lean and mean or something loaded with fat and flavor?"

"Three eggs over easy, hash browns, and a steak, medium rare."

"Good for you. You only live once. Might as well enjoy yourself while you're filling up on cholesterol." She called over her shoulder, "One he-man breakfast, Charlie! And get a move on! This guy looks hungry!" She winked at Stephen. "Want a little OJ to wet your whistle while you're waiting?"

"Sure. Why not?"

She left him alone after that, talking with the UPS driver and auto mechanic.

Stephen shook open his newspaper and read while he waited. He'd been out of the mainstream for a while. Six months in a drug and alcohol rehabilitation center tended to do that to you. He'd only been out for six weeks. He was still treading carefully, trying to stay dry in a wet world. He'd made a conscious decision to leave business behind and focus on recovery. It had been a sound decision.

Unfortunately, he'd waited too long for it to make a difference to his family. The day after he signed himself in, his wife, Kathryn, had closed out their bank accounts and checked herself out of his life, taking his five-year-old daughter, Brittany, with her. He'd faced down his first major temptation when he called home and found out the telephone had been disconnected. It took every ounce of willpower he possessed to stick to the program and not pack up and head home to an empty house and a full bottle of scotch.

He'd calmed down when a friend did some checking and learned Kathryn had moved into an apartment in Sacramento, closer to the brokerage firm where she had worked for the past four years. But when he was served with divorce papers a month into the program, Stephen had really struggled. The old urges returned. The urge to get drunk and escape the pain—until it hit him harder the morning after. Fortunately, he knew this was no solution.

"Irreconcilable differences," Kathryn had claimed.

He'd spent the next few weeks roiling in anger, casting blame, justifying and rationalizing his own behavior over the past few years. Except none of it worked this time. His counselor, Rick, didn't let him get away with it, and the regimen of the twelve-step program kept bringing him face-to-face with himself. He didn't like what he saw in the mirror.

Rick was blunt. "If you quit drinking for your wife and daughter, you'll fail. You have to quit drinking for yourself."

Stephen knew the truth of that advice. He'd tried to quit before, only to fall off the wagon. If he went back to drinking now, he knew he wouldn't stop until he was dead. So he made the decision to turn his life over to Jesus Christ, and live one day at a time. *Live,* the program said. Live and let live, which meant he had to get his own life in order and allow Kathryn to do the same with hers. It meant letting go of the bitterness and wrath that sometimes threatened to overwhelm him. It meant not blaming her for his drinking, and not accepting the role as scapegoat for all of her problems.

He'd signed the divorce papers and contacted an attorney, even though he had already decided not to contest the matter. He took the hard slap across the face when Kathryn told him through her attorney that she wanted the house in lieu of alimony. A clean break, she said, but he knew better. The local real estate market was hot, and she'd make a killing off the house he'd designed and built on a golf course near Granite Bay. He agreed, never expecting her to punch him in the stomach by refusing joint custody of their daughter. When he said he'd fight her, she kicked him below the belt by claiming he had been an abusive husband and father, citing as "proof" that he was living in a rehab center. She demanded exorbitant child-support payments and insisted they be made on a bimonthly direct-deposit basis.

When the attorney delivered the news, Stephen felt like a cockroach pinned to a display board. "Check the records and see if I've ever bounced a check or not made a payment on time. Call the bank! Interview my crew! Talk to my subcontractors! I may have downed a bottle of scotch a day, but I never laid a hand on my wife or my daughter, and I never left a bill unpaid!"

The attorney did check.

Stephen felt small satisfaction. Only a few close friends knew he had a drinking problem, and even they hadn't guessed the depth of it. And the records showed he had run a successful business and made enough to support his family in an exclusive neighborhood. He'd never been arrested on a DUI or created a public disturbance. The only disturbances had been behind the closed door of his well-insulated, luxury home.

"Be thankful she's instructed her attorney to have her name removed from anything to do with your business," his attorney told him. "California is a community-property state, and she's within her rights to ask for half of it."

Stephen knew it wasn't due to any hint of fair play on her part. She'd been through some of the harder years with him. Maybe she was afraid he'd self-destruct, and she'd get caught up in liens against spec housing projects. Construction businesses came and went with every hiccup in the economy. Kathryn just wanted every dime she could get up front. And she didn't care if that left him with only pennies to live on.

"You can fight her," his attorney had said. "You don't have to take this sitting down."

Stephen had almost given in to the temptation to hit back, and hit hard. Instead, he gritted his teeth and said he would think it over. He didn't want to react in anger this time. He wanted to respond wisely, do what was best for Brittany. And Kathryn. He could fight, all right, and probably win some rounds. She had had an affair three years ago, after she'd farmed out Brittany to a preschool. In usual form, she'd blamed him for being too insensitive to her needs, and he'd bought a bottle of Glenfiddich. He could fight her—and fill his attorney's pocket with money—while accomplishing nothing but momentary satisfaction. He didn't feel like punching back this time. They had done enough damage to one another over the past five years. Having Brittany had been an attempt to save their floundering marriage. And it had worked for two years. But how much damage had they done to their daughter during their shouting matches in the last three?

No, this time he'd swallow his pride and let Kathryn have everything she wanted. He'd crush the urge to defend himself. No more casting blame. No more rationalizing or justifying his side of things. Even if he had to go bankrupt.

Maybe when she was on her own, she'd find out he wasn't the cause of all of her problems.

He was going to put one foot in front of the other and live one day at a time. He'd faced up to his drinking problem when he checked into the Salvation Army rehab facility. Knew he was going to live with the urge to drink for the rest of his life. The first few weeks, he'd worked the program on his own terms, determined to win against alcohol, to put a finish to addiction. Loss of his wife, daughter, and home had removed any illusions that he had control over his life. He crashed and burned. But it was in the anguish that followed that he knew everything was changing from the inside out.

It wasn't until he hit rock bottom that he had been willing to look up and cry out to Jesus for help because he finally faced the fact that he was powerless. "Not by might, nor by power, but by my Spirit, says the Lord Almighty." Something happened that night that changed everything. Stephen heard what people who walked the walk were saying. He believed the promises the Bible offered. "Come to me and I will give you rest—all of you who work so hard beneath a heavy yoke."

He had been warned of the enemy on the prowl. "Read your Bible daily," Rick said. "Go to your AA meetings. Find a fellowship of believers. The biggest mistake an alcoholic can make is to isolate, going off by himself and thinking he can make it on his own." Stephen took the advice to heart, knowing it came from the voice of experience.

He'd been out of rehab for six weeks now. He read his *One Year Bible* at five o'clock every morning, attended AA meetings three times a week, and worked out at a gym when the urge to drink hit him. The house had sold two days after Kathryn put it on the market. The few pieces of furniture Kathryn had left behind went into a storage facility until he could find an apartment. By the grace of God, Stephen had a project waiting for him, and would make enough off it to keep Decker Design and Construction in the black for months to come.

A few members of his old crew made themselves available. Carl Henderson, a carpenter dubbed "Tree House" by his friends because of his six-foot-nine-inch frame, and Hector Mendoza, Stephen's "Mexican backhoe," who could be counted on to do the labor of two men. Carl had been one of Stephen's drinking buddies, so he warned him up front, "Those days are over for me." Hector, a naturalized U.S. citizen, was a devout Catholic and dedicated son, helping support his mother, father, and various siblings still south of the border.

All in all, life was bearable. It would be even better when he moved into a place of his own, rather than paying by the week at a motel on Highway 99. He'd run his business out of his house, and now that the house was gone, he was going to have to make some decisions. The thought of going back to the rush of Sacramento depressed him, but Centerville wasn't exactly his style either. He'd have to make do with his truck and fifth wheeler until the project was finished. Six months, at the most. Unless they ran into snags with the inspectors.

"Here you go," Sally said and set down a platter with three eggs over easy, hash browns, and a T-bone steak. She replenished his orange juice and filled his coffee cup to the brim.

Stephen was finishing up the last of his steak when the bell over the door jingled.

"Parson Paul's here, Charlie."

A young man entered, wearing sweats and a damp T-shirt. His sandy-brown hair was cut short. "Hey, Sally," he said with a grin. "How's business?"

"Slow this morning. I expect the crowd to come in around eight. What can I get you?"

"OJ," he said, and waved to the elderly couple sitting in the booth before he slid onto the stool one down from Stephen. "I'm Paul Hudson," he said, extending his hand.

Stephen introduced himself as he shook hands.

Sally plunked a tall glass of orange juice on the counter. "How many miles did you run this morning, Parson?"

"Took the short course. Two."

"Wimping out?" Charlie called through the cook's window.

Hudson laughed. "Something like that." He turned to greet the UPS driver. "How's your wife doing, Al?"

"Getting antsy for the baby to come."

"What does she have to go? Another month?"

"Two weeks."

The mechanic said he enjoyed Hudson's Sunday sermon. "My daughter's planning on coming to the next youth meeting. She said a couple of her friends are attending."

"We're up to twelve," Hudson said. "Tell her to bring as many friends as she wants." He turned his attention back to Stephen. "Are you a Christian?"

"I like to think so."

"Well, we'd love to have you come and visit Centerville Christian. Two blocks down, turn left; look for the steeple. The service starts at nine."

Sally chuckled. "Got to watch out, Decker. Parson Paul is always prowling the pubs for prospective converts." She zeroed in on Hudson with a sly grin. "Mr. Decker's new in town, does a little of this and that." She picked up his plate and looked at it. "Eats like a horse."

"Are you looking for work?"

"Nope. I'm building a house up on Quail Hollow."

Sally put the bill in front of Stephen. "Quail Hollow? Are you going to be working on that big place for the Athertons?"

He nodded.

"A couple of guys working on the foundation came in the other afternoon. Hector Mendoza and a giant who calls himself Tree House. You know 'em?"

"Yes, ma'am. They're the reason I'm here. They told me Charlie's Diner was the place to come for good food and friendly service. They just didn't warn me how friendly."

She laughed with the others. "Well, Hector and Tree House said the place is going to be over six thousand square feet, and only Atherton and his new wife living in it," Sally announced to everyone listening. "Can you imagine? What do people do with that much space?"

Keep their distance, Stephen thought cynically, pulling his wallet from his back pocket. He extracted a twenty and handed it to Sally, who punched the amount into the register and gave him his change. He put a 20 percent tip on the counter as he stood. "Thanks." He'd needed the few minutes of human interaction before he went back to self-inflicted solitude.

She grinned. "Good-looking *and* generous." She folded the bills and tucked them into her apron pocket. "You come back real soon, Stephen, you hear?"

"I plan on making this a regular stop." He gave her a casual salute.

The bell jingled as he went out the door. Maybe Centerville was just the place he needed to be to lick his wounds.

Eunice closed the front door of the parsonage and set off toward Main Street holding Timmy by the hand. She tossed the end of a white woolen scarf over her shoulder to keep off the fall chill and fought tears. Paul usually walked with them, but he was preparing for a meeting today. Time with him was becoming scarce and precious.

It would be Christmas soon—their second Christmas in Centerville. Why was it that troubles often occurred during the holiday season? Which meant that even more time would be taken away from the family. But it couldn't be helped. She remembered how it was growing up in a pastor's home.

Oh, how she missed her parents. The ache of loss was always greater during Christmastime. Memories flooded her, taking her back to childhood in a small Pennsylvania town and the church family her father had served as a lay pastor for twenty-five years. In some ways, Centerville reminded her of Coal Ridge. The congregation had been less than fifty and as closely knit as blood kin. Young people had grown up and moved away. Most had married "outsiders."

During spring break of Eunice's senior year at Midwest Christian,

Paul had driven her home to Pennsylvania to meet her parents. Her father's and mother's reserve had made him doubly conscious of everything he said and did, but he had been single-minded in gaining their acceptance. Not that he needed to worry. They showered him with love and attention. "I was lucky to have five minutes a day with my father," Paul had told her later. "He was always busy with church business."

Paul was becoming busier with each month that passed. She was concerned, but not distressed. She walked along the tree-lined street, thinking about her parents. How had they managed to balance home and church obligations? There had never been any doubt that they were devoted to one another as well as to the body of Christ.

Her mother and father had died within two years of one another. One of the elders had performed her mother's funeral service. Eunice had felt like an orphan when everyone walked away and left her standing at her parents' graves. She had been six months pregnant at the time. Paul had come home to Coal Ridge with her, but had been eager to return to the classes he was teaching. It was the only time she ever argued with him. Her emotions had been such a jumble, her grief so intense. Paul thought it best to go home. He'd wanted to be the one to distribute covenant papers. She'd been so hurt and angry, she said she didn't remember the Lord ever demanding that His disciples sign a piece of paper in order to have a covenant relationship with Him. Paul finally said they could stay another few days, but she knew grief didn't always fit a church schedule and said they could go back to Illinois.

A pastor's wife couldn't expect to have her husband all to herself.

During the few days they had stayed in Coal Ridge, she had tried to imagine what Paul thought of the place where she'd grown up. Shabby houses, more bars than any other kind of business, stores closed. The mine where her father and the rest of the townspeople had worked had closed down for good, and the town was dying. The few townspeople who remained eked out a living on Social Security. No pastor had come to replace her father. What bright young college graduate would want to come to a dead-end town with no prospects for the future?

Still, the church had continued, though it changed. People no longer came on Sundays to hear Cyrus McClintock preach. They came to sit in the creaking pews and pray for everyone and everything the Lord laid upon their hearts. The doors remained unlocked throughout the week so that whoever felt the nudge of the Lord could come and pray. Eunice had no doubt those precious people her father had shepherded for so many years would continue to offer up praise and pleas until the last member went home to heaven.

Centerville Christian Church was changing, too, but Eunice wasn't completely comfortable with what she saw happening. Paul's ambitions for the church were growing just as the church was growing. The pews were filling up with new people. Visitors came out of curiosity, then became regular attendees because they loved Paul's style of preaching.

Lord, what is it that's beneath my concern? Am I being selfish? Why this sense of discontent in the midst of such blessing? Help me through this. Help me see clearly.

She had tried to talk to Paul about it, but found it difficult to put her concerns into words. He still made time for her and Timmy, just not as much as before they had come here. But that was understandable. The responsibilities of a pastor were greater than those of an associate pastor.

"When we got here, there were fewer than sixty people in the pews on any given Sunday, Euny. The idea is to *build* the church, not allow it to stagnate."

Her first thought flew to Samuel and Abby Mason, both of whom lived a vibrant faith, practicing all they had been taught by the previous pastor, Henry Porter. Eunice wished she and Paul had arrived a few days earlier in order to meet this gentleman and his wife who had served so long and so faithfully and were still so well loved. "Just because there were only a few members doesn't mean their faith was stagnant."

"What would you call it when nothing is going on? Sure, they've had their little prayer meetings, and a Bible study that's been going on in Samuel's house for the past twenty years, but are they out there harvesting souls for Jesus? What do you call that kind of faith if not stagnant?"

"It was Samuel's prayers God heard, Paul. It was his prayers that brought you here."

"I know. And Samuel has been praying for revival. He told me, too. That's what I'm trying to bring, Euny. Revival!"

Eunice knew she had chosen the wrong time to talk with him and seek his counsel. Paul was always impatient on Saturday, putting the last polishes on his sermon and practicing it for Sunday morning. "I think I'll go out for a walk with Timmy."

He caught her hand. "Euny, I'm sorry. I didn't mean to sound so harsh. You just don't understand. You came from a little church that had no possibility of growth. There's potential here. God put us in the right place at the right time, but it's up to us to do His work."

It wasn't the right time to tell him he might be trying too hard to follow in his father's footsteps.

"By the way," he said as she opened the door, "we're going to start changing the music to meet the needs of the congregation."

"The congregation loves hymns."

"The older members, maybe, but the new people coming in have other tastes. The suggestion box indicates a change is needed if we're going to turn newcomers into members. We won't change everything at once, Euny, but I'd like you to introduce a new song each week, from the book we used back in Illinois."

Eunice walked along Main Street, wishing she could talk again with her father and mother. They might have been plain folks with little education, but they had possessed more wisdom than she had seen in some pastors who shepherded flocks in the thousands. Sometimes Eunice wondered if Paul wasn't being driven by his past, prodded by his own feelings of inadequacy. He'd always worked hard to prove himself worthy. His father had shown him little, if any, grace. Despite Paul's seeming self-assurance, he was a young man still desperate to gain his father's approval.

Her father had seen that in Paul and told her to encourage and love him through the years ahead, and choose her battles with wisdom. And her mother had said to be patient and willing to step aside for those in greater need. She held their advice close to her heart.

Oh, Lord, You've given me this wonderful husband. I don't deserve him.

It was a miracle Paul had even looked twice at her, a girl from a small hick town, the first in her family to go to college. From the moment she met Paul, the latest in a long family line of educated pastors, she'd thought him far too good for her. What did she have to offer a man like him, other than adoration? Everyone on campus knew who Paul Hudson was, with his impeccable Christian pedigree.

She had resisted going out with him at first because she felt unworthy. She had been flattered when he asked her out, and in love with him by the end of their first date. She had turned him down two times after that, convinced she was headed for heartbreak. But Paul was persistent.

It had been months into their courtship before she began to see the hurt and struggle within him, the burden of pain he carried from childhood. She remembered how uncomfortable she had been the first time she attended the church Paul's father had built. She'd felt out of place among the thousands of affluent parishioners in their expensive suits and adorned with real gold jewelry. And they had all sat mesmerized by David Hudson's preaching. He stood above them on a stage, holding the Bible in one hand and gesturing with the other as he paced back and forth, looking over the massive audience. He was eloquent and elegant, polished and perfect in his presentation.

She had been embarrassed when she realized Paul's mother was watching her closely. Had her feelings of disquiet shown? It was the first time in her relationship with Paul that she had felt that "check in her spirit," as her father called it. As though God was trying to show her something, and she didn't have the eyes to see. She looked closer and listened harder, but still she couldn't put her finger on what was wrong or why she was troubled. The words were right. . . .

She was feeling the same check in her spirit now.

She had few illusions, having grown up as a preacher's daughter. She would always have to share Paul with others. The demands on her husband would always be great. The needs of others would often outweigh her own. She could accept that. Still, she missed discussing the Bible with him. She was as passionate about it as he. But lately, Paul grew annoyed when she had another viewpoint. He became defensive.

Perhaps it was the strain after the elders' meeting.

She had always prayed she would marry a pastor like her father. She had worked hard so that she would qualify for a scholarship to a Christian college, knowing she was more likely to meet godly men in a godly environment. Her father had told her before sending her off on a Greyhound bus that not every young man on a Christian campus was a Christian. She told him a year later that not all professors on a Christian campus were Christians either.

She had never once questioned Paul's faith, nor did she question it now. He loved the Lord. He had been called into ministry.

Oh, Lord, let Paul experience Your grace. Let him feel Your amazing love. He had so little of it from his natural father.

He was pouring his heart into Centerville Christian. Hadn't her mother warned her that the life of a pastor was never easy and harder sometimes for his wife? "He'll get calls in the middle of the night and have to go out in the snow because someone is sick or dying or in distress. And you'll have to fix his breakfast and his lunch and thank God if you have an uninterrupted meal with him."

At least Paul received an adequate salary from the church and didn't have to work a day job in order to support his family. Even at that, she couldn't remember a time when her father hadn't been there when her mother needed him. Or when his daughter had needed him. He had *made* time. Not once had her father ever made her feel she was his last priority.

She had to stop thinking like this. Wallowing in self-pity wouldn't help. She could hunger for Paul's attention, but not be so selfish as to demand it. The other day she had been taken aback when he said, "I never knew you were so needy." She blushed in shame thinking about it. *Needy.* Was she? A clinging woman held a man back from doing what God intended. She must learn to stand beside him instead of standing in his way.

Everything was so jumbled. One doubt led to another until her mind was in confusion. She had come out for this walk to give Paul space to do what he needed. Timmy had been begging Daddy to play soccer with him, but Paul had to prepare for another meeting.

"Cast off those things that keep you from serving Christ wholeheartedly," Paul had said last Sunday.

Was it her *neediness* that made her feel cast off? Or was Paul's focus so fixed upon the task ahead that he couldn't see she needed him as much today as she had on their wedding day? *Lord, You are my constant companion. You always have time for me.*

"Eunice!"

Surprised, Eunice uttered a soft laugh, realizing she had walked over a mile to the Masons' house. "Your garden looks wonderful."

Abby's face shone with welcome as she set her weed bucket aside, brushed off her hands on her apron, and opened the gate. "I was just about to take a break. Would you like to join me for a cup of coffee?"

"I'd love it, Abby."

"Sam!" Timmy broke away and ran toward the house. "Sam!" He sounded like he was calling for help.

Eunice felt the heat pour into her cheeks. "*Mr. Mason*, Timmy. You should call him Mr. Mason."

Abby laughed. "Sam is home, Timmy. And he'll be delighted to see his little buddy."

"Sam!" Timmy stopped on the porch.

Abby opened the front door. "Samuel, you have company."

"Sam-u-el."

"It's all right, Eunice." Abby chuckled.

Timmy made a beeline through the family room to the open door that led into Samuel Mason's small study. "Sam-uuuuuu-el."

Eunice thought of how much her father would have loved Timmy. She pressed her fingers against trembling lips. *Oh, Daddy, I wish you'd lived long enough so that my son could have run to you the way he's running to Samuel Mason.*

Abby's laughter died. Her expression softened as she reached out and slipped her arm around Eunice's waist. "Come in, dear. Let's go in the kitchen. I'll fix us some coffee, and you can tell me what's troubling you."

Eunice felt as though she'd come home.

—————— ❦ ——————

Samuel had been on his knees praying when he heard Abby calling. He heard Timmy, too, and smiled. His old bones protested as he straightened. Paul Hudson had been on his mind all morning, and he took that as a need for prayer. Most of the church ladies thought he was "adorable," but the men were not so enamored, feeling the pinch of new demands.

"You'd think I'd never run a meeting before, the way he talks," Otis had blustered over the telephone a few days before. "He told me he wants an agenda at the next meeting. I always have an agenda! He wants it printed out this time and enough copies to go around. As if that's going to make a bit of difference to the way things always go. And he gave me a list he wants under the heading of *new* business. He wants a new sound system."

Samuel tried to explain that Paul was simply trying to attract more young people, but Otis was on a roll. "Attract them with what? Rock music?"

He'd tried for a little levity. "Keep your shirt on, Otis. I'm sure he wouldn't have Eunice playing rock music. Can you imagine?"

"No, but then there are a lot of other things I couldn't've imagined a few months ago either. Like serving popcorn and sodas and showing movies in the fellowship hall!"

"He showed the *JESUS* film."

"So he showed something worthwhile this time. What's he going to come up with next Tuesday night? I don't remember him even consulting us about whether he should or shouldn't be using the hall for movies. Do you?"

Samuel found himself wishing for the old days when he and Henry Porter would go out for a round of golf and talk about church needs. Now, he had to call and make an appointment with Paul to talk about anything. And the young man was ready with his position statement, which usually started with, "This worked at Mountain High."

It didn't do any good to remind Paul Hudson that Centerville Christian was a long way from a megachurch. And the fact that new people were coming to church merely served to make Paul even more certain that his methods were working. He was like a shepherd using his staff to hook people into the congregation. But Samuel was afraid he was going to use that God-given gift to bludgeon the old members like Otis who couldn't or wouldn't keep pace.

"Sam-uuu-el!" Timmy knocked on the door.

Samuel stepped to one side and opened the door. "Who's there?"

"Me."

"Me who?"

"Mewwww."

They both laughed. It was a silly game they played, but Timmy loved it. Samuel ran his hand over the boy's hair as he welcomed him into the den. Timmy headed straight for the stack of children's books on the bottom shelf beside Samuel's desk. Samuel sat in his easy chair and waited. The last three times Eunice had brought Timmy by, the child had picked the same book. It was now tucked halfway down the pile. Timmy went through the pile, one book at a time, until he reached the one he wanted. Samuel lifted Timmy, plunked him on his lap, and opened the book he'd read more than a dozen times.

When he finished the story, Timmy looked up. "Fish?"

"Yep. I'll bet they're hungry." Samuel set Timmy on his feet. He could hear Abby talking in the kitchen. Careful not to interrupt, he headed through the family room and opened the sliding-glass door. Timmy dashed outside, ran across the lawn to the waterfall in the corner of the yard, and peered into the pool at its base. "Koi!"

Samuel took a handful of food pellets from a plastic bag and poured some into Timmy's hand. Timmy held the pellets carefully and threw one at a time into the water, laughing as the gold-and-white fish surged to the surface and slithered and splashed over one another to get a pellet.

"The Lord made beautiful fish for us to enjoy, didn't He, Timmy?"

"We eat fish."

"So do we. Fish are good for eating. But we wouldn't eat these fish."

"Because they're pretty."

"No, because they're bottom-feeders. See how their mouths are formed? When they finish with these pellets, they'll go down to the bottom of the pond and feed off whatever garbage they find there." He hunkered next to Timmy, watching the swirling koi and thinking how people could swallow little bites of truth on Sunday morning and then dine on garbage all through the week. They could look beautiful, sleek, and healthy and be filled with all manner of evil. But he couldn't tell all that to a little boy. It was a lesson meant for someone older, someone willing to hear. There were other lessons that needed to be taught to a child just beginning to see the world around him, hungry for knowledge of it, openhearted to the One who had created it.

"The Lord has made all the creatures of the earth, creatures great and small, each with its purpose. Perhaps God made them so beautiful because of the dirty job they have to do in cleaning the bottom of the pond."

Timmy lost interest in the koi and wandered toward the rose garden along the picket fence. Samuel walked with him, hunkering again when Timmy pointed to a bud and wanted to know what it was. "It's the beginning of a flower. See how the long stem reaches up toward the sunlight? Soon that bud will open and we'll see a flower like this beautiful red, orange, and yellow one over here. It will last for a time and all the petals will drop, and it will become like the rose apple over here. It can be picked and made into a tea that's good for you."

He turned Timmy and tapped his chest. "Your heart is like that rosebud, Timmy. You'll grow taller, stretching up, and inside you'll want something you can't explain. And then you'll come to know Jesus, and feel the light and warmth of God shining down on you, and your heart will open little by little until you are open wide." He held a flower close so that Timmy could smell it. "People will look at you and say, 'Look how beautiful Timmy's life is because of Jesus.' And someday you'll be an old man like me, and I hope you leave something behind that will help others know that serving Jesus makes us happy."

"I know Jesus."

"Do you?"

"He wuvs me."

"Did your daddy tell you that?"

"Uh-huh. And Mommy."

Samuel felt the prick of tears behind his eyes as he ran his hand tenderly over Timmy's blond hair. "Jesus loves you very much, Timmy." He took his penknife out of his pocket and cut off a new rose just beginning to open. "You give this to your mama."

Timmy headed for the sliding-glass door. Samuel opened it for him and closed it as Timmy ran toward the kitchen. "Mama!"

"Oh, that's so pretty!"

As Samuel came in the back door, he saw Eunice lean down and kiss her son.

"I'll bet the two of you came in for a cookie." Abby held the plate so that Timmy could take one.

Samuel noticed Eunice's eyes looked puffy. Had she been crying? What about? He'd ask Abby later. "I'll just pour myself a cup of coffee, and Timmy can have his milk and cookie in the family room with me. What do you say we watch *Winnie the Pooh* together, Timmy? I haven't seen it since the last time you were here."

"Pooh!"

Settled comfortably on the sofa, feet planted on the hassock, Timmy snuggled next to him. Samuel prayed for Eunice while Pooh danced and sang on the screen. Samuel had no idea what was wrong, but he asked the Lord to be at the center of the conversation going on quietly in the kitchen. Eunice was a lovely young woman with a tender heart. He thanked the Lord for the way she had embraced all the folks in the church, even the ones who grumbled and growled. She'd won their hearts within weeks of her arrival. And she smoothed feathers Paul hadn't even known he had ruffled.

Bless her, Lord, as she has blessed us.

Paul was pent-up energy, zealous and passionate for the Lord, but he was young. He hadn't learned yet to move forward cautiously. A few of his changes had set off sparks in the congregation. Thankfully, God had been gracious enough to bring the danger to Abby's attention so that she could let him know where a little careful dousing prevented a fire from breaking out.

What had happened to Paul's visitations? During the first months of his ministry at Centerville, Paul had visited every member of the congregation. He'd wanted everyone to understand what he hoped to accomplish, and his enthusiasm, if not his ideas, had met with approval. Unfortunately, he hadn't taken people's reservations seriously enough. Now, some were digging in their heels and resisting change of any kind.

Others were disturbed at how many new people were coming into *their* church. Ninety-two people attended the last service. That was fifty-five more than had attended the first service. If numbers were the only thing that mattered, it looked as if Paul was off to a great start.

Paul still did visitation, more often to welcome new people. He had started a class on the foundations of Christianity. It would've been better received by Otis and Hollis if they had been part of the decision-making process. To be honest, Samuel had been hurt to be excluded as well. Hurt and disturbed. The last thing the church needed was a power struggle. He had tried to talk with Paul about it, but the younger man couldn't seem to understand that there were channels to swim through before you set off into deep waters.

"Surely you don't object to a class in what it means to be a Christian."

"We're to work in unity, Paul. A church can't run smoothly without elders being involved. Otis and Hollis are good men who want the same thing you do: to keep Christ at the center of all we do. Be patient." He saw the flicker in Paul's eyes. The young man got the point. He'd stomped on three sets of toes and needed to make amends. Would he be humble enough to do so?

Paul didn't say anything. He looked troubled and a little afraid. Time might help him see things more clearly. And all Samuel wanted to do was help him. "We can avert problems by having the elders read through your curriculum and give their approval."

Paul had readily agreed.

Samuel did what he could to pave the way, but Otis had needed a few weeks to let off the head of steam he'd built up. It took a month before Samuel could get Hollis and Otis to read Paul's curriculum for a six-week course in the fundamentals of Christianity. In the meantime, Samuel had read and studied Paul's course, praying the Holy Spirit would show him anything that might be doctrinally incorrect. The course was a clear presentation of the gospel of Jesus Christ. It was simple and direct with the appropriate authority of God's Word. God's grace and mercy shone through beautifully, and encouraged good works for the purpose of gladness and thanksgiving. Samuel was impressed.

Eunice had been the one to tell him that Paul had written the course while finishing his senior year in college. It was one of the primary reasons he had been offered a position at a megachurch in Illinois. "He's a gifted teacher."

Samuel believed so, too, but it took more than teaching gifts to pastor a church, especially one as small and inbred as Centerville Christian. Samuel had no doubt Paul was the answer to years of prayer. Still, good pastors weren't born; they were mentored.

What looked outstanding in a classroom or thesis was not always easy to put into everyday practice. Paul Hudson had a lot to learn about shepherding people who were two to three times his age. Otis needed correction from time to time, but if it was to come from Paul, it had better be done tenderly as a son to a father, and not as a young ship's captain giving orders to a tired, worn-down old sailor who'd spent the better part of his life in the rigging.

Lord, am I up to this? How do I mentor a young man who thinks he's learned everything he needs to know from a few years in college and watching his father run a big church? He loves You. I've no doubt of that. He's on fire. The problem is he's got a knack for setting off sparks. A sound system, for heaven's sake. Lord, You know how people get all het up over music. He's only been on the job a year, Lord, and I'm already beginning to feel like a fireman running around with a bucket of water. I don't want to put out his fire, Lord. I just want You to show me how to bank it.

12 AM

"Did God make heffalumps?"

Samuel was caught up short until he saw the screen.

"Well . . . ," Abby said from the doorway, Eunice grinning behind her.

"He made the men who thought up heffalumps," Eunice said, smiling at Samuel as she gave her son a hug. A cup of coffee and a few cookies with Abby had cheered up the young lady.

"And woozles," Abby said.

Eunice smiled at Timmy. "Thanks for watching him, Samuel."

"Anytime."

He walked with them to the door.

"Say bye-bye to Mr. and Mrs. Mason, Timmy."

"Bye-bye." He waved.

Abby walked Eunice to the gate. Eunice hugged Abby and kissed her cheek. She said something and then turned away.

Samuel waved back. "Come back soon, little buddy." Samuel waited at the door while Abby closed the gate and came up the walkway.

"Everything okay, Abby?"

"She was missing her mother and father. They haven't been gone all that long. She's still grieving, I think. Moving across country and putting down roots among strangers just brought it to the surface. And Paul has been so busy. . . ."

"Anything I can do?"

She put her arm around his waist as they walked into the house. "Just what you've been doing." She looked up at him. "Keep praying." She slipped free again and headed for the kitchen. "I should get started on dinner."

"Anything specific I should pray about?"

She cast an amused look. "Quit prying."

"Just wondering."

"You can't fix everything, Samuel. Some things only come to rights with time and attention."

"Well, I . . ."

"*Their* time and *their* attention."

He gave her a mock scowl. "You know, you're getting to be a sassy old woman."

She grinned. "Better than being a nosy old man."

——— ❧ ———

Stephen parked his GMC at the Atherton project and gathered his paperwork. A quick check confirmed that a full crew had shown up. Hammers were pounding, saber saws screaming as the work progressed.

The underground and site development had gone smoothly. The hill behind the house had been terraced, the curving driveway from Quail Hollow graded. Forms had been built with stubs up through the floor for underground connections of water, sewer, electricity, telephones, cable television, and computers.

Materials were arriving daily as the walls were framed. Roof components were due to arrive by the end of the week. Everything was under the watchful eyes of numerous inspectors who had been in, around, and over the site and structure, making certain everything was done according to the newest updated building codes.

"Well, Decker, I'd say you don't do anything by halves," an inspector had said yesterday.

"I like building a house that'll be around long after I'm gone."

If everything went according to Stephen's schedule, the project would be finished in ninety days, including the landscaping. Atherton had said initially that an acre of lawn with a scattering of ornamental trees and shrubs would satisfy him, but his young wife had managed to get his approval for a free-form pool surrounded by natural rock. Oh, and she wanted a waterfall spilling into it. Hence, the terracing. A few days later, she added to her list flagstone pathways and a gazebo with various lattices and built-in benches. Stephen did the research and informed Atherton that Sheila's latest "want list" would come to more than one hundred thousand dollars. Did Atherton want to stick to the original plans or proceed with the amendments?

"Just do whatever she wants," Atherton had said in the tone of an executive who had little time to waste and wanted his wife happy.

Building projects, even ones that went relatively smoothly, often caused friction between a husband and wife. But Stephen had the feeling the tensions he sensed between Robert Atherton and his noticeably younger wife had begun long before the ground was broken on this six-thousand-square-foot house.

He heard the crunch of gravel as a vehicle approached. Glancing over his shoulder, he saw a silver Cadillac pull in and park next to his truck. Groaning inwardly, he rolled up the blueprints. A gentleman might have gone over and opened the car door for Sheila Atherton, but Stephen decided instead to keep a safe distance. She rose from her car like Venus from the sea, swinging her long blonde hair over her shoulder as she came toward him like a model down a Paris runway. She wore figure-hugging black leather pants and a scoop-necked white sweater.

The saber saws screeched to a halt, and the hammers were noticeably silent.

If there was any doubt she knew exactly what response her getup would receive, it was quickly obliterated. She cast a radiant smile toward the crew and waved. "Hi, guys!"

Someone whistled.

"Looking good, Mrs. Atherton!" another called.

Annoyed, Stephen realized his men weren't the only ones staring. "Back to work!"

She laughed. "Oh, they don't bother me, Stephen. I'm used to that sort of reaction."

"I'm not surprised." He tried to keep his tone friendly but neutral.

She put her hand on her hip and tilted her head, a glimmer of challenge in her blue eyes. "I was on my way to Sacramento to do some shopping, and thought I'd drop by and see how things are going."

"Everything's right on schedule, *Mrs.* Atherton."

Her smile thinned. "How many times do I have to tell you to call me Sheila? You make me feel so old when you call me Mrs. Atherton." She stepped close enough for him to catch the scent of her expensive perfume. "Why don't you walk me around and show me what you've done since the last time I came by?"

"Not much has changed since the day before yesterday. And I have to get ready for an inspection." The appointment wasn't until four in the afternoon, but she didn't need to know that.

Sheila Atherton shifted. She looked toward the house and then back at him. "I've been thinking."

He knew exactly what that meant, and gritted his teeth.

"We don't have any skylights in the house, Stephen."

"We're building a skylight into the conservatory. Remember?"

"Oh, that one. I forgot about it. Well, it doesn't matter. It's not enough. I want one in the bedroom, a *big* one so that I can look up at the stars at night."

"What does Rob think about the idea?"

"Rob doesn't mind. He isn't interested in anything but business." Her eyes took on the look of steel. "He said I can do whatever I want, and I want a skylight in my bedroom."

"Well, then, I guess we'll draw up plans to put a skylight in your bedroom."

"How much extra will it cost?"

"Depends on how many stars you want to see." His little joke fell flat, so he decided to be blunt. "It'll mean amendments to the blueprints, approval, structural changes, additional time, additional money, additional inspections." You didn't just cut a hole in the roof without it causing a few problems.

"Well, just give me the proposal when it's ready. Rob will probably tell you to hire more men. He's getting impatient to move in."

"I'll work up the drawings and have an estimate ready for your husband to sign by the end of the week."

All smiles now, she stepped close. "I know it's going to be absolutely gorgeous when it's all finished. Everyone is going to envy me." She put her hand on his arm and smiled. "Why don't we have coffee together sometime? There's a lot we could talk about besides the house."

"I don't think so."

"Rob wouldn't mind."

"I doubt that."

"You'd have coffee with Rob if he asked, wouldn't you?"

"He wouldn't ask."

"Why not?"

"Neither one of us has time to waste."

All the amusement vanished as her eyes flashed. "You can be downright rude at times!"

"You and your husband hired me to do a job, *Mrs.* Atherton. That's where all my energy is going right now."

Her eyes hardened. "What makes you think I want anything more from you than that?"

She reminded him of his ex-wife, sleek and blonde, hungry for possessions and power, bored and on the prowl when she got them. Poor

Atherton. He'd probably started out thinking he had a nice, cuddly little kitten to keep him warm through his winter years, and was learning the hard way that he had a tigress by the tail. Stephen looked Sheila straight in the eye and gave her a half smile. Silence said it better than words.

"What an ego you have, Mr. Decker. As if I'd look twice at a blue-collar worker like you!" She marched off to her car.

Relieved she was leaving, Stephen opened the blueprints and started making mental estimates of the time it would take him to add the skylight. For all he knew, she'd be back tomorrow wanting to raise the roof and add dormer windows. She slammed her car door so hard he winced. Backing up, she narrowly missed the driver's side of his truck. She gave him a venomous look before she hit the gas pedal and sent up a shower of gravel from her spinning rear wheels.

"Hey, Boss," Tree House called from the scaffolding. "What'd'ya say to the lady to get her so ticked off?"

"None of your business!" As the work crew laughed, he turned away and muttered, "And that's no lady."

"Senor Decker always has trouble with the ladies," Hector said from a ladder. "Even Sally at Charlie's Diner has been asking about you."

Tree House laughed and lifted a four-by-six into place.

Stephen pointed at his friend. "Keep talking, Hector, and I'll ship you back to Mexico!"

"Hey, no problem, Decker. I was going back this winter anyway, and I'm taking a big hunk of your money with me!"

Stephen laughed.

---— ❧ —---

Tom Hadley, the inspector, came late and went over the place as though he had a magnifying glass in his hand. Stephen laid out the plans, answered his queries, asked a few of his own, and told a couple of jokes. During his years as an apprentice, Stephen had learned that inspectors could turn a seemingly easy job into a nightmare. It only made sense to see them as men or women with a job to do and a life away from job sites. A strong business was built on the right blend of mutual respect and courtesy. Harboring an adversarial attitude toward inspectors was as constructive as using dynamite to dig a trench.

Hadley was a family man, eager to brag about his son and daughter, who were in college. He was still leaning on the front of his truck and talking when Stephen's men started heading for their vehicles.

Glancing at his watch, Hadley straightened. "Didn't realize the time."

Stephen walked the site one last time. Everything looked good. He never tired of the excitement of designing and building something from the ground up. Still, for all the satisfaction he derived from his work, he couldn't shake the restlessness that gripped him frequently. He climbed into his truck, slammed the door, and drove down the hill.

He wondered whether he'd be able to talk with his daughter tonight. The past several days, Kathryn had expertly blocked his every attempt. Remembering last night's conversation set his teeth on edge. "What do you think I want?" he'd asked in response to her less-than-friendly greeting. "I want to talk to my daughter. I've been calling every evening, and getting nothing but your answering machine."

"I've been busy."

"I'm not checking up on you."

"That's good because you don't have the right."

"Could you get Brittany?"

"She's in bed."

"At six? Is she sick?"

"No, she isn't sick. Not that you'd care if she was."

"I'm calling, aren't I? Why is she in bed?"

"She's being punished. She refused to pick up her toys, and I'm not about to do it for her. She acts just like you sometimes. Stubborn, bullheaded."

"Let me talk to her."

"No. She'll see it as a reward, and that would undermine my authority as her mother."

"What about my rights as her father? I haven't gotten to speak with her in eight days, Kathryn. All I'm asking for is a few minutes."

"That's rich, Stephen. You never had time for Brittany or me when we were married. How many times did I plead for a minute of your precious time? All you ever cared about was your business or your construction buddies or some football or baseball game on television."

He clenched his teeth as he remembered the vitriol she'd poured over his head. He'd fought the urge to tell her she'd always loved the martyr role too much for him to interfere. Besides, who would want to spend time with a woman who took every opportunity to spew her litany of complaints? He'd almost asked her if she was still having an affair with her boss.

Kathryn McMurray Decker would have loved to put all the blame on him for her miserable life, but the truth was, she'd been unhappy long before they hooked up. Before he married her, she'd blamed her unhappiness on her mother's weaknesses and her father's abusive tendencies. When he met them, he could only agree, and that put her on the defensive. She started blaming whatever job or boss she had. She always started a job raving about how wonderful everyone was, and six months later would be grousing because supervisors and coworkers weren't treating her properly, or weren't giving her the raise she deserved or the credit she felt she was due.

It had taken him two years of marriage to realize that trying to make her happy was a losing battle. When he stopped trying, she blamed her misery on him. She had self-pity down to a science. But then, to make matters worse, he used her as an excuse to drink. When she told him he'd had one drink already, he'd mix another. If she said he'd had enough, he drank more just to rile her. And so the merry-go-round went, round and round, picking up speed, making them both sick.

Old habits die hard.

Every time he called and heard Kathryn's voice, the urge rose up in him again. The battle against picking up that first glass of scotch was becoming more and more difficult. He passed a liquor store, and it took every ounce of his willpower not to pull into the parking lot. He broke out in a cold sweat because he could almost taste the scotch on his tongue. He gripped the wheel.

Will this ever get any easier, Jesus?

The urge grew worse when he unlocked the door and walked into his empty apartment. The silence closed in around him like a prison. He flicked on the television and found a sports channel. Problem was it reminded him of how he used to sit in his easy chair with a drink in his hand. He flicked the television off and turned on the radio. He opened the refrigerator, but nothing in it appealed to him. Slamming it, he went back into the living room.

He was going quietly nuts in this apartment. He felt as badly as he had the first few weeks he'd checked himself into the Salvation Army facility. In desperation, he picked up the telephone and pressed one of the stored numbers.

"Hello?"

"Mindy, it's Stephen." He glanced at his watch and grimaced. "You're just sitting down to dinner, aren't you?" He could hear children's voices in the background. "I can call back later."

"No, it's all right, Stephen, really. Hold on and I'll get Rick."

Stephen leaned forward, rubbing the ridge of his nose as he held the telephone.

"Hey, Stephen, I haven't heard from you in a while. How're you doing?" His counselor's deep voice was Stephen's only lifeline.

"Not so good."

"Want to talk about it?"

"You've heard it all before. Just tell me something, will you? Does it get any easier?"

"Depends on how you look at it: as a curse or a blessing."

"Right now, it's a curse."

"Well, you made the first step in the right direction by calling me instead of pouring that first drink."

"Don't congratulate me yet."

"Are you reading your *One Year Bible*?"

"Every day."

"Have you found a church yet?"

He made excuses. *No time. Too much work to do.*

"You know what you have to do to make it work, Decker. So what's really stopping you?"

Stephen knew what he had to do all right, but that didn't make it easy. "I've never attended a church other than the services at the facility, and we were all on the same footing. Every man in that place was an alcoholic or drug addict or both."

"Oh, I get it. You figure you have to clean up your life completely before you have the right to set foot in a regular church. Right? You know, you don't have to brand an *A* on your forehead."

Stephen gave a low laugh.

"No one expects you to walk into a church and say, 'Hi, my name is Stephen Decker, and I'm a recovering alcoholic.' Save that for your AA meetings. By the way, I haven't seen you at any meetings lately."

"I know that, but it still galls me that I can't do this on my own."

"It galled me, too, Stephen. And the first time, I didn't make it because I let my pride get in the way. Remember what we talked about? The devil prowls like a lion. Alcoholics tend to live in self-imposed isolation. That makes us easy prey. Have you looked for an AA meeting?"

"There's no guarantee these feelings will go away if I do start going to church."

"And no guarantee they won't. One thing you will have, though."

"And what's that?"

"Accountability."

Back to that again. "Okay. Okay. So what's the procedure?"

"You walk in the door. You sit down, and you listen."

"Easier said than done." The last time he'd walked in, sat down, and listened to a church service, it was because it was required in order to stay in the facility and get the help he needed. By the end of the six months, he'd found himself waiting for Sundays. But he hadn't attended a service since graduating from rehab. He was thirsty again. Better if he drank deeply from the Living Water than from a bottle of scotch. "Thanks, Rick."

"Anytime. I'll pick you up for a meeting or for church. All you have to do is ask. Mindy and I are praying for you, Stephen. Every morning. Just remember. Take it one day at a time."

"Yeah." Some days were harder than others.

He hung up, but he still couldn't rid himself of the restlessness. He was hungry now, but didn't feel like cooking for himself. Grabbing his keys, he went out to find a place to eat. As he drove down Main Street, he spotted two guys from his crew going into the Wagon Wheel Saloon and Restaurant. It would be easy to pull over and join them, and hard to say no when they ordered the first round of drinks.

He found his way to Charlie's Diner instead. The parking lot had two spaces left. People. Too many people. He fought the urge to turn around and head back to the grocery store and home again, but Rick was right. He did tend to isolate himself, and the more isolated he was, the harder it was to fight the temptation to buy a bottle of good scotch and take that first drink that would send him into the black hole again.

"Hey! Stephen Decker came back, Charlie!" Sally called to her husband. "I told you I didn't chase him away!"

"So, invite him to sit down and give him a menu, why don't'cha?"

"Would you like a booth, or would you prefer to sit at the counter?"

Stephen looked around and saw one booth left. It was back in the corner. If he took it, he would have complete privacy. He could eat alone and then go home again to his empty apartment and brood some more. "Counter," he said.

Grinning, Sally waved her hand. "Pick your spot."

He took a stool near the middle and opened the menu she handed him.

"Our special this evening is roast beef with garlic mashed potatoes and baby carrots. It comes with a fresh-baked roll and your choice of homemade minestrone soup or a garden salad."

"Sounds good. I'll take the soup and a cup of coffee whenever you get around to it."

"Coming right up." She clipped the order to the wheel over the cook's counter. Turning, she picked up an orange-capped coffeepot from a burner and a white mug from a rack. She set the cup in front of him and filled it. "How's the construction business?"

"Booming."

She set out a napkin and put a knife, fork, and spoon on it. "That exciting, huh?"

"You know anything about the churches in the area?"

Charlie banged his bell. Sally picked up the soup and set it down in front of Stephen. "Well, you've got your pick. Catholic, Protestant, Mormon, and everything in between. We even have a mosque a few miles down the road, and some Buddhists who meet in a little shrine out on McFarlane. But if you're asking for a recommendation, I say Centerville Christian." She lowered her voice. "It always had good solid Bible teaching, if you know what I mean. Dry as bones, though. Not much going on. Just a handful of old-timers in the congregation up until a year ago when they got a new pastor." She straightened. "Centerville Christian. If you want a happening place, that's where you should go. Charlie and I go there, don't we, honey? At least, when I can get him out of the kitchen. Pastor Paul preaches there. You met him the day you came in for breakfast."

"The jogger?"

"That's him. If you're interested, you can attend the Bible study tomorrow night. Meets at seven thirty in their fellowship hall. Charlie

and I can't go because we're both working. But we would if we could."
She nodded toward an elderly couple sitting in a booth. "That's Samuel
and Abby Mason. They've been members for years. In fact, Samuel's one
of the elders who called Pastor Paul to the pulpit. Hey, Samuel, what're
you studying on Wednesday nights?"

"We just started the book of Ephesians."

"Got room for one more? I got a live one on the line here."

"Plenty of room." He gave Stephen a nod.

Stephen nodded back.

"There, Decker," Sally said, grinning again. "You're all signed up."

"Assuming he wants to go!" Charlie yelled from the back.

"He asked me about churches, you old coot!"

"Don't you have some dishes to wash?"

Sally winked at Stephen as she called back, "He's got to get his dinner and eat it first."

Charlie slid a plate of roast beef, mashed potatoes, and baby carrots
onto the cook's counter and banged the bell.

Stephen laughed with the others supping at the counter. As he ate
dinner, he noticed how Sally talked with her husband as she washed
dishes and put them in sterilizing racks. She laughed at something he
said. He came out and carried the loaded rack into the back room for
her. And then the banter would begin again. Needling without the sting.

Sipping his coffee, Stephen felt lonely again. Even in the middle of
a crowded diner, his walls were going up. And he knew if he allowed
himself to stay inside them, he'd self-destruct. Maybe the Bible study
would be a good start.

If he was going to build a new life, he was going to have to build
new habits.

2:25 A.M.

1/11/15

CHAPTER 4

———— ⟡ ————

PAUL SPOTTED THE CONTRACTOR he'd met briefly at Charlie's Diner. He was entering the fellowship hall with a Bible tucked under his arm. Paul wove his way through the gathering of regulars. "Stephen Decker, isn't it?"

Decker's brows rose slightly. "You've got a good memory."

"It's good to have you join us." He'd worked out a method of name associations while on staff at Mountain High. People felt accepted when their names were remembered. It made them feel significant and cared for, gave them a sense of belonging. When he'd met Stephen Decker at Charlie's, he set memory triggers: *deck, contractor, builder, Decker, Stephen, first martyr.* It was also important to learn what skills people possessed and how they could best serve the church.

They shook hands. "Don't let the noise get to you," Paul laughed. "We start off our Bible studies with refreshments. Gives people a chance to mingle. Let me introduce you around. Did you see the notice about the study in the *Centerville Gazette?*"

"No. Sally told me about it."

"I'll have to thank her." Paul ushered Stephen around and introduced him to everyone, but focused on people with whom he'd have common interests. Matt Carlson was a roofer. Phil Sturgeon was a plumber. Tom

73

Ingersol was an electrician. All had been involved in various projects around Centerville and as far north as Sacramento, and they had become new and valuable members of the church. An architect who was also a contractor would be invaluable as CCC outgrew its sanctuary and fellowship hall.

Stephen shook hands with Tom. "You did the wiring on my Vine Hill project."

"Sure did. That's some house you're building up there. Who's moving into it? Bill Gates?"

Decker laughed. "It's not quite that grand."

"Bigger than anything else we have around this neck of the woods."

With Decker assimilated, Paul felt free to head for the podium, where he made a last-minute check of his notes. "Okay, folks, let's get started. We have a lot to cover this evening." He counted heads as people took seats. Thirty-eight. Good mixture of men and women, middle-aged and older.

He hoped the complainers who continued to come would behave themselves. He didn't want any of them beating newcomers over the head with doctrine. The sooner the church grew, the better. He wanted to revamp the board of elders. If this church was going to grow, men like Otis Harrison and Hollis Sawyer were going to have to retire from leadership. They lived in the past, and Paul was sick of trying to reason with them. If they had their way, this church would remain the same today as it had been for the past forty years.

"Let's open in prayer." Paul prayed fervently that all those present would have open hearts and minds to the lessons God was about to give them, that they would assume the role Jesus had for them, that they would accept God's leadership in the days ahead, and that the Lord would bless them for their obedience.

After reviewing the historical context of Ephesians, Paul moved through the book verse by verse, heavily emphasizing that each person in attendance was chosen of God and should never cease to be thankful. He further stressed that wisdom and revelation would enlighten them as to what service the Lord had created them to do for His church. Samuel Mason raised his hand. Paul ignored him. How many times did he have to explain this was a class and not a discussion group? He had worked out his lesson plan so that it would last exactly fifty minutes, leaving ten minutes for prayer requests at the end. He didn't have time for interruptions or going off on some rabbit trail of discussion.

As the end of the hour approached, Paul closed his Bible and asked for prayer requests. He jotted them down on a slip of paper. To save time, he prayed through the list himself, summarized what he'd taught that evening, and thanked God for His Word. He dismissed the class at nine o'clock. His father had told him years ago that newcomers were more likely to return to a class that had a definite beginning and ending.

Tucking the prayer requests into his Bible, Paul prepared to talk with those who lingered. Now was the time for questions. Several people came up to tell him what a wonderful teacher he was, and how he made the Bible come to life.

"God brought you here, Pastor Paul," Edna Welty said. "Henry Porter was a good man, but he put me to sleep preaching the same thing over and over again."

Samuel and Abby joined them. "Henry Porter taught about grace, Edna," Abby said quietly.

Samuel looked into Paul's eyes. "A lesson that bears teaching again and again because it's beyond the understanding of men."

Paul forced a smile. How long would he have to listen to the plaudits for the old pastor? Did Samuel Mason and the other two elders not yet realize that Reverend Porter had almost led this pathetic little flock into complete oblivion? "Those who receive God's grace are also called to greater responsibility." Most of the parishioners had come to church out of habit, not out of faith. Faith was living and active, not boring and complacent.

"Yes, but the work comes out of gratitude, not obligation."

Samuel Mason was like gum on his shoe! He couldn't shake him off. "Gratitude, yes, but people with a calling upon their lives are useful and vital."

"Every member of the body of Christ is vital."

"But not all are useful. Some just come along for the ride, giving nothing back to the Lord, who saved them."

"Still, it's important not to give the wrong idea."

Paul's confidence evaporated. "What wrong idea was I giving in my lesson this evening?" He had been so careful.

Abby looked distressed. "Oh, I don't think that's what Samuel is saying, Paul."

Samuel didn't amend his words or apologize. "Salvation is a free gift from God, not something we can earn through good works."

"Faith without works is dead." Paul hadn't meant to sound so hard-edged, but Mason deserved a reprimand. The elder had no right to embarrass him. Who had graduated from seminary? Not Mason. Who had spent countless hours poring over the Bible preparing for this class? Who was pastor of this church now?

"Faith and works are interlocked," Samuel said.

The old man was dogged. "A man is justified by works because they show his faith."

"Abraham offered his son Isaac because he *believed* God, and it was reckoned to him as righteousness. It was because of his faith that he was called the friend of God."

Paul smiled stiffly. "Then we both agree, don't we? We just have different ways of getting to the same conclusion." He saw the troubled look in the old man's eyes and leaned closer, speaking in a low tone. "We should end this conversation before others think we are quarreling. The last thing we want is a divisive spirit in the church." He hoped that was enough to shut the old man up.

Abby's face flushed deep red. "Now just a minute!"

"Enough said." Samuel put his arm around her. "Good night, Paul."

Mason sounded tired. Nine thirty was probably past the old guy's bedtime.

Paul felt a twinge of conscience as he watched the Masons leave the fellowship hall. They meant well. He didn't want them to leave like this. As he started after them, a woman stepped into his path and said she'd been nourished by his teaching. Paul looked past her toward the door. The Masons were already gone, and it would be rude to brush past this woman. Maybe he'd call Samuel tomorrow and suggest they have lunch together. They needed to have a meeting of minds if the church was going to continue to grow. This church needed workers. Samuel should realize that better than anyone, considering the years of work he had put in keeping this church going. Why was he resisting now? Surely he wanted Centerville Christian Church to become a beacon in the community and not go on being a dead lightbulb. Samuel Mason was an elder, but that didn't give him the right to challenge Paul's authority.

Locking the doors on the way out, Paul argued with his conscience on the short walk home to the parsonage. Eunice always waited up for him, but he didn't want her getting wind of what had happened between him and the Masons. He thought he had his emotions completely under control when he walked in the front door and found Eunice mending Timmy's coveralls. She glanced up with a smile and her eyebrows rose in question. Depressed, Paul dropped his binder and Bible on the desk. She could read him like a book. "Don't ask." He had blundered with Samuel and Abby and didn't want Eunice to jump to their defense. She loved them like a second set of parents.

His father had told him to be careful how much he shared with his wife. "Women are so easily deceived," he had said. Paul sank into his easy chair.

Euny went back to stitching up the torn seam of Timmy's coveralls, but Paul wasn't fooled. She was waiting for him to say something. Maybe he should talk to her, listen to her take on what had happened. She might be able to advise him on how to make amends without backing down on what he had been teaching.

"We had another newcomer tonight. Stephen Decker. An architect. He's the one in charge of that mansion going up on Vine Hill road." God was sovereign. It was no accident so many people involved in construction were coming to Centerville Christian Church. It was a sign.

"I can see your wheels spinning, Paul."

"I have great hopes for this church."

"Rightfully so, but it wouldn't hurt to slow down a little."

"CCC didn't have a soul under the age of sixty when we got here, Euny, and now we've got a youth group of twenty, and young families are starting to show up. You know as well as I do that the future of the church is in its youth. And Sunday services are filling as well. We had 107 last Sunday."

"You don't have to defend yourself to me, Paul."

"I'm not defending myself!"

She blinked.

He winced. "I'm sorry. I didn't mean to snap like that."

"What happened?"

"Nothing's come up that I can't handle. You know, some people think it's wrong to be ambitious for God's work." He stood, knowing if he sat again, he would pour out his frustrations, and she might end up saying something that would weaken his resolve. "I'm going to take a shower and then hit the sack. I've got some early-morning visitations."

"Are you going over to see Fergus Oslander and Mitzi Pike at Vine Hill Convalescent?"

"No." He hadn't been out to Vine Hill in weeks. He didn't have time. "I'm going to drop by Stephen Decker's job site." He sensed her disquiet. "I can't be in two places at once, Eunice. It would help if you'd go to see them."

"I *have* been going. Every week since we arrived. But sometimes they need to see their pastor."

"Have they asked for a visit?"

"Not exactly."

"I'll try to swing by and say hello to them on my way back into town." Saying he would try didn't mean he actually had to do it.

"Samuel goes every week, too."

"Samuel is retired. He's got plenty of time. He can pick and choose where he goes and who he sees. I haven't got that luxury." He felt that uncomfortable pinch of conscience again. He said good night and left her alone in the room.

Why couldn't she understand that he had to make hard choices? It made more sense to spend the time with a man who could become a vital part of the congregation rather than with two sick old people living out their final years in a convalescent home. They couldn't even attend services anymore and didn't have so much as a dollar to spare for the cause of Christ. Besides, all they ever talked about was their dear old pastor, Henry Porter, and what a good man he was. Porter might have been good, but he had also been ineffective.

Eunice was better with the old folks. He'd encourage her to keep going to see them. But he had to put his energy elsewhere. There were only twenty-four hours in a day, and he needed to use what time he had in cultivating relationships with men like Stephen Decker, who could build this church into something that would glorify God.

———— ✿ ————

Stephen returned to Centerville Christian for the Sunday morning service. He took the program offered by a greeter and slipped into the back row. He hadn't been to a church service since leaving the Salvation Army facility, and he wasn't sure how comfortable he would feel in this one. He'd enjoyed the Wednesday evening Bible study, with Paul Hudson moving confidently through the Scriptures, explaining historical significance, literal meaning, and application. Maybe he'd learn something that could help him get through his days without getting the shakes.

Whoever was playing the piano must've had training. Leaning to one side, he spotted the pretty blonde in front. She looked familiar, but he couldn't place her. Paul Hudson came in from the side door, went up the steps, and took the seat to the left of the pulpit. The blonde pianist finished the last few bars of music, rose, and took her seat in the front row.

For the next hour, Stephen absorbed every word said. Hudson was speaking from Romans, and the sermon seemed designed for Stephen, addressing the struggles he'd been going through over the past five years. It was as though Hudson had an uncanny ability to look into his heart, and was using a laser to point out areas Stephen needed to change, while reminding him what he had learned over six months in an alcohol treatment center. *God, grant me the serenity to accept the things I cannot change, the courage to change the things I can, and the wisdom to know the difference.* Rick always added, "Thy will, not mine, be done." Stephen remembered the essentials. He admitted he was powerless over the alcohol and that his life had become unmanageable because of his addiction. He believed that only Jesus Christ could restore him to sanity. But what had happened to the decision he'd made six months ago to turn his will and his life over to Jesus Christ?

He'd started out okay and then stumbled over that one, which had given him the excuse not to do a thorough searching and fearless moral inventory of his life. It was still easier for him to take Kathryn's inventory than to look at the havoc his own behavior had caused in their marriage and their lives. He'd gone back to living by old habits, rationalizing and justifying his behavior and attitudes.

"If we confess our sins, He is faithful and just and will forgive us our sins and purify us from all unrighteousness."

Stephen winced. Even sitting in the back row—head down, eyes shut—he saw his shortcomings and the areas of his life that needed cleansing. It was easy not to face up to things when you stayed away from people who might actually tell you the truth. He had held off coming to church because he thought he was strong enough to go it alone. And why did he want to go it alone? Because he didn't want to have to apologize if he fell off the wagon. Alone, he could pretend he was accountable to no one. Alone, he could go on pretending his life was his own, that his actions didn't affect anyone but himself, that what he did didn't matter. He could view one drink as a small slip instead of a hard tumble into sin.

I'm here and I'm listening, Jesus. You know I'm fighting for my life. There isn't a soul in this place who knows where I've been or what I'm struggling with. Why should they care? I sat here in the back because I thought I could get up quietly, unnoticed, and walk out that door and do whatever I please without anyone knowing the difference. But You'd know, Lord. You know. That's why everything that's coming out of this guy's mouth is cutting me to the quick. I can't make it on my own. I'm setting myself up for another fall if I try to make it alone. And every time I fall, it's a little harder to get back up.

The congregation stood. Disoriented, Stephen followed suit, bowing his head as Hudson prayed for all those present, that they would heed the calling of Christ on their lives, whatever that calling might entail.

When the service ended, Stephen lingered. Instead of making a bee-line for his car, he went out the side door and down the steps to the courtyard, where coffee and cookies were being served. He recognized a few people. An elderly gentleman approached and extended his hand. "Glad to have you join us. My name's Samuel Mason and this is my wife, Abigail."

"Stephen Decker."

"Are you new to the community, Mr. Decker?"

"Call me Stephen, ma'am."

"Only if you call me Abby, Mr. Decker."

"Yes, ma'am." He laughed. "Abby." She had blue eyes that glowed from the inside. "Yes, I'm new to Centerville. Temporary relocation. I'm building a house up on Vine Hill."

"Oh, you're a carpenter, then."

"More like a jack-of-all-trades."

Samuel chuckled. "Mr. Decker is being modest, Abby. He's the architect and contractor. Am I correct? I read about you in the *Sacramento Bee*. You built several homes in Granite Bay, as I remember. One was purchased by a movie star."

The article had been written almost two years ago. "You have a long memory."

"I liked the looks of the house."

"What movie star?" Abby said.

"Nobody you'd recognize," Samuel said. "We don't attend many movies."

"Last one we went to was *Return to Snowy River.*"

Stephen laughed with them.

Paul Hudson approached, the pretty blonde beside him, a little boy in a neat Sunday suit holding her hand. "Stephen, good to see you again." They shook hands. "I'd like you to meet my wife, Eunice. Eunice, this is Stephen Decker. He dropped in on the Wednesday night Bible study last week. I hope you'll keep coming."

"I plan to."

"You haven't made it to the refreshment table yet, Mr. Decker," Eunice said. "Can I get you something?"

"Don't trouble yourself."

"Oh, it's no trouble." When she smiled at him, he was caught off guard by the shock of attraction. He'd never felt a jolt like that, even in the early days with Kathryn. "Timmy and I were on our way to the plate of cookies."

Others joined their small party. They offered small talk and friendly greetings to make an outsider feel welcome.

Eunice handed Stephen a cup of punch and a small plate on which were several homemade cookies. His fingers brushed hers accidentally. "I enjoyed your music, Eunice."

"Thank you." She blushed.

Was he staring?

An old man with a cane and a sour look interrupted. "Excuse me, Paul, but I'd like a word with you."

Stephen caught the irritation in Hudson's eyes before he covered it. "Of course, Hollis. But first, let me introduce you to Stephen Decker. Stephen, this is Hollis Sawyer, one of our elders."

"Nice to meet you, I'm sure," Hollis said in perfunctory fashion before he glowered at Hudson again. "I'll only take a minute of your precious time, and then you can come back to your hobnobbing."

Paul Hudson's face reddened. He extended his arm and turned aside with the old man.

"Oh, dear," Abby said softly.

"If you'll excuse me, Stephen." Samuel joined the two men heading for the edge of the gathering.

It was obvious Hollis Sawyer was upset about something, and Eunice was distressed as well. An elderly lady drew Abby Mason aside. Eunice glanced toward her husband again, and bit her lip.

"Where did you study music, Eunice?"

She looked at him. "Excuse me?"

"Music. Where did you study?"

She said the name of Midwest something or other. He'd never heard of it.

Stephen nodded toward the three men talking near the front corner of the church building. "I wouldn't worry about that. Your husband looks like a man who can handle himself in a crisis. Besides, it's refreshing for someone like me to know everyone in a church isn't perfect."

Hollis turned and hobbled away. He jammed his cane into the ground with every step. Samuel said something to Hudson. Hudson's head came up and he said something back.

"We're far from perfect," Eunice said softly.

Stephen smiled wryly. "Ah, then, maybe there is space for a divorced recovering alcoholic."

She looked at him again. "That's not the sort of information I would expect anyone to share on first acquaintance."

He rubbed the back of his neck uneasily and gave a soft laugh. "No, it isn't, and I'm not exactly sure why I did." He never blurted out private business. Kathryn complained all the time about how little he shared of himself. She claimed that was one of the dozen reasons she decided to file for divorce. The trouble was every time he did share something, she'd used it as a weapon against him.

Now, he had the programmed excuse: anonymity was an integral part of his recovery. He had to fight his own demons without adding the beast of public condemnation to the mix. So what was he doing blabbing his personal life to this young woman? He didn't know her from Adam, and he'd just put information in her hands that could ruin him in the community as well as the church before he'd even tried to sink in roots.

Maybe he was hoping the opportunity would evaporate.

"It's all right, Mr. Decker." Her smile was gentle and made him weak in the knees. "I'll remember to forget."

Time would tell if she was a woman of her word.

Just to be safe, Stephen decided to shut his mouth and leave before he blurted out the fact that she was the most attractive woman he had met in a long, long time.

———— ❧ ————

Paul watched Stephen Decker leave the gathering in the courtyard. Annoyed and depressed, he let his shoulders slump. "I am sick and tired of Hollis Sawyer's complaints."

"I won't make excuses for him, Paul, but traditions do have their place and should be taken into account."

He wasn't in the mood for more sage advice from Samuel Mason, either. If these old men had their way, the church would continue to die, shrouded in tradition. "It's tradition that's strangling this church." He strove to keep his voice quiet, his emotions hidden from onlookers. He didn't want people noticing that something was amiss between him and another elder. It was bad enough that Hollis had chosen to break up his conversation with Stephen Decker and then march off in a huff. Centerville Christian needed more men like Stephen Decker coming through its doors, affluent professionals in their midthirties with years of service ahead of them. Instead, the church was glutted with tired, broken-down old men and women convinced a church could function without changing its old ways. This church hadn't been working for a long time. "What difference does it make if the Bible on the pulpit is King James or the New International Version?"

"It matters to Hollis. As well as others."

"The idea is to communicate the gospel, not cloak it in language no one uses anymore, let alone understands."

"And they shall know us by our love, Paul."

Heat came up inside Paul. Those gently spoken words cut him to the quick. Was Samuel saying he lacked love? Hadn't he shown his love by pouring every bit of his energy into getting this church back on its feet?

"I can love Hollis, Samuel, and I do. He's my Christian brother. But that doesn't mean I have to give in to him on everything."

"It isn't a matter of giving in. The King James Bible in question was given to the church by one of the founding members."

"Jesus is the founder of this church, Samuel."

"I won't debate you on that point."

"I would hope not."

"Still, it never pays to burn bridges."

Why not, if they were rotting wooden structures that should be replaced with steel and macadam? The elder's remark roused the old fear of failure. "I'm not trying to burn bridges, Samuel. I'm trying to build a church."

"Then a little compromise is in order."

The word *compromise* raised Paul's hackles. When would these old people get it through their heads that the church was a living, breathing organism and stop looking at it like a diorama in a museum? If he gave in to Hollis, he'd have Otis Harrison in his office next, trying to have all the music changed back to dry old hymns. Or some other member would want the order of worship changed back to the way Henry Porter did it for four decades! Their fear of change was what was behind every complaint. Their cry was always the same: Don't change anything! The sooner Paul filled this church with new blood, the sooner he would have help in making this church something that would please God.

In the meantime, he had to resign himself to dealing with these cantankerous old men and women. At the last elders' meeting, Paul had suggested recruiting deacons and deaconesses from the growing congregation. In typical fashion, Hollis and Otis balked. They said they didn't know enough about the newcomers to nominate any of them. Otis insisted men and women should be members in good standing for five years minimum before they should be considered for any kind of leadership. Which, of course, effectively eliminated everyone in the congregation who was under the age of fifty. What better way to deadlock a growing congregation and keep it under the tightfisted reign of a couple of elders?

The meeting had ended with nothing being accomplished. Again. Samuel Mason said, again, to be patient, to pray, and to wait upon the Lord. What were they waiting for? Paul was never quite sure where

Samuel Mason stood. Was he just another one of the good old boys who had been around since the beginning of time and wanted everything to stay the same? Or was he a progressive thinker? Was he willing to risk old friendships to bring the revival he claimed he'd been praying for over the past ten years?

Paul didn't know. So he kept his own counsel and didn't share his thoughts with Mason. Paul thought it better to seek out allies of his own generation who would come alongside him and move this church successfully into the modern age where it belonged, rather than try to change the mind-sets of two old men determined to keep things status quo.

And now, here they were again, going over the same old ground.

"I'll pray about it, Samuel." Mason wouldn't argue with that. "Why don't we join the others and have some coffee?"

Eunice had that worried look in her eyes. "Is everything all right, Paul?"

"We'll talk about it later. Mingle."

As the gathering thinned out, several of the ladies carried the punch bowl and empty cookie trays into the kitchen. The extra paper plates and napkins were put away. Eunice shook out the yellow tablecloths and gathered them up as she headed home with Timmy. She would wash, iron, and bring them back for next week's fellowship hour.

"I'll just be a minute." Paul headed back to lock up the doors of the church. He glanced through the notes in the suggestion box. Mostly complaints from old members. He wadded them up and threw them into the trash can in his office. He went back into the kitchen and encouraged the ladies to move their gab session to a local coffee shop so he could lock up the fellowship hall and head home. They departed quickly.

It was a little after two when he walked in the front door of the parsonage. Eunice had classical music playing on the radio. Timmy sat at the small kitchen table, dipping his peanut-butter-and-jelly sandwich into his tomato soup.

"I'm sorry we didn't wait," Eunice said. "He was starving, and I wasn't sure how long you'd be."

He kissed her. "Gladys was the last one out the door, and you know how she is. I walked her to her car. Even got her into it, but then she rolled down her window and asked me another one of her philosophical questions that would take a college course to answer."

"She's a retired teacher."

"I should've guessed." He sank into a chair with a sigh of relief. Eunice gave him a large mug of hot soup. Then she set a sandwich in front of him and sat with him. Paul took her hand. "Thank You, Father, for all who came to our Sunday service today. We ask that those who were new felt welcome and will return. We ask that You would soften the hearts of others. Give them Your vision so that they can see what can be, instead of what has been. Thank You for this food and for the hands that prepared it. Please bless it for our bodies' use. In Jesus' name, amen."

The troubled look on Eunice's face bothered Paul. What was wrong now?

"Can I play, Mommy?"

"Ask your father."

"Can I, Daddy?"

Paul excused him. "Put your mug and plate on the sink counter, Tim. That'll help your mother." Timmy gathered his things and did as asked.

"Thank you, sweetheart." Eunice kissed their son and gave him a loving pat on his backside. "You can play for a while and then it'll be bath time."

Paul saw the crestfallen look on his son's face and scooped him up. "Maybe we can play later this afternoon." He kissed him and set him down.

"You haven't had much time with him lately," Eunice said.

"I know." When was the last time he'd played in the yard with his son? He'd try hard to make time. "Hollis Sawyer was upset because I put away the King James Bible." He took a bite of his sandwich. "He wants it put back on the pulpit. Samuel wants me to compromise."

"Abby thought it might have something to do with the Bible. She said one of the founders—"

"Samuel told me. It was all right to use the King James Version when it was only the original members attending services, Euny, but we have new members who give me blank stares when I read from it. I'm not using it anymore."

"Where did you put it?"

"In my office."

"In a box or on a shelf?"

He was fast losing his appetite. Was she reminding him of the stir of outrage when he had boxed up all of Henry Porter's old reference books? "On the shelf."

"Maybe you could put it on a stand in the narthex."

"To satisfy Hollis?"

"To give it a place of honor. The Bible is the basis of all your teaching. You agree with these men on that. And this particular Bible has historical significance to Centerville Christian. It would comfort the older members of our congregation to see it before entering the sanctuary. It would give them a sense of continuity. You could talk to Samuel about it first. See what he thinks about the idea. You know he will do everything he can to encourage the others to work with you for the good of the congregation."

He resented being made to feel like a little boy who had to check everything through his elder. But what Eunice said made sense. He had enough trouble with Hollis and Otis without creating more. Until he was able to add new elders who could understand what he was doing, he was going to have to do whatever he could to prevent more waves from swelling and sinking the ship.

"It's too bad Hollis Sawyer and Otis Harrison don't have something better to do with their time than hunt for things to cause dissension."

Eunice smiled tenderly. "I don't think they willfully cause dissension, Paul. They are the last of the old guard who have kept this congregation alive. They think you don't value their traditions and the hard work it took to keep Centerville Christian Church alive."

"They would've had better luck if they'd changed with the times."

"Not all things should change, Paul, least of all our love for one another as brothers and sisters."

His stomach knotted. "I have nothing but respect for their faithfulness."

"I know that, but they don't. You have to show them."

"How, Eunice? Neither Hollis nor Otis can get through a meeting without digressing. And now, Hollis is so mad, I doubt he'll listen to Samuel, let alone me." He was sick of these old men trying to run his church.

"First of all, apologize for removing the Bible, and don't make any excuses."

"Now just a minute!"

"Hear me out, Paul. Please."

He struggled for control over his temper. "Okay. What do you suggest?"

"You could set aside ten minutes in the next few services and have each of them give their testimonies to the congregation. How did they come to Christ? How has this church helped them walk in faith over the decades? What are their hopes for Centerville Christian?"

"Eunice, do you know these men at all?"

"Yes, I do." She spoke quietly.

"Then you're aware that neither one can say anything in under thirty minutes. If I gave Otis a microphone, we'd be sitting in Sunday services until the Second Coming."

"Paul . . ."

"No way."

"Aren't you interested in knowing anything about them?"

"The point isn't whether I'd be interested, but whether the congregation would be interested."

"As pastor, it's your job to teach your people how to love one another. How can you teach them to love these men who are their elders if you can't love them yourself?"

"I do love them."

She looked at him. She didn't have to say another word for him to know what she was thinking. And grudgingly he had to admit she was right. He had been neither patient nor kind to these two venerable old gentlemen. They grated on his nerves and he resented their interference. He had ignored their suggestions and done what he thought best for the church. "Someone has to be in charge, Eunice. Otherwise this place will be in complete confusion."

"Jesus is in charge, Paul. You know that better than anyone. You know, too, that Samuel has prayed for years for this church to be revived."

"That's what I'm trying to do! I'd think you of all people would understand how hard I'm working to that end."

"You've been called here to fan the flame, Paul, not throw fuel on a fire that could burn this church down."

He tossed his napkin on the table. "And removing the Bible from the pulpit could bring everything down? You're a woman. You don't understand about managing a church or—"

Her eyes flashed. "You've always told me I should speak up when I see anything amiss."

"Why are you so determined to find fault with my ministry?" Even as he said it, he knew he was being unfair, but he wasn't about to apologize.

"I'm not finding fault, Paul. I'm trying to help you understand these men."

Her eyes were shiny with tears. For whom? Her husband or those men who were always giving him trouble?

She leaned toward him. "Hollis Sawyer served in the Philippines during World War II. He survived the Bataan death march. Most of the men he served with were not so fortunate. He said it was during that time that he turned to Christ. He needed his faith because when he returned stateside, he found out the high school sweetheart he had married was living with someone she'd met while working in a factory. No one had ever been divorced in his family. He was the first and it was devastating. But then, he met and married his second wife, Denise, after he was in a construction accident. She was the nurse who took care of him. They had three children together. One daughter was born with Down syndrome and died in her early twenties. His two sons married and moved to the East Coast. Denise died of bone cancer eight years ago. Hollis took care of her in their own home up until the last."

She wiped a tear from her cheek. "Otis Harrison served in the Army during the war, but he was on the European front as a medic. He was mayor of Centerville from 1972 until 1976. He was reelected in 1986 and then stepped down due to Mabel's health and served on the town council for another three years. He's now taking care of his wife of forty-eight years. Mabel suffers from congenital heart disease. She's famous around Centerville, Paul. Did you know she won two national cooking contests?

"And Samuel Mason. Samuel was a B-17 gunner and flew more than thirty bombing runs over Germany before being shot down. Abby was a teacher at the local high school. She taught civics. Students still stop by to visit her. One came by the last time I was visiting, and he told me Abby was the one who believed in him and got him to apply to college."

"Okay. Okay, I get your point."

"Do you, Paul? Did you know that Samuel has paid the property taxes on the church for three years running, and Otis and Hollis paid to have the parsonage roof replaced?"

His anger seeped away. "Who told you all these things?"

"I've learned a lot from the people I've been visiting at Vine Hill Convalescent Hospital. They're a wealth of information about the history of the church, Paul, and have served diligently over the years." She smiled tenderly. "All you have to do is ask a question or two and then sit back and listen."

She amazed him at times. A pity he didn't have her talent or the time to develop it. "Can you understand when I tell you I don't have time to spend hours listening to everyone's life story like you do?" He saw the shadow come into her eyes and tightened his hand around hers. "I can respect them for all they've done and love them as Christian brothers and sisters, but I have to move this church out of the past and into the twentieth century, Euny, or it's going to die."

"These people *are* the church, Paul."

His father was right. A woman should learn to be silent and submissive! He shouldn't have talked with her about his problems. "They're *part* of the church." He would concede that much. "But they're already in the minority." Why was it necessary to explain? "There were less than sixty when we arrived, and our attendance is up—way up from what it was. Every Sunday we have visitors now. Every Sunday! And that's not because Hollis or Otis or even Samuel has been out knocking on doors and talking to people all over town or getting involved in community youth activities. I have! It's the younger generations we need to reach. They're the future of the church. And we're accomplishing that. You with your music. Music they didn't like, if you'll remember. I'm not going to allow these old men to ride roughshod over the entire congregation and hold us captive to their personal comforts. I want to build this church, Eunice, not stand by and watch it choke to death on outdated ideas and methods!"

"You have the best of intentions, Paul. I know that."

He could hear the caveat. "Why are you taking their side?"

"It's not a matter of sides, Paul. It's a matter of being united with one another, being at peace with one another. We are all members of the body of Christ. We are all needed."

"So I'm supposed to make peace at any price?"

"Is placing the Bible in the narthex 'any price'? What is the real issue here, Paul?"

"You're my wife, Eunice! That's the issue! You're supposed to stand beside me, not countermand everything I do."

She paled at his words, then spoke quietly, gently. "What is the real issue?"

"The real issue is not allowing those old men to dictate what I should and shouldn't do to turn this church around!"

She bowed her head.

"Daddy? Why are you mad at Mommy?"

Ashamed, Paul winced. "I'm not mad at Mommy, Tim. We're just talking. Go and play with your toys." When his son was out of sight, he looked at Eunice beseechingly. "What's the matter with you lately? You used to stand by me, Euny. Why are you bucking me now when everything is going so well? I fought for you. Remember? They didn't like the music you were playing two months ago. I had to talk myself blue in the face before they agreed to let us have a mix of contemporary and traditional hymns." It might have been his idea in the first place, but she had gone along with him.

Her eyes filled, but she said no more.

Paul felt that jab of conscience again. He resented it. He wasn't trying to hurt her. Had she considered how much her words hurt him? She ought to think about that instead of giving him that doe-eyed look of hers. He was her husband. If she owed loyalty to anyone, it was him. Why did she have to make an issue of this? Couldn't she understand that he was trying to sweep the cobwebs out of Centerville Christian? It was on his tongue to say exactly that, but he didn't because he knew she'd say he was sweeping old members out the back door as the new came in the front. That wasn't his intention. She ought to know that.

Eunice said nothing more about Hollis or the Bible. She asked him if he'd like some more soup. He said no. She cleared the table, squirted liquid detergent into the sink, and ran hot water. He had the feeling she was praying while she washed the dishes. Paul went into the living room and sat in his easy chair. Maybe he should call his father and ask his advice. But why bother? He knew already what his father would say: "Put the Bible away and let God deal with the old men. Get on with building the church and stop worrying about what a few disgruntled people think. There are always enemies in the church, men and women who want to tear down what you're building."

But Euny, Lord? Euny has never fought me before.

"A wife of noble character who can find? She is worth far more than rubies." And Euny was virtuous. Wasn't that why he'd fallen in love with her? For all that, and her beautiful blue eyes and sweet smile. *"She brings him good, not harm, all the days of her life."* Euny had always talked with him about his work for the Lord. She had always backed him. She had always been his helpmate, his encourager.

"What is the real issue here, Paul?"

His pride is what she meant, and the question hurt. What about those two old men? Talk about pride! Hollis was insubordinate. In church council meetings, he and Otis spent half their time in idle chatter about the past rather than getting the business of the church done. Was he supposed to give in every time one of them had a fit about some tradition? Pride had hardened them so that they wouldn't listen.

Paul wanted them to stand aside and allow him to move this church forward unfettered. He wanted them to stop hindering his plans and work alongside him. He wanted Centerville Christian Church to be a beacon in the town. As pastor, he should have their respect.

Eunice came into the living room. She put her hand on his shoulder, leaned down, and kissed him. "I love you, Paul." She went into Timmy's room and told their son it was time to pick up his toys and have a bath. Timmy loved baths. It wasn't long before he was jabbering away in the bathroom, the water running. Eunice laughed and talked with him.

Paul put his hand on his Bible.

You know what I'm trying to do here, Jesus. This church was dry as dust when I came. It was like a valley of dead bones. That's why Samuel called the dean. The elders knew they were in trouble. That's why You called me here. To change things. So why do they fight me at every turn? Why do they quibble and fuss like old ladies over every change I make?

Timmy came out with his wet hair slicked back and his favorite book tucked under his arm. Paul was in no mood to read *The Little Engine That Could* for the five millionth time. "Not today, Timmy." Timmy came closer and held the book out. "I said no." Eunice stood in the hall doorway. "Could you give me a little help here? He's got a library of books in his room and he wants this one. *Again.*"

"It's his favorite." She smiled and sat on the edge of the sofa. "Your mom told me you loved *Peter Rabbit*. She told me she must have read it to you a thousand times."

He remembered and relented. "Okay, Timmy." He set his son on his lap and opened the book. The sooner he read the story, the sooner his son would go to bed. Paul wanted to get back to thinking about more important matters than toy engines and good little boys and girls on the other side of the mountain. "'I think I can. I think I can. . . .'" Timmy tried to hold the page open, but Paul brushed his hand away and turned to the next page. "'I thought I could. I thought I could. I thought I could. . . .'" He closed the book and tossed it onto the coffee table. "All done. Time for your nap." Paul kissed his son as he lifted him off his lap.

"Come on, Timmy." Eunice held out her hand.

The boy's shoulders drooped. Eunice took Timmy's hand and they disappeared down the hallway. He heard her speaking softly. "Daddy has a lot on his mind. No, he's not mad at you." And then she began reading in the other room, slowly, dramatically, rhythmically so that he could almost hear the *chug-chug* of the little toy train.

So what do I do, Lord?

"What is the real issue here, Paul?"

Pride, he thought. *Theirs and mine.* He felt ashamed that he had let his anger get hold of him, but it was understandable. He had been struggling for patience with Hollis and Otis for months. Was it any wonder he lost it when Hollis made an issue of the old Bible missing from the pulpit? He hadn't listened to what was behind Hollis's complaint. Maybe he had been a little short with Samuel. Hollis would undoubtedly go to Otis and complain, and then he'd have two elders mad at him. Three if Samuel held a grudge. No, that wasn't like Samuel. His head throbbed.

Timmy's bedroom door closed softly and Eunice appeared in the hall. "I'm going to take a bubble bath."

"I'm sorry I was impatient with Timmy." He gave her a bleak smile. "Maybe you could hide that book for a while and he'd let me read something else to him for a change."

He knew he'd hurt her earlier. She'd always stood beside him and listened to his problems, advising where she could. He knew he'd said all the wrong things to Hollis. And now, no matter how much it galled him, he was going to have to try to make peace with Hollis. "I'll call

Samuel. If it'll soothe ruffled feathers to put that shabby old King James Bible under glass in the narthex, I'll do it."

She glanced at the mantel clock. "It's still early, Paul. You shouldn't wait." She put her hand on the doorframe. "I'm going to take my bath. I'll be praying for you. It'll all work out if you trust the Lord."

"Trust the Lord."

He waited until he heard the bathwater running before he lifted the telephone. He hesitated for a moment, then punched in Samuel Mason's number.

---- 🙢🙠 ----

Samuel put the phone back on the receiver.

"So?" Abby looked at him over her glasses, her brows raised. She'd stopped rocking her chair when the telephone rang and was still sitting pensively, the pillowcase she had been embroidering resting on her lap, while she waited for him to tell her what the conversation was all about.

"How's the pillowcase coming along?" Every year, she made a new set of embroidered pillowcases for their daughter and son-in-law as well as new ones for their two grandchildren.

"Just fine. Now, what was 'a good idea'?"

"Paul wanted to know what I thought about putting the church's King James Bible into a special glass case in the narthex."

She smiled broadly. "Well, good for her." She lifted the embroidery hoop.

"Good for who?"

"Eunice, of course."

"You think it was her idea?"

"Well, you don't think Paul came up with an idea like that all on his own, do you? It smacks of humility and making amends."

"Abby . . ."

"Oh, don't Abby me. That boy is like a racehorse with the bit in his teeth."

He chuckled. "What do you know about racehorses?"

"Is Paul going to talk with Hollis?"

"He didn't say, but I doubt an apology would get anywhere with Hollis right now, anyway."

"Oh, you can talk Hollis down off his high horse, and then start building a bridge."

He'd do his best. Samuel picked up his book and pretended to read. Instead, he started praying again, praying that if he did manage to build a bridge, Paul Hudson would have sense enough to walk across it.

Stephen was sitting at the counter in Charlie's Diner, sipping coffee and bantering with Sally, when Paul Hudson came in, hair wet with perspiration, sweatshirt tied around his waist and T-shirt sticking to his chest. He slid onto a stool next to Stephen, greeted him, and ordered an orange juice.

"How many miles this morning, Pastor Paul?" Sally called.

"Five, at least," Paul said, puffing.

Stephen's mouth tipped in a half smile. "Something bothering you?"

Paul gave him a sideways glance and grinned. "Human relations."

"Ah." Stephen lifted his mug. "Life's obstacle course."

"I barreled into a hurdle and fell flat on my face last Sunday." He pulled a handkerchief out of his back pocket and wiped his face and neck.

"The gentleman who looked ready to hang you up by your thumbs."

"You don't miss much, do you?"

"I'm always watchful in new surroundings." The world had plenty of minefields.

"Was Sunday your first time in church?"

"Nope. But it's been a while."

"Bad experience?"

"Life-changing experience. Good one. I just wasn't sure I'd find anything close to what I had."

"And?"

If Hudson had been older, Stephen would have figured he was angling for a compliment. Maybe he was just too young to know his power. "I'll be back."

"Good." Thanking Sally, Paul picked up the glass of orange juice and downed half of it. "You're an architect, aren't you?"

"He's building that big place up on the hill," Sally said.

"Then you'd know some craftsmen."

Uh-oh. "A few." He'd been told by a few cynical second-timers at the Salvation Army facility that a church always wanted parishioners to work and give money. "What sort of craftsman did you have in mind?"

"Someone who could build a display cabinet for our narthex."

Stephen thought of Tree House: big, bulky, looked dumb as a post, but was one of the most skilled wood craftsmen around. Tree House built furniture as a hobby. He liked using old tools and methods. "Maybe. I'll see what I can find out for you. How much are you willing to pay and how soon do you need the job done?"

"I'd need an estimate, and the sooner we can get it finished, the better."

"The man I have in mind does beautiful work, but it's a sideline, not his occupation. If he's interested, I'll have him stop by the church and you can tell him what you're looking for."

"Great! Thanks."

"Don't thank me yet. Won't be cheap. Might be a whole lot easier and faster to go to a furniture store and see what you can find."

"Maybe, but I think this particular piece should be something special."

Pastor Paul must have scraped his nose when he fell over the "hurdle." Having crashed and burned a few times himself, Stephen knew what it felt like. "When you work with people, Pastor, you run into trouble. Just comes with the territory."

"You can say that again." Paul finished his orange juice. "And call me Paul." He set his empty glass on the counter. "Seems to me you and I have a lot in common, Stephen. We're both builders, and we both have to deal with inspectors who come in looking for something wrong with our work." He took out his wallet and removed enough money to pay for the juice and leave a generous tip.

"Pays to make friends with inspectors who can impede progress." Stephen turned on his stool and cocked his head. "Is the cabinet a bribe, or a way of making amends?" He saw the color seep into the younger man's face and wondered if it was anger or embarrassment. Maybe he shouldn't have said anything. It wasn't his business what went on inside Centerville Christian Church. Unless he decided he wanted to become part of it.

"Both." Paul grimaced. "But I've been told crow is edible."

"True, but never the bird of choice."

"Maybe the taste of it will keep me from making the same mistake again." He gave a casual salute. "Hope I see you Sunday morning." He thanked Sally and went out the door.

Stephen paid for his breakfast and headed for the work site. He talked to Tree House about the cabinet for the church, but got no for an answer. Tree House was building a china hutch for his mother. "If I start another project before finishing her piece, she'll have my head in a basket."

The more Stephen thought about it, the more he wanted to tackle the project himself. He'd done the finish work on the bookshelves in the den of his Granite Bay house and built the mantel that had been the centerpiece in the living room. Back when he was a kid, he'd made a few pieces of furniture in an elective wood-shop class. A drop-leaf desk that won an award at the county fair. His teacher had told him he had a talent for woodworking, but Stephen had known it was no way to get rich. He'd made a profit of less than a hundred dollars when he calculated the time it had taken him to build the thing. That had been a deciding factor in his decision to be an architect with a contractor's license. The bigger the project, the more money to be made.

The Atherton house would put him in the black again, and the project had already opened up possibilities for more work in the area. But he still had too much time on his hands. Too much time alone. Too much time to think and regret past actions, which only increased the temptation to drink and forget.

He'd never built anything for a church. Why not do the project? It'd keep him busy in the evenings.

Rob Atherton came by late in the afternoon. Before he was out of his car, a Cadillac came up the driveway. Stephen groaned inwardly. Sheila parked next to her husband. They talked briefly. Even at a distance, Stephen could tell Rob was in a foul mood. Probably a rough day at the office. Stephen hoped Sheila would take the hint and not come up with another cockamamie idea that would drive everybody up a wall.

He greeted them cordially and walked them through the house again, explaining how the pace would pick up over the next few weeks as wiring, cables, and plumbing were completed, insulation put in, and Sheetrock put up. Next came the taping and texturing, or paneling, depending on the room. The kitchen and bathroom cabinets were being built and would be brought out for installation by the end of the month. Sheila had already decided on colors, tiles, carpeting, paneling, and fixtures. Everything top of the line, the way Sheila wanted. They had no sooner entered the kitchen than Sheila announced she wanted a Sub-Zero refrigerator and steel instead of black for the convection oven. Stephen exhaled slowly to release steam.

Rob spewed out several four-letter words. Stephen couldn't have voiced his own frustrations any more eloquently. "That's it, Sheila! Enough already! Leave everything as it is now, Decker. No more changes. I want this house to be finished while I'm still this side of sixty."

"But, Rob, I was just telling you what I read. We should upgrade the appliances."

"I said *no*. It's a waste of *his* time and *my* money. What do you care about refrigerators and ovens, anyway? You don't even cook!"

Her eyes went hot. "Well, I would if I had a decent kitchen."

"Decent? Julia Child would be happy to cook in here." His face was red and tight. "Molly never had anything better than what ordinary people have, and she always managed to have a nice dinner on the table at six sharp."

"Then maybe you should've stayed married to her."

"Don't think that hasn't crossed my mind a hundred times in the past three years."

Sheila's mouth fell open. Her blue eyes filled with tears. "You're always blaming me!" Turning abruptly, she left the house. Atherton muttered another expletive under his breath. He took a step after her and then stopped, swore again, and headed for the back of the house. Stephen heard a car door slam, an engine roar, and gravel crunch violently.

Stephen found Rob standing in the barren living room that would eventually look out over a French garden with gazebo and pool, if Sheila's plans proceeded on schedule.

Rob looked up at the beams and around at the alcoves ready to house bookshelves. "Sheila's idea of cooking is to call a restaurant that delivers." He let out his breath, his shoulders drooping. "Nothing like an old fool who thinks he's become cock of the walk, is there?" When he turned, Stephen saw the weariness in his expression, the worn-down look of a man living with a multitude of regrets. "Ever wish you could go back and do things over, Decker?"

"All the time."

"Molly was my first wife." He looked around again. "What's your opinion?"

Stephen wasn't certain what Rob Atherton was asking, but he wasn't going to enter a confessional with an embittered executive who was paying close to seven hundred thousand dollars to house his trophy wife. "Always build with the idea of resale. Men look at garages. Women look at kitchens." Even if they never used them.

Atherton gave a bleak laugh. "There you have it, Decker. Sheila knows where the money's to be made." His eyes were cool and appraising. "I'd like to promise to keep her out of your hair, but I don't think that's possible."

Stephen sensed the message beneath those words. Atherton was no fool. He'd married an adulteress and knew she couldn't be trusted. Too bad Rob couldn't take Sheila off on a two-month vacation to the Bahamas or Hawaii or Timbuktu. By the time they returned, the house would be finished, the landscaping in, and Stephen could hand Rob Atherton or his little tart the key and walk away with the last check due on completion.

He was dreaming.

"I'm already beginning to wish I'd bought land closer to Sacramento," Rob said. "What do you do around here?"

"I attend a Wednesday night Bible study."

"Bible study? You're kidding." Atherton laughed.

"No, I'm not kidding."

"Somehow I didn't think you were that sort."

"What sort would that be?"

Atherton hesitated, assessed. "You really get something out of it?"

He wasn't mocking anymore, and Stephen knew why. For all his money and power, his life was in shambles. "You know where I was before you hired me."

"In rehab." Rob jingled his keys. "Look, I'm not trying to pry. I'm just curious."

"About what?"

"If religion really does improve your life."

"Religion makes life more difficult. God makes life bearable."

"And there's a difference?"

"Life and death difference, but if you want to understand, you ought to check out Centerville Christian."

"Right now, I'd try just about anything."

Stephen smiled cynically. "Well, take a little advice from someone who's been down a few highways. Stay away from booze. Try the church."

8: P.M
1/14/15

CHAPTER 5

———— ❧ ————

As Eunice came out of the parsonage and headed for the church to do her piano practice, Paul was just pulling away from the curb in their Toyota. She waved, but he didn't notice. He'd been up since five, practicing his speech for the Rotary Club.

"Daddy!" Timmy waved.

Eunice crouched down next to her son. "Let's pray for Daddy, Timmy." She put her forehead against his. "Lord Jesus, we know You love us and watch over us. We know You want us to obey You in everything we do. Please be with Daddy today. Give him the words You want him to speak to the men and women at the Rotary Club meeting today. Let Your love shine out of Daddy so that all the people who hear him will want to be Your children. In Jesus' precious name we pray."

"Amen," Timmy said.

She kissed him and stood up. He ran ahead of her to the steps of the church, his arms outstretched like an airplane. Laughing, she followed. She reached into her pocket for the key, but saw the door was already ajar. It wasn't like Paul to leave the church unlocked when he wasn't in his office. She noticed a metallic tan truck parked on the side street near the corner. "Wait, Timmy!" Too late, her son disappeared inside the door.

"Who are you?" she heard Timmy ask.

Hurrying up the steps, Eunice pushed the door wide open. She found a tall man wearing brown work boots, faded Levi's, and a plaid work shirt muscling a dolly carrying a beautiful display cabinet. He glanced back and she smiled in relief. "This is Stephen Decker, Timmy."

Timmy walked closer. "Whatcha doing?"

"Putting in a display case for the church's Bible."

"It's beautiful, Mr. Decker." Eunice admired the curved legs carved with grape leaves and clusters of grapes.

He straightened and ran his hand over the wood framing the glass top. "Call me Stephen."

Her heart did a little fillip at the tone of his voice. She looked into his eyes briefly and then lowered her head, putting her hand lightly on Timmy's head. "Maybe we should come back later and let Mr. Decker finish his work."

Timmy moved away from her. "Mommy practices piano every morning." He stopped and pointed. "You have an owie."

"An owie?"

"What did you do to your thumb?"

"Oh!" Enlightened, Stephen Decker grinned at him. "I smashed it."

"I smashed my finger in a door once."

"I smashed my thumb with a hammer." Stephen pulled the hammer from his tool belt. "This one, as a matter of fact."

"Why?"

"Well, not on purpose, I can tell you. I wasn't paying attention to what I was doing. You have to pay close attention when you're using a hammer."

"Did it hurt?"

"It hurt like—" he stopped, glanced at Eunice—"yeah. It hurt. A lot."

"You need a Band-Aid. Mommy has Sesame Street Band-Aids."

"It's a nice offer, Timmy," Decker said, then looked at her with a broad grin. "But I don't think I'd have the nerve to show up at the job site wearing a Big Bird Band-Aid."

Eunice laughed. "I can see how that might cause some difficulties."

"I'd never live it down."

She withdrew a step. "Come on, Timmy."

"Don't put off your piano practice on account of me, Mrs. Hudson. I'd enjoy listening while I finish up here."

For the first time in a long time, Eunice felt shy about her playing. "I make a lot of mistakes."

He smiled. "I promise not to tell anyone."

"As long as you promise to pay attention to what you're doing."

He slipped the hammer back into his work belt like a gunfighter holstering his gun. "You bet."

She took Timmy's hand and went into the sanctuary. Once her son was settled with some toys she kept in a basket under the front pew, she sat at the piano and began her scales. It had been cold out this morning, an autumn snap in the air, and her fingers were stiff. She ran through all the scales and then went to chords, then runs. Then she just played whatever came to her, bits and pieces of hymns, classical movements, popular songs, Broadway musicals, and some of her own compositions as well. She loved the challenge of making it all flow from one part to the next so that it blended without seams. Paul called her practices "improv-venue."

He hadn't listened to her practice since becoming a pastor. No time. And since arriving at Centerville Christian, his only real interest in her music was to make it work in the service. Paul wanted her to play music that appealed to the people he was trying to attract to the church. Several of the senior members of the church would then come to her and complain, gently, about the music she played and ask why she wasn't playing the hymns she had when she'd first come. She couldn't bring herself to say Paul had told her the kind of music to play. That would only exacerbate the tension between her husband and some of the older members of the congregation. Worse, it would make her feel like she was protecting herself rather than standing beside her husband in his mission to serve the church the best way he knew how.

"Sounds sad."

Startled, she saw Stephen Decker sitting in the second pew. She lifted her hands from the keys.

"You looked pretty caught up in it."

Her face went hot. "I thought you'd be gone by now."

"Hoped I'd be gone, you mean."

"No, I didn't mean . . ."

"I should've kept my mouth shut so I could've enjoyed the rest of the concert. What were you playing?"

"A little of this and that."

"Never heard of it."

She wished she didn't blush so easily. "And likely never will again."

"Ah. You make it up as you go."

"It's the way I warm up." She shrugged. "I just play whatever music comes to mind."

"I recognized a lot of it, but not the last portion. Who wrote that music?"

"I can't remember." She looked away and opened the book of music on the stand.

"Sure you do. You're just too shy to say it came from you."

She watched him walk back down the aisle. He troubled her. For one thing, he was far too attractive, and there was something about the way he looked at her. Refocusing on the music in front of her, she began to play again, following the notes on the page this time. The song was contemporary and designed for praise and worship in more charismatic services than the seniors at Centerville Christian were used to hearing. She'd questioned Paul's choice. "They'll get used to it," Paul had told her. She agreed it was a beautiful song, but so were any one of the four hundred hymns in the books set out in each pew rack. The new song was so easy; she had it memorized in a few minutes. The words were clear, concise, and simple. A child would be able to sing the stanza by heart after the first Sunday.

"Boring!" Stephen Decker called loudly from the back of the church.

"Excuse me?"

"You heard me. It's repetitious."

"What do you mean, repetitious?" Annoyed, she wished he would leave and let her practice in peace.

"Repetitious, as in repeating the same thing over and over again."

"The words . . ."

"I know the words."

She put her hands on her jean-clad knees. "It's the latest music, Mr. Decker."

"Latest doesn't necessarily mean the greatest, Mrs. Hudson."

"It appeals to the younger generation." She felt the color mount in her cheeks as he laughed.

"Thirty-four and I'm part of the older generation, huh, Mrs. Hudson? But I guess to a twenty-what-year-old, that must seem over the hill and sliding into the grave."

"It spells out the gospel message in basic terms. It's meant to give people something to take home with them. Something they can remember and think about during the week. People have so many things to do these days. It's not like fifty years ago when the church was people's social life and singing hymns was enjoyable."

"I didn't know we came to church for enjoyment."

"Not entirely." She was uncomfortable with the tack the conversation was taking. "Don't you enjoy being a Christian?"

"*Enjoyment* isn't a term I'd use. Trying to turn the tables on me, Mrs. Hudson?"

"Just curious."

"So am I. Why don't you play some of your own work?"

She shook her head. "It's not good enough."

"It's better than what you were just playing."

"Well, thank you." She dismissed his praise easily.

"Just chicken, I'm thinking."

She'd never met a more disturbing man. "I've never finished anything, if you want to know."

"Why not? You don't strike me as someone who would give up easily."

She tried to think of a response quickly. "I haven't given up." She'd put it aside. Paul needed her. Timmy needed her. "There's just not time right now. Someday. Maybe."

"When your husband's retired from the ministry and your son's grown-up and moved away?"

She lifted her head at his dry tone. He was standing at the end of the church aisle, arms crossed, leaning his hip against a pew. Why was he baiting her? "My music is not as important as my husband or my son."

"Good cop-out. I guess there's no way for people to stay married and still be all God meant them to be as individuals." He straightened. "Sorry to have interrupted your practice." He picked up his jacket and left.

What he said bothered her. Sometimes she did feel restless. She felt a changing tide in her life and in her marriage. Every evening, Paul seemed to have a meeting scheduled. He accepted invitations from any organization that asked him to speak, viewing them as opportunities from the Lord to "get the word out." But the word about what? The gospel? Or Centerville Christian? Or were they still one and the same? Sometimes she wondered.

Paul was driven to build the church, but she wasn't sure what he meant by that anymore. Shouldn't his wife and son be a priority?

She missed Paul. She missed the times when they would sit and talk about the Lord and what they had learned in their morning devotions together. She missed the walks they had taken early in their marriage. She missed sleeping in on Saturday morning with Paul's arms around her. She flipped a page in her sheet music. She shouldn't feel sorry for herself. It would only make matters worse.

Her fingers moved over the keys. Scales again, with one hand, up and down, higher and higher, then with both hands. The music on the stand blurred. *Oh, Lord, Lord . . .* She had no words to pray, but her fingers moved, speaking through her music, from major to minor key, soft runs, and a melody she knew she wouldn't even try to put onto paper because it was only between her and the Lord.

And there lay Timmy, on his stomach beneath the front pew, chin resting on his crossed arms while he watched and listened.

As Samuel ushered Hollis into his den, he wondered what complaint his old friend would lodge this time. Abby was in the kitchen preparing coffee and refreshments. She always thought coffee and cookies could cure anything. Sometimes she was right.

Closing the door, Samuel offered Hollis his leather chair. It was worn and comfortable and much easier to get out of than the rocker Abby preferred. Hollis thanked him, eased himself into the chair, and set his cane aside. "I've had it, Sam. I'm done."

"Why don't you tell me what happened?"

"Nothing I can put my finger on." Hollis shook his head. "I'm just tired of feeling useless and old. He doesn't listen to us. You know that as well as I do."

"He's young."

"Being young is no excuse for disrespect."

"I'm not trying to make excuses for Paul. But consider. He showed respect for what you had to say when he put in the display cabinet in the narthex. And he apologized to you personally, didn't he?"

"If you can call explaining why he removed the King James Bible an apology. He never actually said he was sorry. And that cabinet . . ."

"It's beautiful."

"Sure, it's beautiful, but he was being expedient, Samuel. The more new people that come into the church, the less that kid is going to feel he has to consider anything we say."

Samuel was afraid Hollis might be right. "The first thing we have to do is remember he was called here to be our pastor."

"He acts more like a dictator."

"Did you and Paul have words again?"

"No." Hollis looked more hurt than angry. "Maybe it's what he doesn't say, or what he does or doesn't do about what *we* say. I look into his eyes and see impatience. I can almost hear what he's thinking: *What does this old man want now?* Well, Sam, I'm tired of fighting. And what am I fighting for anymore? To keep things as they were? I don't know most of the people coming to church anymore. All new faces."

"That's a good thing, Hollis. The church is growing."

"All *young* faces." His mouth tightened. "And I'm sure they want *young* elders in keeping with their *young* ideas."

"They need leadership."

"They've got Paul, their anointed one."

Samuel frowned, troubled by his words. "We're all anointed, Hollis. Every believer receives the Holy Spirit."

"You and I know that, but to hear some talk, Paul Hudson has more of an anointing than the rest of us common folk. Maybe that's why he doesn't want to submit himself to his elders. Maybe he has private audiences with God Himself. Maybe he . . ."

Samuel leaned forward. "Sarcasm isn't going to help us bring unity."

"Unity ended the day Henry Porter left Centerville. We were a family as long as he was standing in the pulpit. His sermons might not have drawn the people Hudson's do, but we never had to wonder if he loved us."

Abby tapped on the door before entering. She carried a tray in and set it on the desk. She poured coffee, added cream, stirred, and gave the mug to Hollis. "There are some nice pecan nougats here for you, Hollis. I know you like them."

"Thanks, Abby." He took one.

Abby quietly left the room, closing the door behind her.

"I'm resigning from the eldership, Samuel."

"Don't do that, Hollis, please." Samuel was sick at heart for all he had expected it. What would happen to the parishioners if there were only two elders remaining to oversee the church? "We have 150 new people coming each Sunday."

"Most are transfers from other churches. Hudson can tap some of them for service."

"We don't know anything about these new people, Hollis."

"I don't fit in at Centerville anymore, Sam. And you know it." He put his coffee aside. He seemed to have no taste for his favorite cookies. "I can't stand the new music, for another thing. How many times can we sing the same four lines? I feel like I'm singing some Christian mantra. They're dumbing down the church just like they're dumbing down America. And before you start defending him, I'll tell you I've heard all the rhetoric behind it. If it's going to bring new people to Christ, then so be it. But that doesn't mean I have to sit in a pew and feel assaulted every week."

"You've made up your mind." The old guard was giving up his post.

"I wrote my letter of resignation and mailed it before coming over." Hollis couldn't look him in the eye. "I knew if I waited, you'd talk me out of it again. And it's time, Samuel." His eyes were glassy with moisture. He looked away and picked up his coffee mug. His lips shook as he sipped. "I should warn you, Otis has resigned as well."

Samuel felt as though he'd been punched in the stomach. *Lord, am I to stand alone in this battle?* "I'm sorry to hear that." His voice choked. He wondered if it would make any difference to Paul that two-thirds of the elders were leaving the church because of his methods of increasing membership. The younger man appeared to have the hide of a rhinoceros, but Samuel knew from things Eunice had shared with Abby that appearances were often deceiving. Paul Hudson had grown up in the shadow of his famous father. Was that what was driving him so hard? Fear that he wouldn't make the grade?

Right now, Samuel was more concerned with the old friends who had served with him over the years. "Where will you go for services?"

"Stay right in my own living room, I guess. Can't drive anymore, and Otis is tied down with Mabel in the condition she's in." He gave a brittle laugh. "I guess we're down to watching TV evangelists. God help us. There are enough of them on every week. The gospel in a box. Send in a donation and get a blessing."

"There are some good ones, if that's the route you intend to take, but be careful."

"Yeah, and the best part is, you never know what shenanigans are going on behind the scenes. All you see are smiling faces in the pews. Probably weed all the misfits out at the door. And then you have the glitzy professional worship team and the main man who speaks like Charlton Heston opening the Red Sea."

"Why don't we have a Bible study here? Just for old fogies like us who long for the good old days. I'll invite Otis and Mabel and a few others who haven't been coming to church lately."

"Trying to keep us in the family, Samuel?"

"We *are* family."

Hollis's eyes filled. "Sounds good. What day? What time?"

"Any day but Sunday."

"You're sticking?"

"Until God says otherwise."

"Or Paul Hudson gives you the boot."

A plain white envelope with Paul's name handwritten lay on the desk blotter when he came into the church office the next morning. When he tore the end off, a key fell out. He read the one-line note: *I no longer feel welcome at Centerville Christian Church, and therefore resign as elder. Otis Harrison.*

Paul sat down heavily. Depressed, he sifted through the mail and saw an envelope with Hollis Sawyer's name and return address. Probably another litany of complaints. Annoyed, he sliced the letter open with his penknife. *All my efforts to work with you have failed,* he read. What efforts? Hollis had tried to block him at every turn. Even when he'd contracted Stephen Decker to build the display cabinet, Hollis had shown no sign of gratitude. Did the old man realize how much that had cost and that the money had come out of savings he and Eunice had managed to put aside for Timmy's college fund? He had a good mind to tell Hollis Sawyer, but his anger evaporated as he read Hollis's last few lines. *I have loved and been a part of this church for longer than you are old, and now find there is no place for me. What can a man do when he is made to feel old and useless by the pastor? You have left me with no choice but to resign with some semblance of dignity.*

Heart sinking, Paul read the letter again. He felt Hollis Sawyer's frustration and hopelessness and was filled with remorse. Not once did Hollis recount past arguments. Instead, he summed everything up in a way that punched a hole in Paul's confidence. These were two of the three men who had called him to the pastorate here, and they were saying he had failed them. Closing his eyes, he asked God to forgive him. He'd never intended for these men to leave the church. He'd just wanted them to step aside. They had called him to revive Centerville Christian. All he'd ever wanted from them was their backing in his efforts. Instead, Otis and Hollis had criticized and fought him on every front. Now he had to find a way to deal with the inevitable gossip about why two elders had resigned and left the church.

At least he was now free to fill their posts.

Let me find men who are like-minded, God—men who will help me make Centerville Christian the center of worship I know it can be.

He prayed for more than an hour and ended up feeling drier than he had when he started. Sometimes he felt as though his prayers bounced off the ceiling and landed back in his lap. He opened a drawer and took out the church roster. He jotted down the names of men who shared his vision. Two stood out as though the Lord Himself had put a light on them. Both were transfers from other churches, where they had served as deacons and elders.

Marvin Lockford and his wife, LaVonne, lived twenty minutes north of Centerville, which put Marvin within easy commute of the church. He was manager of a local branch of a nationwide real estate firm, and was listed as one of their top salesmen. "We were looking for a congregation as on fire for the Lord as we are," Marvin had told Paul when they discussed membership six months ago. He and his wife had sat right in this office and talked about their faith and service before coming forward the following Sunday during the worship service.

"Frankly, Paul, Centerville Christian was dry as bones the one time we attended," Marvin had told him. "They had an old man in the pulpit who rambled, and they were singing hymns from a hundred years ago. So we made the commute north. We liked the other church well enough, but it was too far away to get involved in any of the programs. And we miss being involved. We like to serve. When we heard Centerville Christian had called a new pastor, we thought we'd give it one more try. So here we are, happy as clams."

And they were generous with their financial support.

Paul put a star next to Marvin Lockford's name.

The next one who struck him as being a prime candidate for eldership was Gerald Boham. His wife, Jessie, was a school nurse at one of the high schools south of Centerville. Gerald was a financial planner who ran his business out of his home. He had run a big firm in Los Angeles, but decided it would be better for his clients and his family life if he set out on his own. Apparently, he was doing well; he'd just purchased a Jaguar.

If these two men would agree to serve as elders, Paul knew he would have men working with him instead of against him. Marvin and Gerald were exactly the kind of men he needed to keep the church growing.

Paul tapped his pencil, wondering if he should call the other pastors and ask for some kind of reference. But what would they think if he asked for references and did a background check on a Christian brother?

He needed more than three elders to manage operations now. Centerville Christian hadn't had deacons in the last ten years because of small membership. The elders had done everything from the down-and-dirty work, counseling members, and planning functions to managing the financial end of the church. The church was filling up, and he needed men who could paint, plumb, build cabinets and shelves, change lightbulbs in the high ceiling of the fellowship hall, and take on some of the gardening work like mowing the lawn and trimming the hedges. He had more important things to do. It would be an added bonus if the men organized and taught adult Sunday school classes, and their wives taught the children.

Deacons would save money by not having to hire a professional— money better spent on a sound system, educational supplies, new praise books for the pews, banners for the walls, new cushions for the pews, and a TV for videos for the growing number in the youth group. Paul had done most of the menial work himself. Of course, Samuel Mason had helped as much as he could for a man in his late seventies, but when he did, Paul had to suffer through his sermonizing on one subject or another. Paul had to tune out the old man so he could get through the work faster and move on to more important things. Custodial jobs took time away from what Paul knew he should be doing—studying and teaching, spending more time meeting important people in the community, building bridges from the outside world into Centerville Christian Church.

All the men he had in mind were married with children, except one. Their wives were capable women who might also be called upon to serve in some capacity in the church. Abby Mason had already drafted several of them to help in the nursery and take on teaching some of the grade school classes, but more were needed. Abby was terrific in the nursery, but the lesson plans she gave the others were outdated. Grade school and high school children should be hearing modern-day stories that incorporated biblical principles rather than the same timeworn tales of Daniel in the lions' den, David and Goliath, or Moses opening the Red Sea.

The more Paul thought about it, the more convinced and excited he was that the resignations of Hollis Sawyer and Otis Harrison were blessings straight from the Lord. Their departure heralded a new era at Centerville Christian Church. No more fighting over music and the order of worship! No more comparisons with Henry Porter! No more meetings that lasted two hours and accomplished nothing!

Eunice could start an adult choir and a children's choir. With all her training, she should be able to organize and orchestrate cantatas that would bring in the public at Christmas and Easter. If the programs were good enough, visitors would become regulars at the services.

Lord, give me five years and I'll make this church a focal point in the community!

Pulsing with excitement, Paul picked up the telephone. He knew church protocol said he should inform Samuel Mason of his plans before beginning the process, but Samuel might want him to seek out the other two ex-elders and try to get them back. No way! He didn't want them back. Let their resignations stand. Let them leave the church. Good riddance. No, he wouldn't call Samuel. Hollis, Otis, and Samuel had been a trio for years. Better if he called Marvin and Gerald first and found out if they were willing to serve as elders. Once he had their agreement, he would call Samuel. Otherwise, Samuel would want him to wait. He'd call for caution, references, background checks. He'd throw up a dozen other roadblocks that would take up valuable time. One thing was clear to Paul: this church could not function with one pastor and one stubborn old elder.

He punched in Marvin Lockford's work number.

"Of course!" Marvin was eager to serve. "I've been an elder before. I know what the job entails."

Paul called Gerald Boham, who was equally willing. "I'd be honored to serve," Gerald said. Paul explained again that the matter would be settled as soon as the church body took a vote on it, but that he didn't think there would be any problem with gaining members' approval. The new members now outnumbered the ones who had been here for decades, and the newer ones would follow his leading.

Paul felt a niggling discomfort in the pit of his stomach. Maybe it was something he had eaten that morning. Or had he eaten? He went through the rest of his mail, tossing the bills into a basket, perusing the brochures on church growth instead. He jotted ideas into a notebook he kept in his top-right drawer. The phone rang once, twice, thrice, and the answering machine picked up. He hated using it, but he had to screen his calls so that he could get some work done. If he answered every call that came into the church office, he'd be spending all his time running around and visiting various members of the church rather than preparing sermons and lessons.

What he needed was a handpicked associate who shared his vision and was qualified to shoulder some of the load. He glanced over the financial reports. Offerings had increased during the last few weeks since he had begun writing his sermons to a seeker audience. Perhaps an associate could be the first order of business for the new eldership. But first there would have to be an increase in his own salary so that he and Eunice could move into a house of their own. It didn't have to be very big. Three bedrooms would be nice so that he could have a home office. He'd have more time with Eunice and Timmy that way. And the parsonage would be available for another staff member and his family when they came along.

But he was getting ahead of himself.

Paul made a list of men who would be good deacons. He reached half of them before noon. When he went home for lunch, he didn't tell Eunice about Hollis and Otis. She would only get upset, and want to know the details. He didn't want to talk about it. He didn't tell her about Marvin or Gerald either. Nor did he tell her about the new deacons he'd selected. He'd tell her tonight, after he had spoken to all of them and before word spread and she heard the news from someone else. Like Samuel or Abby Mason. He'd have to prepare a roster on which the church members could vote. If all went smoothly, he would call for a church-wide meeting after this Sunday's service. It wouldn't take long. Everyone knew the church needed workers. And next year, he'd let the congregation nominate the deacons and deaconesses.

"Is everything all right, Paul?"

"Couldn't be better." He finished his sandwich and downed his glass of tomato juice. "I'm going to be doing visitations all afternoon." A personal visit from the pastor was more likely to win agreement to serve than a telephone call. "So I'll be late."

"Do you want me to keep your dinner warm?"

He wiped his mouth with his napkin and tossed it on the table. "No." He would go down to Charlie's Diner and see if he could connect with Stephen Decker. Sally said Stephen ate breakfast at seven and dinner between six and seven. He gave Eunice a quick kiss. "Go ahead and have dinner without me."

"It's getting to be a habit."

"It can't be helped." He ruffled Timmy's hair. "Be a good boy for Mommy."

"Paul?"

"I've got to run, honey."

"Couldn't you stay for thirty minutes? Even a businessman gets a lunch hour."

"I'm not a businessman." She, of all people, should understand, having grown up the daughter of a pastor. "I have a lot of work to do and hardly enough time as it is. Did you want to talk about something specific? Is it important?"

"I guess not."

He kissed her again. "We'll talk later this evening." He would tell her all his good news when it was all settled.

———— ❦ ————

Stephen Decker was surprised to see Paul Hudson enter Charlie's Diner at dinnertime. If Stephen had a wife like Eunice at home, he wouldn't be eating in a café, even if all she could cook were hot dogs and macaroni and cheese. Stephen gave him a nod as Hudson approached his booth.

"Mind if I join you?"

Surprised, Stephen gathered up the paperwork with the final details of the Atherton project. "Have a seat." He raised his brows. "Did you and your wife have a spat?"

Paul laughed. "No. Actually, I came here to talk with you."

"Pastoral visit. Sounds serious." He hadn't been near a bar. So that couldn't be the reason for this tête-à-tête.

"I need a few good men to serve as deacons."

Stephen leaned back. "And you think I qualify?" He laughed.

"Yes, I do."

Eunice must not have shared their little chat with her husband, which raised his opinion of her another notch. "You don't know anything about me except what I do for a living, and that I can do a reasonable job at building a display cabinet. Or was that what you had in mind? Day laborers for the church who'd work evenings and Saturdays."

Pastor Paul made no pretenses. "Labor, yes, but also men who love the Lord and are willing to work with me to make Centerville Christian Church the church it could be."

"And what kind of church is that?"

Paul leaned forward, eager to tell him. "A center for Christian worship for Centerville as well as the surrounding areas, a place where families can come and be involved and nurtured in their faith, a place that will set people on fire for the Lord and encourage them to go out and fulfill the great commission of making disciples of all nations."

Whoa. Paul was on a fast horse.

"We have every kind of religion in the Central Valley, from Islam to Buddhism to New Age, Stephen. And right now, there are a pathetic few Christian churches doing outreach programs to lead nonbelievers to salvation. We need younger men with new and progressive ideas that can help us build the Kingdom of God, and bring the church into the twenty-first century."

Intrigued, Stephen closed his file and dropped it into his open brief-case. He recognized ambition when he saw it, but as far as he could tell, there was nothing wrong with being ambitious about building a church. Where would he be now without the Lord? At the Wagon Wheel. What would he be? A drunk. "I'm all for giving back to the Lord."

"That's what I thought."

"But before we go further, there's something that could eliminate me as a deacon."

Paul frowned. "What would that be?"

"I'm a recovering alcoholic. I was in a rehab center for six months. While I was there, my wife divorced me and was given custody of our daughter." He saw the troubled look come into Pastor Paul's eyes, could almost hear the wheels in his brain spinning and trying to find a way to renege on his proposal.

"How long since you had a drink?"

"Eleven months, one week, and three days." Just so the pastor knew it wasn't easy staying sober.

"The Bible says a deacon shouldn't be a man given to drink, and since you're not drinking, I can't see any reason why you can't serve as a deacon. If everyone had to have lived a perfect life in order to serve the Lord, there wouldn't be anyone serving." He grinned. "What do you say? Do you want to be in on planning the future of Centerville Christian?"

"Okay," Stephen said slowly. "You can count me in."

"Great!" Paul extended his hand to shake Stephen's. "Welcome aboard."

Stephen felt as though he had just made some kind of contract with the pastor.

"I'm preparing the roster tomorrow, and am planning to call a church membership meeting following the service on Sunday morning. The congregation has to take a vote on it, but I don't see that there's going to be a problem. As soon as those details are taken care of, we can have our first meeting and see where we're going."

A regular mover and shaker.

Sally appeared with Stephen's salad. "Are you staying for supper, Pastor Paul?"

"If Stephen doesn't mind company. Dutch, of course."

"Nonsense," Sally said. "Whatever you want is on the house." She left and came back with a menu.

Paul smiled. "I've heard Charlie's meat loaf is terrific."

"His steaks are better," she said.

"Steak it is. Medium-rare."

"Mushrooms?"

"Sure. Why not?"

"You got it." Sally called the order to Charlie as soon as she was behind the counter.

Stephen found himself curious about Paul Hudson. He was young to be heading a church. "How did you end up at Centerville Christian?"

Paul told him about the previous pastor's collapse and the phone call from the dean of the college he and Eunice had attended. "I was working for a big church in the Midwest at the time. But I knew God was calling me to this post. When we arrived, I got to know people and felt the hunger in them. They hadn't been fed for a long time. Not that Henry Porter didn't try to fulfill his responsibilities. He did, admirably. The parishioners loved him, loved him so much they almost worked him to death. They just needed a younger man."

"And they sure got one. How old are you, anyway?"

Paul told him. "I'm young, but not inexperienced. I was a PK."

"Preacher's kid." Stephen had heard the expression. "Did you go the route that some do?"

"Diving off the deep end into the ocean, you mean?" Paul chuckled. "I thought about it a few times, but didn't dare go through with it. I never wanted to bring embarrassment on my father or my mother. And, even more than that, I wanted to please the Lord. I gave my life to Him when I was seven years old."

"Did your father baptize you?"

"No. Actually, my mother did. Well, my dad did later. Officially. I can't recall where my father was when I told my mother I'd decided to give my life to the Lord. She took me straightaway into the bathroom and baptized me in the tub, clothes and all." He laughed. "She's always been a little unorthodox."

"Well, it must've taken," Stephen said, laughing too.

"My father had me rebaptized in front of the congregation on Easter Sunday."

Stephen wondered why Paul's expression became suddenly solemn and withdrawn. Paul caught himself and continued. "I grew up seeing how a church is built. My father started with a handful of people and built the congregation into thousands. Maybe you've heard of him. David Hudson."

"Sorry. Can't say that I have."

"They televise his services. And my grandfather was also a pastor. Not a successful one, but he tried, I guess. He was a traveling evangelist who did tent revivals in little towns across the country."

"So you come by the gift naturally."

"The gift?"

"Speaking. You must know you're the reason so many new people are coming to check out Centerville Christian."

Paul was clearly pleased by the praise, though he tried to downplay it. "I can't think of anything else I'd rather do than work for the Lord."

"That's as it should be."

Sally brought Paul's salad, then served their steaks. They lingered over dinner, talking about the church, the Atherton house and other projects Stephen had built, programs Paul had been involved in and wanted to start up at Centerville Christian.

Stephen let Paul do most of the talking. The young pastor had a dream—a big one—of building the Kingdom for the glory of God. A spark caught fire in Stephen. Maybe that was what he needed to still the restlessness in him. He needed to work at something that occupied him longer than the six months to a year it took to build a house or an office building. He knew Paul was speaking of people when he talked about building the Kingdom, but if he succeeded, the congregation would soon reach the boundaries of the small church building in which they were now meeting. Multiple services would help. For a while.

Sooner or later, Centerville Christian would need a bigger facility.

What would it be like to design and build a church? What a challenge that would be!

The more he listened to Paul, the more excited he was to be a part of what was happening at the church. He and Paul might come from divergent backgrounds, but they had one major thing in common: they both wanted to build something that would last.

PART 2

In Sight of the
PROMISED LAND

———— ❧ ————

CHAPTER 6

1/17/15
5:05 P.M.

5 yrs. pass

1992

Eunice fought the physical exhaustion and depression that invariably hit her at Christmastime. She didn't know how she would make it through to New Year's. It was her third cantata and rehearsals were going well, but there had been the usual squabbling among choir members. Tensions always mounted as the day of the performance approached.

She'd had to remind several participants again of the hours of labor two senior saints had put into making the beautiful costumes. They should be thanked and not treated to further complaints. The point was not to put on a Broadway production, but to present the gospel. Unsaved members of the community would be coming, and they needed to learn the true meaning of Christmas: the birth of God's only begotten Son, Jesus Christ. Yet, week after week, the same three women clustered and grumbled, their attitudes and words far from the angelic presences they were supposed to portray in the pageant.

Thankfully the rehearsal was over. Her head was pounding. She felt sick to her stomach. When the last person departed, Eunice shut off the lights, locked the fellowship hall, and went into the sanctuary. She sank to her knees and tried to pray, but every thought was less than honoring to the Lord. Should she come before Him and grumble about those who grumbled?

Oh, Lord, Lord . . . I used to love Christmas. When I was a little girl, we sang carols for the pure pleasure of it. No one cared that we were dressed in clothes purchased from a thrift store. They listened with delight! I remember being invited in for hot cocoa and homemade cookies.

Eunice sang softly to the Lord. "'Hark! the herald angels sing, "Glory to the newborn King . . ."'"

She sang the same songs women in this congregation were going to sing in two days, unless three of them quit in a snit because they couldn't get over the size of their wings or how much glitter was glued to their white robes! "We're supposed to glow!" Why couldn't they get past themselves long enough to see that this cantata wasn't about how they looked onstage, but what God had done for mankind? Everyone became so caught up in the sets and costumes and decorations that she couldn't bring them back to the simplicity and beauty of Christmas. Instead of being a play about the passion of God's love, it had become a Hollywood production.

Forgive me, Lord; please forgive me. You know the desire of my heart is to bring You glory, and what I'm seeing is so far from it. I want to love these women, Lord. I want to love them as You love me. Help me.

Longing for a few more moments to bask in God's presence, Eunice went back to the church office and phoned home. Maybe Paul would be willing to give Timmy his bath.

"Where are you?" He sounded frustrated.

"I'm still at church. I was—"

"It's late, and Timmy needs a bath."

"I was hoping maybe you could take care of that. It's not that difficult to fill the tub, Paul." She tried to instill some humor into her voice.

"I haven't got time to play games with him—or you. I'm in the middle of studying."

She wanted to say she had just finished a grueling two hours of rehearsal, not to mention dealing with three obstinate, self-centered women who would send her to the funny farm soon. She needed time to pray. She needed time to beg the Lord for His patience and love. "Couldn't I have a few more minutes? . . . Paul?"

He'd already hung up.

1/17 , 10:30 P.M. ✓

Hurt and angry, Eunice went out the front door of the church, locked the door, and headed for the parsonage. The house was silent, Paul hunkered down in his chair, books and notes scattered around him.

"Where's Timmy?"

"I sent him to bed."

"I thought you said he needed a bath."

"I told him you'd give it to him in the morning."

"He has school in the morning."

His eyes darkened. "So get him up early, and he can take a shower before you take him."

She put her satchel of music aside and sat slowly. "What happened?"

"You've spoiled him rotten."

His voice was loud enough to carry through the closed door of Timmy's bedroom. Did he realize how cruel his words sounded, how condemning? "Paul—"

Paul slammed his book shut. "Eunice, the boy is eight years old, but he whines like a baby. He wants to watch a video. He wants a story. He wants a bath. He wants, wants, wants—"

"He wants time with his father."

"Don't give me that. I spend time with him."

"Five minutes here and there isn't enough time, Paul. You should know that better than anyone." She saw the change in his expression and knew she should have said something less volatile, something that didn't compare him to David Hudson. She might as well have waved a red flag in front of a bull's face.

"I helped him with his homework last night."

For five minutes before sending him into the kitchen to her.

"I played baseball with him on Saturday."

Until his pager went off ten minutes after they'd gone outside.

"I took him to Charlie's Diner."

And brought him home in tears less than an hour later because Gerald Boham had called and invited Daddy to a round of golf at the country club.

"If I spent all day, every day with him, it wouldn't be enough. He can't seem to get it into his head that *I have responsibilities*."

"You needn't shout." Every word stabbed her heart. And the walls were so thin, poor Timmy could hear everything his father said. She watched Paul gather up his papers. "Where are you going?"

"To the church office, where I can get some work done!" He shoved his notes into his briefcase.

"It's nine thirty, Paul."

He headed for the hall closet, where his coat was hung. "Some of us have to work for a living." He shoved an arm into his coat.

Eunice clenched her hands as he went out the front door, closing it none too quietly behind him. She waited a few minutes, giving him time to change his mind. Then she turned on the porch light.

When she opened Timmy's bedroom door, she could hear his muffled sobs. She didn't turn on the light, but sat on the edge of his bed and rubbed his back. "He loves you, Timmy."

"No, he doesn't."

"He loves you very much. It's just that he's working so hard." Places to go and things to do. For the church. He had to set priorities. Unfortunately, Timmy was way down on his list. So was she. After elders' calls, deacons' meetings, and parishioners' needs. "And it's hardest on him this time of year because . . ." Timmy rolled over and came into her arms. She held him close, fighting tears as she stroked his back and rocked him tenderly. "Lots of people struggle with Christmas, Timmy. They call Daddy, and he has to be there to counsel them. He's under a lot of pressure."

"Will he be home for Christmas?"

"We'll all be together for services Christmas Eve and Christmas Day." And in between—unless Paul received a call from a family in crisis. Last year, Paul had been called away from home just as the turkey was being taken from the oven. She and Timmy had eaten alone. Grandma Hudson had called at a little past eight to wish them a blessed Christmas. Eunice had waited one more hour before allowing Timmy to open his packages. She had finally put him to bed at eleven. Paul had come in so late, he was too tired to get up and spend the morning with them. Still, he had risen in time to prepare for the Christmas Day services.

Would this year be the same?

"Did you say your prayers, sweetheart?"

Timmy shook his head against her shoulder.

"What do you say we do that right now while we're thinking about it?"

They prayed softly together, thanking God for His love and mercy, His provision and guidance, and thanking Him especially for His Son, Jesus. Timmy prayed for her and the cantata. He prayed for Samuel and Abigail. He prayed for Grandma and Grandpa Hudson. He prayed for his friends in school and his teacher. He prayed for peace in the world. "In Jesus' name, amen."

"And Daddy," Eunice said softly, prompting. "God bless Daddy."

Wiping his nose on his sleeve, Timmy lay back against his pillows and turned his back to her. He pulled his teddy bear close. The night-light from the hall cast a soft glow in the room. She saw his shoulders were trembling and knew he was crying again, trying to stifle the sounds against his worn stuffed animal. It broke her heart. "I love you, Timmy. And Daddy loves you, too." She stroked Timmy's soft hair. It was sandy brown, like Paul's. Timmy drew his knees up and burrowed his head deeper into the covers. Heart aching, throat tight and hot, Eunice leaned down and kissed him. "You are so precious to me. I love you so very, very much, Timmy." She kissed him again. "You are God's blessing to Daddy and me." She ran her hand over his hair once more. Rising, she rearranged the covers so that he would be warm and closed the door quietly on her way out.

Sitting in the living room, Eunice covered her face and wept. Paul had more compassion for rebellious members of his church than he did for his own son. Or her, for that matter. How many times had she asked for his counsel regarding grumbling, gossiping parishioners, and he would hurriedly tell her to be patient, hear them out, and bend as much as possible so that they would enjoy their service for the Lord? And then out the door he'd go again. Did Paul want her to treat these women with kid gloves because all three were elders' wives? Was she supposed to make special rules for special people? How could Paul command her to bend for them and then refuse to bend at all for his own son? Did Paul even listen? Couldn't he understand that Timmy acted up because he desperately wanted his father's attention? Negative attention was better than no attention at all. Paul always managed to rearrange his schedule so that he could have lunch or play golf with one of his elders. Why not for Timmy? Why not for her?

"Do this, Eunice." "Do that, Eunice."

Paul had told her to form a choir, then told her to organize a cantata for Christmas and another for Easter. Even as she obeyed, he made it clear in a dozen ways that she should not expect his help as she tried to accomplish his goals. He didn't have the time. He had more important things to do. Places to go and people to meet.

She kept telling herself that Paul was doing all this work "for the Kingdom," but sometimes a betraying thought would grip her heart. Which kingdom? He was making and carrying out plans so fast, she wondered how he had time to ask God's counsel, let alone hear it.

And yet, everything seemed to be moving ahead just as he said it would. Paul took every success as a sign from God that he was on the right track, that he was accomplishing what God wanted, that his methods were appropriate to the work God had given him. Centerville Christian Church was growing so fast, Eunice didn't know many of the people now attending on a regular basis. Paul did two Sunday services now, and he had the backing of the elders to add staff. Reka Wilson, a retired office manager, had offered to take on the job of church secretary at minimum wage. Over the past month, Reka had fielded calls and saved Paul countless hours of paperwork. Eunice had hoped Paul would be able to spend more time with her and Timmy, and more time writing wonderful Christ-centered Bible studies like he had during his senior year in college.

Instead, Paul scheduled more speaking engagements. "The only way I can be an influence in the community is if people know who I am and what I stand for." Paul had become well known and well liked in the community. When the mayor came to services, Eunice noticed how Paul cut back on the number of quotations from the Bible and brought in more stories and illustrations, excusing the softened message by saying he wanted people to come back to church again, not come once and then never return because "they've been beaten over the head with some dry lesson on doctrine." And Paul had canceled the Wednesday night Bible study several months ago, because so few people turned out in the middle of the week.

The clock chimed eleven.

Ashamed, Eunice realized she'd spent more than an hour wallowing in self-pity, assessing her husband's faults without examining her own.

Lord, please remold my thinking, reshape my heart, burn away the anger that's threatening to sink roots of bitterness into my marriage and my life.

She went into the kitchen, warmed a cup of milk in the microwave, and sat at the table where she and Timmy ate most of their meals alone.

Lord, You are my shepherd. You have given me everything I need. Your strength and power, Your love and guidance keep me on the path You've laid out for me. Protect me, Lord. Keep the enemy away, Father, please. I'm vulnerable right now, Jesus. I know in my heart it's who You are and not what I do that's important. But it's so easy to get caught up in the show of it all. Let my life be a light by which others can see You. I want to do what's right, but sometimes it seems there are so many things going on, so many irons in the fire, I don't even know where to start.

The front door opened.

Eunice put her hands around the warm mug of milk. She heard the soft catch as the coat closet door was opened and then closed. Footsteps on the linoleum. A weary sigh. "There was a message on the answering machine from Marvin Lockford. LaVonne is feeling unwell and may not be able to be in the performance."

"That's just as well." She was tired of the struggle. She imagined Jessie Boham and Shirl Wenke would be calling sometime tomorrow with the same lame excuse.

"Just as well? What do you mean, 'just as well'?"

Lord, please don't let me speak in anger. "They have the wrong idea about the cantata."

"It was up to you to give them the *right* idea, Eunice. Do you have any idea the trouble you've caused me by not handling this situation with more delicacy?"

"You're blaming me for something I have no power to change."

"You're in charge. The buck stops with you."

She wasn't about to throw his failures in his face. "All right, Paul. Then as the one 'in charge,' I have this to say: The point of the cantata is not the size of LaVonne's wings or the amount of glitter on her robe, but the proclamation of the birth of our Savior and Lord, Jesus Christ."

His face tightened. "I'm sure she understands that as well as anyone."

"If she did, you wouldn't have received a call from her husband."

"I called Marvin and said you'd call LaVonne tomorrow and apologize for the misunderstanding."

He assumed she would comply. Fuel on the fire she had asked God to snuff out. *Daddy, is this one of the battles you meant? So be it.* "I will call and tell LaVonne how sorry I am that she's too ill to be a part of the cantata."

"Why are you acting like this?"

"I'm not acting, Paul." Tears filled her eyes. "I will not be held hostage by LaVonne Lockford's emotional blackmail."

"You're letting your pride get in the way of unity with a Christian sister."

Was LaVonne Lockford a Christian sister? "How can I have unity with a woman who wants the spotlight on *her* rather than on *Jesus?*"

"You're overreacting."

"You're not listening, Paul! You haven't listened to anything I've said to you in months!"

He scraped a chair out and sat. "Okay. I'm listening now. Tell me what your problem is."

Her problem. Not theirs. She looked across the table at him, the mug of warm milk growing cold between her hands. "You've already assigned blame to me. Why is that?" Was she just a convenient scapegoat?

He said nothing, but the look on his face made her want to scream at him.

Lord, Lord, Your words, not mine. Please. Your will, not mine. "It's not my problem with LaVonne, Paul. It's her relationship with Jesus. Does she have one?"

"Her husband is one of our elders, Eunice. Of course LaVonne has a relationship with Jesus."

"I'd like to think so, but I haven't seen any evidence of it since she joined the choir." *Nor before that,* she wanted to say and did not dare. The Lockfords had seemed a nice enough couple when they had joined the church, and they had apparently served in several other churches before moving to Centerville. Still, she had been shocked three years ago when Paul had informed her of Hollis Sawyer's and Otis Harrison's resignations and sprung the nomination roster with Marvin Lockford named as a candidate for eldership. They hardly knew the man. No one had questioned the names Paul gave the congregation, except Samuel, who voiced his reservations to Paul in private and was summarily ignored. "I told him I'm not about to conduct a CIA investigation on a Christian brother and sister!" Everything had gone smoothly with Marvin, who encouraged and backed Paul's endeavors to build the church membership, but from the beginning, LaVonne tended to use her husband's position to gain a platform for herself.

"Eunice, why are you making such a big deal out of such a little thing? What harm is there in putting more glitter, or whatever it is she wants, on LaVonne's costume?"

Was she overreacting? It was true she liked LaVonne less and less as time went on. Perhaps her own feelings were getting in the way of her judgment. On the other hand, wasn't there something fundamentally wrong with repeatedly giving in to a person's petty demands?

"It is a little thing, Paul. I know it is. And Abby made changes to the costume to please LaVonne, but it wasn't enough." It was never enough. "There have been lots of little things over the past three years. Haven't you noticed? And all of it adds up to one big question: Is she saved?"

His eyes darkened. "I would hardly have asked Marvin to be an elder if I wasn't convinced both he and his wife were saved."

There was no use reminding him that he hadn't known the Lockfords that long before drafting Marvin to assist in the running of the church. He hadn't known the Bohams that long either. Or the Wenkes, for that matter. "Paul, it matters more to me that we know where LaVonne stands with Jesus than whether she sings one of the solos in the cantata."

Paul scraped his chair back, his cheeks red. "And you think it doesn't matter to me? You call her, Eunice, and you apologize. Do you understand me? You're my wife, and you're supposed to be building bridges, not burning down the ones I've built all by myself without any help from you!" He headed out of the room.

Battered and bruised by his accusation, she sat stunned and hurt. *Lord, is he right? Am I burning bridges? Help me let go of hurt feelings and concentrate on the needful issues, God. Help me . . . help me.* "Paul?" *Oh, God . . .*

"What?" The long-suffering look on his face made her feel she was nothing but trouble to him.

She fought tears. *Needful things, Lord. Please, make him listen this time.* "We need to talk about Timmy."

He closed his eyes, exasperated. "Not tonight. I'm tired."

"When?"

"Tomorrow morning."

But when Eunice awakened in the morning, Paul was already gone.

He'd left a note on the kitchen table. *Breakfast with SD. Lunch at the country club with the mayor. Might be home for dinner.*

She knew better than to keep it warm.

By the time Stephen arrived at the Christmas cantata, the fellowship hall was packed. He stood in the back corner, along with half a dozen others who, like he, had had to park six blocks from the church. The way he saw it, if the membership of Centerville Christian kept growing like it was, the powers that be were going to have to consider building a bigger facility to accommodate the flock. This pen was becoming too small.

He could relax now that he had found a space to stand. The air smelled of pine mingled with gingerbread. The hall looked like something from an old-time Victorian Christmas card with pine-and-holly garlands tied with red velvet bows on windowsills, podium, top of the piano, and front of the stage.

Everyone quieted when Pastor Paul entered—elegantly dressed in a black suit, white shirt, and black tie—and announced the cantata. Paul's prayer was a bit long, but eloquent as always. He looked downright regal as he nodded and then took a seat in the front row. Stephen wondered why Timmy wasn't sitting with his father. The boy was perched on a chair between Abigail and Samuel Mason.

When Eunice entered, Stephen caught his breath. Her blonde hair hung down around her shoulders. She was wearing a single strand of pearls and a long black dress. Stephen swallowed hard and spent the next hour watching every move she made, relishing the pure pleasure of the experience from the dark corner of the fellowship hall. He had never seen a woman so completely, inwardly, outwardly, breathtakingly beautiful.

This was her third Christmas cantata, and each was better than the last. More sets, more singers, more cookies, more punch, more decorations. More work! When the performance was over, Stephen lingered in the back. He'd save his congratulations for later. The choir members in their costumes were mingling with those who had come to listen and watch the show. People had to draw back quickly when LaVonne Lockford passed by, glittering wings flopping. Stephen almost laughed. She looked more like a giant mutant fairy than an angel.

Now that the show was over, thanks and congratulations offered, the flock stood grazing at tables laden with Christmas cookies and hot apple cider. Eunice was smiling, Timmy at her side, but Stephen recognized fatigue when he saw it. At a guess, he'd say the adrenaline rush had worn off and collapse was near at hand. Paul was busy serving punch to the mayor and his wife.

Stephen made his way through the crowd. His gaze met hers, and he felt a shock of awareness heat his blood. It always caught him off guard. He hoped she didn't have a clue how much he admired her. He didn't want her to put up walls and withdraw from their friendship. "Hey, sport, how're you doing?" he said to Timmy. "What do you say we go get a gingerbread cookie before they're all gone? Unless your mother nixes the idea."

"Mommy?"

Smiling, she ran her hand over his slicked-back hair. "Go ahead."

Stephen took two cookies and filled an extra cup of punch, but when he turned, he saw that Paul had signaled his wife to join him with the mayor. Eunice rose from the chair where she'd been sitting with the Masons and threaded her way through the crowd to shake hands and offer greetings to Paul's illustrious guests. When Eunice looked around, Stephen raised his hand so that she spotted him. He pointed down. Timmy was still safe at his side. She smiled and beckoned.

"Do you want to meet the mayor, Timmy?"

"No. I want to go back and sit with Sam and Abby."

Dead set on that, Timmy took off. Stephen shrugged and pointed again. Timmy was already sitting between the Masons. Stephen followed and handed Abby Mason the cup of punch he'd poured for Eunice. "Quite a crowd tonight."

"Over three hundred," Samuel said. "Some standing."

"I was one of them."

"We were here an hour early or we wouldn't have gotten a good seat," Abby said.

Samuel put his arm on the back of Timmy's chair. "The fire marshal was here and chewing his nails. If he wasn't a member of the church, he'd have to cite us for violations."

"Might be better if they put on the performance two days running."

Samuel nodded. "I think so."

"Too bad we don't have a bigger church building." When Samuel raised his head, Stephen grinned and lifted one hand. "Not that I'm looking for work, mind you. It was just a thought."

Abby smiled tightly. "A thought I'm sure has occurred to Paul Hudson."

"Abigail. We wanted growth."

"Growth, yes, but—"

Samuel cleared his throat. Abby closed her parted lips and said no more.

Amused, Stephen drew a chair from one of the rows and sat with them. He looked between the two elderly people. "I've never seen that happen before."

"What?" Samuel said, bemused.

"A man able to silence a woman without saying a word."

Abby slapped his knee. "You'd do well to take a few lessons from my husband instead of trying to stir up mischief."

Stephen grinned. "Yes, ma'am."

"My wife is seldom quiet for long," Samuel said with a chuckle.

Stephen leaned back. "Do you think we should keep the church small?"

"Depends on how you define *small*," Samuel said.

Paul had complained about the elder's caution several times over breakfast at Charlie's. "Say fewer than three hundred."

Samuel looked at him. "God has never been concerned with numbers, Stephen. He's concerned with focus and the heart. Growth in numbers is a blessing as long as spiritual growth and maturity come along with it."

Stephen nodded. "I agree, but sometimes growth comes fast. Remember, the church gained three thousand members in one day during Pentecost."

"Yes—" Samuel smiled—"and Christ had reared 120 individuals for leadership. They had lived with Jesus, heard His teachings, seen what it meant to live by and practice faith. The Holy Spirit came upon them as they were praying together in that upper room, and it was through the Spirit of the Lord that hearts were stirred that day. It wasn't because of a good show."

Stephen felt his hackles rise. "Are you saying we shouldn't have programs like this?" He jerked his head toward the stage, thinking of how hard Eunice must have worked to bring it all together.

"Not at all," Samuel said, and Stephen felt the probing behind the elder's look. "Clearly, Eunice's motivation was to put together a program to please the Lord. Anyone who knows her also knows she loves the Lord and seeks to serve Him. And everyone who attended tonight heard the heart of the gospel, Jesus Christ, proclaimed in every song and scene. The birth of mankind's Savior is the reason for celebration. Eunice is a prime example of the right focus and heart I'm talking about."

Others joined them, steering the conversation to weather, visiting family members, holiday plans, Christmas shopping, and complaints about prices. Stephen found his attention wandering until Abby leaned close. "As babies grow, they need something more than milk, Stephen. They need *meat*." She patted his knee as though he were a little boy. "And now that the men are talking football, it's time for me to see what needs to be done in the kitchen."

Babies? Meat? Had his mind drifted so long he'd lost complete track of the conversation? Bemused, Stephen caught Samuel looking at him. He had the feeling the Masons were trying to tell him something and he didn't have the ears to hear it.

The crowd thinned. Stephen stayed to help stow the folding chairs beneath the stage. Paul stripped off his suit jacket and helped. Eunice had returned to the parsonage to put Timmy to bed. "It went well, don't you think?" Paul said.

"Better than well, I'd say." Stephen leaned his weight against the trolley of chairs and rolled it into the storage space. "Packed house."

"I told Eunice she'll have to plan on two nights this Easter. Word will spread about the quality of the cantatas. We won't be able to get everyone in with only one night. I had one lady come up and tell me that the performance was as good as anything she's seen in San Francisco."

"Maybe you ought to sell tickets."

Paul laughed. "Don't think I haven't thought about it." He straightened after locking the storage-compartment door. "The congregation is outgrowing the building."

"I was saying the same thing to Samuel Mason."

Paul's expression clouded. "Some people see growth as a threat. Any kind of change scares them." He called out thanks to two other deacons who had finished stowing chairs. "Just leave everything else. Some of the deaconesses are coming back in the morning to sweep up and finish cleaning the kitchen." Paul fell into step with Stephen as he headed for the door. "The problem is parking."

"You could say that." And parking would remain a problem. The church had been built when Centerville was just forming and most parishioners were within walking distance. Things were different now. Most church members were from outside Centerville itself. Some came from twenty miles north.

"I was thinking." Paul paused on the steps between the sanctuary and fellowship hall and shrugged on his coat. "The elders increased my salary last year. It would be a stretch, but I think I could afford to buy a home in one of the new suburbs. If I moved my family out of the parsonage, we could demolish it and turn that part of the property into a parking lot."

"Nice idea, but it'd cost more than you might think, and it would only be a short-term fix. Not to mention the trouble you'd create with your neighbors over turning that sweet little place into a slab of asphalt." Stephen shook his head. "Nope. Bad idea all the way around, Pastor. Better and more cost-effective if you looked for property and started from scratch. Build with the idea of expanding as the congregation grows."

Paul tipped up his collar. "Sounds right up your alley."

Stephen wasn't so naive he couldn't see where Paul's thinking was heading. "I've never designed a church." Not that he hadn't thought about it on occasion since becoming a deacon of CCC.

"There was probably a time when you'd never designed an office building or a house either." Paul went down the steps and started across the courtyard lawn.

"You couldn't afford me!"

Paul laughed and waved without looking back as he headed for the parsonage, where Eunice would be waiting for him.

Hunching into his leather jacket, Stephen made for his truck.

Snug and warm in faded yellow- and blue-flowered flannel pajamas, pink chenille robe, and fuzzy slippers, Eunice curled her legs on the couch and sipped a cup of hot herbal tea. Her headache had gone away as soon as the cantata was over and the crowd was dispersing. Handel's

Messiah played softly on the stereo. Closing her eyes, Eunice listened and thanked the Lord she would have a month's respite before she would have to start making plans for the Easter cantata.

The telephone rang. She started. She was still too tense. *Please, God, don't let it be another emergency to call Paul away from home before he's even walked in the door.*

"It's Mom, Euny. How did the cantata go? Better than you expected?"

Eunice relaxed at the sound of her mother-in-law's voice. They had talked often over the past months, and Lois Hudson had given sound advice and wise counsel. "Everyone enjoyed the evening."

"Did any feathers fly?"

Eunice laughed. "No. The angels all behaved themselves."

"That's good. You sound tired."

"Exhausted."

"Is my son home?"

"Not yet. He probably got waylaid on the way home."

"The plight of all pastors. How would you like visitors? David is actually going to take a few days off in January, and I suggested we come up and see how our son is faring in the pulpit. We'd stay in a hotel, of course. Is there one close to you? I can't wait to hug my grandson again."

"A bed-and-breakfast opened last month. It's just down the street. But I'm not sure how much they charge."

"Whatever they charge will be fine." She gave several possible dates. "Check your calendar and see which days fit your schedule the best and go ahead and make the reservations. Then let me know."

They talked for another half hour about Timmy's progress in school, the Sunday school program Paul wanted her to organize and facilitate, and Paul's many commitments. Eunice sensed more than weariness in Lois's voice. Something was wrong. When she asked, her mother-in-law became evasive. Lois said both she and David just needed to get away from all the pressures and stresses of work. "Warn that son of mine that he'd better block out some time for his mother," Lois said. "And, honey, I love you. Keep the faith."

"I love you, too, Mom." Eunice's throat closed as she hung up the phone. Lois Hudson had always been there for her, especially during the dark days after Euny's mother and father had passed on to be with the Lord. Whenever she needed advice on how to handle various difficult situations that arose, she knew she could count on Lois for sound and sensitive counsel. Lois had faced all manner of difficulties in her years as a pastor's wife. The only thing Eunice never talked about with her mother-in-law was Paul. As far as Lois knew, everything was perfect in the younger Hudson household, and Eunice never wanted her to think otherwise.

The door clicked open. Euny watched Paul shrug off his suit coat. "The deaconesses are going to finish cleaning the kitchen tomorrow," he said without looking at her, "but the floor needs a good scrubbing and waxing." He hung his coat in the small closet. She knew he meant he wanted her to do it—or to call someone who would get it done.

"The program went well, don't you think?" She had received many compliments from others, but so far, Paul had said nothing about the outcome.

"Sure. It was fine." He loosened his tie. "What about the kitchen floor? You'll need to get it done tomorrow so it's ready by Sunday."

She looked away, throat tight. "I could use a day of rest, Paul."

"I could use a day of rest, too." He headed toward the kitchen. "You know, Stephen and I were talking, and he thinks it would make more sense to build another building than try to make this one work for a bigger congregation."

She closed her eyes. She could hear the refrigerator door open. "I'm hungry," Paul called almost petulantly. "Isn't there anything to eat in this house?"

There hadn't been much time for cooking over the past week with all the last-minute preparations for the cantata. "The rest of the meat loaf is in a Tupperware container on the top shelf. Other than that, there's lunch meat, cheese, some peaches."

"When are you going to go shopping?"

"I was going to go tomorrow." She would have to go early so she would have time to scrub and then wax the church floor. It was a good thing supermarkets opened at the crack of dawn. "Will you be around tomorrow to watch Timmy?"

"No. I'm going to meet Gerald at the club."

Which meant she would have to ask Abby to babysit or have Timmy play alone in the fellowship hall while she was working in the church kitchen.

"I haven't had a toasted cheese sandwich in a while."

A less-than-subtle hint. She was too tired to get up from her chair, let alone stand at the stove and cook for him. Did he even care about the months of work that had gone into the cantata? Did he understand the energy expended to put on tonight's performance? Or the stress of being peacemaker between LaVonne Lockford and half the choir? Sometimes it seemed a job well done meant adding another job and another until a person was crushed beneath the weight of responsibility.

"Eunice?"

"You know, I didn't even get one cup of punch this evening, or a single Christmas cookie." She hated sounding like she was feeling sorry for herself.

"I don't remember getting any either."

"Oh, yes, you did, Paul. When you served the mayor and his wife, you served yourself as well. While we were all talking together. Remember?" He hadn't even thought to offer her something to drink, and she hadn't wanted to embarrass him by excusing herself to go and get a cup for herself. And now, judging by his look, she would've been better off saying nothing at all.

"Okay, since you're so tired, what can I fix you to eat—assuming you didn't already fix yourself something before I got home?"

She rose slowly, walked past him into the kitchen, poured her cold tea down the drain, and put the cup in the sink. "I'll do your dishes in the morning, if you decide you can manage to toast yourself a cheese sandwich." She headed for the hallway.

"We need to talk, Eunice."

She looked back at him. "I've tried, Paul. For weeks, for months, I've tried. Tonight I'm too tired." She felt like a rabbit in the sights of a rifle loaded for bear. But even a dumb rabbit knew how to escape obliteration. "Mom called."

"Mom?"

"She and your father are coming up to spend a few days with us in January. She asked that you block off some time on your schedule for your mother."

The great David Hudson in the flesh. She had tried to love Paul's father as she had loved her own, but the two men were very different in method and theology, not that Paul could understand that. He was still striving to attain his father's approval and praise. She could see Paul was already making plans.

"That's great! I'll spread the word. It might even get Otis Harrison back into church for a service. Didn't you tell me once that his wife— what's her name? . . ."

"Mabel."

"Mabel likes to listen to my father's television service. Maybe the rest of the older members will come for a special service."

Eunice felt a twinge of alarm. "Are you planning to let your father preach?"

"No. He wouldn't anyway unless we gave him an invitation ahead of time, and even then . . ." He shrugged. "I don't think so."

What was the going rate these days?

Centerville Christian could ill afford a big honorarium, and Eunice doubted David Hudson would do anything gratis, even for his own son. She hated how cynical she was about Paul's father. What was it about David Hudson that made her dislike him so? His neglect of Paul as a boy wasn't enough to cause her to dislike him forever. It was something else, something more, something hidden and elemental about him that made her tense, watchful, uncomfortable.

"But we should have a fellowship hour so that people can meet him." Paul started taking leftovers out of the refrigerator. "My father would like that. You'll need to call all the deaconesses tomorrow and set up a meeting so you can make arrangements. We'll need refreshments, decorations. Maybe you could plan a church-wide potluck dinner with them as our honored guests."

More work, and he was missing the point. "Paul, don't turn this visit into an event. Your parents are coming for a visit *with us*. They're not coming to Centerville to make a public appearance. Wouldn't it be nice if you and your father could kick back and talk about anything and everything? No interruptions. Just the two of you." How many times had he told her that he'd never had time alone with his father? Something had always come up to interfere. And they had always been the ones to drive south for a few weekdays so that Timmy could get to know his grandparents.

"My father isn't the sort of man who wants to sit on a porch and talk all day."

3:15 P.M. 1/18

She knew the little jab of disdain was aimed at her father, who had spent hours sitting on the porch. It was one of the many things she'd loved about him. He'd always had time for people, especially his daughter. "We can always hope, Paul." She turned away before he saw the tears. "Good night."

Paul was changing and it filled her with sorrow. He had been so on fire for the Lord. He had respected her father, despite the short time they had known one another. Or had he just been pretending? Who wouldn't respect and love her father? He had always made time for her and his flock. He had made time for Paul, too—hours, in fact—on that front porch her husband now mentioned with such contempt. Never in all her life had her father made her feel unworthy of his love, unworthy of his time and attention.

She had always thought Paul was a man like her father, a man after God's own heart. But was he? Sometimes she wondered.

"Eunice, I didn't mean that the way it sounded."

"I hope not." He just spoke without thinking, then said he was sorry later. Which part should she believe?

Did he know he was neglecting Timmy the same way he had been neglected by his own father? She tried to tell him gently, but he was unwilling to listen. She loved him as much as she always had. She loved him more than anyone else in the church did, more than all of them put together if it came to that. Did it ever occur to Paul how much she cared, how many times she sacrificed to please him, how she compromised her own views to accommodate his? She was just like him in some ways. She worked constantly to gain his approval and attention.

"I'm just hungry and tired, Euny. I'm not myself."

Excuses. Issue forgotten. Don't bring it up again. He had more important things to think about, like making his own toasted cheese sandwich and a honey-do list for her so that everything would be perfect by the time his father arrived. If David Hudson didn't cancel at the last minute. Like the last time and the time before that. Something better always came up. A television talk show. A speaking engagement on a cruise boat. She knew she shouldn't have expectations of any human being, not even her husband. No one was perfect. Everyone was a sinner.

She closed the bedroom door quietly and knelt beside her bed. *I'm drowning, God. I've never felt so alone. Who can I turn to but You, Lord? Where else does a pastor's wife go for help when her marriage is failing and her life is out of control? Who can I trust with my anguish, Lord? Who but You?*

Grasping her pillow, she pressed it tightly to her mouth so that her sobs would not be heard.

The last time she saw her father alive, they had sat on the porch talking. "Center your life on Jesus." As he had done. "Don't put your hopes in people, sweetheart. If you do, you'll only add to their burdens and bring grief upon yourself. Love God, and He will enable you to love others, even when they disappoint you."

Her father had known her better than anyone but the Lord. Had her father known Paul as well? Had he seen what the future would hold for her?

"Give your heart to Jesus, Euny, and you can rest assured that He will keep every promise to you, and He will bring you through whatever happens."

It was a lesson her father oft repeated. Maybe he had seen the trouble coming.

I don't think Paul even loves me anymore, God . . . if he ever really did. And I'm not speaking from self-pity, Father. I just want to know. I want to understand. What was it Paul saw in me that made him believe I would make him a good wife? Because I can sing and play the piano a little?

You love Me.

Yes, I love You. Oh, Lord, I do love You, but does life have to be so full of pain and loneliness? You are sovereign, so I have to believe I am the wife You chose for Paul. But help me understand him! Every day that passes, we have less to say to one another, less in common. The harder I try, the less time and interest he seems to have for me or our son. I want to cleave to my husband, Father, but he sways with every wind that blows, and Timmy and I are tossed with the storm and left to fend for ourselves.

Cling to Me, beloved.

I'm trying, Jesus.

She rose from her knees and curled up in bed, blankets over her head. Maybe she was more like Paul than she realized. Maybe she was caught up in her impoverished but idyllic childhood with a father who had been steady on course every day he lived. *Serve the Lord with all your heart, mind, soul, and strength.* She thanked God she had grown up in the shadow of her father's faith.

Unfortunately, Paul had grown up in the shadow of his father's ambition.

———— ❧ ————

Samuel went into the kitchen and poured himself a mug of milk. He set it in the microwave and pushed two minutes. How could he be so physically exhausted and mentally awake? He'd tried meditating on the Twenty-third Psalm for the past hour and still couldn't slow down his whirring thoughts. They were like the currents below a waterfall, sucking him down into discouragement, frustration, and anger.

"Can't sleep?" Abby said in a drowsy voice. She stood in the doorway.

"Nope."

"Who's on your mind tonight?"

"Eunice."

She drew her blue chenille robe more tightly around her. She opened the refrigerator and took the milk container out, lifted a mug off the shelf, and poured. "So it's come to this, Samuel. Two old coots sipping hot milk in the kitchen at three o'clock in the morning."

Ping! Samuel took his mug from the microwave and put hers in, pressed the buttons. "Take mine."

"You're a sweetie. Why don't we live dangerously and add chocolate?"

"Why not? We're getting too old to play it safe."

She opened the pantry. "On a note like that, we'll shoot the works and add some of those marshmallows we keep on hand for Timmy."

Samuel sat with her at the nook table, mug of hot chocolate between his hands. The warmth eased the pain in his arthritic fingers, but didn't touch the ache in his heart. "She's struggling."

"Yes, she's struggling."

"Has she talked with you about it?"

"She doesn't have to, and she will resist talking about it until it becomes too much for her. Every time she does talk, she feels guilty, as though she's somehow being disloyal to Paul for having to confide in someone else. I was watching her after the cantata. She'll probably come over in a day or so, and we'll have tea again. You and Timmy can go out into your garden and feed the koi."

"I'm not sure waiting is advisable. I'm worried about her."

"We're not the only ones."

He raised his head at her dry tone and looked at her. She scowled at him as though he were as dense as a post. "I may be wearing trifocals, Samuel, but I've got eyes in my head. Stephen Decker has more than a normal parishioner's interest in our pastor's wife."

He pursed his lips, and wondered if anyone else had noticed. He always seemed to sense things, and Abby was too perceptive for her own good. "That does not mean he'd do anything about it."

"No, it doesn't. Nor does it mean that if he did consider doing anything, whatever he might think up, that our Euny would fall head over heels into trouble. She's the most godly young woman I've ever met, Samuel. I don't think she has a clue that Stephen Decker is in love with her."

"I didn't say he was in love with her."

"I doubt he knows it. And maybe that's a good thing."

"So what do we do to protect her?"

"Pray."

He rolled his eyes in exasperation. "That's all I do. Pray. And pray some more."

"And after we pray, we mind our own business. You can hardly confront someone for something they haven't done yet or might not even have in their mind to do. Worse, you might be planting an idea."

He fought his anger. "Paul is blind as a bat."

"On the contrary. Paul has twenty-twenty vision. Unfortunately, it's not focused on his pretty little sparrow." She leaned forward and planted her elbows on the table. Tenting her fingers, she gave him her impish smile. "Why don't we invite Stephen Decker to our Wednesday evening Bible study?"

"Oh, I'm sure a thirtysomething man will dive at the opportunity to spend the evening with eight old fogies."

Her smile broadened to a grin. "If he resists, accuse him of age discrimination. These young businessmen break out in a cold sweat whenever that word is mentioned. It breathes lawsuit."

"Use coercion, you mean."

"Such a nasty word. All I'm saying is, Stephen needs strong encouragement. I'll fill his tummy with homemade cookies and cider, and you fill his head and heart with sound doctrine. And who knows?" She spread her hands. "Stephen Decker might just end up an ally instead of an adversary."

"Stephen is not an adversary."

She gave him a level-eyed look. "Of course, you're right." Crossing her arms, she tilted her head. "If you want my opinion, he's more like a carnivore who's been living on milk and has his eye on a tasty spring lamb."

"Abigail."

"Don't Abigail me. You're the one who woke me up at three o'clock in the morning because you couldn't sleep for worrying."

"I'm not worrying."

"Excuse me. I should've said you can't sleep for being *concerned*."

"Have I ever told you that you're downright crabby at times?"

"And you're Mr. Peace and Light?" She put her hands on the table and pushed herself up. She put her mug in the sink and ran water into it. She patted him on the back and planted a kiss on his bald spot. "I love you despite your disposition."

He harrumphed a soft laugh and swatted her backside as she passed. "I love you, too, old woman."

Her backless slippers flip-flopped to the doorway. She yawned. "Well, you hash everything out with the Lord and let me know in the morning what He decides."

"Assuming He'll tell me."

She paused in the doorway, that sassy smile back on her face. "Oh, I imagine He'll tell you the same thing I did. Pray. Mind your own business, and trust Him to handle things."

"You can't resist having the last word."

She put her fingertips to her lips and blew him a kiss.

Returning from a two-day business trip, Stephen punched the button to listen to his messages and shrugged off his jacket. The first three were offers of work. He jotted down names and numbers. The fourth message was from Kathryn asking for more money. She wanted Brittany to have piano lessons, which meant she needed a piano, a good one. She'd checked prices and they ranged from three thousand to ten thousand dollars, but he could afford it. And it would be good for their daughter. She always said "our daughter" when she wanted something.

Clenching his teeth, Stephen wrote a note to talk to Brittany about piano lessons and see if this was her idea or Kathryn's. If his daughter wanted music lessons, he'd pay for them, directly to her instructor. And he'd order and pay for the piano as well rather than trust Kathryn with the money. Messages five, six, and seven were salesmen. Eight was Kathryn again, pushing. He deleted it before she was finished haranguing.

"Stephen, this is Samuel Mason. Abby and I would like to invite you to our Wednesday evening Bible study. We have a small group of people interested in studying the Bible. You can ask any questions you want. If we don't know the answers, we'll look them up. We start at seven thirty with coffee, tea, cookies, and conversation and then go into an hour of in-depth study, then end with prayer. We hope you'll come."

Stephen's first impulse was to erase the message and pretend he hadn't heard it. He wondered if he could come up with some excuse to decline the invitation. If he responded at all. An AA meeting was scheduled for Wednesday nights, but he had opted for the Friday morning meeting in Sacramento because he was usually there on business, and then spent afternoons with Brittany whenever Kathryn would allow, which wasn't often. He didn't know Samuel and Abby Mason very well, other than that Samuel was a thorn in Paul Hudson's side. In fact, Stephen couldn't remember Paul's ever saying anything particularly nice about this elder. "I can always count on Sam Mason to vote against whatever plans I have," Paul had said not long ago. That seemed odd considering that Eunice and Abby were friends, and Timmy hung around Samuel as though the old man were his grandfather.

Still, a Bible study with some old people wouldn't be an exciting way to spend Wednesday evenings. He dismissed the idea and went into the kitchen to see what he could rustle up for dinner. Nothing looked particularly appetizing, but he wasn't in the mood for Charlie's Diner either. Sometimes Sally's sense of humor grated his nerves. He yanked out a Swiss steak frozen dinner, punched holes in the top with his pen, and tossed it into the microwave. He unbuttoned his shirt and stripped it off on his way into the bedroom. A good hot shower would put him to rights.

He was restless, annoyed at nothing in particular. The sound of Kathryn's voice always did that to him. Her catlike screeching always made him want to smash something. She was a thorn in his side, a charley horse, a pulsating hemorrhoid.

The urge to buy a bottle of scotch gripped him again.

He took a cold shower instead of a hot one and then dressed in worn jeans and an old Cal sweatshirt. Barefoot, he went back into the kitchen to check on his dinner. It was cooked as close to perfection as mystery meat could get. Probably stray dog from the alleys of Los Angeles. He ate it while standing at the counter and going through his mail. Junk, mostly. Grocery ads, lost women and children. He wished Kathryn would get lost. Maybe then he'd have some time with his daughter before she was eighteen and on her way to college or married and moving to another state. He opened two bills and set them aside and then opened a statement from his broker. His finances were in better shape now than they had been in ten years. Even with the monthly payments to Kathryn for Brittany, he had enough money to buy himself another house in Granite Bay. Or build a house in Centerville.

Always buy with location in mind. Best place to invest is Vine Hill. Oh, boy, he could buy the five-acre parcel next to the Athertons and have Sheila ringing his doorbell and asking for a cup of sugar. Last Sunday, she'd waltzed into church and plunked herself down next to him. "Rob's in Orlando on business." Her meaning was all too clear, especially when she put her hand on his thigh. He'd gripped her wrist and shoved her hand away from him. And she'd just smiled.

Several friends in Sacramento had asked him why he didn't buy one of the luxurious condos he had designed near Roseville. It would certainly be closer to "the action." Whatever kind of action he might want. Several friends were divorced and dating. Stephen hadn't been out more than a dozen times since his divorce and only with women he met through work: three real estate agents, one broker, a bank officer, two loan agents, and an attorney. He'd come close to sleeping with several of them, but backed off. He knew from experience that sex tended to attach a woman to a man like a barnacle to the underbelly of a ship, and he didn't need or want that kind of complication at this time of his life.

Only one woman tempted his resolve to keep his walls up, and she was as unavailable as she was unaware. Which was just as well.

Tossing the empty TV dinner tray into the trash bag under the sink, Stephen went into the living room and turned on CNN, but he'd heard all the news on the drive north from LA. He channel surfed until he stopped on another news program, but quickly grew irritated by the commentator's constant interruptions and combative, know-it-all attitude. He punched off the TV, tossed the remote onto the coffee table, and reached for the novel he'd bought at Costco. Ten minutes later, he tossed the book back on the coffee table in disgust. Putting that rubbish onto good paper was a waste of trees.

He wanted a drink. Badly.

Swearing under his breath, he tried to get his mind off how good a glass of fine scotch would taste right now. But the harder he tried, the more the urge persisted. His sponsor had told him to flee temptation. He needed to get out of the apartment or he'd go nuts. But where could he go? It was too dark and too cold to run. Too far from Sacramento to make it worthwhile driving up there "for some action."

He flipped through the newspaper until he found the theater ad. Only one movie playing, and it was about a serial killer who had a taste for human livers.

His hands were shaking again. They hadn't done that in two years. Why was tonight such a crisis?

Glancing at his watch, he saw it was only 7:10. He never went to bed before ten thirty. Nothing on television. Nothing worth seeing at the theater. Not interested in reading a novel. Not enough room to work out in his living room, not that that held any appeal either. Nothing in his movie collection he wanted to watch. So what was he going to do to get through the evening without going out to buy a bottle of scotch and ending up back in the pit?

Help me, God. This is only Wednesday.

Wednesday.

Something clicked.

Surging to his feet, Stephen headed for his home office. Frustrated, he jabbed the button on his phone and listened again to the message about the Masons' Bible study. Why not? He'd try it once. He went into his bedroom, put on socks and sneakers, yanked off his sweatshirt, and pulled on a T-shirt and sweater. He grabbed his black leather jacket on the way out the door. Swearing under his breath, he unlocked the door again and went back in to look up the Masons' address.

When he pulled up in front of their house, he saw three other cars—one a Buick with a wheelchair mount on the back. What was he doing here? This was crazy. What did he have in common with a houseful of old people? The dash clock said 7:28. In three more minutes, he would be late and could drive away with a clear conscience.

And go where?

He shifted into park and jammed on the parking brake. Climbing out, he locked his truck, pulled up his leather collar, and headed for the gate of the Masons' white picket fence. The porch light was on, casting a warm glow over the attractive lawn and neatly pruned rosebushes lining the cobblestone walkway to the front steps. He heard the sound of voices and pressed the doorbell.

He saw the gathering just inside the screen door. No one under seventy. Abigail Mason spotted him. "Stephen!"

"Maybe I should have called first." He took a step back.

"Nonsense!" She pushed the screen door open. "I'm so glad you're here!" Looping her arm through his, she drew him in, closing the door firmly behind him. He couldn't escape without being rude.

The diminutive, white-haired old lady ushered him through the tiny entry alcove into the living room, where eight others were gathered, one in a wheelchair near the refreshment trolley. Otis Harrison's wife. Everyone in the room was more than twice Stephen's age, except for the little boy perched next to Samuel Mason.

Apparently Abigail Mason noticed he noticed. "We're babysitting. Eunice had some last-minute shopping to do before her in-laws arrive in town. She'll pop by later."

His heart gave a little lurch. "Does she attend the Bible study?"

"No." She gave him a sidelong look he couldn't decipher. "Not usually."

Meaning Eunice might attend on occasion? He shrugged out of his leather jacket and entered the living room. Conversation ceased.

"Friends, we have a newcomer," Abigail said brightly. "Let's make Stephen Decker welcome, shall we?" Several greeted him warmly, including Samuel and Timmy. Abigail released his arm and looked up at him.

"Now, what can I serve you, Stephen? We have macaroons this evening. How about some coffee? Or would you prefer a nice hot cup of tea?"

Tea! Stephen laughed. "Coffee, please, Abby."

"Regular or unleaded? Sugar or cream?"

"Regular and black, ma'am. And thank you."

"Coffee it is." She gave him a cheeky grin. "We're glad you're here. We've been praying you'd come."

Thus began an evening full of surprises, not the least of which was how fast time passed, or that he didn't even notice when Eunice Hudson took Timmy from the gathering. Samuel Mason held his attention. The old man had pulled them all into the Bible, outlining historical aspects, culture, and meaning along with current applications. And he'd posed questions that made Stephen think. Mason had covered only four short verses, but Stephen knew he'd be thinking about those verses for the rest of the night and probably for the next few days as well. He'd never thought the Minor Prophets had anything vital to say about today, so he had skimmed them at best, or skipped them entirely on occasion. He couldn't have been more wrong—or more delighted in the discovery.

"So how did the meat taste, Stephen?" Abby handed him his jacket.

"Meat?" Maybe she had a touch of Alzheimer's.

She chuckled and patted his arm. "That's all right."

The others filed out ahead of him, Otis pushing his wife's wheelchair out first as Samuel said good night at the door. When it came Stephen's turn to depart, Samuel extended his hand. "Good to have you join us." The old man had a strong handshake. Stephen liked that.

He stepped out onto their front porch and looked around. Tipping up the collar of his leather jacket, he looked back. "See you next week." He went down the steps feeling better than he had in weeks.

CHAPTER 7

PAUL STOOD AT THE FRONT DOOR of the church, shaking hands with people as they filed out of the sanctuary. Several said his message was anointed. Most said they enjoyed the service immensely. Yet his despair deepened. It didn't matter how many complimented him, his father's opinion was what mattered most, and all David Hudson had said was, "Not bad. I'll give you a few pointers later."

His father could still reduce him to nothing with just a few words.

From the night Eunice had told him his parents were coming, he had worked constantly. Now, his parents were in the fellowship hall, his father undoubtedly surrounded by admirers, feted by the deacons and deaconesses who had prepared an elaborate potluck and program to honor David Hudson, famous TV evangelist.

What was so wrong with the sermon he had given? Flawless alliteration, poignant illustrations, light touches. The congregation had laughed when he'd wanted them to laugh, become silent and thoughtful when he'd wanted them to be silent and thoughtful. He'd even roused their tears.

"Not bad."

The curse of faint praise.

Days of hard work, and still he didn't measure up to his father's expectations. He never had, and probably never would. Several new people came around the corner, talking together. Paul kept the smile tacked to his face. He needed to be upbeat or they might walk out the door and never come back. And he would've failed again.

"Great sermon, Pastor."

"I'm glad you joined us this morning. I hope you'll come back."

"We wouldn't have missed it. Is David Hudson really your father?"

What was that supposed to mean? That his sermon was a shadow to his father's oratory talents? "Yes, he is."

"Will he be speaking at the evening service?"

"No."

"What a pity. We were hoping to hear him in person."

Paul's stomach tightened. "My father is here on vacation, but you have an opportunity to meet him in the fellowship hall. We're having a potluck lunch to honor him."

The husband and wife looked at one another in dismay. "We didn't bring anything."

"We planned for visitors. We have plenty. The fellowship hall is right around the corner. You're more than welcome to stay and meet my parents as well as members of our congregation. Everyone will make you welcome." He watched them go down the steps toward the gathering, and then he turned to meet several others filing out of the church.

Maybe he'd disappointed his mother as well. She'd smiled at him, but said nothing before going down the steps with his father. In fact, she had barely looked at him. He wished he could go into his office, close the door, and have a few minutes to get his emotions under control before he joined everyone in the fellowship hall. He felt like smashing something.

Where was Eunice when he needed her? Was she off shooting the breeze with some of the old biddies again? She should be talking to people like LaVonne Lockford and Jessie Boham, women who could actually *do* something for the church.

Never had he been more acutely aware of the small scale of this old church than today with his father sitting in the front pew. CCC must look small and shabby compared to his father's church. And most of the people were common workers rather than the affluent members of his father's congregation. But that was changing. The mayor was now coming regularly, and so were the Athertons, as well as others who owned their own businesses. Still, Paul had seen the way his father looked around.

Paul hurried the last few stragglers to the potluck and strode up the aisle. Eunice was tucking her music into the piano bench. "What's taking you so long? We should be in the fellowship hall."

She came down the steps. "You asked me to play a postlude. We can use the side doors." She paused. "Are you all right?"

"Of course I'm all right. Let's go before everyone wonders where we are."

"You go on ahead. I have to get Timmy."

"Abby will bring him into the fellowship hall."

"I need to sign him out. We have new rules. Remember?"

"I forgot."

"What's wrong, Paul?"

The same thing that had always been wrong. He wasn't good enough. "Nothing."

She put her hand on his arm. "Everyone loved your sermon."

Eunice was easy to please. Anything he did for the Lord, no matter how insignificant, made her happy. "Not everyone." He wanted to sit in the last pew and bury his head in his hands. "Apparently, it wasn't up to my father's standards."

Her eyes flashed. "Did he say that?"

"Not exactly. Never mind. We'd better join everyone. I hope the deaconesses got it all together."

"All the decorations are up, including the banner welcoming your father and mother. And there's enough food to feed an army. You've no need to worry."

As they came in the door, Paul was stunned by feelings of betrayal and the surge of jealousy that welled up at the sight of his father surrounded by *his* parishioners. Paul swallowed hard. Usually, those same people surrounded *him* the moment he came in the hall. Those same people told *him* how wonderful his message had been. Now, they didn't even notice him, so intent were they on getting close to the great David Hudson. His father stood with a beatific smile of humility on his handsome face, inclining his head to one and then another like a king before his lowly subjects. Even Hollis Sawyer had shown up to fawn over him!

"I just love your show on television, Dr. Hudson."

"Thank you."

"My wife has been watching you for years! She swears by every word you say."

"I only speak what the Lord gives me."

"God has anointed you, Pastor Hudson. That's for sure."

"We're so honored you're here, Pastor Hudson."

"It's a pleasure to be here."

"Oh, would you please autograph my Bible?"

"Of course."

His mother touched his arm. "I'm sorry, Paul."

"Sorry about what?" Was she going to tell him his sermon stank, too?

"This." She nodded toward his father.

Paul forced a laugh. "It's all right, Mom. He's famous. It stands to reason people would want to shake hands with him and tell him how much he's meant to them through the years."

"They don't know him like we do."

Paul bristled. "He's worked hard all his life to be what he is today."

"Yes, he has worked hard. And made sacrifices along the way." She watched the crowd around him. "We both know about that."

"I'm proud of him, Mom. I always have been." It wasn't anyone's fault that these simple people saw David Hudson as ecclesiastical royalty holding court in this humble hall. "People are drawn to him."

His mother took his hand. "Charisma is a powerful thing, Paul. Your father—"

"I know, Mom. Believe me, I know. As far back as I can remember, I've seen how people look up to him. They're in awe. People hang on his every word."

"Not bad."

"Do you remember how we talked when you were a little boy, Paul? Do you remember your dream?"

"Sure. To serve the Lord."

"Then you keep your focus on that, Son. Take your lead from the Lord, not your father."

"It would appear I'm failing dismally at taking a lead from anyone." This wasn't the place to catalog his shortcomings. And he didn't want to talk about his father or what a success David Hudson had always been in the pulpit. He would only feel more inadequate. David Hudson had built one of the biggest churches in the nation, a charismatic evangelical powerhouse that set souls on fire. Paul wanted to know if he was on the right path in his own ministry, if there was any hope of his getting the job done here in Centerville. He was trying so hard, sacrificing so much. "What did you think of my sermon?"

She looked away. "You have your father's eloquence, Paul. And his charisma."

He was surprised and pleased. "I thought after what he said, I'd fallen flat on my face."

She sighed. "You're very much like him, more like him than I ever realized."

His spirits rose. "I never thought I'd hear anyone say that to me."

She looked at him intently. "I've no doubt if you keep on as you are, you'll end up with a church every bit as large as the one he's built. But is that what you want?"

His smile came freely this time, set loose by his mother's praise. "Of course it's what I want. Hasn't that always been what I've wanted, to build something for the Lord? Something *great*. Something the world would notice." He lifted his mother's hand and kissed it. "You've always been my mainstay of encouragement."

Her mouth curved slightly. "Don't give me any credit, Paul. What you decide to do with your ministry rests on your shoulders."

"There's Eunice, Mom." He waved his wife over, annoyed to see Samuel and Abigail Mason coming with her.

Eunice opened the way for the elderly couple. She smiled radiantly as she kissed his mother's cheek. Lois scooped up Timmy and kissed him. "I'm sorry it took me so long, Mom. We've set up new rules since the congregation has grown. We're all supposed to sign our children into class and out as well, and I can hardly break the rules. Mom, say hi to Samuel and Abigail Mason, dear friends of ours. Samuel, Abby, this is my mother-in-law, Lois Hudson."

As greetings were exchanged, Paul excused himself. "I'd better call this gathering to order so we can begin the program."

Once settled at the head table, David Hudson would be separated from the Centerville flock, and Paul could take charge again.

———— ❧ ————

After the potluck, Paul ushered his father into his church office and offered him the easy chair. "Make yourself comfortable, Dad."

His father sat and looked around. "Pretty tight space you have here."

Paul forced a laugh. "Makes reaching everything easy."

His father leaned over pointedly and ran his hand along a shelf of books. "Doesn't give you much room for expanding your library."

"We're using every room we have for classes."

"I noticed your service was full."

"*Both* services are full, and the Saturday night service is filling up fast."

Grimacing, his father flicked a speck of lint off his dark-gray slacks. "You'll need a new facility. This place looks as though it was built a hundred and fifty years ago."

"Pretty close to that. It's one of the most important historical landmarks in Centerville."

"Historical landmark? Kiss remodeling this barn good-bye. You should look for a piece of land where you can grow and put this building on the market."

Paul lolled back in his office chair. "I've already thought of that, Dad. I've been checking around to see if there are any five-acre plots available."

"Five acres? Is that all? I started with fifteen."

"And it was thirty years ago. Prices were a lot less than they are now."

"It's all relative, Paul. Think small and you stay small."

Paul knew better than to say things took time and he had only been pastor of Centerville Christian Church for five years. Within the first five years of his ministry, David Hudson had already laid the foundations for a twenty-thousand-square-foot building with sanctuary and two floors of classrooms. Within ten years, he'd added a Christian school that went from kindergarten through ninth grade. Five years after that, he had a high school on the grounds. They owned a fleet of buses and a media center of which his father made expert use, gaining a nationwide following. Donations flooded in from all parts of the country, filling the coffers for the building program.

Glancing around, Paul could imagine what his father thought of this little backwater church. "We're not exactly in the same kind of high-density area you were."

"When word spreads, you'll be drawing people from Sacramento, Paul. You just haven't gotten your stride yet. It'll come, if you want it to come. You have talent, but you need to hone your skills."

Paul tried not to show how deeply his father's words hurt. "Could you be a little more specific?"

His father raised his brows. "Are you sure you want to hear this? I don't remember you ever asking for my advice before."

Trained in letting the subtle digs glance off, Paul smiled. "I'm grown-up now."

"Glad to hear it. I was afraid you were going to be a mama's boy for the rest of your life."

The barb pricked, but Paul didn't show it. This wasn't the time for accusations that would only eliminate any possibility of eliciting his father's advice. "How did you get your congregation to agree to a building project?"

His father laughed. "Get their agreement? I can see we have our work cut out for us." He crossed his legs. "Listen to me, Son. You are the shepherd here. Aren't you?"

"Yes, sir."

"Does a shepherd ask his sheep for directions? You have to remember you're the leader. The first thing you need is a vision of what Centerville Christian Church can be, and then go for it. You don't ask them if it's okay with them. You bring them along. You guide them and grow them up into what they should be. If you wait around for them to tell you what they want to do with this church, you'll never do anything."

There was something wrong with what his father was saying, but Paul couldn't put his finger on it.

His father's eyes narrowed. "I can see you're hesitating already. There's your weakness. You're supposed to be the one with the vision. You have to act upon it. God anointed you to be pastor of Centerville Christian Church, and God put you here to build His church. And the only one stopping you from doing just that is you."

"You make it sound easy."

"It is easy. The secret is getting to know your people. You have to find out what makes them tick on an individual basis. Figure out what it is they want as a whole. The money and talents of your people should be used to glorify God, but they don't understand that any more than sheep understand their wool is valuable. You have to teach them. Make them feel good about opening their pockets. Praise them for using their talents. Build them up and make them feel good about themselves while they're building the Kingdom. That's the secret to success. The real question is, do you want to succeed?"

"Of course I do."

"Can you make the hard choices along the way?"

"What sort of hard choices do you mean?" He'd already made some hard choices, but he wasn't going to share them with his father.

His father leaned back. "There are always people who want to keep things the way they are. They're in a rut and like it." He raised his hand. "They cling to old buildings and ideas."

Like Otis Harrison and Hollis Sawyer. "I've had a few of them. Two out of the three elders who called me to this church." They were gone now, thank God.

"Hold it right there, Paul. Back up a little. You need to change your thinking. The elders of this church did not call you here. God did. You need to remember that every time someone gets in the way of progress. Since this church was probably built shortly after the time of the California gold rush, I'll use a stagecoach as an illustration. Most of your parishioners are like passengers sitting inside. They bought a ticket. They know where they want to go, and they're leaving it up to you to get them there. Then you have the horses, the ones who do the work to get you to your destination. You're the one with the reins, Paul. It's your job to steer and set the pace so the workers will last and you'll get everyone to the goal. So what happened with the troublemakers?"

"They made my life miserable for a while."

"Did you win the battle?"

"Well, I don't know if you'd call it winning or not. They resigned from their elderships and no longer attend church." Except today when Hollis showed up to get David Hudson's autograph.

"Did anybody quibble about them leaving?"

"Not that I heard. We had so many new people coming by then that I don't think they were missed."

"Good for you."

Paul felt a flush of pleasure at his father's approval. "The only one who was upset about the whole thing was Eunice."

"Women!" His father chuckled. "You know I love your mother, but she hasn't always made things easy for me. In fact, I think the hardest battles I've fought have been with her over various individuals who caused me trouble. You know your mother. She listens to every complaint as though it had merit."

As she had listened to him for countless hours as he was growing up. If not for his mother's love, Paul wondered where he'd be right now.

His father laughed. "If you and I listened to everything everyone had to say, we'd spend the rest of our lives doing nothing else."

Paul laughed with him. "Isn't that the truth? I finally got sick of listening to those two old men grumble about everything."

His father became serious again. "You're lucky they didn't poison your ministry." His eyes hardened. "Next time you run into that kind of trouble, don't wait for them to resign."

There was one more thorn in Paul's side, but the sting was negligible now that he had other men standing with him against any arguments Samuel Mason wanted to raise.

His father stood. He never could sit for long. "Anytime someone starts throwing stumbling blocks in your way, Paul, you'd better get them out of your church fast. If you let them get away with it, you'll be tripping over yourself every step of the way. Keep close watch. Assess whatever situation arises for its destructive potential, make a decision, and stick to it. Don't allow yourself to be swayed, especially by your wife. As intelligent as they are, women are run by their emotions."

It didn't help Paul that Eunice was so attached to Abigail Mason.

"Is there a good steak house in this town?"

His father probably hadn't had a chance to eat much at the potluck with all the people vying for his attention. "The golf course has a nice restaurant." He felt bolstered at the way his father's brows rose. Paul grinned. "The manager is a member of our church. All I have to do is make a call and he'll have a table waiting for us."

"So make the call."

Paul picked up the phone and pushed the speed dial while his father glanced through the volumes on the bookshelves. He took one out and leafed through it, shoved it back, took another, scowled.

"Everything's all set," Paul said, dropping the receiver back into its cradle. "Table for four." They could drop Timmy off at the Masons'.

"Let's leave the women at home, all right? I doubt they'd be interested in shoptalk anyway."

Paul was flattered that his father wanted to spend more time alone with him. He'd go over to the parsonage and let Eunice know she didn't have to hold supper for them.

His father snapped the book shut and dropped it on Paul's desk in disdain. "I know the guy who wrote that."

"I take it you don't think much of him." Eunice had been impressed with the book and asked him to read it.

His father shrugged into his sport coat. "Oh, he writes well enough, but he bleats a lot of nonsense about patience and humility. Both are admirable qualities, but if you took his advice, you'd sit around twiddling your thumbs and waiting for the Spirit to move you."

Paul frowned slightly. "That bad?"

"Well, go ahead and read it if you don't believe me. I just thought I'd save you a little time."

"I'll pass it along to the library." Picking up his keys, Paul followed his father out of the church.

―――― ❦ ――――

While Paul took his father to the church office to talk after the potluck, Eunice took Timmy and her mother-in-law home. "Would you like to stretch out on our bed, Mom, and rest for a while?" She had never seen her mother-in-law look so downcast, nor known her to be so quiet.

"You know what I would like, Eunice? A nice long walk with you and my grandson. There must be a park somewhere in this little burg, and a coffee shop where we can sip café lattes and Timmy can have hot cocoa."

"Can we, Mommy? Can we, please?" After his initial shyness around two grandparents he had seen only four times in his life, Timmy had warmed up to Lois Hudson quickly.

"There's a little park down the street from where you're staying—and Charlie's Diner on Main Street." She'd been there only a few times with

Paul, but she had liked the homey atmosphere and camaraderie between Charlie and Sally Wentworth. "The owners are members of the church. You'll like them."

"I don't want to meet anyone, Euny. I've done my schmoozing for the day. I just want time with you and Timmy. Is there any place in town where Paul is *not* known?"

Eunice set her purse on the side table. "The truck stop on Highway 99." The clientele just passed right on through to other places. Paul had never seen a point in sitting at the counter with someone who wouldn't end up in one of Centerville Christian's pews.

"Sounds perfect."

Eunice looked back at her. "You want to go there?"

"Sounds like a delightful place to me. Besides, truck stops are supposed to have the best food in town."

Eunice thought she saw a sheen of tears in her mother-in-law's brown eyes, but before she could ask if everything was all right, Lois clapped her hands. "Let's go. Let's go. You and Timmy change into something you won't mind getting dirty while I leave a note for Grandpa and Daddy. And then we'll walk down to the bed-and-breakfast so Granny can get out of her Sunday suit and toe-pinching high heels and into some nice comfy sweats." Timmy laughed. "What? You didn't know grannies wore sweats? Well, you've got a lot to learn, my boy." She leaned down so that she was at eye level with him. "Better wear your running shoes, Timmy, because I'm going to race you to the slide." She straightened and looked at Eunice. "Assuming there is a slide."

"There is!" Timmy ran for his bedroom.

"And swings, I hope!" Lois called after him.

"Enough for all three of us." Eunice laughed. "We'll be ready in a minute or two."

Timmy had never been inside the Bedfords' bed-and-breakfast, but he wasn't the least bit impressed by the Victorian parlor, oriental silk rug on the polished hardwood floor, needlepoint cushions, or Royal Doulton figurines on the massive carved mantel.

"She'll be down in a few minutes, sweetheart," Eunice said. "Just sit and don't touch anything." He plunked himself into a brocade-covered wing chair and swung his legs back and forth. As soon as Lois appeared, he bounded out of the chair and raced to the front door.

"Hold up at the gate, buster," Lois called after him. "This is going to be a fair race." She rolled her eyes at Eunice. "How far is the park from here?"

"One block down, turn right at the corner, and another half block."

"Thank the good Lord. I think I can make it that far." She went down the steps and stooped beside Timmy. "Ready? Set? Go!" Timmy took off down the sidewalk, but Lois wasn't far behind him. Laughing, Eunice closed the gate behind her and followed at a more leisurely pace.

It was a beautiful afternoon—brisk, clear, quiet. She didn't want to waste a minute of it worrying over what kind of advice Paul was receiving from his father. Unfortunately, whatever David Hudson did say would be gospel to Paul. She was equally certain that Paul wouldn't share a fraction of it with her.

"You've never liked him," Paul had told her once.

"It has nothing to do with like or dislike, Paul. Just because he's your father doesn't mean he knows everything."

"He knows more than I do about building a church. I'd be stupid not to listen to him!"

Eunice knew whatever suggestions were made by David Hudson would be presented to Paul's handpicked elders, Gerald Boham and Marvin Lockford, both of whom were ready and willing to come alongside any plans Paul had for building the church.

And here she was doing exactly what she had set her mind not to do: worrying.

She came around the corner and saw Timmy going down the slide first, Lois following right after him. She adored her mother-in-law. She was as warm as David was cold. Her father-in-law had lost interest in Timmy after five minutes. "Give the book to your grandmother. She'll read it to you. Daddy and I have important things to talk about." Politics they had no control over. Baseball scores. The state of the economy and how it affected church giving. Delighting in her grandson, Lois had settled Timmy on her lap and read to him until it was his bedtime, then asked if she could pray with him and tuck him in. After half an hour, Eunice went to see if everything was all right, and heard Timmy chattering away like a little magpie while his grandma listened to every word he said with complete attention. How could she not adore a mother-in-law like that?

A pity David Hudson came with the package.

Hands in the air, Lois gave a delighted shriek as she whooshed down the slide. She straightened and stepped out of the sandbox. Timmy clambered up the slide and flew down again while his granny headed for the swings. Euny grinned as her mother-in-law took the one next to her. They both kicked back and lifted their feet. "This is the life," Lois said, no sign of the tension Eunice had seen in her face earlier in the day.

"Granny, watch me!" Timmy shouted from the top of the slide.

"I'm watching you! Let's see how fast you go this time!" Timmy dropped onto the slide and shoved off, shooting down the curve of shiny metal and flying off the end. He barely made it to his feet. Lois applauded and praised his efforts. Beaming, Timmy raced up the ladder again while she chuckled. "Imagine what I could do with a tenth of that energy." Lois let her legs dangle. Euny let her swing drift back and forth while she studied her mother-in-law. She knew something was on her mind, but she was not going to press her.

They stayed at the park for an hour before walking the mile to the truck stop on Highway 99. Timmy didn't complain about the distance. He was soaking up the attention Lois poured on him, relishing her laughter, chattering about everything he saw and anything that popped into his head. Euny loved the sound of Lois's laughter, open and trilling. Lois leaned down once and cupped Timmy's face. "I love you, Timothy Michael Hudson. You warm my tired old soul."

"How old are you, Granny?"

"Well, it depends. I felt a hundred years old this morning, but right now, I feel younger than your mother." Straightening, she ran her hand over his hair.

Perplexed, Timmy looked up at Euny, but he didn't ask for an explanation. "Can I have a hamburger?"

Lois laughed. "You bet."

"Yippee!" He ran ahead.

"No farther than the end of the block, Timmy," Eunice called. They were within sight of the truck stop, and the parking lot was full of semis, pickups, and several recreational vehicles.

"Must be a good place to eat," Lois said.

Timmy waited for them at the Stop sign. Lois took one hand while Euny took his other before they crossed the last intersection. They headed across the parking lot. Four Harley-Davidson motorcycles were parked near the front double doors. Eunice glanced at Lois, but her mother-in-law opened the front door without blinking. Four men in black leather jackets sat at the counter. One had a tattoo of a dragon around his neck, its horrifying mouth open as though sinking its fangs into his jugular. Eunice looked down at Timmy. She put her hand on his shoulder. "Don't stare, sweetheart."

He couldn't seem to help himself.

"The sign says to seat yourself." Lois looked around. "How about the booth there by the windows overlooking the parking lot, Timmy? You can watch the trucks come and go."

"Okay." His eyes were still fixed upon the man at the counter, who sensed his attention and glanced over. Timmy shrugged Eunice's hand from his shoulder and went over to the counter. "What's that thing on your neck?"

The man raised his brows in surprise. "Nosy little fella, aren't you?"

Heart pounding, Eunice took the four steps to retrieve her son. "It's a tattoo, honey." She looked into the man's eyes. "I'm so sorry, sir."

"Sir! You hear that, Riley?"

She put her hand on Timmy's shoulder and held on this time. "Come on, sweetheart."

All four men were looking at her now, and she could feel heat surging into her cheeks.

"But he's got a dragon on his neck, Mommy! Look! And it's got its teeth in him!"

"Timmy."

"Granny, come and see!" He looked at the man again, resisting Euny as she tried to pull him away. "Does it hurt?"

The men were laughing now, all except the one with the dragon tattoo. He looked pained, perplexed, tired, and annoyed.

"Our apologies, gentlemen." Lois took Timmy's hand and pointed him toward the booth. "It comes of living a sheltered life."

"Where you been hiding him?"

"He's growing up in the church." Lois nodded toward Eunice. "This is his mother, the pastor's wife."

"Pastor's wife!" One laughed and gave a wolf whistle. The man next to him uttered the Lord's name in vain. A third grinned, turning around and leaning his elbows back on the counter as he gave Eunice a once-over. "If I knew pastors had wives that looked like this one, I'd've gone back to church years ago."

"That will do, gentlemen." Lois's boldness stunned Euny.

By now, everyone in the small restaurant was watching the exchange. Two of the men turned their stools slowly as Lois and Eunice passed them, Lois holding Timmy by the hand. Eunice kept her eyes downcast, but she could feel the men's perusal. The last one leaned forward as she came abreast of him. "What's a nice girl like you doing in a place like this?"

"Shut up, Jackson!" The tattooed man glared at him.

"I'm just having a little fun."

"Open your mouth again, and I'll make sure you don't open it for a month. You got that?"

Face burning, Eunice slid into the booth, her mother-in-law and son on the opposite side. Lois handed Timmy a menu so that he would have something else to look at besides the man at the counter. Thankfully, the four black-leather-clad men turned around again, devoting their attention to the plates of food the waitress set before them.

Lois smiled at her across the table. "That took me back to the days when a group of my friends would go down into the barrios of Los Angeles. We'd talk about Jesus to people on the streets."

"You and David?" Eunice couldn't imagine either of them standing on a street corner, talking with prostitutes, drug addicts, or derelicts.

"Oh no. No, no. During my high school years, before I met David." She opened her menu, then dipped it to peer at Euny over the top. "Dinner is on me, by the way. Order whatever you'd like."

Eunice wasn't sure she could eat anything. She was still rattled by the attention of the men at the counter. Hell's Angels! What had she been thinking, agreeing to bring Timmy to a place like this?

Lois lowered her menu again. "Euny, they've forgotten all about us. And even if they haven't, I'm sure the gentleman with the tattoo will make certain the rest of them behave themselves."

Eunice concentrated on the menu. It wasn't extensive, but the aromas emanating from the kitchen were tantalizing. Timmy was stacking sugar cubes into a tower.

Lois set the menu aside. "I'm going to have a steak. You still want a hamburger, Timmy?"

"Yep." The sugar cubes tumbled and he started over.

Lois brushed some hair back from Timmy's forehead. "Does Daddy come home every night for supper with you and Mommy?"

Timmy lifted one shoulder and said nothing as he played with the sugar cubes.

Paul was hardly ever home for dinner, but Eunice wasn't sure she should tell Lois that. "He comes as often as he can."

"Well, I know what that means." Lois shook her head as she looked out the window at the semis and pickups and motorcycles. "I've prayed and prayed . . ." Her eyes welled with tears and she shook her head again.

"Most of the time it can't be helped. Someone is always calling and—" Eunice shrugged—"well, you of all people must know what I mean. A pastor's life isn't his own."

"I'm sorry, Euny. I am so very, very sorry."

Before Euny could ask what she meant, she heard the creak of leather. Glancing up, she felt her pulse shoot up in alarm as she looked into the dark eyes of the tattooed man standing over her. He winced, his mouth tipping up in a wry half smile as he held up his hands in a calming gesture. "Sorry to startle you, ma'am. Just wanted to apologize for the way my friends behaved." He jerked his head toward the three men filing out the door. He stepped back.

Eunice's lips parted. Before she could think of a word to say, Lois started talking, and in the space of less than two minutes, she spelled out the entire gospel of Jesus Christ to the man standing at their booth. *Everyone has sinned and needs God's grace and mercy to be saved. And the Lord God in power and mercy has made a way through His Son Jesus Christ, who died on the cross as the blood sacrifice to atone for all the sins of mankind from the beginning of time to the end. When Jesus arose, He showed He had power over sin and death. All those who believe in Him will not perish but have everlasting life.*

Eunice had never heard the gospel spoken so quickly or so clearly to anyone in her entire life. No leading questions or lengthy preparation lessons gradually leading into the meaning of the Cross and Resurrection. Just the simple, unvarnished truth, spoken with a boldness that took her breath away. And the man's as well, if she could judge by the look on his face.

His mouth curved in a bleak smile. "You cut to the chase, don't you, lady?" He moved back.

"Considering the fact that you're backing toward the door, I thought there was no time to lose."

He planted his feet, his face darkening. "I doubt you could even imagine some of the things I've done in my lifetime."

"A pastor's wife hears more than most priests in a confessional, young man, and you need to know the truth. Nothing, I repeat, *nothing* you have ever done is too much to be washed away by the blood of Christ. He loves you. He died for you."

"I've been in prison."

"So have we all."

His laugh mocked. "Not the same kind."

"The walls we build around ourselves can lock us up tighter and longer than concrete and steel. Now, listen, dear. If God could create the earth and the universe and everything in it, do you really think your sins can defeat Him?" She held his gaze. "Never. I say never. Christ Jesus has already proven His love for you." She smiled at the man tenderly. "Not to mention the fact that He's the one who brought you over to us so that you could hear what He has to say to you personally. He whispered in your ear and you responded. That tells me He's chosen you to hear His Word. Now He's leaving it up to you to choose Him."

Three Harleys roared outside. A worn-down look came into the man's eyes. Face hardening, he headed out the door. Eunice watched as he swung his leg over his Harley and put on his helmet. He raised his head as he pulled his motorcycle back. His gaze met hers in a piercing look as his black-booted foot went down hard on the starter. The Harley roared to life.

"Is he going to come to our church?" Timmy stretched to look out the window.

"We can hope, Timmy." Lois waved. The biker gave a slight nod before turning the bike and speeding toward the freeway on-ramp heading north. She rumpled Timmy's hair. "If he does, you make him feel welcome. You say hello to him and sit with him. All right? That man probably has a lot in common with one of Jesus' disciples, Simon the Zealot. Do you remember him?"

"No."

"No?" She looked across the table. Eunice blushed. She hadn't spent much time on the disciples. She concentrated on Jesus.

"Well, Simon was a Zealot."

"What's a Zealot?"

"In our day and age, a zealot would be a terrorist, someone who plans and carries out acts of violence and murder for political reasons. Zealots were sometimes called Sicarii because of the curved knives they carried."

The waitress took their order.

Timmy knocked over the paper-wrapped sugar cubes and started building again. Lois watched, amused. Eunice felt uneasy with her surroundings. "Paul is going to be furious with me for bringing you here."

"You didn't bring me. I brought you. Besides, we needn't worry. David will have his head so full of plans for building the church that neither one of them will even wonder where we went or what we did. Assuming they will even be at the parsonage when we return."

Eunice had never heard Lois speak with such cynicism. She studied Lois as her mother-in-law looked at the patrons dining at the long counter and in the tight booths and clustered tables. Her smile was wistful. "It's been a long time since I've been in a place like this. I've grown too used to church functions, conference centers, club restaurants, and private homes."

"The same is true for me."

"A pity, isn't it? This is where Jesus would've come to eat."

Eunice saw the sorrow in Lois's eyes. "What's wrong, Mom?"

"Oh, nothing. And everything." She smiled faintly. "What's bothering you, my dear?"

"Nothing. Everything." She shook her head. "As afraid as I was coming in the door here, I look around, Lois, and see how much these people have in common with our parishioners. They come in for service. They sit for an hour, expecting to be waited on. They nibble at what Paul teaches them, and then they ride off to life as usual, nothing changed."

"And you're the waitress?"

"No." She laughed bleakly. "I'm the jukebox. Drop some money in the plate, tell Paul what you want to hear, and he'll make sure I fill the requests."

"And the rest of the time?"

"Entertainment and background music. CCC has become a spiritual truck stop."

"Why aren't you writing songs anymore?"

"There's no time."

Lois's face softened. "Oh, Euny."

"That doesn't matter, Mom, but Paul spends hours perfecting his sermons. He never speaks longer than fifteen minutes because someone told him people like short messages. Speak for any longer than that and the men start thinking about the football game they're going to miss if they don't get home soon, and the women are making shopping lists. A thousand other things consuming their thoughts. So he works fifteen hours on fifteen minutes of preaching that never gets deeper than their earwax."

"And probably goes in one ear and out the other with weekly regularity. Wait until the Christian schools start teaching courses in advertising. Then we'll probably be having three-minute commercials for God."

Eunice's laugh broke. "I've never heard you talk like this."

"Comes with age and experience. God allows us to suffer the slings and arrows of our own stupidity." She rested her arms on the table. "Does Paul listen to you anymore, Eunice? Do you get *your* fifteen minutes? And don't give me a shrug. What you say to me won't go further than this table. I want the unvarnished truth."

"No. He doesn't listen to me."

"Does he listen to anyone?"

"Other than Dad, you mean?"

"His father is a given, but what about others? His elders? Close friends in the church?"

"Paul spends a great deal of time with Gerald Boham and Marvin Lockford." His handpicked, yes-men elders. "And he has lunch with Stephen Decker every week or two."

"Who is Stephen Decker?"

"He designs and builds high-end houses and office buildings."

"Oh." Lois closed her eyes.

The waitress brought their meals. Lois joined hands with Timmy and Eunice and prayed quietly. Timmy picked up his hamburger and tried to get his jaw to open wide enough to accommodate it. Euny laughed and cut it in half, took out half of the lettuce and some of the onions, and pressed it down for him.

"David is considering retirement."

"You're kidding! I never thought Dad would ever retire."

"Things change. Sometimes for the better." Her expression was enigmatic. "He should step down." She stabbed a tomato wedge. "It's high time."

Eunice couldn't imagine David Hudson retiring from the pulpit for any reason.

Lois gave her a bright, if somewhat-brittle, smile. "Of course, things could always change again. We'll just have to wait and see what the Lord decides." She asked Timmy how he liked his hamburger, then how he liked school, who his friends were, what he liked to do for fun.

The sun was going down as they walked the mile back into town. Timmy skipped along the sidewalk to the corner and back. Lois chuckled. "He's covering twice the distance we are."

"He'll sleep well tonight."

Lois took her hand. "About David retiring. David would be annoyed if he knew I'd mentioned it to you."

"I won't say anything." She doubted anything would ever come of it, but if talking about it disturbed Lois, Euny would never mention it again.

Lois squeezed her hand before letting go. "I'm very glad Paul married you, Eunice. You're the daughter of my heart."

When they reached the parsonage, a note had been scribbled below Lois's. She handed it to Euny. "Can you decipher this?"

"Paul's taken Dad to the Centerville Golf Course clubhouse for dinner. He left the number in case anyone needs to get in touch with him."

"And I suppose he wrote *fly* at the end because he was in such a hurry."

Eunice laughed. "That's an *I*, Mom, not an *f*. It means 'I love you.'"

Lois removed her Windbreaker. "Nice that he goes to such lengths to let you know."

Stephen put his pencil down and straightened. Raising his arms, he stretched, trying to ease the cramping in his shoulders. Looking over the sketches and ideas, he grinned. He hadn't had this much fun in years!

He glanced at his wristwatch. Three in the morning! Tapping it, he got up and checked the clock on the microwave in the kitchen. It said the same thing. He was going to have a hard time hauling himself out of bed at six so that he could get to Sacramento for an eight o'clock meeting. He opened his refrigerator and took out a piece of cold pepperoni pizza. Might as well pull an all-nighter, then stop at a Starbucks and toss off a couple of espressos. He took a soda from the fridge door.

Paul Hudson probably had no idea of the seed he had dropped. Nor that it had taken root and was consuming Stephen's imagination. What sort of church could he build in order to glorify God? One question overflowed into another until Stephen found himself researching, calling other architects he knew, ordering books on churches across the nation and around the world. He studied everything from chapels to glass cathedrals.

Samuel Mason talked about living a life that glorifies God. What better way to accomplish that than to build a church that would stand and proclaim His name to everyone who saw it? Of course, it would take money, lots of money, to build the kind of facility he was sketching. But the congregation was steadily growing. As was the church budget.

Polishing off the soda, Stephen crushed the can and tossed it into the recycling container in the corner. He finished the last bite of pizza, tossed the pizza crust into the trash, washed his hands, and went back into his home office.

He hadn't been this jazzed about anything since . . . he couldn't remember when.

He set the alarm on his wristwatch so he would have time enough to shower and shave before he headed north to Sacramento. Then he settled himself on the stool, picked up his pencil, and went back to sketching. He doubted Centerville Christian would ever go for something this grand. But that didn't stop him from dreaming.

Dreaming never cost a dime.

CHAPTER 8

———— ❧ ————

Abby took her apron from the drawer and tied a bow behind her back. "Why don't you gentlemen go out on the patio and enjoy the last bit of sunshine while I clean up the kitchen? It's hot enough in here without you two adding your steam."

Samuel chuckled. "What do you say, Stephen? You think it'll be cooler outside?"

Abby turned at the sink. "You can always turn on the sprinklers."

Samuel opened the screen door, inviting their dinner guest to follow. "Never argue with a lady, Stephen. If you win, you just end up feeling guilty." The younger man laughed as he pushed his chair up to the kitchen table.

It was considerably cooler in the backyard. Samuel turned on a faucet and the soothing hiss of sprinklers started. "One of the disadvantages of having an older house is the sorrowful lack of central air-conditioning." He settled into a lawn chair beside the glass table shaded by a large green canvas umbrella.

Stephen sat and stretched out his long legs. "Ever think about adding it?"

"Every summer when the temperatures hit the high nineties." And every time, he and Abby decided there were better places to invest their money: a Christian hospital in Zimbabwe, a missionary in Thailand. Besides, they had four fans. And sprinklers. When the sun went down, they opened all the windows and let in the cooling air.

Stephen grinned at him. "Are we going to finish the book of Romans tonight?"

"Well, I don't rightly know, son," Samuel responded in mock solemnity. "Depends on how many questions you have and how long we end up talking about whatever comes up." He looked at Stephen over the rim of his glasses. "It's only been six months since we started Romans."

Stephen laughed and crossed his arms behind his head. "The longer I live in Centerville, the more time I seem to have."

"Are you running out of work in these parts?"

"No. Just not as obsessed about getting the big-money projects as I was. I've made enough in the last three years to give me breathing space. Time to think. Time to dream."

"Time to spend with your daughter?"

Stephen frowned. "Not much hope of that. I called my ex to ask if I could take Brittany on a trip to Disneyland. I thought she and her new husband might appreciate a little time alone. She said she'd already made plans for Brittany to stay with a friend."

"How long since you last saw Brittany?"

"Three weeks, and then only for a couple of hours."

The screen door banged as Abby came out with two tall glasses of iced tea. "Something to wet your whistles."

Stephen stood. "Why don't you join us, Mrs. M.?"

"Sit down, Stephen. I'd rather have the heat than the gnats." She waved her hand in front of her perspiring face. "Otis called."

Samuel took her hand. "He's not coming?"

"Oh, he's coming. Said he wouldn't miss it, but he's beside himself about Mabel again. She's not eating anything at the convalescent hospital. She told him everything tastes like paste. I'm going to make some peanut-butter cookies. You know how she loves peanut-butter cookies." Her voice was husky.

"We can go for a visit tomorrow. We can drop by that Chinese place where we all used to go for lunch and pick up some chow mein for her."

Abby nodded and went back inside the house.

Stephen watched her go. "Abby's taking it hard, isn't she?"

"Abby and Mabel have been friends for decades. They used to do most of the cooking for the church potlucks. They organized the family picnics and vacation Bible schools. We don't have many close friends left." He gave Stephen a rueful smile and sipped his tea. "It's gotten so Abby lets me open the mail. She doesn't want to be the first one to read about another friend ending up in convalescent care or dying."

"It's too bad about Mabel."

"Mabel is tired and ready to go home to the Lord. It's Otis who's having the hard time. He doesn't want to let her go. They've been married fifty-eight years." Samuel looked out over the lawn to the garden he and Abby had first planted together when they were young and their children small. The roses were in full bloom along the white picket fence. "I understand how he feels." Someone had to pass through the pearly gates first. Selfishly, he hoped he would be the first to go. He couldn't imagine living out whatever time he had left on this earth without Abby beside him. Just the thought of losing her put a hitch in his throat. He took another sip of tea.

Stephen leaned forward. "There's a lot of talk about building another church."

Samuel set his glass down carefully. Stephen must have had lunch with Paul in the last few days. "It comes up every now and again."

"What do you think about the idea?"

Had Paul Hudson put Stephen up to asking the big question? "It takes a lot of money to build a new church."

"Sure it does, but we have a congregation of givers and two services running full every Sunday and a full one Saturday night."

"Yep."

"But you still have reservations."

"Yep, but I've been praying about them." He was well aware of Paul's conviction that the old church building wasn't big enough—or good enough—for his growing congregation. Samuel had tried to discuss the matter quietly with him, but Paul wasn't into discussing anything. He wanted action. He wanted to keep things "moving forward." Every time Samuel spoke to the young pastor, he came away feeling as though he had been in a spiritual battle. Paul Hudson treated him with respect, probably due to Eunice's attachment to Abby, but Samuel still had the feeling that Paul saw him as an old man, out of touch with the world and a boulder in the way of progress.

"Would you mind sharing your concerns with me, Samuel?"

Samuel took his glasses off and pulled out his handkerchief. "What do you need before you start putting up a building, Stephen?"

"Most projects begin with an exploratory phase and a feasibility committee. Then you retain an architect to come up with a conceptual drawing to fit the needs and land. The elders vote, the design phase begins, the architect is hired, the design team gathered, and a critical path for the work organized, and you go for it."

Samuel cleaned his glasses slowly. "Back up a little."

"How far?"

"Permission might be a good start."

Stephen sat up. "Well, sure! That goes without saying. You take the idea and the drawings before the congregation and get their okay."

Samuel put his glasses back on. He could see Stephen was excited about the idea. Did he want to be the one to design and build it? And if so, what were his motivations? He was still young in the Lord, learning to take baby steps in his walk with Christ. A building project could knock him flat on his face. Worse, it could injure him and put him out of the race. "I wasn't thinking of the congregation."

"Planning commission? County supervisors?"

"Someone a lot higher up the ladder, son. You go to the Head of the church. You go to the Lord. You lay everything out before Him in prayer, and then you wait and you listen and you watch. You do those things first, and when you get an answer, assuming the answer is to move ahead, then you proceed. Not before. You shouldn't start something and then pray the Lord will come and help you finish it."

Stephen's mouth tipped. "What about the leap of faith everyone talks about?"

Everyone meaning Paul. "Faith is based on knowledge." *Not unbridled personal ambition.*

"And what about the great commission? What about expanding our territory?"

Samuel had been to services, too, and listened to week after week of Paul preaching on boldness in faith, moving forward, expanding God's territory. He grabbed hold of every new catchphrase. But was it really

God's territory Paul wanted to expand? Was it coincidental that his determination hardened every time David Hudson visited? Just because the father had built a church that housed five thousand members didn't mean the son had to do the same thing. Samuel wanted desperately to give the young pastor the benefit of the doubt, but sometimes he found himself wondering which father Paul Hudson was following.

"David Hudson never had the time of day for his son," Eunice said once. "He was too busy building his empire." The girl had blushed and apologized for saying such a horrible thing about her father-in-law. But her short lapse in familial loyalty had given Samuel and Abby a hint of what was behind Paul's drive for success. And all the slights and veiled insults Samuel had suffered from Paul over the past five years ceased to hurt so much. He realized the boy was still struggling for his father's approval. The realization filled Samuel with compassion for Paul, as well as trepidation over the spiritual battle raging inside the younger Hudson. Paul seemed oblivious to it, for he saw nothing wrong in the worldly methods and thinking that were creeping into his programs and teaching. Eunice said she'd fallen in love with Paul because he had a heart for God. Samuel had sensed that in Paul, too, but right now, Paul was badly in need of open-heart surgery.

Samuel had tried hard to build a relationship with Paul Hudson. He was still trying. If not for Eunice and Timmy, he'd have no insights into what made Paul tick or what troubles he was facing and needed brought before the Lord in prayer. Samuel had spent more hours on his knees in prayer for Paul than for any other member of the congregation. Except possibly Stephen Decker.

"Samuel?"

"Sorry." He gave Stephen an apologetic smile. "Just lost in my thoughts. You mentioned the great commission and taking a leap of faith."

"A building project would accomplish both."

If it was God-directed. "Sounds like you've already made up your mind." Or Paul Hudson had made it up for him with subtle prods and incentives.

"Not exactly, though some might accuse me of having a vested interest." He leaned his forearms on the patio table, his eyes glowing. "I've been doing conceptual drawings for months. Just toying around with some ideas. Not that I'm trying to talk anyone into building."

1/22/15 8:30 P.M.

"You know what it would entail?"

"From the purchase of land to moving in, you bet I know. A building project would test the commitment of the congregation."

"And there's the rub, Stephen. Commitment to build a church facility doesn't necessarily mean commitment to the Lord." He could see Stephen didn't understand what he was saying, but he couldn't explain without sounding as though he were set against Paul Hudson, which he wasn't.

"Centerville Christian is bursting at the seams, Samuel. What's your answer?"

"I don't have an answer. Just questions waiting on answers." More than half of the new members were attending Centerville Christian because they had found their previous church "too fundamental and intolerant." Paul had softened his message. He no longer taught the foundational classes. His sermons brushed over the gospel and zeroed in on the good life in Christ. He'd forgotten that God wanted followers to live a godly life. That called for obedience, and sometimes meant suffering and sacrifice. The heart had to change before a life changed, before one experienced the bounteous joy that came from a personal relationship with Jesus Christ, an indwelling of the Holy Spirit, a complete soul overhaul.

"So you're not set against exploring the possibility of a building project?"

"I'm for taking the time to find out what the Lord wants us to do. What's the motivation behind building a new facility?"

"We're growing. We need more space."

"Just because something grows doesn't mean it's healthy, Stephen. Cancer grows. How many of those who came to hear Paul's preaching on Sunday morning are interested in a midweek Bible study? We need to make disciples of those who are attending now. They need to learn the Bible. They need to mature as Christians. What does God want from members of His church? How do they live lives pleasing to the Lord? How do we offer ourselves as living sacrifices?"

Stephen listened, but he had been primed. "The more people you have, the more talent you can tap for leadership."

"And you think you have to have a big, new building to do that? The apostle Peter in the power of the Holy Spirit preached the gospel on Pentecost and brought three thousand new members into the church. I don't think their first order of business was a building project."

"They gathered in the Temple, didn't they?"

Samuel chuckled. "You've been reading your Bible."

Stephen grinned. "I thought it might be a good idea with you as my teacher."

Samuel was pleased. "Yes. They spoke before the Temple. They met in the corridors and on the steps and in private homes. They continually devoted themselves to the apostles' teaching and to fellowship, to the breaking of bread and to prayer. They weren't asking for pledges to build another temple. God is building the temple, one living stone at a time. You and I are talking about two different kinds of building projects, Stephen."

Stephen relaxed in his lawn chair. "I think I see what you mean." He grew thoughtful.

"So, you've done some conceptual drawings." Had Paul asked for them?

"Quite a few. For kicks. Better to spend an evening doing that than pouring scotch."

"Still a struggle?"

"Always will be. It's the thorn in my side."

"We all have besetting sins, Stephen. They're the trouble that brings us to our knees and keeps us depending on the Lord for strength."

Stephen gave him a wry look. "I haven't yet gotten to the point in my faith where I can call alcoholism a blessing."

"You will."

"What I'd like to know is your besetting sin."

Samuel laughed with him. "Let's just say I wasn't always the cool, calm, and collected man you see before you now."

The screen door creaked and Abby stuck her head out. "Hollis is here."

"We're on our way in." Samuel stood and picked up his empty glass. "Why don't you bring your conceptual drawings over, Stephen? I'd like to see what you think a church should look like."

"I think I got ahead of myself."

Samuel smiled. "Depends on who was nudging you."

What Samuel feared most was Centerville Christian Church ending up the victim on the field of battle over Paul Hudson's soul.

———— ❧❦ ————

"It's your mother's birthday, Paul." Eunice couldn't believe he was going to allow it to pass without even calling Lois.

"You sent her a gift, didn't you?" He took his coat from the hall closet.

"Yes, but she'll want to hear from you."

"Okay! I'll call and wish her a happy birthday."

She had to bite her tongue or she would say something she'd regret. Paul loved his mother. She knew he did, just as she knew he loved her. He just allowed other responsibilities to get in the way. He gave his time to a dozen people who called every week wanting his counseling. He gave his time to his deacons and his elders. Except for Samuel Mason. Then Paul was "busy" or "out on visitation" or some other excuse he insisted she pass on to a man she had grown to love and admire like her own father. "You're spending too much time with the Masons," Paul had said the other night. He had grown to despise Samuel. He didn't say so. He might not even realize it, but she heard it in his tone every time Samuel's name came up. And she knew the cause of Paul's animosity. Samuel Mason never caved in to "popular opinion."

"Happy birthday, Mom!" Paul said into the phone.

Eunice was shaking. She went into the kitchen and started the water. Maybe a cup of tea would calm her down. *Lord, Lord, kill the root of bitterness growing in me. I don't want to feel this way about my husband. My sun doesn't rise and fall because of him. You are my God, my help in times of trouble. And, God, oh, God, I'm in trouble!* She could hear the steady drone of Paul's voice as he talked to his mother. Talked, not listened. His voice came closer. "Tell Dad hello. Tell him everything is going well up here. I may have some really great news soon. Here's Eunice." He handed her the telephone and headed for the living room.

"Hi, Mom."

"Hello, dear. Did you have to dial for him?"

"No. Of course not." A small lie to spare her mother-in-law's feelings. She heard the front door open and close as Paul went to meet the mayor at the country club.

"How's the interior decorating going?"

She and Paul had recently moved to a new home, vacating the

parsonage just in time for the new associate pastor to move in. "Slower than Paul would like, but it's moving along." She talked about the painting, wallpapering, and making drapes for the living room and master bedroom. "And the landscaping is almost done."

"I didn't get a chance to tell Paul, but his father is retiring."

"Really?"

"The board of directors is throwing a big bash for him in six weeks. Put it on your calendar." She gave Eunice the date.

"He's really going to do it?"

"He wouldn't dare change his mind."

"Are you relieved?"

A long silence followed her question. Sometimes silence said more than words.

"I'll miss all the friends I've made in this church."

"Just because Dad is retiring doesn't mean you have to leave the church."

"Of course it does, sweetheart. The new pastor would have a very hard time leading this flock if David Hudson was still sitting in one of the rows, don't you think?"

"I hadn't thought of that."

"I think it would be best to move out of the area. But I promise not to move within a hundred miles of Centerville."

"I would love to have you as a neighbor."

"And risk your husband's church to his father? If we lived close enough to commute to CCC, David would have his hands in Paul's ministry within weeks, and how would Paul feel about that?"

Like a little boy who couldn't do anything right. Again. "Maybe you'd like Oregon. Or Washington. How about Maine?"

Lois laughed with her. "Actually, I was thinking a desert island would be nice." There was a catch in her voice. "No more board meetings. No more elders' retreats or discipline intensives or private tutoring sessions in the deeper meanings of the Bible. If David wants to travel, he'll have to take the old ball and chain with him. No more private counseling sessions . . ."

Eunice knew something was wrong, but she didn't want to pry. "Mom?"

"I swore I wasn't going to do this." Lois blew her nose quietly. "I'm all right, Euny. Really I am. I'm just so angry I'm ready to explode. And I can't even tell you who I'm most angry with. God in His sovereignty who sees everything and waits so patiently? David for being what he is? Members of the church leadership who chose to overlook David's weaknesses because he was bringing in the people who were filling the offering plates? Or friends who knew what was going on and didn't have the courage to tell me?"

Knew what? Eunice was afraid to ask. She was afraid she already knew.

"I've always tried to believe the best about people, especially my husband. Euny, I have to talk to someone, and I'd rather it was you than anyone else. But you have to promise to keep it all to yourself."

Lois unloaded her burdens, and Eunice was weighed down by them, filled with righteous wrath and sorrow. "Oh, Mom. I'm sorry. What does Dad say?"

"That it's all a misunderstanding. That there are tares among the wheat that are trying to strangle his ministry. That this is all about jealousy and ambition. That he's being persecuted just like Jesus Christ. He fought back at first. Like a wolf in a trap. Maybe that's why the board members started banding together. Whatever the case, the last meeting settled the matter. I've never seen David so angry, but he wrote the letter of resignation. And now, the congregation is going to hold a big party to say thank you and wish us well. They have no idea what's happened. And that's the last I'm going to say on the matter because I'm too close to the whole thing to be objective. How's Timmy? Tell me what my grandson is up to these days."

Eunice took her cue and spent the next fifteen minutes talking about Timmy's activities. He loved soccer and riding his bike, but he was having difficulty "staying on task" in school.

"Paul was the same way. Now, what about you? Is everything all right with you?"

"I'm busier than I like to be, and Paul is working harder than he should, but other than that, everything is just fine."

"Uh-huh. I can hear how fine it is."

"I've been learning hard lessons since we came to Centerville. A pastor's life is not his own. How have you managed all these years?"

"The Lord is my first husband, Eunice. My faithful companion."

She laughed softly. "The hardest part is learning that you can't pray on Monday and expect God to answer by Tuesday morning."

Eunice plucked a tissue from the box on the counter. "Wouldn't it be nice if He did?"

"Set a timer for five minutes. *Ping!* Problem solved. Of course, it would be down the chute and into the fire instead of grace and mercy, wouldn't it?" She reminded Eunice of the date of the retirement celebration. "If Paul gives you any hassle, tell him his father needs him. Don't tell Paul anything of what I've shared with you. I want David to be the one to explain all this, if he has the courage."

Paul went through the mail Reka Wilson had put on his desk. A letter from an attorney caught his attention. He sliced it open and read that Centerville Christian Church was the sole beneficiary of a Bjorn Svenson. His pulse jumped. He turned to his computer and typed in the name. Nothing came up. He tapped speed-dial number five. "Eunice, do you remember someone named Bjorn Svenson?"

"No, I don't think so. Why?"

"I just received a letter from his attorney informing me the church is Svenson's primary beneficiary." He wondered how much money was involved. *Let it be a lot, God! Let it be enough for me to move ahead with my plans. We need a bigger facility. If it isn't enough for that, let there be enough to buy land.*

"Samuel might know."

He wasn't about to call Samuel. "Did the office furniture arrive yet?"

"All the pieces made it without a scratch."

"I want my desk and the credenza by the front windows."

"Everything is exactly where you said you wanted it, Paul. Don't forget we're supposed to meet with Timmy's teacher this afternoon."

He had forgotten, but how important could it be? "I haven't got time today, Eunice."

"It's important that you be there this time, Paul."

"You can handle it."

"We should be together on this, and his teacher asked to speak to both of us. He's been in two fights in the last month."

"So ground him again. For more than a few days this time."

"Paul—"

"Look, Eunice. You know I love him, but I have a full day scheduled. Everyone wants a piece of me."

"It's only twenty minutes, Paul. And this is your son."

The heat came up beneath his skin, his muscles tensing. "I don't remember my father ever attending one of my parent-teacher conferences. My mother was the one who went."

"And you told me once you never felt as though you mattered to your father."

Why did she have to bring up something he'd said in a weak moment and throw it in his face?

"The appointment is at three thirty."

"All right. I'll do my best to be there." He hung up. He looked at his calendar, glanced at his watch, and picked up the phone again. He wanted to find out more about the Svenson bequest. This might just be the answer to his prayers.

Paul didn't even think about the parent-teacher conference until he was on his way home from Rockville. Eunice would be disappointed, but as soon as he told her the news, she'd understand.

He turned onto the cul-de-sac of new houses, pulled into the driveway of the largest one in the back curve, and pushed the remote on his visor. He felt a warm glow of pride as he looked at their new home. Four bedrooms, two bathrooms, a large family room, and a formal dining room adjacent to a living room with a fireplace. The door rolled up smoothly and he drove his new Saturn into the two-car garage, parking next to his old Toyota.

Unlocking the side door, he came into the kitchen and smelled pot roast and apples baking. The nook table was set for two. Eunice stood at the sink, peeling potatoes. He put his hands on her hips and kissed the curve of her neck. She didn't move. "I'm sorry I missed the parent-teacher conference." She continued peeling potatoes. "You'll understand as soon as I tell you why."

"I'm sure you have a good reason. You always do." She cut up the potato over a pot on the counter, ran the tap water until the chunks of potato were covered, and shut the water off. She stepped away from him and set the pot on a burner.

"I didn't intentionally forget about the appointment. I told you about the letter I received from the attorney."

She turned. "What attorney?"

"The one who sent me a letter about Bjorn Svenson, the man who made the church his sole beneficiary." A look came into her eyes that he couldn't decipher. He opened the refrigerator and took out a can of soda. "Svenson was a merchant in Rockville. He ran a clothing store there for forty years." He popped the top and took a long swig. "When his wife died, he tried to sell. There was a recession, so the place just sat on the market for a couple of years with no offers. The Realtor advised him to take it off the market, which he did. When Svenson's health declined, he moved into a residential-care facility north of Sacramento and left the attorney to handle the details of his estate. The property taxes have been paid on time each year, but the store sat vacant. I went out to look at it with a Realtor this afternoon."

He grinned. Maybe she'd be more enthusiastic when he told her the great news. "Take a guess what the property is worth on today's market, Eunice."

"I wouldn't know."

"Five hundred and fifty thousand dollars! Can you believe it?" He laughed. The last of the soda bubbled over his tongue. He put the empty can on the counter. "This is what I've been praying for: a clear sign that I'm to move ahead with the building project."

"It could mean other things, Paul."

"No, this is a sign from God, Euny, a clear sign that we should move ahead on the new facility. This windfall is the money I need to start. I've called a board meeting on Friday night. The Realtor said she could have the report on comparable values ready by then."

"You're assuming everyone will see it the same way you do."

"Everyone will. Even Samuel will agree this is provident." He cupped her face. "So, are you going to forgive me for missing the parent-teacher conference and set a place for me at the dinner table?"

"Your place is set. Timmy's spending the night with the Masons. We need to talk."

Warning bells went off, but he didn't want anything to spoil the rush he'd felt since he'd talked with the attorney and the Realtor. He didn't want anything to dampen his joy. "You know, this is the first time in ages that we've been alone together."

"Paul . . ."

He kissed her again, the way he had when they were first married. "I love you. I know I haven't said it often enough, or shown you . . ."

It took only a moment for her resistance to melt.

They could talk about Tim's problems in the morning.

CHAPTER 9

SOMETHING WAS WRONG. Paul could see it in the way his father shoved his hand into his pocket and jingled his keys as they waited for the retirement banquet to begin. Paul's mother sat on the leather sofa between Eunice and Timmy, looking lovely but older than the last time he'd seen her, seven months ago. Was her health the reason his father had decided to retire?

"Sit down, David." She smoothed the skirt of her peach silk suit.

"I don't feel like sitting down."

"You're not facing a firing squad."

He gave her a venomous look and went to his high-backed leather armchair near the built-in mahogany bookshelves. The office had been redecorated again. Everything was first-class. "If you're going to attract corporate types to your church, you have to look the part," he'd told Paul earlier in the evening. "You can't usher an executive into some tacky little hole-in-the-wall and convince him Jesus is the way to a good life." The cherry wood paneling, custom drapes, brass lamps, and plush forest-green carpeting probably cost more than Paul's annual salary, and that didn't even count the new desk and credenza.

His father drummed his fingers on the red leather chair.

Someone had better say something to ease the tension in the room. "I doubt I'll live long enough to have an office like this," Paul said, hoping the envy didn't come through in his voice.

His father stood and paced again. "You will if you work hard enough."

"Paul works very hard," Eunice said.

"Did I say he didn't?"

Paul gave Eunice a warning frown. She knew better than to be argumentative. The last thing he needed was his father making some crack about a husband who needed his wife to defend him. "A church of five hundred can't be compared to one of six thousand, Eunice."

"Jesus began with twelve." His mom patted Eunice's hand. "Some people forget that work is just work if it isn't guided by the Holy Spirit."

His father turned his back on them and stared out the window.

"Who's taking over your pulpit, Dad?"

"Joseph Wheeler."

"He's been an associate pastor for five years," his mother said. "He's a man after God's own heart."

Paul couldn't remember him. "I've never heard him preach. Is he any good?"

His father snorted. "The elders think he is."

His mother smiled. "He's an excellent teacher with a solid foundation in the Bible. People can trust him."

His father moved away from the windows and glanced at his Rolex. "What's taking them so long?"

"Try to relax, Dad. You're making all of us nervous."

"This evening wasn't my idea." He pulled a monogrammed handkerchief from an inside pocket of his Armani suit coat and dabbed at the perspiration beading on his forehead. "I don't like having things planned for me." Refolding the handkerchief, he tucked it back into his pocket.

"At least it isn't a surprise party," Paul said, trying for a little levity.

"I'd like to surprise them." His father's eyes were dark.

Paul's mother looked at her husband with a faint smile. "I wouldn't advise it."

"I was asked to say a few words about what it was like to be your son."

"Whose idea was that?" He looked at his wife. "Yours, Lois?"

"You can trust Paul to be kind, David." She crossed her legs and smoothed her skirt over her knees. "I thought it might be good if your son spoke for you."

Paul wasn't about to admit it had taken him three days to write a five-minute speech—and hours of recounting how many times his father had hurt him. What honor would result from his telling the whole truth? "I'm going to tell them that I grew up seeing firsthand the devotion it took to build a church. Anyone who knows you has seen your passion for the ministry—and your dedication to your calling. I hope to follow in your footsteps." David Hudson had dedicated his life to the church, and that's what Paul intended to tell the audience waiting to wish him a fond farewell.

"Well, let's hope you come out better in the deal than I have."

Paul was stunned. "I think you've done all right for yourself, Dad."

His mother laughed. "Indeed he has. And he would be the first to tell you how God has blessed him."

The door opened. "We're ready for you, David."

"Thank you." His father headed for the door and then paused, looking at his wife.

"Lois," the man said respectfully and gave her a nod before stepping back into the corridor.

"It's time, Lois."

"Yes, it is time. High time." She sat looking up at him, her expression enigmatic.

Eunice blushed and looked at Paul uneasily.

"Dad?" Paul had never seen his father look vulnerable or uncertain, and it shook him. "What's going on here?"

"Nothing that should concern you." He held out his hand to his wife. "Lois . . ."

"For the last few years, I've been on the sidelines watching the game, David. And now you want me by your side." She pressed her lips together. "This is your evening. You're the one they all came to see. You go on out there and receive your just reward." Her dark eyes glistened with tears. She shook her head.

He paled. "Please, Lois."

A look of anguish filled her eyes. She shut them tightly for a moment and then rose gracefully. "On with the show." She tucked her hand into the crook of David's arm and walked out the door with him.

Paul put his hand on Tim's shoulder. "You're with us, Son. Stick close." He leaned toward Eunice. "Would you please smile? You look like you're going to a funeral."

"Has your father talked to you about why he's retiring?"

"He said he was tired and needed a rest. And he wanted to spend more time with Mom."

"Well, that's good," she said in an odd tone before following the usher.

Two more dark-suited ushers were waiting for them at the double doors that opened into the church's gymnasium. Paul heard the low rumble of a large crowd and soft music from a string quartet.

"Dr. Hudson, Pastor Wheeler will be here in just a moment to escort you and Lois to the head table. I'll show your son and his family to their table. They'll be right in front of the podium. We have a beautiful evening planned for you. We hope you'll enjoy it." His smile was faint and cool. "Joseph will speak first, and then dinner will be served. As soon as the dessert is served, the program will start. Several of our associate pastors will say a few words, and then your son will speak. Five minutes," he said, looking at Paul. "Whatever you say will act as an introduction to a video the staff put together to sum up your father's career. We've planned special music at the end, and then it's over."

It's over. He made it sound like an ordeal to get through rather than a celebration of a man's life.

"Ladies and gentlemen," someone said into a microphone, and the crowd quieted to a low hum. "Please welcome Dr. and Mrs. David Hudson." As the doors opened and Paul's mother and father stepped forward, a man stood waiting for them. People began to rise from their seats and clap as his parents were escorted to the front of the gymnasium, where a dais and long head table had been set up. Soon the entire congregation was on its feet. The applause was thunderous.

Paul and Eunice, with Timmy between them, were escorted to their table. The applause continued even after his father and mother had reached their seats. And still the applause went on as his father seated his mother. His father sat for a few seconds and then rose as though embarrassed by the adoration and praise, and spread his hands and nodded and gestured for everyone to be seated. Paul's mother tugged on his jacket and he sat again, and the rest of those standing at the head table sat as well.

Jealousy raged inside Paul. Would there ever come a day when his congregation would hold him in such high esteem? Damask tablecloths, fine china, silverware, and real crystal goblets, a floral centerpiece that wasn't out of someone's garden. The cost of his father's retirement send-off would wipe out Centerville Christian's entire budget for two years. Paul felt small and insignificant.

Joseph stepped to the microphone. Chairs scraped as people took their seats. He opened in prayer, calling upon all present to give thanks to the Lord for their many blessings. Then he spoke briefly about the evening's program.

As the evening progressed, Paul became more aware of his father's tension. His father said little to the man on his right, and he rubbed his fingers back and forth on the tablecloth until Paul's mother put her hand over his. When he raised her hand and kissed it, Paul was shocked. He'd never seen his father do anything like that before. His mother snatched her hand away and folded both hands in her lap before returning her attention to the salad that had been placed before her. Neither of his parents seemed to have much appetite.

Nor did he. His palms were sweating. Everything he had planned to say went out of his head. His heart pounded. His stomach churned. The only time his father had shown interest in him was when Paul disappointed him. And that had been often when he was a boy. His grades weren't high enough. He wasn't athletic enough. He dressed inappropriately. His hair was too long. He was a mama's boy. It was true that his father had dedicated his energies to building this church, but he had done it at the expense of a son who had wanted nothing more than to please him and make him proud.

"Paul?" Eunice put her hand on his leg.

She always sensed when something was bothering him. This time, he was relieved. "Things aren't right between my mother and father. I can't put my finger on it. And I'm not sure what I planned to say suits the occasion. Pray the Lord gives me the words, honey. Pray hard."

She took his hand and squeezed it. "The leadership is shifting the attention away from your father and putting it on the Lord and His work. That's good, Paul. That's as it should be."

"Look at my father's face."

"Focus on the Lord, Paul. If you look at the program, you'll see that the whole intention is to take the focus off your father and put it on Jesus Christ."

She was right. Had it been his father's idea to shift the spotlight? It seemed out of character, but appropriate. His retirement could change the direction of the whole ministry here. The program must have been designed to reassure his father that his work for the Lord would continue. His ministry would continue long after he left.

The salad plates were removed and beef Wellington served, followed by chocolate mousse for dessert.

Paul could hardly swallow any of it. *Lord, give me the words You want me to speak.*

Joseph Wheeler stood and introduced Paul. Paul rose, took the microphone, and faced the multitude. He hesitated for only a few seconds and spoke in love of the respect he had for his father as he watched him dedicate his life to the church. He encouraged everyone present to nurture faith in their sons and daughters, prompting them to follow the Lord wholeheartedly, for that would be pleasing to Him. When he took his seat, he looked up at the head table. His mother was smiling, tears streaming down her cheeks, but his father was looking up at the screen as the lights were dimming and the video encapsulating his ministry was starting.

Eunice took Paul's hand beneath the table and leaned toward him. "That was perfect, Paul. You couldn't have said anything better."

A pity his father wasn't satisfied.

Eunice knew her father-in-law had said something to Paul before leaving the church because Paul said a curt good-night that included the whole family before going downstairs to the spacious guest suite in his parents' North Hollywood Hills luxury home. Tim headed for the bathroom.

Lois let out her breath. "What did you say to your son this time, David?"

"Nothing that should put him in a childish snit." He loosened his tie and headed for the master bedroom.

"Maybe you should talk to Paul and see if he's all right," Lois told Eunice. "You can tell him I'm proud of him."

Lois met Tim halfway down the hallway. "How would you like to watch a movie with Granny in the den? Have you ever seen *Ben-Hur*? You'll love the chariot race. We can have popcorn and hot cocoa."

Eunice opened the guest suite door and saw the suitcase on the bed. Paul came out of the closet with an armload of his clothes. She closed the door behind her and crossed the room. "What are you doing?"

"What does it look like? I'm packing."

"Paul, we can't leave."

"That's what you think!"

"How will your mother feel?"

"She'll understand."

"But, Paul, you said we would be staying until Friday."

"*You* stay. I'm going back to Centerville. You can tell them something came up. I have work to do. That's the truth."

"I take it you and your father had words after the banquet."

He gave a hard laugh. "Just enough to make me want to get out of here as fast as I can. I shouldn't have said anything. I shouldn't have come."

"What did he say, Paul?"

"He said he expected more from his son than a paltry tribute to fatherhood any first-year seminary student could write in five minutes."

"And what would have pleased him? To say the ministry will fall apart without him? God willing, it won't." She stepped toward him. "We can't leave, Paul. This is the first family vacation we've had since you took the pulpit in Centerville. Six years, Paul. We promised to take Timmy to Disneyland and Universal Studios. What about all that talk about Zuma Beach and La Brea Tar Pits and all the other places your mother took you when you were a boy? It's not fair to him."

"He'll get over it." His back was to her as he yanked open another drawer.

"When are you going to stop living your life to please your father?"

He stopped packing long enough to glare at her. "You don't know what you're talking about!" He dumped some shirts into the suitcase.

Eunice was so angry, she was shaking. She knew exactly what would happen if he went through with this. "If you leave tomorrow morning, your father is going to say you tucked tail and ran."

He turned so sharply, she didn't know what he meant to do. She fell back more in shock than from the slap across her face. She put her hand over her stinging cheek and stared at him, horrified. When he took a step toward her, she stepped back. "Euny," he said, his face ashen.

Her heart was thundering. "Sometimes I wonder if I know you at all."

"I'm sorry," he said hoarsely. He sat on the bed, his shoulders hunched, and wept.

She ran a trembling hand through his hair as she did to Timmy when he was deeply upset. Usually over something his father had done—or not done. "Paul, your father was upset tonight and he took it out on you."

He took her hand. "Will you forgive me?"

"I already have."

"How is it possible to love someone so much and hate him at the same time? My father makes me crazy!"

Was that an excuse for what Paul had done to her? "Your father will have a lot to answer for, Paul." She couldn't say any more than that without breaking confidence with Lois. No matter what she knew about her father-in-law, she had no right to condemn him, or try to assassinate him in the eyes of his son. The truth would have to come from his father or Lois. And if not from either of them, Eunice prayed that God Himself would make the truth known to Paul, and his father would cease to be his idol.

She sat on the bed beside her husband. "You asked me to pray for you, Paul. And I did. I prayed with all my heart and soul that you would speak God's words. *You* prayed, too. And you said what the Lord gave you to say." She took his hand between hers. "The Lord is pleased, Paul, even if your father isn't."

"I felt certain God was speaking those words through me, Euny. So certain. I haven't felt that good in a long time."

Oh, Lord, let him see clearly how lost he's been. Let this be the time. Please.

"Sometimes I think my father cuts me down deliberately. There's always been something between us that agitates him." His eyes were filled with anguish. "There's something in me that sets him off."

Lord, please, Your words not mine. Let Paul hear the truth with love.
"Sometimes things aren't as they seem, Paul."

"What do you mean?"

Her heart fluttered as her nerves tightened. *Let my motivation be pure, Lord.* "Just because a man says he's a Christian doesn't mean he is one. Even if he is standing in a pulpit."

He stared at her, searching her eyes for a few seconds, and then he let go of her hand. "Are you saying what I think you are?"

The anger was back in his voice. So be it. "We can't know your father's heart, Paul. But we can see what fruit is being produced."

He rose. "You've got it wrong, Eunice. It's unbelievable how wrong you are."

Paul was only a foot from her, but she felt the growing distance in her heart. Even while he looked down on her, she felt he'd turned his back on her. "I hope so, Paul."

"How could you even think my father isn't a Christian? Look at what he's built for the Lord. Did you see the hundreds of people in that hall? They were all there to say thanks for his years of service. Did you hear what they were saying to him when they came through the receiving line? They couldn't thank him enough for all he's done for them! If not for him, they never would have received the gospel! Some wept!"

Eunice wondered how he could be so easily swayed. He'd studied the Bible even more than she had. It was God, not David Hudson, who softened hearts. It was the Word of God, Christ Jesus, who saved. It was by His death those people were redeemed. All through the centuries there had been men who had proclaimed the gospel for their own gain. And God had used even them to accomplish His good purpose. David Hudson had never saved a single soul in his entire life, nor would he. She wanted to cry out against the man who had ridden Paul all his life, the man who could crush him with a few words or a look, and whose favor Paul was so desperate to win. But what was the use? She had only to look into her husband's eyes to see he wasn't ready to listen.

Weary, frustrated, hurt, she stood. "You do and think as you will, Paul." She walked to the bedroom door.

"I suppose you're going to go whine to my mother now about what a lousy husband and father I am."

Hand on the doorknob, she turned and looked at him. Did he really think so little of her? Or did he just say things to hurt her the same way his father said hurtful things to him? "I'm going to go and sit with Timmy and Mom and watch *Ben-Hur.*"

She would leave Paul alone to sulk by himself.

When Eunice came to bed late that night, Paul pulled her into his arms and apologized again. Everything seemed right between them—more right than it had been in months—until she awakened in the morning and found herself alone in bed. She sat up quickly, and was relieved to see Paul's suit, slacks, and shirts on hangers in the closet and his suitcase in the corner next to hers. The clock on the bedside table said seven.

Pushing back the comforter, she slipped her feet into her slippers. Pulling on her pink chenille robe, she went to check on Timmy in the upstairs guest room. On the way past the den, she saw Lois, dressed in black slacks, a white blouse, and a hip-length purple sweater, closing up the sofa bed. "I thought I should get up before Paul or Tim knew I was sleeping in here."

The master bedroom door was closed.

"Paul and Dad must be in the kitchen having coffee."

"I don't think so."

"Then Paul's probably out for a run."

"So he's still jogging."

"Not as often as he'd like."

Lois smiled. "He lettered in track in high school. He won so many sprints a scout came to talk with him about training for the Olympics."

"Why didn't he?"

"God called him into the ministry."

The kitchen was full of Southern California sunshine. Lois had decorated in blue, white, and yellow. Eunice sat at the breakfast bar while Lois ground coffee beans, poured the fresh grounds into a filter, and slipped the holder into place on the coffeemaker. "What was bothering Paul last night?" She poured in the water. "He did so well at the banquet."

Eunice shrugged. She didn't want to say anything about Paul. "Dad must be enjoying his first day of retirement. He doesn't usually sleep in."

"He's up and gone just like Paul. I closed the door to the master bedroom because I haven't had the chance to make the bed yet." Lois gave her a dry smile. "He went out to play golf at Lakeside."

"Oh. Well, maybe Paul is with him."

"No," Lois said, looking out the kitchen window. "He's just coming in now."

The front door opened and closed. Paul came into the kitchen in sweatpants and a sleeveless T-shirt, his sandy hair dark with sweat. "Good morning, ladies!" He kissed Eunice and then kissed his mother's cheek. Opening the refrigerator, he took out the orange juice, found a glass, and filled it. Still puffing, he raised it in salute. "Cheers!" He emptied it and put the glass in the sink.

Lois tossed him a kitchen towel. "Before you sweat all over my clean kitchen floor."

He wiped his face and draped the towel around his neck. "Where's Dad?"

"He . . . had to go out this morning." Lois shot Eunice a look of warning.

"I was hoping to take him out to lunch. When's he getting home?"

"I don't think he's going to be home until late this afternoon, Paul." Lois set up cups and saucers. "Which means you can go with Eunice and Timmy and me to Griffith Park and the zoo."

"Oh, joy." He held both ends of the towel.

Eunice saw that Lois had no intention of telling Paul that his father was playing golf. "I'd better take a shower," Eunice said. Maybe if she was out of the kitchen, Lois could talk to Paul.

"Let me get mine first." Paul headed for the door. "I need a shower more than you do."

She sat on the stool again, depressed. Sooner or later, Paul was going to find out where his father was and be hurt that he hadn't been invited.

Lois poured Eunice some coffee. "If Paul comes with us, he'll have a good time and he won't be around to see his father stroll in with his golf clubs. I think David is avoiding the moment when Paul asks him why he retired."

More excuses.

Lois took a container of half-and-half from the refrigerator, filled the little cream pitcher, and placed it carefully on the counter beside the sugar bowl. "I'm glad last night is behind me."

"It was a very beautiful program."

Lois's face softened. "Yes, it was. The leadership managed to kill gossip before it started. A few people left the church, but they did so quietly." She poured a cup of coffee for herself and sat down. She added cream and sugar and stirred slowly. "Last night went a long way toward making the transition easier on the congregation."

"Are you going to be all right, Mom?"

"Actually, I'm doing better than I expected."

"In the den?"

She smiled sardonically. "My sciatica is acting up."

That would be the story Paul would hear if he asked why his mother wasn't sleeping with his father.

Paul went with them to Griffith Park. Timmy stayed with his father, drinking in every word Paul told him about the various animals, while Lois and Eunice hung back and talked.

"Everything has been handled quietly," Lois said, "which is best for the church. The last thing I want is to cause disunity in the body, not to mention the disillusionment to some of the newer members. David is sorry about everything, of course."

Was he repentant, or just sorry that his ministry had come to an end? Eunice wanted to ask, but she didn't want to cause Lois any more hurt.

Her mother-in-law had prepared a picnic lunch. They found a quiet place in the shade near an expanse of lawn. Lois had also thought to bring along two gloves and a baseball. The smaller one looked well used; the larger, new. Eunice couldn't remember the last time she had seen Paul play catch with their son. She relished every moment of it.

"Hold the glove up, Tim," Paul called to their son. "That's it! Good catch, Son!" Tim beamed.

The day was almost perfect until they pulled up in front of the house. The garage door was open and Paul's father was lifting his golf clubs out of the trunk. "He *had* to go out, you said." Paul jammed on the parking brake. "Nice try, Mom."

Lois leaned forward in the backseat and put her hand on his shoulder. "We had a very nice day, Paul."

Paul took the keys from the ignition. "I'm heading back to Centerville tomorrow morning."

"I thought we were going to Disneyland," Tim said from the backseat.

"Another time, Son."

"But, Dad . . ."

"I have more important things to do than go to an amusement park!" Eunice turned in the front seat and forced a smile. "You know your father wouldn't break a promise to you, Tim. He has to go back, but we don't. You and me and Grandma will head for Anaheim tomorrow morning, and spend the entire day at Disneyland. We'll rest a day and then go to Universal Studios."

"Cool!" Tim bounded out of the car and headed for the house. Lois got out and followed him.

Paul glared at Eunice. "What about school?"

"Tim's teacher knows he won't be back until Monday."

"I suppose I'm supposed to drive back down here and pick you two up on Friday."

"Don't put yourself out, Paul. We can always ride a Greyhound bus home."

"Suit yourself." Paul shoved the door open, got out, slammed it, and strode up the walkway.

Eunice sat in the car for a moment, watching her father-in-law polish his Ping golf clubs before she got out and followed her husband into the house.

Samuel leaned his weight into the edger as he trimmed the last foot of grass from along the pathway to the front steps. He swept the blades of grass into a dustpan, dumped them into the green recycling bin in the garage, and hung up the broom and edger. He was tired, but he felt good. He loved the smell of freshly cut grass.

In deference to Abby, he took off his shoes and left them next to the step before entering the house through the garage. He could smell banana bread baking. Abby wasn't in the kitchen. Samuel headed for the door to the backyard, but the timer pinged. He turned off the oven. Picking up the pot holders, he opened the oven and pulled out two loaves of banana bread and set them on the cooling rack.

Abby wasn't in the backyard. He came back inside. "Abby?" He found her sitting on the bedroom floor, fighting for breath, her back against the edge of their bed.

"Abby! Honey, what's wrong?" He gathered her in his arms, trying to slip his arm beneath her knees.

"No!" she gasped, her lips blue. "Don't lift me."

"I'm calling the doctor. Don't move!" He scrambled for the phone, knocking it off the side table onto the floor. He righted it and punched in 911. As soon as he gave the dispatcher the information she needed, he hung up and knelt beside Abby. Drawing her into his arms, he held her tenderly. "Hang on, honey. They're on their way. Hang on. Hang on."

He could hear sirens in the distance. Easing Abby back onto the floor, he grabbed the bedpost and pulled himself up. Wincing against the pain in his knees, he hurried along the hallway, opened the front door, and went out just as the paramedics pulled up. "In here." He beckoned them and hurried back inside and down the hall. "Abby. They're here, honey. They're on their way in. Hang on, honey." He was fighting tears.

"The bread."

"It's on the counter, sweetheart. I turned the oven off. There's nothing to worry about. You're going to be fine. You'll be fine." He took her hand and felt her squeeze his weakly.

"Calm down, Samuel, or we'll have to call another ambulance." Her forehead was beaded with perspiration. He kissed it and held her close, unable to say anything past the lump in his throat.

Don't take her from me, Lord. Please don't take her. Not yet.

When the paramedics entered with their equipment, there was no room for him. He stood back, watching as they took her vitals, talked to a doctor, started an IV drip, and lifted her gently to the gurney. "I'm going with her." Samuel followed them down the hall and out the front door. Millie Bruester was waiting at the front gate, asking him what she could do to help. "Lock up the house, would you, please?" The paramedics were lifting the gurney into the ambulance, and Abby was lifting her hand. "I've got to go."

"Don't worry about anything, Samuel. Just go. Go!"

The ride to the hospital seemed to take forever. When they arrived, the paramedics wheeled Abby into the emergency room, where a doctor met them and was apprised of her vitals as they wheeled her through double doors. Samuel tried to follow, but a nurse intercepted him. "I need some information, sir. You need to fill out these forms."

"But my wife—"

"Dr. Hayes is with her, sir. He's an excellent doctor. She couldn't be in better hands." She held out a clipboard with the forms. "I'll be at the registration counter when you're finished."

A few minutes later, he held the clipboard out to her. "Is there a telephone I can use?"

Smiling, she took it back and nodded toward his right. "The telephones are at the end of the waiting room between the restrooms."

Pay phones! He dug in his pocket. It was empty. He reached into his back pocket and remembered he had left his wallet on top of his dresser in the organizer his daughter had given him. What need did he have for his wallet while mowing the lawn?

Lord, Lord . . .

"Samuel." He saw Eunice hurrying toward him, Tim right on her heels.

"I thought you two were in Southern California."

"We returned about an hour ago. I was just unpacking when Millie called. We came right away. How is she?"

"They won't tell me. She's with the doctor." His voice cracked. Eunice wrapped her arms around his waist and hugged him tightly. He put his arm around Timmy's shoulders and pulled him in close. They all wept together.

"Don't give up, Samuel." Eunice rubbed his back and began to pray aloud as naturally as she took in air. Timmy pressed closer, and Samuel held on tighter as Eunice asked Jesus to be with them, to heal Abby's body, to give them strength and patience. When she finished, the three of them remained in the embrace.

"I was going to call my daughter, but I haven't even got a dime in my pocket and I forgot my wallet."

Eunice reached into her shoulder bag and pulled out her change purse. "You forgot something else, too, Samuel." She smiled at him through her tears.

"What?"

"Your shoes."

———— ❦ ————

As soon as Stephen heard the news about Abigail Mason, he called his work site, told them he wouldn't be coming, and headed for the hospital. He bought an arrangement of flowers in the gift shop and asked the receptionist where he could find Abby. When he reached the private room on the second floor, he tapped on the door before easing it open.

Abby smiled at him from behind her oxygen mask as Samuel stood and shook his hand. Stephen was shocked at how small, thin, and pale Abigail Mason looked in the hospital bed. And Samuel had aged in the last few days.

"More flowers." Stephen grinned and put the arrangement of pink rosebuds alongside a small basket of daisies on Abby's bedside table. Another rolling table had three more arrangements with cards tucked in them, and two more were on a shelf. "You could start up your own shop, Mrs. M."

She chuckled. "When I woke up, I thought I was attending my own memorial service."

Samuel took her hand between both of his.

Stephen had to agree it wasn't all that funny. "I was in Sacramento and didn't hear you were in the hospital until this morning."

"Were you seeing your daughter?"

He had picked up Brittany at Kathryn's new digs in Gold River. For the first eight months of her new marriage, Kathryn had actually been polite to him and cooperative in allowing him more visitation privileges. But when Kathryn answered the door this time, he knew things were already going wrong. She had that look in her eyes. Disillusionment, anger, looking for a target. Her husband was off on another business trip, and she had plans for the day. Brittany told him over lunch, "Mom wanted to go with him to Paris and London, but Jeff wouldn't hear of it." They had a fight and Brittany hoped he wouldn't come back even if it was his house they were living in. She hated her stepfather for making her mother cry. Stephen found himself wondering if Brittany hated him for the same reasons.

"We had a full day together this time."

"That's good," Samuel said.

"It didn't go as well as I'd hoped." By the end of the day, he had developed a hardy dislike for his own flesh and blood. She was a miniature Kathryn, complaining and carping about everything. The only word in her vocabulary seemed to be *boring*. The movie they saw together was boring. The lunch was boring. Everything was *boring*. He assumed she thought he was boring as well. He tried to be thankful her favorite word had more than four letters.

But he'd finally had it by two in the afternoon when he suggested they rent bicycles and ride along the riverfront. "Oh, that's so boring!" When he asked her what she wanted to do, she said shopping.

That did it. "You know something, sweetheart? That bores me."

She'd rolled her eyes and let out a heavy, long-suffering sigh. "So you're going to make me go on some *boring* bike ride."

She'd sounded so much like Kathryn that his temper had lit. "Boring people find life is boring. If the only thing that interests you is spending someone else's money on things you don't need or even want, you've got a problem, honey—a big one." Just like her mother. Kathryn was only eight months into her new marriage and already she was complaining. Stephen felt sorry for the poor fool who'd slipped the ring on her finger and now had to deal with her endless list of demands.

Still, he should have kept his cool instead of allowing an eleven-year-old girl to get his goat. He was still regretting his words. He'd flung them in anger, heedless of the damage they'd cause. Now it was too late. The bridge he'd been trying to build for the last five years went up in flames. The chasm yawned wider than ever. Just because Kathryn had skin like a rhinoceros didn't mean Brittany did.

"Since I'm so boring, Daddy, don't waste your precious time on me next month!"

"It's not my fault I only get to see you once a month. Talk to your mother about that."

"I don't care. *I hate you both!*" She didn't say another word for the rest of the day. Another unfortunate skill she was learning from Kathryn: how to use silence and tears to make a man feel like a worm after a rainstorm—washed-up and helpless. He apologized, but it did no good.

"It didn't go well?" Samuel was waiting.

"A complete disaster. Like walking across a minefield." He hadn't made it across in one piece. Nor had Brittany.

Abby motioned to Samuel, who stood and pressed the button to raise her bed a little more. When she was more comfortable, she patted the bed and gestured for Stephen to sit. "Little girls idolize their fathers, Stephen."

He snorted. "She hates my guts." Kathryn had taught her well.

"No, she doesn't."

"She said point-blank she hated me."

"You probably gave her cause to be upset."

"It's always the man's fault."

"Stop wallowing in self-pity, and listen to me. Chances are your daughter is going to go out and look for a man exactly like you to marry and then try to fix whatever's wrong between the two of you now."

Abby might as well have punched him in the stomach. He tried to make light of it. "Someone good-looking and smart, you mean?" It was more likely his pretty little girl would marry someone rich who'd take care of her in the manner in which she wanted to become accustomed.

Abby was having none of it. "I'm old and sick, Stephen, but I still possess all my faculties. Well, most of them." She grimaced at Samuel, then faced Stephen again, expression solemn. "I've seen a lot more of life than you have, and I've seen girls make that mistake time and time again." Her hand was like a little bird claw on his. "You need to connect with Brittany and sort things out between you. Soon. Do you hear me? She's not your wife, Stephen. She's your daughter. They are two very different people, no matter how much they seem alike to you. And another thing. You need to forgive Kathryn."

"I have."

"In your head, maybe, but not your heart. Every time you speak about her, there's an edge to your voice and a look in your eyes. Your daughter isn't blind. You're going to have to pray about all that, Stephen. Long and hard, but it's got to be done if you're going to move ahead and grow up in Christ. It's been five years, young man, and you're still grinding your ax. And whether you know it or not, you're sinking your ax deep into Brittany."

The truth of it struck him. What chance did his daughter have when he looked at her and saw everything he had despised about his ex-wife? It had become too convenient to blame Kathryn for the way Brittany was behaving. As her father, he carried a heavy share of the responsibility.

"Since I'm so boring, Daddy, don't waste your precious time on me next month!"

He'd heard the hurt and accusation in her tone, even with her face averted. How could he claim he loved her and cared about her if he wasn't willing to fight for more time with her? One day a month wasn't enough to build a relationship with anyone, least of all your own daughter. Kathryn used Brittany as a weapon.

Abby smiled tenderly. "Christ forgave you, Stephen. How can you withhold forgiveness from Kathryn?"

He couldn't if he wanted to call himself a Christian. No matter what his ex-wife did, he had to keep his eyes fixed on how to be a better father to Brittany. "I'll work on it."

"You'll do better than that. I know you will." She patted his hand. "And you're going to be surprised how much will change between the three of you when you do."

Another tap on the door. "Anyone home?" Stephen's heart leaped, and he felt heat in the pit of his belly as Eunice Hudson peered into the room. She saw him and smiled. "Hi, Stephen." He offered a lame hello as Samuel rose to welcome her with a hug and kiss on her cheek. "How's our patient today?" Eunice took Abby's hand. She was so close; Stephen inhaled the scent of her perfume. Or was it just the scent of her skin? He stood and stepped away from the bed to give her room. Samuel was watching him. Did his feelings show? He was such an idiot. Unfortunately, reminding himself that the object of his passion was married—and to his pastor, no less—didn't help.

"I'd better get going," he said.

Abby protested. "But you only just got here. You aren't running off because of what I said, are you?"

Eunice lifted her head.

"No, ma'am. I just . . ." Just what? He couldn't think up a good enough excuse when Eunice was looking at him.

"I didn't mean to interrupt your visit, Stephen. I only have a few minutes."

His heart was hammering. "I think Abby was finished lecturing me about my poor behavior anyway." He watched as Eunice took his place on the edge of the bed.

"I brought you a copy of the service." She took a tape out of her shoulder bag and put it on the bedside table. "And the children made cards." She gave Abby a stack of envelopes tied with a yellow ribbon. They talked for a few more minutes, their conversation as easy and open as a mother and daughter, and then Eunice leaned over and kissed Abby's cheek. "You should rest, Abby."

"That's all I've been doing."

Eunice took her hand again and squeezed. "I'll come back and see you this evening with Tim." As she stood, she looked at Stephen. "And I'll see you in church, Stephen."

"Yeah." He watched her go out the door.

"Euny and Timmy sat with me in the waiting room for six hours the morning Abby came into the hospital." Samuel took Abby's hand again.

Abby chuckled. "She even got his shoes."

"His shoes?" Stephen looked between them.

"Abby always makes me take off my yard shoes in the garage."

"I don't want him tracking dirt and grass onto our nice clean rug."

"When I found Abby, I forgot all about putting on another pair."

"So he came to the hospital in his stocking feet."

Samuel lifted her hand and kissed her palm. "The loss of my mental capacities is proof of my devotion." He spread her fingers against his cheek and held her hand there. Stephen was struck by the tenderness of the gesture and the pallor of Samuel's face. He was exhausted and worried. Abby Mason wasn't out of the woods yet.

They all talked for a few more minutes, and Stephen knew it was time to leave. Abby looked exhausted; Samuel, concerned. "I'd better be on my way."

"Samuel is still holding the Bible study tomorrow evening, Stephen."

He looked at Samuel. "You sure?"

He wasn't, but he'd do it anyway. "Abby insists."

As Stephen left the room, he saw Eunice at the nurses' station. He'd stayed an extra ten minutes to avoid speaking with her, or worse, asking her if she'd like a cup of coffee, even the lousy stuff in the hospital cafeteria. "Stephen, I'd like to introduce you to someone. This is Karen Kessler. Karen, this is Stephen Decker."

An attractive brunette stood from her workstation and extended her hand. "It's nice to finally meet you, Stephen."

"Likewise." He had seen that look in women's eyes before.

"Karen is one of our new members. She's starting up a singles group."

Uh-oh. "Yeah, well, good luck." He stepped back and lifted his hand in a see-you-sometime gesture.

"Why don't I call you and fill you in on what we're doing at the next meeting?" Karen said.

"Sorry. No time." *And not interested.* He headed for the exit, fuming.

"Stephen!"

Eunice came through the automatic glass doors. She looked troubled. "Did I do something wrong back there?"

He dug in his pocket and pulled out his truck keys. "No." Why was he so steamed?

"You look like something's wrong."

Yeah. Something was. His feelings for her were way out of line. All she had done was try to hook him up with Florence Nightingale. Maybe it was good Eunice didn't have the slightest idea how he felt about her. What a mess! He steadied his nerves and tipped a smile. "Nothing's wrong, Eunice. At least, nothing you could fix." Paul was his friend, but that didn't mean Stephen didn't envy him his wife. Which was wrong— all wrong. It didn't help matters that he knew there was tension between the Hudsons. He recognized a marriage in trouble when he saw it. He was tempted to assuage the hurt he saw in her eyes. Neglect. Loneliness. Stress. He had a feeling if he asked Eunice to go for coffee right now, she might say yes. And that meant trouble with a capital *T*. "See you."

"Stephen?"

His heart thumped. He couldn't have moved from the spot if his life depended on it. *Help me, Jesus!*

"Can I ask you something in confidence?"

"Shoot." *Me, right between the eyes.*

"Paul said you've done some conceptual drawings for a new facility."

"That's right."

"Did he ask you to do them?" She searched his eyes.

"No. He told me last December that we're outgrowing CCC. That got me thinking. I've never designed a church. Started playing around with the idea. No—" he shook his head—"your husband did not ask me to do any drawings." He saw relief flood her eyes before she glanced away. She didn't trust her husband. He wondered why, then kicked himself mentally. *It's none of your business, Decker. Get that through your head. And get in your truck and get out of here now.*

She looked at him with those clear, innocent, blue eyes. "He said they're good."

Heat spread across his chest and down his legs. *Oh, Lord, give me strength.* If she had been any other woman, he would think she was coming on to him. But Eunice Hudson? No way! He could just imagine the look on her face if he invited her over to his place to see his work. "I incorporated a lot of ideas from various facilities. When I dream, I dream big."

"So does Paul."

It was good that she brought her husband's name into the conversation. It had a cold-shower effect. He looked into her eyes and held her gaze. "Yeah, well, so do a lot of people. Dream, I mean. It doesn't mean anything will come of it. Or that anything should." He let his feelings show just enough for her to understand.

He expected her to look away, but she didn't. She held his gaze, her cheeks turning pink, her eyes growing moist. "Stephen . . ."

Oh, Lord, help. He hadn't expected to see what was in her eyes. "I'd better get going."

"Yes."

Neither moved.

"I'm sorry, Stephen."

He wasn't sure why she said it, but he didn't want her worrying about him on top of everything else she had on her plate. He was a big boy. He could take care of himself. "Thanks for introducing me to Florence Nightingale. Maybe I'll give her a call."

She seemed to breathe again. "Her name is Karen."

"Karen," he said dutifully. He couldn't care less.

"She's very nice."

"I'm sure she is." Not that it would make any difference.

Samuel sat in a quiet room on one side of a long table. On the other side sat Dr. Shaeffer, a social worker, a counselor, and someone from the patient referral department of the hospital. He felt sick at heart.

The doctor was young and well educated. Samuel had seen the framed diplomas on his office wall. He also didn't have time to waste and got to the point quickly. Abby's condition was irreversible, her prognosis not good. He finished what he had to say in less than two minutes. Staccato facts. He asked Samuel if he had any questions, but his tone implied he'd already spelled it all out and didn't have time to waste on amplification. Samuel said no. And down the line it went from the social worker to the counselor to patient referral. They all felt he and Abby would be better off if she were moved to a convalescent hospital.

The doctor excused himself. It was down to three against one. "I'm taking my wife home tomorrow morning." He could see they had met with resistance before and were prepared to fight him.

"That's noble, Mr. Mason, but unwise."

"You can't take care of your wife by yourself, Mr. Mason."

"She's had nursing care around the clock. No one can do that by himself."

"I appreciate your concern, but my mind is made up."

The social worker sighed heavily and clasped her hands on the table. "We know it's difficult, Mr. Mason. But we need to make you aware of the facts. You are older than your wife. You had a minor heart attack four years ago. If you take care of your wife full-time, your own health is going to suffer."

"I'll take my chances."

"And what happens if you end up in the hospital, Mr. Mason? Your wife will still need constant care."

They knew how to apply the screws.

"She would receive top-quality care in Vine Hill Convalescent Hospital. If you don't want to go that route, then we encourage you to arrange for help."

"You need to conserve your energy for the long haul, Mr. Mason."

"The doctor has already made it clear your wife is not going to get better."

Samuel felt outnumbered.

"She's going to need more care as time passes. And that care is going to increase your burden."

It was that last word that strengthened his resolve. "Abby has never been a *burden*."

"Mr. Mason . . ."

Samuel stood. "If given a choice, I'm sure each of you would choose to die in your own bed." His mouth jerked as he restrained his tears.

He didn't dare go back to Abby's room in his present state, so he headed for the hospital cafeteria and downed a cup of their foul-tasting coffee. He waited another half hour after that, but still Abby took one look at him and knew.

"Oh, Samuel, don't take it so hard."

"They talked to you, didn't they?"

"Of course they did. I have a heart condition. I haven't lost my mind."

He swore for the first time in years.

Abby snorted. "If that isn't a sign of sheer exhaustion and frustration, I don't know what is."

"I'm not putting you in a convalescent hospital, and that's final!"

"Well, I'm glad to hear that, but you are going to get help. If I have to wear diapers, I don't want you being the one putting them on me."

He laughed, then wept. She wept, too, her hand on his bowed head. "For heaven's sake, Samuel, we knew one of us was going to go first. Let's not make it a race to see who gets to go through the pearly gates first."

He grasped her hand and held it against his cheek tightly. He couldn't utter a word past the lump growing in his throat.

"You need a shave, Samuel." He could tell she was starting to doze off again. "Promise me you won't turn into a bristly old coot."

He stood and leaned down, kissing her firmly on the mouth. "I promise."

She smiled. "A shower, too."

Samuel watched Abby fall asleep before he left.

1/24 12:A.M. ———— ❦ ————

Paul's mouth tightened when the intercom buzzed. Couldn't people leave him alone for one measly hour? Even Jesus could get away for a while. He jammed the button. "I told you to hold my calls, Reka." He needed to read through the real estate papers.

"Samuel Mason is on line one."

"Oh." His anger evaporated. Abigail Mason had been in the hospital over a week, and he hadn't made it over yet. He should've called. "Did you send the flowers?"

"Yes."

Thank goodness, Eunice had gone to the hospital every day. She had been telling him something about Abby's condition last night, but he couldn't remember what. "Did he mention how Abby's doing?"

"He sounded as though he'd been crying, Paul. I was afraid to ask."

Paul rubbed his forehead, ashamed he hadn't gone to the hospital and talked with the two of them. But it seemed something had come up every day. "Okay," he told Reka. He pushed line one. "Samuel, how's Abby?"

"About as well as can be expected. I'm bringing her home tomorrow."

Thank God. At least Abby was still alive. "I'll have Reka call the deaconesses. They'll prepare meals for you and Abby . . ."

"That's not why I'm calling, Paul. I'm resigning as an elder."

"Excuse me?"

"I said I'm resigning as an elder."

Stunned, Paul sat back in his chair. He had been trying to figure out a way to remove Samuel gracefully for the past two years, and now Abby's heart attack had accomplished what he couldn't. The Lord's timing couldn't be more perfect.

"I'm sorry, Samuel." And he was sorry. He wished Samuel had rowed with him instead of going against the current. "I know we haven't always agreed, but I know you've always had Centerville Christian's best interests at heart. I want you to know I've appreciated all you've done for the church. Your service won't be forgotten."

"Thanks."

"Would you like me to put you on the list to receive copies of the services?"

"Please."

"We'll miss you."

"Nice of you to say that, Paul."

Paul shifted in his chair. "When Abby's settled, Eunice and I will come by for a visit."

"You're welcome anytime, Paul. If you ever need to talk, you know where to find me."

"Thanks, Samuel."

Paul hung up and raised his hands in the air, giving thanks to God. He now had a green light to move ahead with his plans for the church.

PART 3

Wandering in the
WILDERNESS

———— ❧❧ ————

CHAPTER 10

—— ❧ ——

1996

"All right! Let's go!" Paul took his place in the backseat of the rented white convertible. He slapped the newest associate pastor on the back. "Come on, Ralph. Let the town know we're here!"

Ralph Henson blasted the horn as he started the procession of cars toward the center of town. He laughed. "Good thing the chief of police is a member of the congregation."

Every driver in the caravan following was applying the horn until the noise was deafening. People on the sidewalk gawked. Others came running from stores to see what was happening. Paul stood and used a bullhorn to let them know Centerville's old Christian Church was on the move, leading the way to a new life. Laurel Henson waved like the Rose Parade queen. "Wave, Tim! Come on! Get with the spirit!" Tim stuck his fingers in his mouth and gave an earsplitting whistle.

Paul leaned down to where Eunice slunk in her seat. "What's the matter with you?" She looked as though she wanted to hide in the bottom of the car. "Do something! Don't just sit there!" She waved, but there was no hooting and hollering from her.

As soon as they were through town, Paul put on his seat belt. Ralph roared down Highway 99, streamers flying. Laurel shrieked and raised her hands. Glancing back, Paul saw the rest of the cars following and grinned. Relaxing, he enjoyed the wind in his face.

It was amazing how fast things had come together once the stumbling blocks were removed. Samuel Mason's departure from the board of elders three years before had cleared the way. It had taken Paul less than two years to put his dream team together. Once the new elders gained the congregation's approval to build, a green light came on. What little opposition had come up in the beginning had been quickly put to rest. His team orchestrated a public relations campaign within the church body. All it took was a handful of people in leadership positions to bring the whole church into line. Marvin Lockford posted Stephen Decker's conceptual drawings in the fellowship hall. Stephen hired a professional to build a model of the projected complex. The leaders began talking up the "twenty-year project." Paul figured the plans would be completed long before that, especially with the increasing numbers CCC was drawing since he'd changed his preaching format to seeker-friendly services.

"If we build, they will come" was the rally cry for the church. Twelve hundred people were attending the ground-breaking ceremonies today! *Thank You, Jesus!*

The old folks who had been such a headache were silent. Otis Harrison had died a few months after his wife, Mabel. Hollis Sawyer's memorial service was last week, and the pathetic turnout showed how little he was missed. Only Samuel Mason was still around, but he had his hands full taking care of his ailing wife. He never came to church anymore, though he did request copies of the sermons.

Ralph shouted, "There it is!" Laurel shrieked and raised her hands again as Paul spotted the billboard identifying the future site of the Valley New Life Center. Thank God Stephen Decker had gotten it up in time. The congregation had voted in the new name only a month ago. It was in keeping with the expansion. *Valley* was easily decided; the church would no longer be in Centerville. The fight had been over the word *Christian*. Many newer members said they never would have set foot inside the church if not for close friends who had brought them. *Christian* was associated with fundamentalism and intolerance. So the new name was chosen in keeping with the new direction of the church.

Eunice had been against the name change, but out of respect for

Paul's position she had not made her opinion public. However, nothing had stopped her from voicing her opinion at home. "We're supposed to be a beacon to the world, Paul. How are we going to be any different from the world if . . . ?"

He had gotten sick of listening to her. "The only way to get the message across is to get people in the door first. Once they're in, we can start training them."

"It's deceptive, Paul. How is this any different from what cults do?"

Ralph drove to the middle of the forty-acre parcel and parked. Laurel leaped from the car and danced around like a Texas cheerleader. Why couldn't Eunice be as enthusiastic? Couldn't she see how God was working and bringing people into the fold? Was it a coincidence that the sale of the Svenson property in Rockville was just what the church had needed as a down payment on the first twenty-acre parcel? Three months later, the landowner had donated a second twenty-acre parcel as a tax deduction. Surely that indicated God's approval. Maybe the fund-raising campaign did get off to a slow start, but as soon as Gerald Boham started posting donations in the fellowship hall, the money had poured in. People liked to see their names on the chart. They needed to feel important.

When giving had slowed down again, Paul got the idea of calling on older members of the congregation, especially those in Vine Hill Convalescent Hospital, where several of the wealthier members were living out their final years. Mitzi Pike and Fergus Oslander had welcomed him with open arms and hearts. Neither had any family left. Every Thursday, he brought Mitzi doughnuts and played checkers with Fergus. He always went on the same day so that they would come to expect him. He never stayed more than an hour, and he never mentioned the building project. Instead, he talked with them about death being the gateway to heaven and an eternity with Jesus. He asked them how they would like to be remembered. Only when they began to talk about leaving something to the church did he bring in the miniature model of the proposed facility. They had been as excited as he.

Mitzi Pike died and bequeathed her entire estate to CCC. One hundred eighty-seven thousand, five hundred forty-two dollars, and fifty-three cents! Paul had been blown away by the bounty. And rumor had it that Fergus's estate was far larger than hers.

Oh, the Lord was good. Look how Jesus was blessing the church. The floodgates of heaven were opening and money was raining down.

People swarmed across the open space, picnic baskets in hand. They sat around the marker where the pulpit would one day stand. LaVonne Lockford and three of her friends sang opening songs. Paul kept the service short. The sun was going to be beating down well before noon, and he didn't want people to become uncomfortable.

Stephen Decker presented him with a brand-new shovel with three colored ribbons tied around the handle—white, for the purity of Christ; green, for the living Word; and purple, for the royal priesthood of all people of faith. Paul had chosen Rob Atherton to pitch the first shovelful of dirt, but Sheila said her husband insisted she do it. Since Robert Atherton had donated thirty-five thousand dollars to the building fund, Paul thought it fair that his request be honored.

Stephen had protested. "If you're going to have a woman do it, it should be Eunice."

Had Eunice been asked, she would have refused.

The ground was rough, and Sheila, wearing white spaghetti-strap sandals, trod carefully to the front. She looked like a movie star in her snug-fitting, white leather pants and powder-blue, scoop-necked top. "Thank you, Pastor Paul." She smiled at him as she took the shovel. The dirt had been loosened for her, so it was easy for her to scoop a shovelful and dump it aside.

"Hallelujah!" Paul said, a rush of adrenaline surging through him. "Thank You, Jesus!"

Hundreds of people joined in, shouting and raising their hands. "Praise the Lord!" Someone started singing "Firm Foundation."

Sheila looked at him, eyes bright. "It's all because of you, Pastor Paul."

Paul was filled with pride over his congregation. *Look at them! They're on fire for the Lord. No wonder God is blessing us.*

———— ❧ ————

Samuel wanted to call for an ambulance, but Abby said no. "You're in pain, Abby. Don't tell me you aren't." He could see it in her face and couldn't bear it.

Her mouth curved sadly. "I want to die in my own home, Samuel.

I love you. You know that. But this is no way to live." Her lips were blue, her skin ashen. "Let me go." He fumbled for a nitroglycerin pill, but she shook her head and tapped her fingers against the fresh linen sheet the visiting nurse had put on that morning. He turned up the oxygen that fed into the small plastic mask over her mouth and nose.

"Today was the ground-breaking ceremony," she said, each word a struggle.

"Don't talk, Abby." Tears came. He held her hands between his, trying to warm them. "I love you."

"A gentleman always opens the door for a lady."

He was in no mood for her humor. His chest ached as he listened to her breathing. The door was being opened, but not by him. He had done everything he could to keep it closed for a year now, and he watched helplessly while she slipped away from him. He wanted to plead with her not to be so eager, to hang on to this life a little longer. For his sake. He knew it was the cruelest kind of selfishness to press her. And futile. God wanted Abigail to come home.

"Today was the ground-breaking ceremony." It was a whisper this time.

Had she heard the blaring horns an hour ago? Or was she talking about something else? Her lips moved. Samuel leaned down to hear. "Poor Paul." He felt her fingers move, a soft fluttering, a last hesitation. "Keep praying for him. Keep praying . . ."

Her breathing slowed. He could see the pain ebbing, the peace spreading across her face. Her eyes flickered briefly, as though Someone had struck a match and lit a candle within. She caught her breath and then gave a long, slow sigh. As her body relaxed, her head turned toward him, her lips faintly curved. Like a child sleeping. Samuel's own heart stopped for a moment. He wished it would stop forever and he could go with her.

Cupping his wife's face with trembling hands, Samuel leaned down and kissed her eyes closed. Then he kissed her lips. He stood and tucked the covers around her, brushed his fingers over her white hair, and went out of the room, closing the bedroom door quietly behind him as though she were merely sleeping. He went into his den. Leaning heavily on the desk, he lowered himself to his knees.

"Lord, in all things thanksgiving . . . Lord . . . Lord . . ."

Samuel sobbed.

———— ❧ ————

Shrinking inwardly, Eunice spread the picnic blanket while Paul spoke to Timothy. She tried to smile and go through the motions of being happy about this auspicious day, but she wanted to weep.

"I don't care if you want to play or not," Paul snarled, his back to others gathered while he upbraided his son. "You'll go and pretend to like it, unless you want to spend next week in your room." Several people called greetings. Paul turned, smiled, waved.

Tim sneered. "You're all hypocrites."

Paul's body went rigid. "What did you say to me?"

Tim's jaw jutted. "You're all hypocrites, and you're the worst one of all!" He stalked off.

Paul turned toward Eunice. Her stomach clenched. *Here it comes again.*

"Hey! Pastor Paul! We need you over here!"

Smiling, Paul raised his hand. "Be there in a minute, Marvin." He leaned down, his eyes cold. "You'd better get a handle on your son, Eunice."

She took three bundles of silverware from the picnic basket. "He's *our* son, Paul, not a suitcase."

"Your attitude is worse than his. Try to remember you're my wife. This is the most important day of my life, and you and Tim are doing your best to spoil it for everyone. Maybe you ought to pray about that." He stood and walked away.

Fighting tears, Eunice finished putting out the sodas, napkins. *Pray,* he said. That's all she did—pray. Tim was too close to the truth. That was the problem. Paul bent with every wind that blew, but he was a stone wall where the two of them were concerned. Paul would spend the day smiling, laughing, mingling. She looked for Tim and spotted him with Ralph and Laurel Henson. No matter how upset he got, Tim always ended up doing what Paul asked. Did Paul even realize?

"You have a nice spot here, Eunice," LaVonne Lockford said, smiling. "Mind if we join you?"

Jessie Boham waved toward the far end of the property. "Our guys are all over there playing softball."

Paul was heading that way now.

"They'll probably have strokes in this heat," Shirl Wenke said.

They spread their blankets around Eunice.

"You know, Eunice, it should've been you breaking ground instead of Sheila Atherton." Jessie plunked her basket on her blanket. "That woman is something else."

Shirl snorted. "Leave it to *her* to wear white pants to a picnic."

"And a sweater when the weather forecast says it's going to be in the eighties!" LaVonne rolled her eyes. "Guess what she wanted everyone to notice."

Eunice cleared her throat, but they didn't take the hint.

"She was just showing off her new body enhancements," Jessie said.

They all laughed. Eunice blushed and tried to change the subject, but the verbal lynching went on.

"I thought Marvin's eyes would pop right out of his head."

One of the women new to the church joined them and the conversation. "My husband used to work for Rob Atherton when he was married to his first wife."

"His *first* wife!" LaVonne's eyes brightened. "How many has he had?"

"Well, only two."

Eunice leaned forward. "Ladies . . ." She caught LaVonne's gaze and frowned.

"Sheila was Rob's secretary," the visitor said.

LaVonne looked at her. "What happened to his first wife?"

"She took his children and moved to Florida."

"Children! That home wrecker."

"Ladies, please!"

Jessie Boham looked at Eunice in surprise. "Did you want to say something, Eunice?"

"Yes." Her cheeks were burning with shame over their conversation. "Sheila Atherton is our sister in Christ."

Jessie gave a coarse laugh. "You've got to be kidding!"

LaVonne's eyes narrowed. "No. She isn't. And she's right. We shouldn't be talking about Sheila Atherton. She's not worth our time. There are lots of things far more interesting." They talked about the weather, the low test scores at Centerville High School, the influx of migrant workers. Everything they said was stilted.

Eunice couldn't stand it. "I'm going to see if I can help the ladies at the potluck tables. Would anyone like to join me?"

"Maybe later, Eunice."

She wasn't out of hearing range before they picked another target.

"Well, who does she think she is? She didn't have to embarrass me like that!"

"It's not as though we were saying anything untrue about Sheila Atherton."

"Just because she's the pastor's wife . . ."

"Thank God Paul isn't like her. He always makes people feel good about themselves instead of making them feel small."

Eunice pretended not to hear, but their malice hurt.

The women at the potluck tables didn't need any help. Everything was running like a well-oiled machine. She offered help with the youth, but Paul had hired two Energizer Bunnies to help him. She felt in the way. Worse, she felt like an alien among these people.

"You look lost, little girl."

Her heart did a fillip as she turned and faced Stephen Decker. "I was looking for Tim."

"He's probably off having fun with his friends." He handed her a can of soda. "You look like you just lost your best friend."

Eunice didn't have to look behind her to know that LaVonne, Jessie, and Shirl were probably staring at them. What would they make of Stephen giving her a soda? Anything they wanted to make of it! She looked around uneasily.

Stephen lifted his can of soda and took a swig. "If you're looking for Paul, he's over there talking with the Athertons."

"Oh." Paul was probably schmoozing, as Lois put it, hoping for another donation down the road. *Lord, I don't like the train of my thoughts. I'm becoming cynical.* "They've been very generous to the church."

"Oh, no doubt about that. And equally generous to the Central Valley Committee on Cultural Diversity."

She felt like the air had been punched out of her. "I beg your pardon?"

"Rob was their honored guest last month. Didn't you hear?"

"No, I didn't."

"You've got to give big bucks to have a luncheon thrown in your honor." He raised his brows and took another long swig of soda. "It made the paper."

She didn't read the paper every day, but Paul did.

"Rob must need tax deductions." Stephen crushed the can and tossed it into one of the garbage bins the youth group had set up for collecting aluminum cans.

"Every penny counts," Paul always said.

"What do you think of all this?" Stephen's nod included everything.

"It's a wonderful day for a picnic."

He laughed. "Well, tell me what you really think."

That I'm sick to my stomach? That I have this awful feeling Paul knew about the Athertons and didn't care? Oh, God, help us. "I hope the Lord brings it all together."

"So far, it seems He has."

Eunice looked away. What could she say to that? God had despised the offerings of the Israelites when they had shared themselves and practiced the ways of the people around them. They had worshiped under every spreading tree and high place just as the pagans did, then had the audacity to bring offerings to the Lord in His Temple and expect to be blessed for it. God wanted the wholehearted love of His people. He warned them through the prophets, and when they wouldn't listen, He disciplined them. He'd destroyed them in wars, sent them into exile, scattered them across the face of the earth. "Be holy, because I am holy," God said. No compromise!

She looked around at the gathering. What kind of message would it send to these poor people if they knew the couple at the top of Paul's charts was also helping fund an organization promoting sinful lifestyles and pagan religions? Surely Paul didn't know. "If only I'd known." She could have said something. She could have warned him. He could have spoken to Rob and Sheila and taught them God's ways more clearly. *Come out and be holy! Honor God and leave no room for the flesh!* Rob and Sheila might have the wrong idea about what it meant to be a follower of Christ. How many others were in a similar state of confusion?

"I'm sorry I told you, Eunice. You're taking it harder than Paul did."

She glanced up. "Paul knew?"

"After the fact. Rob invited him to the luncheon."

Eunice felt sick. Had he gone?

"He didn't go, Eunice. He had an out and took it. The luncheon was on a Wednesday, and Paul and I have a standing appointment for lunch on Wednesdays. We spent most of that lunch talking about that donation. Paul said the Lord works in mysterious ways, and there's no condemnation in Christ." He shrugged. "He's the pastor. He knows a lot more than I do."

"Just because Paul is the pastor doesn't mean you haven't the right to voice your opinion."

"I did voice my opinion, but he said he was afraid turning down Atherton's donation might be like closing the door of heaven in his face."

Eunice wanted to go home, hide in her closet, and weep.

"We've missed you at Bible study, Eunice."

"I've missed coming." She didn't dare tell him that Paul had asked her not to go . . . or that she had agreed for reasons she couldn't share with either man.

The ground-breaking celebration lasted all afternoon. Eunice hadn't spoken with Paul since he'd walked away from her early in the day. She had caught only glimpses of him as he socialized.

The gathering began to disperse before sunset. Tim asked if he could spend the night with Frank Heber. The Hebers were solid Christians who had moved from Missouri to Centerville and who also attended the Masons' Bible study. Eunice saw no harm in Tim spending the night. They attended church every Sunday. She walked with him to the Hebers' car, talked with them briefly, and said she'd stop by later with his church clothes.

Tim bent to kiss her cheek. "Thanks, Mom. I don't want to be home tonight and have to listen to Dad gloat." Before she could say anything, he was in the car and they were on their way.

She went back to collect their things. As she picked up the blanket and shook it, Paul came over. "Where's Tim?"

"He's spending the night with the Hebers."

"I wish you'd asked me first. They're a little too legalistic for my liking."

"Do you want me to go over and pick him up?"

"No. Forget it. It's been a fantastic day, hasn't it? Ralph and Laurel have all the equipment loaded. So anytime you're ready, we can go. I'll meet you at the car. I want to thank the Athertons again."

"Paul, did you know—?"

He turned his back. "I'll talk to you later."

She watched him walk away. As she put the blanket on top of the plates, silverware, and cloth napkins already in the picnic basket, she watched Paul approach the Athertons. He talked with Rob over the top of their new Jaguar as he opened the door for Sheila.

Depressed, Eunice picked up the basket and headed for Ralph and Laurel. *Oh, Father, all this show! And for what? It's not right! How do I get through to Paul that we're compromising? He won't listen. Am I wrong? Have I misread Your Word? Is Paul right and everything that's happening is affirmation of Your blessing? But You laid waste to Israel in the midst of prosperity.*

"Great day, huh?" Sunburned and smiling, Ralph opened the car door for her.

"I'm exhausted!" Laurel slid down and rested her head against the back of the seat. "Did you know we had over five hundred children here today? Vacation Bible school is going to be a zoo! I don't know how I'm going to handle it. We need more staff. The sooner, the better."

Paul arrived in time to hear Laurel's comment. "You and Ralph did an outstanding job today. But you're right. We do need more staff. And we're going to have what we need."

The royal *we*.

Ralph and Laurel talked all the way back to Centerville. Ralph dropped them off at the church. Paul and Eunice drove home in separate cars. Paul always had to be at church ahead of everyone else. She couldn't remember the last time she and Paul and Timothy had been in the same car together.

Eunice arrived home first and saw a blinking 7 on the answering machine. Paul expected her to screen messages for him. She emptied the basket onto the kitchen counter, put the plates, silverware, and plastic cups into the dishwasher, tossed the blanket into the wash basket in the laundry room, and tucked the picnic basket into the hall cabinet before she took a pad of paper and pen and pushed the Play button.

The first three calls were from parishioners who needed counseling appointments. She jotted down their names and numbers and deleted the messages. The fourth phone call was from Jack Hardacre, Tim's principal. Unfortunately, she didn't need to write down his name and number; she knew it from memory. What had Tim done this time? She made a note on her personal calendar to call the principal first thing Monday morning. Just a click on the fifth call. And the sixth.

The last call was from Millie Bruester. "Abby died this morning," she wept. "I thought you'd want to know." The telephone beeped twice . . . and then silence.

Eunice sat, stunned. She was just reaching for her purse as Paul came in from the garage. "What's the matter?"

"Abby died." She dug in her purse for her keys. Unable to find them, she dumped everything on the counter. Crying, she rummaged through the things scattered across the counter—pocket organizer, lipstick, notepad, sunglasses, checkbook, change purse, wallet, keys to the church.

"I'm sorry, Euny." He spoke quietly. "I know how much she meant to you."

"How much she meant to *all of us*, Paul. She nurtured *everyone*, and Samuel . . ." Her voice broke. Poor Samuel. She knew why he hadn't called. He would've known everyone was out at the ground-breaking ceremony. He wouldn't've wanted to interrupt the festivities. Clutching her keys, she stuffed everything else back into her shoulder bag. "I need to call the Hebers. I don't want Tim to find out at church tomorrow."

Paul took the keys from her hand. "We'll pick him up and go over together."

Surprised, she glanced up and saw the moisture in his eyes.

The man still had the power to surprise her.

———— ❧ ————

Stephen left the ground-breaking celebration early and headed for Sacramento. He called Kathryn on his cell phone, hoping to set up a time to visit with Brittany sometime during the week. "She's gone."

He knew it was within his rights to press the issue. He was supposed to have time with his daughter each month, but it had been almost six weeks since he'd last seen her. Things still weren't right between them. He felt the chasm widening. Was it just her age? Or was it something deeper? "I need to talk with her, Kathryn."

"Why?"

"I'm trying to build a bridge."

She gave a harsh laugh. "Well, good luck. She doesn't listen to anyone these days."

"I thought you two got along."

"Are you being sarcastic?"

Even when he spoke in a neutral tone, Kathryn took offense. "No, I wasn't. How long have you been having trouble with her?"

"I don't remember a time when I *haven't* had trouble with her. All she does is gripe. I've dedicated my life to making sure she has everything she wants, and she treats me like I'm nothing. I'm sick to death of fighting with her."

He winced at the vitriol in Kathryn's voice. Brittany had always been a weapon in her hand, a way of wounding him repeatedly. But the animosity in his ex-wife's tone now went deeper. There was a hard edge of dislike that worried him. "You want to talk about joint custody?" Maybe there would be light at the end of this tunnel.

"I'm not fed up enough to give her to you."

Every time he gave her an opportunity to bury the hatchet, she sank it deeper into his heart. He was done with fighting back, answering in kind. He didn't want her taking out her wrath on their daughter. "Okay," he said carefully. "When would be a good time to call Brittany?"

Kathryn didn't answer immediately, and when she did, her tone was weary. "Your guess is as good as mine, Stephen. She's hardly ever home, and when she is, she's so sarcastic I end up sending her to her room. I'm so tired of trying to keep peace in this house. Jeff and I aren't getting along, and it's her fault."

So she was blaming Brittany for her marriage problems now. He had to stop and remind himself that he had made a habit of blaming Kathryn for most of what went wrong between them. "I'm sorry to hear that, Kat." *Live and let live.* His ex-wife would have to find her own way. Maybe she'd find it easier if he lit the way instead of blowing out the candle every chance he got.

Another hesitation. Stephen waited for the next barb.

"You haven't called me Kat in years."

"Sorry."

She sighed. "Brittany left a note saying that she's with friends. That's all I know right now, Stephen. I have her cell phone number, if you want it."

"Sure." He flipped up the center console, where he had a pad of paper clipped. "Shoot."

She gave it to him. "Not that there's any guarantee she'll answer. I tried calling earlier, but she has caller ID."

If she and her mother were at odds, Brittany wouldn't answer. "I'll give it a try."

"Good luck," she said dryly and hung up.

Brittany didn't answer. He left a message that he wanted to spend some time with her. "I'm staying in Sacramento for a few days. I'd like to see you." He told her he was staying at the same Residence Inn as his last visit. "I have my cell phone with me." She had the number, if she'd bothered to keep it. "I love you, Brittany. It may not seem that way sometimes, but I do. More than you'll ever know."

He called Kathryn on Monday night and left another message for Brittany, then spent all day Tuesday in business meetings with possible clients. His daughter didn't call. Wednesday, he checked out and headed south.

The tension left him as soon as he took the on-ramp to 99. Maybe he just wasn't a city boy anymore. He missed his friends in Centerville. Especially Samuel. Wednesday night Bible study was even more important to him than Sunday worship. It had become his lifeline. For some reason, he came away from church dissatisfied. As though he'd had hors d'oeuvres, but missed the main course.

The mail was piled up below the chute. He went through it quickly, tossing junk into a wastebasket. He had just enough time for a micro-waved TV dinner before heading for the Masons'.

The porch light was on. He saw people through the sheer curtains in the living room of the little American bungalow. He checked his watch, wondering if he was late. Nope. He was thirty minutes early. He picked up his Bible. As he got out of his truck, he spotted Eunice's white Saturn. His pulse jumped. It had been a long time since she had attended the home group.

The Masons always left the door unlocked. The minute Stephen stepped inside, he knew Abby was gone. Instead of laughter and lively conversation, people sat around the living room speaking in subdued tones, their faces solemn. Samuel sat in the wing chair everyone had dubbed "the rabbi's seat," and Eunice was on the edge of the sofa, holding his hand and talking with him. Stephen's longtime friend and mentor looked old and frail.

Samuel squeezed Eunice's hand, rose, and came to greet him. "Stephen." He extended his hand. "I thought you were in Sacramento."

"I just got back an hour ago. When did it happen?"

"Abby went home Saturday morning."

Stephen felt as if someone had hold of his throat with both hands, choking him. His eyes were hot. "Sorry."

Samuel's face softened. His eyes filled with tears. He bowed his head and gestured. "Sit. Please."

Eunice gave him her space on the sofa. When she put her hand on Stephen's shoulder, he felt the warmth run the course of his entire body. "Would you like some coffee or tea, Stephen?"

He didn't meet her eyes. "Coffee. Black. Thanks."

"So . . ." Samuel took his seat again. "How did things go in Sacramento?"

It was so like Samuel to think of others at a time like this. "Not so good, but I'm not giving up." He clasped his hands between his knees. "What are your plans?"

"Abby's memorial service will be on Saturday."

Stephen figured Samuel couldn't look any further ahead than that. He couldn't even imagine what it would be like to lose a wife of sixty-two years. He'd known in the first year with Kathryn that their marriage wouldn't make it. And in truth, he hadn't done much of a job trying to keep it together. It took resurrection power to make love last through the long haul. And it took a man and woman willing to surrender themselves to one another and to the One who came up with marriage in the first place. He'd fouled up his chance, but that didn't mean his heart didn't yearn for the kind of relationship Samuel had shared with Abigail. "She'll be missed." *Sorely.* He could already feel the difference in the house. Abigail Mason was gone. He could already see the difference in his friend. Samuel couldn't hide the raw pain in his eyes—or the fact that he probably hadn't slept since Saturday.

Eunice returned with a mug of black coffee. His fingers brushed hers as he took the mug. She looked as worn down as Samuel. He ached for her. She took a seat across the living room beside Marilyn Heber.

Gradually, people began to talk again, sharing memories of Abby and how she had impacted their lives. Stephen talked about the time he visited her in the hospital. "She wouldn't let me get away with anything."

"Me neither," Samuel said.

The others laughed. Everyone shared funny stories and the mood lightened. By the end of the evening, the focus had changed from losing her to knowing she was with Jesus, that her pain was over, that she was no longer trapped in a body that kept her in bed. Not that everything said had made losing Abby any easier on Samuel.

It was after eleven when people started leaving. The ladies put all the food away. Samuel had enough to last him for a month. Stephen was one of the last two to leave. Samuel walked with him to the door. Stephen shook his hand. "Mind if I drop by tomorrow? See how you're doing?"

"Anytime, Stephen."

The night air was cold, without a whisper of wind. Stephen tugged up his collar and went down the steps. As he opened the gate, he looked back and saw Eunice and Samuel holding one another in the doorway. Samuel patted her cheek. He lifted his head and looked at Stephen standing at the gate before he closed the door. Strange how one look like that could give a word of warning.

Stephen held the gate open for Eunice. "How's Tim taking it?"

"Hard."

He didn't ask about Paul. He knew enough about the strained relations between Samuel and the pastor not to bring that up. Still, he had never heard Abby or Samuel say a single word against Paul Hudson. Paul was the one who did all the talking. Too much talking, now that Stephen thought about it. Why wasn't he sitting in that living room, sharing stories about Abby?

Eunice drew her coat closer around her. Stephen could see the sheen of tears. He should stand aside and let her go home. "Abby was a good friend to a lot of people."

"She was the best friend I had in this town. I don't know what I'll do without her."

Her comment troubled him. "You have a lot of friends, Eunice."

"Precious few I can trust." He saw her grief in the soft glow of the streetlight. "A pastor's wife has to be very careful what she says and to whom she says it. I never had to worry with Abby. I could talk about anything with her and know it would go no further than her own heart.

And maybe Samuel." He heard the soft catch in her voice, the helpless grief grabbing hold again. "I don't know what I'm going to do without her, and that makes me so angry."

"Why?"

"Because it's so selfish."

"I'm not taking it that way."

"She was suffering, Stephen, and here I am feeling sorry for myself."

He wanted to comfort her, but kept his distance. Still, he couldn't help but wonder. Were there problems between her and Paul? He knew there was trouble between her and other members of the church. Surely her husband should be her best friend. He knew some people were uncomfortable around Eunice Hudson. She walked into a room and people changed the course of their conversation. It was as though Jesus had entered with her, and people became aware of what they were saying and doing. Jesus was everything to Eunice Hudson, and everyone knew it. "I'm your friend, Eunice."

She looked up. "I shouldn't have said anything."

"Anything you say to me now won't go beyond this gate." He felt her stillness and knew she'd heard him. He sensed she heard even more than he said.

"I can't."

"Because I'm Paul's friend?"

"Partly."

"Because I'm a man?"

"That, too." She searched his eyes. "You're dangerous."

"Dangerous? Me?" He started to make light of it until he realized what she meant.

"Good night, Stephen."

The soft, broken sound of her voice made him give her the room she needed. He shoved his hands into the pockets of his leather jacket as she stepped past him. He wanted to follow her to her car and tell her he'd never do anything to hurt her. She could trust him.

Yeah, right! He had good intentions. He'd make promises. But a man of character kept his promises, and Stephen knew he wouldn't have the strength to run from temptation if it ever came to his door in the form of Eunice Hudson.

Stephen liked Paul, even admired him as a pastor who could move and shake his congregation. But that didn't mean Stephen was blind to his friend's faults. Paul took his wife for granted; he was so caught up in building a church that he paid little attention to the stresses and strains within his own family. Stephen recognized disaster on the horizon because he'd been as self-absorbed while helping destroy his own marriage.

Was it possible for a church to rip a marriage apart? And would Paul be wise enough to make sure that didn't happen?

Stephen had seen Tim stalking away from his parents at the groundbreaking celebration. He had seen Eunice hunched and setting out the picnic things while Paul talked down to her and then went off to spend the rest of the day with other people. Stephen had left early because he knew if he didn't, he would say or do something he'd regret.

Tonight, Eunice was vulnerable. Grieving and unguarded, she had spoken frankly. It didn't take a rocket scientist to see she was already regretting it.

Stephen's heart hammered as he got into his truck and jammed the key into the ignition. She knew how he felt. She'd drawn the line once before. Tonight she'd drawn it again. But it was thinner this time, and not as straight. He watched the taillights on her Saturn as she turned left at the corner. Starting his truck, he had the urge to follow. She was lonely and hurting, maybe a little confused. He could pull up beside her at the next intersection, ask her if she wanted to have a cup of coffee out at the truck stop. It wasn't a place CCC members patronized. They could talk, maybe sort some things out between them.

He knew where he was heading. *The mind tends to justify whatever the heart has chosen.*

"Lord," he said under his breath, "Lord, You'd better help me out here."

Stephen pulled up to the corner and stopped. He saw her taillights again. She was within easy reach. He let the truck idle a moment longer before he made his decision.

He turned right and headed home.

Fewer than a hundred people came to Abby's memorial service. Ashamed, Eunice sat at the piano, fighting tears as she played her friend's favorite hymns. Samuel sat in the front row, Tim beside him. Paul would open the service and then quietly depart, leaving Pastor Hank Porter to stand in the gap. Eunice had been told only this morning.

"This is wrong, Paul! Wrong!"

"It couldn't be more right. Just listen."

"If it's so right, why did you wait until the last minute to tell me?"

"Because you've been so emotional lately. Sometimes you aren't reasonable, Eunice. Listen to me for a minute! Hank Porter is a gift from God. He couldn't have come at a better time. Howard MacNamara is the key to the planning commission. I'm not about to cancel on him and risk delays with the building project."

"What about Samuel's feelings? What about Abby's years of service to this church? Don't they matter to you?"

"Hank Porter arrived from Oregon yesterday. I've already spoken to him, and he's more than willing to take over the service. God's hand is in this. Can't you see that? Porter should be the one conducting the service anyway, Eunice. He was Samuel and Abby's pastor for forty years! I'll start the memorial, say a few words about Abby, and then step down. No one will even notice when I leave."

"I'll notice."

"I'm doing this for the church!"

"Abby was important to this church."

"She was important for a time, Eunice. Most people don't even know who she is or care that she's passed on."

"And that's a symptom of what's going wrong in your ministry, Paul. They should care." It was the wrong thing to say.

"There's nothing wrong with my ministry! If there was, the church wouldn't be putting on four full services. You're the only one in the congregation who doesn't seem to think I'm fit for the job! New people are coming every week to hear my sermons. They're opening their pocketbooks and falling all over themselves to give us the money to build a bigger facility. You tell me that isn't God's blessing on my ministry."

"Just because something grows, doesn't mean it's good, Paul. Cancer grows."

She'd never seen such a look on his face.

"What do you know about anything, Eunice? You didn't grow up the way I did. All you ever knew was that little shack in the hills. How many members did your father have at the last? Fifteen? Twenty? You call that a church? That's nothing!"

She had almost retaliated, almost lashed out in anger that her father had been more of a pastor than his father had ever been. But she had lowered her head, shut her eyes, and prayed frantically that God would keep her silent, that God would keep her from throwing stones back at him, heavier stones than his contempt of her and her heritage. She had said too much already, and not a word she had said in the last five years had been heard.

Now here she sat, struggling to keep a peaceful facade for those who happened to look her way. She was Pastor Paul's wife, after all. Never had her role pinched her more uncomfortably than today!

Hank Porter was short, balding, slightly overweight, and though not eloquent, he spoke brokenly of Abigail Mason. No one doubted his love and respect for her. "She had a servant's heart," he said and took his handkerchief from his pocket.

Others shared humorous stories about her outspoken manner. "I was whining about my parents once, and she told me I was a self-centered little pip-squeak," one young man said. Everyone laughed. "She said some other things, too, but I don't think I want to go into how big a jerk I was at the time. Anyway . . . what I really wanted to say is, if it'd been anyone else but Mrs. Mason, I wouldn't've listened. I knew she loved me."

Hank Porter's wife stood, wearing a rather garish outfit that made people twitter. "Some of you are probably wondering how a pastor's wife could dare wear a getup like this, but I did it to honor Abby. She gave me this red hat and this purple blouse on my sixty-fifth birthday." Everyone laughed, including Susanna Porter herself, who dabbed tears from her eyes.

Tim stood, tried to speak, and sat again. Samuel put his arm around him, and they leaned their heads together. Eunice stood, took the mike offered, and told everyone about Abby's untiring service to the church, her compassion for others, especially a shy, young pastor's wife. She looked at Samuel through her tears. "She was like a mother to me, and my dearest friend. Whenever I have been with Abby or Samuel, I have felt the presence of God." Unable to say more, she sat on the piano bench again.

When all were silent, Hank Porter brought the service to an end. "The last thing we can do for Christ in this world is to die well. Abby's last words to her husband, Samuel, were not about herself, but of her concern for another. I have no doubt when our Abby opened her eyes again, she was looking straight into Jesus' face and He was smiling and saying the words we all long to hear . . ."

There was a soft rumble of voices as the older members of the congregation spoke in unison with him, "Well done, good and faithful servant."

Hank Porter bowed his head and prayed simply, "Lord, receive our beloved sister, Abigail Mason. She has been an example of Your love to everyone who knew her. Help us to honor her by living our lives as she did, our eyes fixed upon Your precious Son, Jesus, in whose name we pray."

Again the soft rumble of voices as they said, "Amen."

Eunice was thankful she knew all of Abby's favorite hymns by heart. She could not have seen the music through her tears. She played one after another until the sanctuary was almost empty and everyone was on their way to the fellowship hall, where the deaconesses had prepared a luncheon buffet.

"Why didn't Dad stay?" Tim asked on the way home.

"Hank Porter was Samuel and Abby's pastor for forty years."

"You didn't answer the question."

"He had an important meeting."

"Sure. And I have a bridge I can sell you, Mom." He glared straight ahead. "The Masons are the best friends we've ever had, and Dad's too stupid to know it."

"Don't talk that way about your father."

"Why not? It's true."

She pulled into the driveway and pressed the garage door opener. Paul's new Buick was parked inside. She pulled in next to it. Tim was still a boy, but his face had a hardness that hurt Eunice. "Your father doesn't need your condemnation, Tim. He needs your prayers."

"Why should he need my prayers? He's got God's ear. Just ask him." He got out of the car and slammed the door.

"Tim!" She got out of the car as quickly as she could, but he was already on his bike. "Where are you going?"

"Anywhere but here!"

Paul was full of good news. The luncheon meeting with MacNamara had gone better than he hoped. "We hit it off. He as much as said he'd grease the wheels and make sure everything goes ahead on schedule."

"Aren't you going to ask how Abby's memorial service went?"

"I'm sure it went well. You know, I used to get so sick of hearing Henry Porter's name all the time, and last night I couldn't have been happier to meet him. God works in mysterious ways."

"Don't you mean convenient?"

He ignored her comment and launched into more details about his meeting with the planning commission and how everything was coming together the way he had been praying.

Not once did he ask about Tim, who was taking Abby Mason's death even harder than she was.

CHAPTER 11

———— ❧ ————

1996 -

3 yrs. from per. chap.

1999

Paul flipped through the pages of *Christian Worldview* magazine, scanning articles with progressive ideas. In the middle was the bestseller list with his father's book, *Building a Church for the Twenty-First Century*, at the top. Dropping the magazine on the desk, Paul leaned back, depressed. Turning his swivel chair, he looked out the window of his new office and watched a crew working on the skeleton of the third wing of Valley New Life Center. He had come a long way in twelve years, but not far enough. The sick feeling in the pit of his stomach was all too familiar. Would he always live in the shadow of his father? He should be rejoicing for him, not feeling this plague of envy.

Resolved, he picked up the telephone and pressed a speed-dial button. Looking out over VNLC, he tried to bolster himself. He was winning souls, too, wasn't he? "Hey, Mom, how are you doing?"

"Fine. How are *you*? It's been a while since you called."

"Well, you know how things are. Never enough hours in the day. The building project is ahead of schedule."

"How nice for you."

"I just saw Dad's book on the bestseller list. Not that I'm surprised."

"Not that you should be."

Sometimes he wondered at his mother's tone. "I'm calling to congratulate him. Is he around or off playing golf with some big muckety-muck?"

"Oh, he's here, working and scheming as always. Hang on, Paul. We have a new phone system. If I push a wrong button and cut you off, I'll call you right back."

His parents had moved into a new house in North Hollywood soon after his father retired. It was in the hills overlooking San Fernando Valley. The last time he and Eunice had gone down for a visit, his father had shown him the new office they'd added over the two-car garage. It was every bit as grand as the one he had vacated at the church he'd built.

Paul drummed his fingers. Two minutes passed before his mother came back on the line. "Your father will be with you shortly, Paul. He's on another call."

He was probably talking to the publisher about a sequel.

"So, how's Eunice? How's Tim?"

Delaying tactics? "Euny is still playing piano and singing, though not as much now that we have a full-time music minister. And Tim is doing his thing." He glanced at his watch again. "Look, I can call back later."

"You can't talk to your mother for five minutes?"

"Sure. I didn't mean—"

"What 'thing' is Tim up to these days?"

"What most teenagers do. Hang out with friends. He comes to church every Sunday."

"I'm certain of that."

Again, that tone.

The phone clicked. "Hey, Paul. How're things in your little neck of the woods?"

His father never missed a chance to get in a dig.

"I'll leave you two to talk." His mother hung up abruptly.

"Did you call for advice again? You know, one of these days I'm going to be singing with the angels and you'll have to figure things out for yourself."

Paul bristled, but he managed a laugh. "I didn't call for advice. None needed. I just called to say congratulations on making the bestseller list. When do I get a copy?"

"As soon as you order one." His father laughed. "Just kidding, kid. I already put you on my influencers list. You should be getting a copy from the publisher any day. In fact, I'm surprised you haven't received it already."

Nice personal touch. "No autograph?"

"You sound a little jaundiced."

Paul was careful to lighten his tone. "Far from it. I'm proud of you, Dad. I should get you up here to speak. You'd draw people from Sacramento. We could make a day of it."

His father laughed. "My fee has gone up."

"What are you charging these days? We have two thousand members now, Dad. We can afford the best."

"Well, good for you. What's it taken you to get that church on its feet? Fifteen years?"

"Twelve." Paul curbed his irritation. "I started with thirty-eight members."

"I had fewer than that when I started. How's the building project going, by the way?"

Paul was glad his father brought up the subject. "Ahead of schedule." It was his turn to boast. "The third wing is going up. I got a call yesterday that *Architectural Digest* is going to do an article on our designer, Stephen Decker."

"I've never heard of the magazine."

"Because it's not Christian, Dad. It's what the *Atlantic Monthly* is to literature, only in the world of architecture. You can't even get a Christian magazine in the racks these days. The *Digest* is in every supermarket across the country. And our sanctuary is going to be on the cover in August." Paul tossed *Christian Worldview* into the wastebasket and tipped his chair back. "I'll send you a copy when it comes out."

"I've got a few other irons in the fire."

Paul relished his father's jaundiced tone. "Good for you, Dad." He tipped his chair forward. "Look, I'd like to talk longer, but I've got to run. Give Mom a hug." He hung up before his father could say more.

He'd won this time, and wondered why he felt curiously empty despite his victory.

———— ❦ ————

There were days Stephen wished he'd never submitted the proposal to build the Valley New Life Center. He knew the minute Paul came through the door of Charlie's Diner, briefcase in hand, that this was going to be anything but lunch with a friend.

Dealing with a demanding executive intent on building his dream house or a landowner designing a business park was a cakewalk compared to building a church. Paul—and the rest of the building committee—seemed to have forgotten that the usual fee for a contractor was 10 percent of the construction cost. Stephen had written up the contract for 5 percent, considering the difference to be his gift to God. And still some were convinced he was lining his pockets with gold.

"How soon before this phase is done?" was becoming an irritating litany, along with "You need to cut costs."

Stephen had explained the critical-path concept a dozen times. The schedule had been set up to make the best use of time in coordinating subcontractors, materials, and order schedules. He'd built in float time so that the project would be cost-effective, even in the event of delays. Still Paul pushed, harder and harder.

"You told me last week the next shipment of lumber was arriving on Monday."

"Coast Lumber's semi broke down on I-5, so there's a two-day delay. It's no big deal."

"No big deal?" Paul raised his brows. "Time is money."

"I warned you there are always delays, Paul. I'm not God. We're all working hard. The dozers are preparing the back parking lot, and the tractors are getting the ground ready to plant the olive grove."

"Yeah, but . . ."

Stephen hated *yeah, buts*. They drove him nuts. He didn't like being taken for granted, either. Nor did he like the members of Paul's building committee coming at him from all directions with ideas, thinking a change here or there didn't mean much. How many times over the past three years had he reminded them why he had written up a *twenty-year plan*?

"You're moving too fast, Paul. You're going to drive our church so deep into debt, we'll never dig our way out."

"The money's coming in."

"Not fast enough. Not for the work you want done."

"You've got to have more faith, Stephen." Sometimes Paul had the eyes of a bulldog with his teeth in the leg of a mailman.

"I've got faith. I also have experience. Businesses that try to grow too fast go under."

"We're not a business. God will provide."

Yeah, but . . .

Gerald Boham would probably come up with another one of his harebrained fund-raising schemes. And Marvin Lockford didn't mind holding bills for sixty days or longer.

The church wasn't the only one going into debt. It had always been a matter of honor to Stephen to make sure his subcontractors and workers were paid on time. But he only had so much in the way of resources. And he was tired of waiting for reimbursement.

"Documentation," Lockford always said. "We need more documentation." What was the Bible verse about returning a man's cloak to him before nightfall so he had something to sleep in?

Stephen didn't hire strangers. He hired men with whom he had built relationships. He was on a first-name basis with the structural engineer, framing contractor, civil engineer, and landscape architect. Stephen kept a close eye on things because he didn't trust Marvin Lockford to keep the accounts straight. He didn't like feeling as though he had to use a crowbar to get money owed out of Lockford's clenched fist.

Stephen doubted Paul ever had to wait for his paycheck.

Bills were always coming due. Acoustical engineers putting in the sound systems; the mechanical engineer in charge of the heating, ventilation, and air-conditioning systems; the electrical engineer, the plumbing engineer, and the fire-suppression engineer. Woven into all their work were the constant stress and flow of inspectors who could bring a project to a grinding halt if everything wasn't done right.

Some days Stephen felt like a traffic cop at a Manhattan intersection. It would be easier if he lay down in the middle of the street and let them all run over him. Unfortunately, it wasn't in his nature.

Lord, who's in charge of this project? You or Paul Hudson? I want to do Your will, Jesus. I'm trying to get it right.

Stephen wanted this church to stand long after he and Paul Hudson were dead and gone. He wanted people to see Christ in each board and brick of it. But every time he glimpsed one of the building committee guys walking around the site, or heard about another one of Gerald Boham's "events," or saw Paul walk into Charlie's with his leather briefcase in his hand, his blood pressure shot up.

Sally Wentworth poured coffee. Paul smiled and chatted briefly with her, then got straight back to business. "I don't see why we can't cut some costs here and there."

How many times did they have to have this conversation? Stephen strove for patience. "Cut costs and the quality goes down. You get what you pay for, Paul. This church is being built to honor God, and it's going to be built with the best materials available." As long as he had any say about it.

Paul flushed. "Did I say to build it with cheap materials?" As he talked about the pressure he was under from his building committee, Stephen almost sneered. Paul had handpicked those men; they rubber-stamped everything Paul wanted.

What's going on here, Lord?

Stephen knew something was wrong, but he couldn't put his finger on it. Things were changing—Pastor Paul, most of all. Stephen used to respect Paul's charisma in the pulpit, his ability to organize programs and pick staff that worked with him as a unit. But over the past few years, he had seen some of those same people goose-step over anyone who disagreed with "the vision." Paul Hudson could still motivate people and tap talent and resources, but Stephen was feeling more and more uneasy about him.

Maybe it's because I feel tapped to the limit, Lord. Is it just about money, or is there something else going on here?

He wondered if anyone else had misgivings. He was seeing a hard edge to Paul's fierce determination to build VNLC ahead of the proposed twenty-year schedule. What had happened to the easygoing friend who used to slide onto a stool at the counter of Charlie's Diner after a four-mile run?

Stephen shoved his half-eaten lunch aside and clasped his hands on the table. "Let's back up, Paul. Let's slow it down. There's a reason I wrote it up as a twenty-year project. The best materials cost more, but they last longer. We dreamed of building something that would last."

"I know, Stephen, but at the rate we're going, we'll be lucky to live long enough to see the complex finished."

"Does it matter if we live to see it? We wanted it done right. It used to take hundreds of years to build a cathedral." Stephen was perplexed by Paul's frustration and impatience.

Paul laughed without humor. "I wish it *were* a cathedral."

"We're ahead of schedule, Paul. Ease up. Give the congregation a breather from fund-raising programs. Let them settle in."

Paul nodded. "Okay. Let's put off the gymnasium. But we'd like to have the fountain up and running by the end of the year."

Stephen breathed out slowly. *Is he listening, Lord?* "The fountain is in the last-phase plans. One of those options to consider down the road, *after* the twenty-year plan is completed."

"It looks spectacular on paper, Stephen. The living water gushing up from the earth and flowing over those statues like a cleansing stream. It would be awe inspiring. It would draw people."

"It was a conceptual drawing."

"So you don't know how much it would cost."

"Somewhere in the neighborhood of three hundred thousand dollars. Probably more by the time we get around to putting it in. *If* we do."

"I suppose you could design something simpler, but incorporating the same ideas. You've always had great design concepts, Stephen."

He saw where Paul was going. He wanted another set of blueprints for a nominal fee—or no fee at all. It was time to call a halt. He couldn't keep giving away his time and savings. He had to make house payments and buy groceries. "I haven't got the time. I've got three other jobs lined up."

"That might be one of your problems right there, Stephen."

Stephen stared at him, pulse rocketing. "What are you saying?"

"The committee thinks you're stretched too thin."

The committee, meaning him. "I have to work for a living, Paul. VNLC isn't paying the going rate for any general contractor, let alone what I normally make. I'm not even breaking even."

"We all know you're doing it for the Lord, Stephen, and I know He's going to bless you for it. We're all grateful to have a man of your reputation heading up this project. But it will be quite a coup for you, too, won't it? Your first work for the Lord. It made the cover of one of the most prestigious architectural magazines in the country. People are watching to see how you do on this project."

Did Paul think he was that naive? He recognized manipulation when he faced it. "Gratitude and free publicity don't pay the rent. I've had to make good on bills Marvin Lockford doesn't pay on time." He was relieved when Paul looked surprised. He didn't want to think Paul was the one telling his treasurer to hold back the funds.

"He's not paying?"

"Sixty to ninety days late these days." Stephen leaned his forearms on the table. "My men have families, Paul. They can't wait for their paychecks. I've paid the day laborers out of my own pocket, but I can't keep that up." He watched Paul's expression change, but couldn't decipher what he was thinking. It was like a veil coming down, and that bothered Stephen. He didn't know Paul anymore. Worse, he wasn't sure he wanted to know him. All he knew was he didn't like feeling guilty when he asked for his pay. And he didn't like feeling used.

"I'm sorry." Paul reached for his wallet. "I'll talk to Marvin. What do you say I pay for lunch today?" He extracted a twenty.

Stephen decided not to quibble about the check. Paul was certainly clearing more this month than he was.

Eunice sat in the waiting room outside Paul's office. She had hoped to speak with Paul on the telephone, but Reka informed her that Paul had given orders that he not be disturbed unless it was an emergency. He was counseling someone. Eunice knew he wouldn't consider the situation earth-shattering enough to interrupt him. "We'll come down and wait to see him."

Paul made it abundantly clear to her that she was never to start any speculation. He had said more than once, "Deal with it and fill me in later." She supposed it was democratic to treat her and Tim like any other member of the church asking for help, but she resented it. How many times had the telephone rung during a family dinner and he would spend an hour or more talking with someone who was in crisis? How many times had he gotten up in the middle of the night to go to someone's side? He always found time for others, but when it came to his own wife and son, he had no energy or time left. She tried to squelch the resentment as she sat beside Tim in the waiting room.

Reka gave them a pained smile. "I slipped him a note. He knows you're here. I'm sure he'll be done soon." She went back to her typing.

Fifteen minutes passed. Timothy was beside her, grim and silent.

Reka offered to make coffee. Eunice said it wasn't necessary. Another fifteen minutes passed before the door opened and Rob Atherton came through it with Paul on his heels. He patted Rob on the back. "Thanks for coming in, Rob."

Rob looked worn down. He gave Eunice a nod. Was Paul trying to extract another donation from the man?

"Eunice, you can go on into the office," Paul said. "I'll be with you and Tim in just a minute." He walked out into the hallway with Rob.

"I'm surprised he has the time," Tim said as he got up.

Eunice sat on the plush leather sofa. It was another ten minutes before Paul was back in the outer office. "It's almost four, Reka. You can finish the church newsletter in the morning." He strode into his office and closed the door behind him. His smile was gone. So, too, was the look of tender patience he so often wore when speaking with people like Marvin and LaVonne Lockford or Jessie Boham.

"You both have trouble written all over your faces. Couldn't you have kept whatever this is all about at home for us to talk about later instead of coming in here and sitting out there where anyone can see you?"

Eunice felt her defenses going up. "You told me this morning you wouldn't be coming home until late because you had another important meeting with the building committee. And I did call. Reka said you told her to hold all calls. And we couldn't wait." Some things couldn't be put off and shoved aside. Not anymore. And she didn't want Paul hearing the bad news from someone in the church. Jessie was sure to tell Gerald, and Gerald would tell Paul . . .

"Okay. Okay. Get to the point. What happened this time?"

"Why don't you ask me, Dad?" Face white, Tim glared at his father. "Why take it out on her?"

"I'm not taking anything out on her, but maybe you ought to think about how your behavior affects others. Especially *me*. What you do affects *my* reputation." He turned on her. "So are you going to tell me or not?"

"If you'd give me a chance."

Tim lowered his head.

Paul sat, looking exasperated. "Just spit it out." He glanced at his watch. "I have to leave in forty-five minutes for an important meeting."

"Tim has been suspended from school."

"Great! Just what I need!" Paul stood and paced. Arms akimbo, he looked up as though searching through his counseling books for the one that would give him a quick, easy way out of this latest crisis. "What is it with you, Tim? Are you trying to embarrass me in front of my congregation?" He looked at their son as though he despised him. "Are you trying to make me a laughingstock to everyone in town?"

"No."

"What about your mother? How do you think she feels when you pull some stunt that gets her called into the principal's office? She can't defend you for the rest of your life. When are you going to get out from behind her and grow up? Don't you know everyone watches our family? We're important to this community. People look up to us as examples. And what kind of example are you with your black eye and split lip? What are people going to say when they see you Sunday morning?"

"I don't care what they say."

"Because you don't care about anyone but yourself."

Eunice was afraid he was just getting warmed up. "Paul—"

"When are you going to grow up?"

Eunice tried to interrupt.

"You stay out of this, Eunice. You're always protecting him. You don't seem to get the point. If people think I can't manage my own son, they're going to begin to wonder if I can manage my church."

Paul hadn't even asked what had happened to bring about the suspension. Did everything have to come down to *his* church, *his* reputation? Since when was truth measured by what others might say? People invented gossip, and the wives of some of Paul's elders were the worst offenders of all.

"You're not giving him a chance—"

"He's had chance after chance."

Paul seemed blind to the hurting boy who was becoming an angry young man. His attention was fixed on his pastorate, his ministry, his reputation.

Eunice realized she was sick of a few things, too. Sick of Paul's public graciousness and his private bullying.

Tears welled in Tim's eyes as he glared back at his father. "The only thing you care about is your church."

"I care about everyone in this church, including you."

"Not that I've ever noticed."

"Don't you dare talk to me that way!"

"Paul, hear him out!"

He rounded on her. "If you weren't always trying to fix things for him, he wouldn't be in another mess."

She was just following his instructions, dealing with problems and trying to tell him later. Only he never listened!

"Why are you always blaming Mom? Why don't you try looking at yourself for a change? Mr. Picture-Perfect Pastor Paul."

"Do you think I don't know what it's like being a PK? I know it isn't easy. But you don't even try. I got top grades all the way through school! I lettered in track! I never missed a youth group meeting! I went on mission trips! I attended conferences with my mother! I did *everything* I could to make my father's life easier. And here you are." He gave a dismissive wave. Planting his hands on his desk, he leaned toward Tim. "Every time you act up, you're serving Satan. You're opening the door of this church and inviting him in."

"*That's enough!*" Eunice stood, cheeks on fire, gripped with wrath. Paul and Tim both stared at her, and no wonder. She had never shouted at anyone in her entire life. She was shaking with anger. "Tim, you go home." Her heart ached at the look on his face. She put her hand on his shoulder. "I need to talk with your father alone."

Tim stood, his eyes awash with tears. "I'm sorry, Mom."

"So am I."

Paul glared at her. "You're the biggest part of his problem, you know that? He doesn't even listen to me."

"Why should he listen to you? You didn't even allow him the opportunity to tell you what happened."

"I didn't have to ask. He's got a black eye and a split lip. He was in another fight."

"Shirl Wenke called me last week."

"What's that got to do with anything?"

"She was full of praise about how patient and understanding you were with her son, Bobby, when he was caught writing graffiti with a permanent marker in the church bathroom."

Paul's eyes hardened. "He repainted the wall."

"And Shirl said you took him out for a hamburger and talked with him for more than an hour." She picked up her purse. "Yes, Paul, Tim was in a fight. One of the boys from our youth group was being beaten up in the locker room by some of the football players. Tim interceded. It was four to one. Tim could've ended up in the hospital."

His eyes flickered. "Then why was he the only one suspended?"

"He wasn't. They all were. Even Frank Heber, who took the most damage."

Paul sank into his chair. "Fighting isn't the answer."

"Maybe not, but sometimes you can't stand by. And I doubt Tim did as much damage with his fists as you just did with your tongue."

His head came up, eyes darkening again. "Where do you get off accusing me after shouting at me in front of our son?"

"You didn't wait thirty seconds before you condemned and passed judgment on him!"

"You're not being fair! Why don't you stop and consider the position he's put me in?"

"Don't talk of fairness, Paul. I watch you coddle members of your congregation, even those who are blatantly sinning. Men and women living with one another, deaconesses gossiping, elders who withhold money from workers."

"What do you know about that?" His eyes narrowed. "Have you been talking to Stephen Decker?"

"No. I overheard one of the day laborers in the bank the other day." She swallowed the hurt. "I cling to hope that everything will be all right, but sometimes I wonder, Paul." She searched his eyes. "You've changed."

"So have you, Eunice. You're far from the submissive girl I married. You buck me every chance you get."

What was he talking about? "You're not even listening to me, are you? You're so caught up in building this church that you haven't time left for us."

Paul let out a long-suffering sigh. "I'm tired. Maybe I overreacted.

But what do you expect when you hit me at the end of the day with something like this?"

"I suppose it would have been better if Tim had gotten himself suspended earlier in the day." She put her hand on the doorknob. "You know, Paul, I can't remember the last time you extended grace to me or Tim."

"He doesn't need grace. He needs discipline."

Was there any use in talking to him? Did he have eyes to see or ears to hear? She couldn't keep walking around the issue. "You're treating Tim the same way your father treated you."

His face reddened. "Don't you talk about my father. What do you know about the pressures of building a church? I'm a better pastor because my father pushed me. Now that I'm standing in his shoes, I can look back and understand the stress Dad was under, the constant battle going on to build something for God. I'm not a little boy anymore, running to my mother every time my feelings are hurt."

Every word pierced and wounded.

"There's no excuse for cruelty, Paul." She searched his face, wondering what had happened to the young man she had loved so much. She had watched Paul become harder and more obstinate. Sometimes she wondered if the only reason he attended school functions at all was to be seen by the other VNLC parents. He spent most of the time talking with the other parents, other people's sons and daughters.

Tim saw. Tim knew. Tim took it into his heart. She could almost hear her son asking himself if he even counted in the scheme of things— other than as a poster child for Paul Hudson, pastor of the fastest growing church in the Central Valley.

Sometimes she wondered the same thing about her own role. She could sing. She could play the piano. Take that away and who was she? Just little Eunice McClintock, girl from the hills of Pennsylvania who gave her life to Christ before she was nine years old. She was no one special. She'd always wondered what Paul saw in her.

Maybe he was wondering the same thing.

"Neither one of you seems to care about the trouble this situation can cause me." Paul waved his hand over his desk. "As if I don't have enough to deal with already."

That was always his excuse.

She knew their marriage was floundering, but where did a pastor's wife go for counseling? "Why don't you just tell everyone your son almost became a Christian martyr?"

Paul looked as though he might consider the idea.

"I'm going home, Paul. Is there anything you want me to tell Tim?"

"He's grounded."

The future stretched out ahead of her—bleak, lonely. *Help me, God.* "If you keep on as you are, Paul, you're going to drive Tim out of the church."

He might even drive their son away from God.

When Samuel heard the doorbell ring, he thought maybe it was one of the Mormon boys in their crisp white shirts and black trousers. Last time, they accepted his invitation to milk and cookies and left their bicycles locked by his front gate. After half an hour, one of the young men had been eager to leave, but the other couldn't be pried from his chair. Samuel invited them both to Wednesday evening Bible study.

"Tim! It's been a while." He opened the door wide. "Come on in."

"Thanks."

Samuel grimaced. "Are you all right?"

"Yeah."

"And the other guy?"

"Guys." Tim stepped through the front door and stood in the living room. Samuel wondered if the boy was remembering how Abby used to ask him if he wanted some cookies as he came through the door. Tim's shoulders shook and a sound came out of him like a wounded animal. Sinking onto the old sofa, he held his head and started to sob.

Samuel put his hand on Tim's shoulder and sat beside him.

Tim rubbed his face on his sleeve and sat hunched over, forearms resting on his knees. "Sorry. I didn't mean to come over here and blubber like a baby."

"I've had my moments, Tim. If we didn't, we'd bust wide open."

Tim gave a bleak laugh. "Or bust someone else wide open." He released a long breath through pursed lips. "I hope I didn't interrupt anything."

"Nothing that can't wait." Samuel patted Tim's shoulder, put his hands on his knees, and straightened. "Why don't you come on in the kitchen and help me figure out what to rustle up for grub?" Tim followed and stood at the back door, looking out. Samuel peered into the freezer. "I've got TV dinners. Swiss steak, meat loaf, lasagna. Or we can throw one of these pizzas in the oven."

"Whatever you want."

Samuel knew Tim liked pizza. He turned on the oven, opened the pizza box, removed the cellophane wrapping, and slid the pizza onto a cookie sheet. "Should be ready in half an hour." He took two sodas from the refrigerator. "Or when the smoke alarm goes off." He popped the top of one soda and slid it across the table.

Tim took a long swig of soda, set the can down, and rested his arms on the table. "Did you get along with your dad, Samuel?"

Samuel smiled. "We butted heads on occasion."

"I got suspended. Got hauled into the principal's office again." He stared at the can. "I'm sick of all of 'em, Samuel. They're all a bunch of stinking hypocrites. I'm sick of the principal bending over backward to excuse the jocks. I'm sick of my teachers telling me I'm wasting my natural talent. As if they really give a rip. I'm sick of Dad blaming Mom every time something happens. Most of all, I'm sick of *him*." He took another swig of soda. "I don't care what any of them think of me."

Samuel could see how much he didn't care. He thought of a dozen platitudes. *It's not easy growing up. You'll get through this. Your dad loves you. It's not easy being a parent these days. Life is tough.* All true. But Tim was the one who needed to talk. Not him.

So Samuel let him. He already knew most of it. He'd been involved in Timothy Hudson's life since the boy was being pushed around in a stroller. It had only been the last couple of years, when Tim's visits had dwindled to once every month or so and lasted fewer than thirty minutes, that he'd had to rely on Eunice. She still took long walks and stopped by for tea. She filled him in about Tim. A toad set free in Sunday school, difficulty with homework, soccer meets interfering with youth group, church camp escapades. Tim had written a skit, a full-fledged satire about the church, that hit a little too close to home for comfort. Jessie Boham thought she saw him smoking pot behind the bowling alley. It turned out to be someone else, but people tended to believe gossip.

Tim stood and walked around the table, opening the cabinet door under the sink and putting his can into the recycling bag. "I'm not going to church anymore."

Samuel had no doubt where that speech was aimed. "Mind telling me why?"

"I'm sick of sitting with a bunch of hypocrites, Samuel. Mrs. Lockford and her gestapo checking up on everyone. Mr. Boham telling the youth group we have to sacrifice for the Kingdom while he goes out and buys himself a new car every year. Mrs. Boham yapping about the moral decay of America's youth. Did you know she records three soap operas a day?"

"How do you know that?"

"Trudy. She's as hooked as her mother. She eats the stuff up! And her mother looks down her nose at me because I listen to heavy metal." He straddled the chair again. "You're lucky to be out of it."

He wasn't out of it. He'd just found another way to be in it. "You need to change your focus. Look up."

"Yeah, right. Up at the pulpit? At my dad? All that talk about how we're supposed to *love one another.* He's the biggest hypocrite in the whole place."

At least he didn't include his mother in his sweeping condemnation. "Look higher, Tim."

"What's to see? A couple pieces of wood nailed to the front wall? It doesn't mean anything. Not to them. Not that I can see." He bowed his head. "I don't even know if I believe in Jesus anymore. Or even if I want to."

Of all the things Tim had said over the past hour, that grieved Samuel the most. He knew what it was like to feel cut out, cut off, defeated. Even after years of loving and serving the Lord, Samuel had his moments of discouragement. He'd had his times of shaking his fist at heaven and asking why. Every day demanded a decision, and some days Samuel pleaded for Jesus to take him home. *Lord, I miss my wife. Why do I have to stick around without her?* He knew what Abby would say to that. "You'd better pray, Samuel. You're in a battle. Let the Lord arm you. You can't face the enemy in spiritual underwear."

So, Lord, what do I say? The boy's in no mood for a sermon.

Tim sat silent. Samuel could only hope the boy was waiting for a rebuttal.

"People fail all the time, Tim. It's our nature to mess things up. The only man who ever made it through life without botching it was Jesus, and He's God. Look to Him. Don't expect your father to have all the answers you need."

"No kidding." His mouth twisted. "Sometimes I wonder if Dad even believes. What's he need God for, anyway? He thinks he can do everything all by himself."

Timothy Hudson had more wisdom than he knew. "You were on fire for Jesus once."

"Maybe."

"I was there the day you were baptized."

"It didn't take."

"What part of you didn't get dipped?"

"Well, then, let's say I can't see that it's changed anything."

"I'll tell you what. You follow your faith, as weak as it is, rather than your doubts, as strong as they seem to you right now. You do that and leave the rest up to God. He'll make sure everything goes according to plan."

Tim tilted his head and looked at him. How could one so young have such a cynical smile? "It'd be a whole lot easier if I weren't going to church."

Paul tried to focus on the meeting, but his mind kept slipping back to Eunice and Tim. He shouldn't have lost his temper. He should've listened to his son's side of the story. But he'd just spent a grueling hour with Rob Atherton, trying to get that man to open up. He might as well have been digging clams in high tide. Sheila had been the one to ask for marriage counseling, but he wouldn't get far if Rob wasn't going to cooperate.

After an hour with the reticent Rob, he'd been tied up in knots of frustration over trying to help a couple without turning the husband off to the church. Rob was on the fence, and Paul didn't want the man throwing his resources in the wrong direction. The sight of Tim with another black eye had obliterated what little patience he had left.

And now this meeting. Couldn't these men do anything without him?

"So, what do you want us to do, Paul?"

"The only thing we can do right now. Shave money off missions and pay the subcontractors. I don't want to have the same conversation with Stephen Decker next week that I had with him last time. If we're going to get things done, we're going to have to make sacrifices."

Marvin nodded. "That's what I've been saying all along. We need to keep the money here, not off in some foreign country with people we've never even met."

"We have to do what's best for our congregation," Gerald agreed.

They talked for a while longer. Everyone wanted to do what was best for the church. And what was best was to keep it growing.

On the way home, Paul called Stephen on his cell phone and left a message that Marvin Lockford would have a check ready for him in the morning. "I'm sorry about the delay, Stephen. I didn't know about it." How many other things had slipped by him? He was going to have to be more diligent. Too bad he couldn't be cloned.

Maybe he should stop at the market for a bouquet. It had been a long time since he'd brought flowers home to Eunice. He leaned over and took a fresh package of Tums from his glove compartment. His dash clock showed 9:48. If he stopped, it would just mean another fifteen minutes later getting home. Maybe longer if Maggie O'Brien was at the checkout stand. She talked his ear off every time he saw her and, at this hour, customers would be few and far between and he wouldn't have a ready excuse to escape. No, he'd better wait on the flowers. He could always send Reka over tomorrow to buy a bouquet. He chewed a second Tums.

The living room lights were off when he pulled into the driveway. He pressed the garage door remote. Tim's bike was leaning against the wall, his helmet hanging from a handlebar. Tim. *What am I going to do about that kid, God? He's driving me crazy. Could You help me a little? Turn him around, Lord.*

Paul took off his jacket and loosened his tie as he went upstairs. The television was playing in the den, Tim sprawled on the couch.

"You know I don't want you watching that show." Paul picked up the remote and turned the television off. "And it's after ten."

Tim stretched and came to his feet. "You're home early."

Was he trying to pick a fight? "Look, I'm sorry about this afternoon in my office. I had a tough day."

"So did I."

Paul leaned against the doorjamb. "Your mom said it was four to one."

"I wasn't keeping score."

"You want to tell me about it?"

Tim picked up his sneakers and walked to the door. "It's a little late, Dad."

"Not too late."

The telephone rang. Tim gave him a wry look and stepped past him.

"Tim . . ." The phone rang for a third time, the sound grating on Paul's nerves. It was late. Couldn't people leave him alone?

"You'd better get it, Dad. It might be someone important." Tim went into his room and closed the door.

The phone stopped ringing. It was about time Eunice answered. Paul tossed the remote onto the couch. He paused at Tim's door, but decided to leave him alone. Better to wait until morning after they'd both had a good night's sleep. He opened the door of the master bedroom and shrugged off his jacket.

"Paul . . ."

"Take a message. I'm beat."

"It's your mother."

He could see something was terribly wrong. He took the phone. "Mom? What's happened?"

"Your father, Paul." She was crying. "He's dead!"

CHAPTER 12

PAUL SAT IN THE FRONT ROW of his father's church, his mother on one side, his wife and son on the other. Staring straight ahead, he struggled against the anger gnawing. Old hurts rose, taunting him as he listened to the speakers praise his father. Representatives from the community, the state, the nation were in attendance. Five thousand people were here to pay their respects, among them state politicians, movie stars, well-known evangelical preachers, as well as other religious leaders who lauded David Hudson for his love of all mankind. There was even a guru in the crowd, along with a dozen of his robed followers sitting in the pews. Flowers and messages of condolence had been pouring in. *People* magazine had called his mother for an interview.

He should have known his father would find some way out of the world before the Valley New Life Center was complete. Another five years and Paul might have earned his father's respect and approval.

Too late now. David Hudson, renowned evangelical preacher, was being laid to rest, his eloquence silenced forever. Other than what he had to say in the book that still topped the bestseller lists.

His mother refused to speak to anyone in the press. "If you love me, Paul, you will say nothing. You will sit beside me and hold my hand and help me get through this three-ring circus!" She was pale, dark circles under her eyes, and so distraught he didn't argue. "I don't want his funeral to be a golden opportunity."

Opportunity? The word stung.

So here he sat among thousands, silent, holding her hand and his tongue while others outside the church praised his father. He could have said more and said it better than newspaper reporters and those in front of the TV cameras. Who knew a father better than his own son? Would people wonder why he wasn't speaking? Would they take it as an affront to the memory of the great David Hudson? But he'd abide by his mother's wishes. Unless she changed her mind. He leaned down, but her hand tightened. Her face was rigid, her ashen face streaked with tears.

Everything was being done according to her wishes. Even the simple service with Joseph Wheeler presiding. Paul wondered how many attendees were offended by the gospel message. He could hear the shifting in the pews, the soft murmuring voices. Wheeler didn't falter. He spelled it out in simple, uncompromising steps to salvation. Jesus saves. No one else. He gave the benediction, and the praise orchestra began the postlude. Eunice probably loved the hymns. The ushers came forward to escort him and his mother up the aisle. Eunice and Tim followed close behind.

Photographers, cameramen, and reporters were waiting out front. His mother's hand tightened on his arm. "Stay beside me."

"They will expect someone to speak for the family."

"I don't care what 'they' expect. This is the last time your father will be in the public eye, and we're going to do what's right! Say nothing! Do you understand me, Paul? Not a word." She drew the black veil down over her face and walked with him out the front doors of the church.

Cameras flashed. Reporters pushed forward. Questions came from all sides as microphones were held up. Excitement beat through Paul. Several of the ushers moved in to block the press as Paul escorted his mother down the steps to the waiting black limousine.

"Mrs. Hudson, can you give us a few words?"

"Mrs. Hudson!"

"Mrs. Hudson!"

"Mrs. Hudson!"

"Mrs. Hudson!"

"Mrs. Hudson!"

The driver opened the car door and his mother almost dove inside. Paul held back, waiting for Eunice and Tim to get in ahead of him. There was so much he wanted to say about his father. He recognized some of the news reporters. He had seen them on television.

"This is Paul Hudson, David Hudson's only son. Reverend Hudson, your father was one of the greatest evangelists of the last century. And now, we've been informed you're building a church in the Central Valley to rival his efforts. Are you hoping to follow in your father's footsteps?" A beautiful blonde thrust a microphone forward.

The ushers moved in front of him, putting their arms out to block the press advance while the limo attendant beckoned behind Paul.

"Paul!" His mother reached out to him. He couldn't ignore her without it making the press.

Sliding into the limo beside her, he looked out as the door was closed firmly, shutting off his last chance to say anything. As the limousine moved swiftly away from the curb, Paul looked out at the sea of faces. "A few words wouldn't have hurt, Mother." She could have given him one minute, at least. "They'll think I don't care."

She looked away.

"Let them think you're too bereaved to say anything," Eunice said, glaring at him through her tears.

What was wrong with her?

Tim peered through the tinted one-way windows. "Is that the governor?"

Paul glanced out, fighting his resentment. "Yes." He hadn't even had a chance to shake his hand.

"Wow!" Tim said. "And there's Tom Davenport! He's got a new movie coming out next month. I didn't know Grandpa knew him."

"He's no more important than anyone else, Tim."

Paul's resentment boiled hotter at Eunice's remark.

"Don't forget why we're here."

"Sorry, Grandma."

His mother stared straight ahead. "A lot of people came to get their faces in the papers or on the evening news."

———— ❧ ————

Paul was surprised and disappointed that his father's memorial service received only five minutes of news coverage. The anchorwoman summed up David Hudson's illustrious career using clips of Paul's father preaching in the church he had built, then another clip when he was preaching to fifty thousand in a football stadium. There were clips of him shaking hands with President Ronald Reagan and, later, President Bill Clinton. The governor, Tom Davenport, and several other celebrities interviewed had a couple of seconds' coverage each. The last shot was of Paul and his mother coming down the steps of the church, Eunice and Tim behind them. The news commentator tapped her papers and set them aside as she moved on to other newsworthy events.

"The world will continue to turn without him, Paul."

He glanced up sharply and saw his mother standing in the doorway. Why should he be embarrassed for watching the news? Why should he feel guilty? What was wrong with wanting to see what the media had to say about his father's death?

He was still upset over the news that his father's body was being shipped to Midvale, Missouri. His father would have hated the idea. Paul remembered his father's assessment of his own father. "Your grandfather moved us from town to town for twenty years and never preached to crowds bigger than a few hundred! Don't listen to your mother. She's got some Pollyanna idea about who my father was and what he accomplished. Just because he was a nice old man doesn't mean he ever did anything worthwhile for God. The Bible says a man who doesn't take care of his family is worse than an unbeliever. I grew up wearing shoes and clothes my mother got from church rummage sales! My father could barely pay the rent on whatever dilapidated shack we lived in. I can remember going to bed hungry! If you want to be a great man of God, don't look to Ezra Hudson. Your grandfather was a complete failure as a preacher—and as a man."

"You're still angry with me, aren't you, Paul?"

"Not angry. Disappointed. I want to understand, Mother. Why wouldn't you allow me to say anything on behalf of Dad?"

"You used to call me Mom." She sighed. "There's a lot you don't know, Paul."

"Then tell me."

She searched his eyes for a moment and then shook her head. "Some of it you know already. Some you're not willing to remember." She sat in a wing chair near the window and pushed the sheer curtain aside so that she could look out. "Another time." She was pale and strained. "I loved him, too, Paul. A lot more and for a lot longer."

"I know he wasn't perfect, Mom. But we're supposed to forgive. We made our peace. I thought you understood that."

"Oh, I know. I saw the change in you."

"We should have made a statement."

She lowered her hand and the sheer curtain floated back into place. "Don't you think it was enough for that news lady to say, 'The grieving family departed without making a statement to the press'?"

"No."

Her mouth tipped in a melancholy smile. "Why not?"

"Because he would've wanted more."

"A national holiday in his name, perhaps?"

"Don't joke, Mom."

Silence fell between them. He struggled against the tears choking him. He was so angry he wanted to smash something. He felt his mother's eyes on him, watching, waiting. He felt small and petty beneath her tender perusal. She let out her breath slowly and leaned her head back. "He was on his way to Chicago to discuss the details of his latest venture."

"Another book?" He didn't want to sound envious or bitter, but he knew both emotions were eating at him.

"His alma mater offered him a teaching position. He was going to conduct seminars for Christian leaders on how to build a church."

"All he ever told me is he had other irons in the fire." Despair filled Paul. So much for thinking he and his father had any kind of relationship. "I thought Dad and I were getting closer over the last few years." He'd never measured up to his father's expectations. He'd never quite made the grade. Even with everything he had accomplished at VNLC, he still fell short.

"He was a sinner, Paul, just like you and me. I didn't want you to say anything because he had been elevated high enough already." She shook her head. "I didn't want you to say something that would have pleased him. Enough has been said. Far too much. And anything you might have added would have been a lie."

His head came up. "What do you mean by that?"

"If you don't understand, you've forgotten everything I ever taught you about the Lord and what He wants of us." Her voice was low. "That grieves me even more than your father's death, Paul."

He had never been able to gain his father's approval, and now it seemed he had failed his mother as well. His eyes blurred with tears. "I would have spoken about what he did right, Mom, not what he did wrong."

"I wanted the gospel presented at your father's memorial service. I wanted the truth proclaimed clearly and simply. Christ glorified." Her voice was husky with strain and sorrow. "I wanted the last words uttered in that service to be about the One who redeemed us and made a way for us to return to God's embrace."

"How can I argue with that?"

"I shouldn't think you would want to. Maybe now you'll be free to become the pastor God intended you to be."

Paul clasped his hands between his knees. "I'd hoped . . ." He cried. Hoped for what? To hear the words *I'm proud of you, Son*?

His mother came to him and cupped his face as she had when he was a boy. She kissed him. Her gaze was fierce and tear-soaked. "Only one thing is needed, Paul. In the midst of your grief, remember whom you serve."

Alone in the den, Paul wondered why his mother had felt the need to remind him. Her words were like salt in his wounds.

He was a pastor. If anyone should know more was expected of him, he did.

——— ❧ ———

Eunice didn't try to convince Paul to stay in Southern California. Why plead when he wouldn't listen? She simply announced her own plans. "I'm going to stay with your mother for a few days longer. I already made some calls and lined up a few women to substitute for me at the church while I'm gone."

"Nice of you to let me know."

"It'll be easier on Mom if we don't all leave at once, Paul. I thought you'd be pleased, and I thought it might be good if you took Tim home with you. It's a long drive. The two of you will have some time alone together to talk."

He dropped one of his father's books into a box. Three others were already taped shut. "Don't make plans for me, Eunice. Tim hasn't said five words to me in the last four days. The thought of being cooped up in a car with him for five hours is less than appealing."

"You haven't sought him out either. You've spent most of the time up here in your father's office."

He threw another book into the box. "What do you expect me to do? Go out and sit by the pool with him? I'm not a kid with time to waste. Mom said I could take whatever I wanted from Dad's library." He waved his arm. "As you can see, I have a lot to do."

How do I reach him, Lord? How do I break through the walls he's building around himself? Eunice looked around the room. On a display table was the model of David Hudson's church. She walked over and looked at it and then looked up at the wall of photographs. David Hudson shaking hands with President Clinton. David Hudson with a movie star known for his martial arts, another for her body. David Hudson shaking hands with an ambassador from China. David at the front door of his church, his hands together as he bowed welcome to a visiting guru. The same guru who had attended the memorial service the other day and said David Hudson was one of the most enlightened pastors of the past century, a true man of peace and love. All the photographs were expensively matted and framed. David Hudson's trophy wall.

Disturbed, she looked around the room slowly, carefully, searching. Nowhere in the room was there a picture of David Hudson's wife, David Hudson's only son, David Hudson's only grandson. Or of Jesus.

"You can stand there all day, Eunice, but I'm not going to change my mind. And you can't make me feel guilty about it, either. I haven't got time to police Tim. I can't be driving him to and from school and then keeping track of where he is when I'm not there."

"That's a mother's job. Right?" One he liked to remind her she hadn't done right from day one.

"I have too much on my plate already." He selected another book to add to his personal library and dropped it on top of the others. When was he going to have time to read all those books? Eunice wondered. "I've been gone for four days," he said, his back to her. "You know as well as I do that I'll have a pile of messages to go through." He perused the bookshelf, looking for treasures. "And I have to meet with the building committee again and make sure they followed up on a few things. Stephen Decker wants his money. You'd think he could wait a few weeks." He yanked another book off the shelf and tucked it into the box. "It's not like all I have to do is play a couple of songs on Sunday morning and chat on the telephone for the rest of the week."

Another barb aimed at her heart. "If you prefer I not counsel women in your congregation, just tell me, Paul, and I will refer them to whomever you like."

"Have I struck a nerve?"

She could see she wasn't going to get anywhere with him. "Since I have so little of importance to do, you and the church won't miss me if I decide to stay a week instead of a few days."

"Stay a month if you want!"

Who was the fool who said sticks and stones could break bones, but words could never hurt you?

"Look. I'm sorry." He sounded more frustrated than apologetic. "I didn't mean that. You know I didn't mean it."

"No, I don't know that, Paul. I don't know anything anymore. I don't know *you* anymore!"

"I said I was sorry. What more do you want from me?"

"Sincerity would do. *Sorry* is just a word, Paul. It doesn't make everything better."

He caught her before she could walk out the door. Pulling her back against himself, he locked his arms around her waist and held her close. "I lost my father a few days ago. I'm not myself."

More excuses.

"Forgive me."

She fought the urge to dig her fingernails into his arm to gain her freedom. Seventy times seven, the Lord said. *Seventy times seven.* "I forgive you."

His arms loosened. "You can't understand how much the last few years have meant to me. For the first time in my life, I felt I had a relationship with my father. And now he's gone." He let go of her. "You know what depresses me most? He's never going to see Valley New Life Center completed."

Why did everything always come back to that?

Paul was already back at the bookshelf, back to work. He glanced from book to book, pulled one out, flipped through it, weighing its usefulness. He slipped it back into place on the shelf. Maybe she shouldn't have been so quick to forgive. Was he even repentant? *If not for You, Lord . . .*

"Why don't you go downstairs and visit with Mom?"

He was brushing her off again. It had become a habit. "What do you see when you look around your father's office, Paul?"

He didn't attempt to hide his impatience this time. "Would you let me get to my work? I'll be down later, Eunice."

"Tell me what you see, Paul, and I'll go."

"A lifetime of achievement. Fame. Respect. The world took notice of David Hudson. That's what I see reflected in this room. Why, what do you see?"

"I see what's missing, Paul. I see what he cast aside." Worse, she had never seen any evidence that David Hudson regretted throwing aside those who loved him most—his wife and son.

She went downstairs and out the sliding doors to the backyard. Lois sat beneath the umbrella, her Bible open in her lap. Shouting like a banshee, Tim took two big steps, bounced, and made a cannonball into the pool. "It's nice having a boy around again. I'm sorry Paul and Tim have to leave so soon."

"I've decided Tim is staying with me."

Lois put the ribbon marker back in her Bible, closed it, and placed it on the patio table. They watched Tim go off the diving board again. "He gets to be more like his father every day."

"Paul? Or Tim?"

Lois smiled ruefully. "Both."

Eunice got up with Paul the next morning. He had already loaded the boxes of books into the trunk of his Buick. She started breakfast for him while he packed his clothes and shaving kit. Lois came into the kitchen wearing her bathrobe. The shadows beneath her eyes were more pronounced. Opening the cabinet, Eunice took down another cup and saucer and poured coffee for her.

"Thanks, honey. I just came down to wish my son a safe trip."

Eunice cracked an extra two eggs into the frying pan.

"Did Paul take all the books he wanted?"

"Six boxes full."

"Any files?"

Paul entered the kitchen. "No time to go through the files this time, Mom." He poured himself a cup of coffee and sat at the nook table. "Besides, I thought someone in the church may want to read through them, use them to write his biography."

Lois set her cup on the saucer. "Dennis Nott suggested the same thing."

"I was going to ask you about him. Who is Nott, anyway? He left a couple of cryptic notes in Dad's office. Was he Dad's secretary or what?"

"He was your father's ghostwriter."

Paul held his coffee cup suspended. "Ghostwriter?"

"He wrote your father's book."

Eunice divided the eggs onto three plates and put the frying pan in the sink to wash later. She served Lois first, then Paul. He looked pensive. Eunice hoped he was thinking about his father's lack of ethics. Was he wondering if David Hudson was capable of other kinds of deceit, if he could allow the public to believe he had written a book someone else had written for him?

"I wish you could stay a few days longer, Paul," Lois said. "There are a lot of things I wanted to talk over with you."

"I wish I could, Mom, but I have a couple fires to put out at VNLC."

"Trouble?"

"Nothing that can't be fixed when I get there. The general contractor is turning into a royal headache." He stood. "I'd better get a move on. I've got a long drive ahead of me." He leaned down and gave his mother a kiss. "You know if you need anything, you only have to ask." He straightened. "Walk with me to the car, would you, Eunice?"

She went out with him, praying for words of reconciliation.

"Tell Tim good-bye for me." He gave her a perfunctory kiss and slid into his Buick. "Keep a tight rein on him. I don't want him getting into more trouble down here. Mom doesn't need it. And don't stay longer than a week. You can't leave your responsibilities to others, whatever you'd like to do."

Heart sinking, she watched him back down the driveway. He couldn't wait to get back to his mistress, the church.

Lois was still in the kitchen. "He's still annoyed that he didn't get his face in the news, isn't he?"

Eunice took her seat again. "He just has a lot on his mind." She tried to raise enough appetite to eat her scrambled eggs. Lois rose and poured herself more coffee, sat again, and remained silent for a long time. Giving up all pretenses, Eunice got up and dumped her eggs into the garbage disposal and put the dishes in the washer.

"It would seem neither of us has an appetite." Lois stretched out and put her hand over Eunice's. "Don't stay away from home too long, honey."

"I was only kidding about a month, Mom."

"I know that, but there are times in a man's life when he is particularly vulnerable. This is one for Paul. He's very confused. There was a lot of unfinished business between him and David." She squeezed Euny's hand and leaned back in her seat again. She turned her cup around in the saucer. "I keep hoping God will open Paul's eyes. I thought going through his father's things might jog his memory about the past."

"He saw what he wanted to see, Mom." Saying even that much made her feel guilty. It wasn't her right to speak against David Hudson. Lois had made her privy to information the public would never know. And it would be up to Lois to tell Paul, if she ever decided to do so. To know more of her father-in-law's sins would only add to the temptation of exposing him. And all that would accomplish was an annihilation of her already-crumbling marriage.

Who would ever guess that a pastor's wife could feel so trapped in despair?

"I'm not sure what I'm going to do about finances," Lois said.

"The church didn't give Dad a pension?"

"Oh, of course. He received a generous retirement. Unfortunately, it won't extend to me."

"Oh, Mom."

"I'll manage. I have Social Security. I'm not counting royalties on

David's book. I'm keeping only enough of it to pay the taxes on the income. I've arranged for Dennis Nott to receive 25 percent, and the rest is going to missions."

Eunice wished Lois had said all this to Paul.

"Sometimes I think I should tell Paul everything." Lois sipped her coffee. "I've thought about it so many times. But every time I think it's time to lay everything out on the table, something stops me. I end up examining my own motives and realizing they're less than pure. All those years of hurt, the years of watching David play at work. I don't want to use truth as a weapon of revenge, Euny." Her voice broke. She looked out the window for a long time before speaking again. "I kept hoping God would get through to David and he would repent. The Bible says, 'God gave them over to shameful lusts.' I saw that happen from up close. Too close. God kept reminding me that a man may be won over by his wife's submission." She looked at Eunice. "I left David once and took Paul with me. Has he ever told you about that?"

"No."

"Maybe he doesn't remember. He was just a little boy and we weren't gone long."

"Where did you go?"

"Morro Bay. I couldn't afford a motel room, so we slept in the car. It was in my head to keep following Highway 1 up the coast all the way to Canada, but I headed home the next day. It was Saturday. Everyone would've been asking questions if I wasn't seen sitting in the front-row pew on Sunday morning."

At least Eunice would be saved those speculations. She had the ready excuse of a death in the family.

Lois pushed her cup and saucer away. "Enough whining about the past. I'm going to make some changes in my life. First thing tomorrow, I'm going to call a Realtor and put this house on the market." She looked around the kitchen. "One person doesn't need a place this big."

Eunice leaned over and touched Lois's arm. "You can come stay with us for a while."

"I don't think so, Euny. I don't think I could stand to watch . . ." Lois shook her head. "A pastor's life is difficult. It would bring back too many memories."

"Maybe you should wait on making any decisions."

"No. I need to unload this house. I need to unload a lot of things. No more reflected glory for me." She looked fragile and broken. "You know what hurts most, Euny? I can't seem to hear the Lord's voice anymore. It used to be so clear that it was like a trumpet call—like the shofar of ancient Israel. But I can't hear Him anymore. Not even the still, small voice. And I want that more than anything." She took Eunice's hand, her eyes filled with anguish. "Don't let it happen to you, honey. Please, don't let it happen."

CHAPTER 13

Stephen Decker knew how the wind was blowing the minute he opened his church newsletter and read the headline: "Building Stones for New Life." He had said everything he could to dissuade Paul from agreeing to Gerald Boham's latest fund-raising scheme—a program designed to give special recognition to all those members who gave a thousand dollars or more to the building fund. Designated gifts would also receive recognition. If you paid for a pew, a small brass plaque with your name would be attached. Give a stained-glass window and your name would be etched on it. Names of those donating smaller amounts would be posted each Sunday. Courtyard paving stones would be marketed between the sanctuary and the education complex.

Father, forgive us. Crumpling the newsletter, Stephen slam-dunked the wad into his wastebasket. They would need Jesus and His whip to clean out the new temple. Stephen reached for the phone and punched the speed dial for VNLC. The machine picked up. Everyone was busy, but someone would be with him soon. Then a recording clicked on, advertising the upcoming events at the church. Stephen banged the phone back onto its cradle. What he had to say was best said in person.

Reka's eyes widened when he walked in the door. "You want me to buzz Pastor Paul?"

"Don't bother."

"Stephen, he's counseling—"

Stephen was too mad to care. He rapped twice on the door and opened it. Sheila Atherton sat on the couch, eyes wide. "You scared the life out of me, Stephen."

Stephen knew that look. "Why? Did you think I was Rob?" She was dressed to kill.

Pastor Paul was on his feet. "Who do you think you are barging into my office like this? I'm in the middle of a counseling session."

Pastor Paul was pretty quick to her defense. Sheila noticed, too, and looked smug. Was Paul naive or just plain stupid? "Five minutes is all I need, and then you can get back to business as usual."

Sheila smirked as she picked up her purse. "Jealous?" She mouthed the word, her back to Paul.

"You don't have to leave, Sheila. Stephen is the one leaving." He was so solicitous, so careful of her feelings. A goldfish courting a piranha.

"It's all right, Pastor Paul. I don't think Stephen would behave in such an unseemly manner if it weren't important." She closed the door behind her.

Paul's face was red. "It better be good, Stephen."

Stephen thought of Eunice, loving and faithful, and turned his head, staring into Paul's eyes. "*You'd* better be good." If he saw so much as a flicker of guilt, he was going to smash his jaw.

"What're you talking about?"

Pastor Paul didn't have a clue. Stephen let it go and got to the point of his visit instead. "'Building Stones for New Life'?"

Paul sat. "You said you needed more money. We're getting you more money."

"Don't you dare lay this at my feet! I said we need more *time!*"

"We won't need more time if we have more money, and it's been pouring in since that newsletter went out. Ten thousand dollars came in just this morning."

"For what? The cross? Whose name are you going to carve on that, Paul?"

"*You're out of line!*"

"And seeing the light." He shook his head. "You're way off track, my friend."

Paul made a noticeable effort to rein in his temper. "You have no idea the pressure I'm under. If we hadn't finally sold that old church building, we'd be drowning in debt."

Stephen had warned him. "Pressure from whom? Pressure from what? You're the one pushing every Sunday, browbeating the congregation into giving more and more. You're using coercion, Paul. What's next? Are you and General Gerald going to start selling shares in the church? You going along with that idea, too?"

Paul's eyes flickered. "Not shares. Bonds. There's nothing wrong with it! It'll give us what we need to finish the project." Paul tried on a smile, but it didn't fit. "You won't have to worry about paying the sub-contractors anymore."

There was no talking to him, no heading him off from disaster. By the time the church was finished, it would just be another big project brought to fruition. Stephen wished he had never gotten involved. He wished he had never done the conceptual drawings and the blueprints. *God, forgive me. Please. I didn't know what I was getting into. I didn't know what I was getting these people into.* He felt sick. "I'm contracted to fin-ish the west wing. It's almost done. After that, I'm out. I can't in good conscience move forward. Not in the direction you're going."

Paul looked grim, but not surprised. He folded his hands on his desk. "Gerald didn't think you'd have the staying power."

"Is that so? Based on what information?" He'd never left a project unfinished until now. Then again, he had never worked with a pastor and board who thought they had unlimited resources. They ran this place like the government, a new tithe increase every term.

"We've had our disagreements, Stephen, but I hoped you would see this project through. The end result will be every bit as fantastic as we first envisioned it."

The end result was exactly what Stephen had been talking about for months, but Paul didn't seem to get it. "I was under the impression a church wasn't just a building, Paul. A church is built on faith."

Paul's eyes darkened. "I don't need to be told that. It is being built on faith. *My* faith in the ability of the people of this church to come through!"

"Come through for what? For whom? You?"

"You're the one without faith, Stephen. You had enough to get us started, but not enough to endure to the end. And that's saving faith. You don't even have as much as a mustard seed." He took on an expression of profound disappointment. "Who'd have thought you would be the stumbling block to a project like this? Something that will bring credit to your name whether you finish it or not?"

"I don't want my name mentioned. I never did."

Paul shook his head. "The least you can do at this point is give us some recommendations."

Stephen couldn't believe his brass. "Someone with more faith than I have, you mean? Someone who'll work for 3 percent? Other subcontractors who'll walk when I do because they will know Marvin Lockford holds the key to the money and they'll have to use dynamite to get into the vault?"

"It's always the money with you, isn't it? So much for all your rhetoric about building something for God!"

Stephen clenched his fist. *Lord, help me think straight. Don't let my anger get the better of me.*

"How about giving me the name of someone who values his reputation?"

Stephen felt a cold wave of shock. "Is that a threat?"

"It's what people will say when word gets out that you quit in the middle of building our church. And what will the papers make of it? I wonder. Did you think of that before busting in here with your demands? Stephen Decker doesn't finish what he starts. He's not dependable. That's what people are going to say. I don't think you'll be welcome at VNLC after word gets out. I doubt you'll find much work in the area either."

"And you call yourself a man of God."

"You're the one turning your back on the church, Stephen! You're the one deserting Jesus Christ!"

Stephen couldn't believe the man sitting behind the mahogany desk was the same man who had befriended a stranger at Charlie's Diner. Or had all that just been a good cover for what he really was underneath the surface? "It's because of Christ I'm walking away from this project, Paul. And it's because of Christ I'm not coming over the top of your desk right now and pounding your face into a bloody pulp."

His eyes widened in fear. "Try it and I'll have you arrested for assault."

"You know your real problem, Paul? You've forgotten who you work for." Stephen yanked open the door.

"Finished so soon?" Sheila crooned, rising like Venus from the sea.

Stephen figured Pastor Paul could fend for himself in shark-infested waters.

Samuel sat in his DeSoto across from the old Centerville Christian Church, a newspaper lying beside him on the seat with the headline that had sent him out for verification: "Historical Landmark Sold." The front doors of the church were open. A cherry picker was parked on the curb, a two-man crew at work on the steeple. Samuel saw a pickup pull up. A man got out and pried up the For Sale sign with a Sold banner across it, heaved it into the back, and drove off. A local sign company was at work mounting a new marquee on the front of the building.

He heard shouting from the basket of the cherry picker. The wooden cross that had stood above the treetops of Centerville for over a hundred years toppled, bounced down the roof, and fell, splintering into pieces on the front steps of the old church. Samuel made an anguished cry, but no one heard him. Who cared about an old man in an old car watching progress come to town?

Two young men came out of the church. One held a box. They talked animatedly as they put letters up on the marquee. When they finished, they embraced. The crew from the cherry picker gathered up the pieces of the cross and tossed them into the back of the truck, then received a check from one of the young men. As the cherry picker pulled away, Samuel was able to read the marquee:

New home of the Science of the Mind Church
Services every Sunday at 10:00 a.m.
Visitors Welcome

Bowing his head, Samuel wept. Sobs shook his body. He could hardly catch his breath. Soul-weary, he started his old DeSoto and drove home, praying every foot of the way that the Lord wouldn't leave him on this earth much longer.

———— ❧❧ ————

Paul answered the phone on the second ring, and his heart leaped at the familiar voice on the other end. "Paul, I have to talk with you."

He glanced toward the kitchen, where Eunice was peeling potatoes. "I told you never to call me at home."

"I couldn't help it. Rob was an absolute monster before he left yesterday. He said the meanest things to me. I need to talk to you. I'm desperate."

Paul could hear her soft weeping. "Sheila, I've explained before. You have to call the church office and make an appointment through Reka. The last thing either of us wants is misunderstanding about our relationship."

"Reka doesn't like me."

Eunice looked his way. He shrugged and rolled his eyes, pretending it was someone unimportant. "Why do you say that?"

"I can tell. Every time I call for an appointment, she leaves me on hold for five minutes."

"We get a lot of calls."

"You know I would never bother you without reason, Paul. I know how important you are."

"Maybe I should call Carol Matthews. She has a master's in family counseling."

"I don't do well with women, Paul."

"She's well trained."

"It doesn't matter how well she's trained. It never works."

Eunice was looking at him again. He carried the phone into the living room, but found Tim lounged on the sofa, reading his American history textbook. Sliding the glass door open, Paul went out to the patio.

"They don't like me, Paul. I think they're jealous. I have money. They don't. I do everything I possibly can to look my best for my husband. And they gossip about everything from the age difference between me and Rob to the size of my bustline. I'll bet you didn't know that, did you?"

"No, I didn't." A small white lie.

Paul conceded Sheila was the most beautiful woman in the congregation. And he had overheard gossip. LaVonne Lockford made a crack at a dinner party not long ago about Sheila Atherton having a body like a supermodel. Whether it was manufactured by plastic surgeons, Paul didn't know. But he was a healthy male. He couldn't help but notice her body when she came to counseling sessions in figure-fitting pants and sweaters. Sometimes she moved in such a way that his mouth went dry.

"I've been holding back, Paul," Sheila had told him last week. "I didn't want to seem disloyal to my husband. But I guess it's best to be honest and get things out into the open. I think there's something wrong with Rob. I wanted him to go in for a checkup, but he says he's fine." Paul had pressed her. "Well, I don't know how to say this . . ." She had explained in embarrassing detail what the problem was.

No wonder the poor girl was unhappy.

She said she wanted children, but there didn't seem much chance of that happening. Besides, Rob already had three children by his first wife and a grandbaby on the way. "I've tried to be friends with them, but they hate me. They think I'm the one that broke up their father's marriage to their mother. But it was over and done with long before I came on the scene."

The more she talked, the more his mind wandered into realms he knew he should avoid. She'd given him a hug the last time, and he had been shocked by his physical response. Of course, she hadn't meant anything by the embrace. She'd just been thanking him for all the time he spent counseling her and trying to help her fix her marriage. She was so grateful.

"Could you come out to the house? Rob left this morning and I'm so upset. I don't think I can drive without getting in an accident. Please, Paul."

"I can't, Sheila." Rob was out of town. "It's inappropriate."

"Inappropriate?" Her voice broke. "Why? You're my pastor, aren't you?"

"People would get the wrong idea."

"The wrong idea about what?"

She was so innocent. "I have to be especially careful about my reputation."

"And you think I'd ever do anything to hurt you? Oh, I wouldn't. I swear I wouldn't."

"I know you wouldn't. But people can easily get the wrong idea.

They talk." A reputation that had taken years to build could be undone in a few minutes. He felt a twinge of conscience. Stephen Decker had little business in Centerville or the surrounding area anymore because Marvin Lockford and Gerald Boham had said Decker wasn't as upstanding as people might think. Did they know he'd spent time in an alcoholic treatment center? Paul had stayed out of it, but his silence had helped fan the sparks into a firestorm against the contractor. And Stephen had said nothing to defend himself. The first few Sundays after the gossip started, he had come to church and sat near the front, looking up at Paul. After a month, Stephen left VNLC.

Sometimes Paul regretted it, but at least no harm had come from his leaving. The building program was on schedule. The new contractor wasn't a Christian. He didn't quibble about cutting corners.

"I'm sorry, Paul. I guess I'm asking too much again. Rob says I'm always asking for too much." She was crying harder now. "It's just that . . . that I'm so miserable. Sometimes I wish I was dead. Sometimes I think Rob would be happy if I drove my car into a tree! Or took a bottle of pills."

Paul felt a prickle of fear. He'd learned in training never to take a threat of suicide lightly. "Don't talk that way. He cares about you. *I* care about you." Maybe he should go to her house. She needed him. And she didn't trust anyone else. Ordinarily he could take Eunice along for something delicate like this, but Sheila thought women didn't like her. She would never open up if Eunice was there.

"I'm sorry I called you," Sheila said in a broken voice. "I shouldn't have bothered you."

"You're no bother."

"I'll be all right. You don't need to worry about me anymore." She fumbled the telephone as she hung up.

How desperate was she? What had Rob said to get Sheila into such a state? Could he believe her that she would be all right? And if she wasn't, how could he live with the knowledge that she'd called him and made a desperate plea for help? He couldn't in good conscience abandon her.

"I've got to go out for a couple of hours." He put the telephone back on the power source and headed for the back door to the garage.

"Who was calling?"

He pretended he didn't hear her as he grabbed his car keys. "I'll try to call you later."

She dried her hands on a towel and followed him as he went out the door. "Paul?" She stood in the doorway.

All he could think about was getting to Sheila before she did anything crazy.

———— ❧ ————

Stephen sat at the counter of Charlie's Diner. "Haven't seen you in a while, handsome." Sally poured his coffee.

"Pastor Paul still warming a seat in here?"

"Oh, not in ages. Not since he moved up to that new housing tract. I don't think he jogs down our way anymore. At least, not that I've seen." She set the pot back on the burner. "Still going to church?"

"Not lately. You?"

She lifted one shoulder. "Not as often as we used to. CCC's gotten too big for us. Sorry. Forgot. Valley New Life Center. Beautiful facility though. That fountain is really something, Stephen."

"Lot of splash."

"You okay?"

"Why do you ask? Did you hear I fell off the wagon? Don't believe everything you hear, Sally."

She made a fist and stopped it just short of his jaw. "You should know me better than that. You just look a little down today."

"Down, but not out."

"So what are you building these days? Hotel? Hospital? New airport?"

"Nothing." He still had business offers, but none that had excited him as much as building that church. In the beginning, at least. It was a good thing he'd made some sound investments. He needed time off.

"Sure miss going to church. You could sure feel the Spirit moving. . . ."

"You should stop by Samuel Mason's house if you want to feel the Spirit moving. He's still holding his Bible study every Wednesday night." It was the only port in the storms battering Stephen's life.

Brittany had run away. The private detective ran into a wall in San Francisco. "She's probably living on the streets. . . ."

Stephen had bought a bottle of bourbon that night and come close to taking his first drink in years. Then he remembered what his AA sponsor had told him: "It's the first one that kills you." He didn't want his little girl coming home and finding her father had turned into a drunk again.

"Might just come to that Bible study," Sally said. "Wednesday's a slow night. Charlie and I could close up early. You sure Samuel wouldn't mind?"

"He always leaves his door open. You might have to sit on the floor, but there'll be room for you."

Others came in. Stephen ate his breakfast alone, praying for his daughter's safety, praying she'd come home soon. He even prayed for Kathryn. She was a mess, her marriage tumbling down around her ears.

The only thing that kept him from selling his house and moving back to Sacramento was the Wednesday night Bible study. It had become a lifeline. He dropped by Samuel's a couple of times a week. Every time he did, they sat in the kitchen or out on the patio talking about the Bible. Stephen had gotten hooked on it. It filled the holes life had punched in him. Stephen always felt God's presence during those short hours with Samuel. He came away feeling better, believing that God was at work somewhere, somehow. Just not in his line of vision.

"Don't make yourself so scarce," Sally said when he set the bell ringing on his way out the door.

Stephen headed out for a drive. He had the inexplicable urge to go to Rockville. The little town fit its name, the only apparent business a sand-and-gravel company on the outskirts of town. As he drove down the main street, he spotted a building for sale. Pulling over, he looked at it. It could have been an old five-and-dime at one time with an apartment upstairs for the proprietor. Brick and mortar with turn-of-the-century touches. An iron bench was out front, a derelict with a newspaper over his head sleeping on it.

Stephen got out of his truck and walked the street from one end to the other. It was lined with old maple trees and run-down buildings, a third empty due to businesses going under. Still, there was something about the down-on-its-luck town.

The place fit him.

Laughing at himself, he took his cell phone out of his pocket and punched in the number of the real estate office listing the building. Teresa Espinoza said she could be in Rockville in an hour. He spent the time driving up and down the rest of the streets. Half the houses were built on bare ground, having been put up before zoning laws would have prevented their construction without proper foundations.

Teresa was a small woman with graying black hair and intelligent dark eyes. "The bank foreclosed three years ago. I don't think there have been any offers on it." She unlocked the door and entered. "As you can tell, it needs a lot of work."

That was an understatement. He walked around the big room, looking at the floors, walls, ceiling. The stairs creaked as he went up to the apartment over the vacant store. It had a great view of Main Street, assuming anyone would want to look at that depressing sight.

"How much?"

"You're kidding."

"Why would I kid you?"

"I saw the name on your truck. Decker Design and Construction. Haven't you built a couple of places in Granite Bay?"

"Three or four." Thank God she didn't mention VNLC.

As they came outside, she grimaced in distaste as the bum slumped on the front bench, a half-empty bottle next to him. "Frankly, I can't picture you here, Mr. Decker." She locked the door again.

He looked into the drunk's eyes. "I can." His own battle was far from won.

She told him the price.

Maybe taking on a challenge like renovation was just what he needed to keep his mind off what he couldn't change or control. God had begun a complete renovation of his soul and remodel of his life. Why shouldn't he take on this project?

Brittany, baby, where are you? God, keep her safe.

Let go. Let God. Live. Let live. Easy does it. Easier said than done, Lord. Easier if his mind and hands were busy.

He told Teresa Espinoza he'd sign as soon as she had the papers ready.

Principal Kalish tossed a stapled document across his desk. Eunice could tell by his expression that he had had it. Timothy would receive no mercy this time. "It's called a *zine*, Mrs. Hudson, short for underground magazine."

She flipped through the photocopied pages, heat coming up her neck and filling her face. One article was titled "Who's Really in Charge" and dealt with gangs roving the hallways while teachers looked the other way. The second page had a satirical article on school athletes. Every page had a cartoon. One was unmistakably Principal Kalish, his balding head and widening girth exaggerated by the button-popping shirt he was wearing. He was pictured sitting in his big office chair, feet propped on his desk, a cigarette in one hand, a bottle of Johnnie Walker scotch in the other, a sign on his back wall: Just Say No. Another cartoon showing two PE teachers in a fistfight on the football field was captioned "It's all in how you play the game." "Safety in schools" had students passing a bazooka around the side of a metal detector while a teacher was closely examining a girl's nail file. The last had the school nurse saying, "If it doesn't work, I can always drive you to the abortion clinic," while handing out condoms to students getting off the school bus.

Numb, Eunice sat, convinced she had failed as a parent. Tim sat beside her. She hoped he realized anything he said now would be held against him. How was she ever going to tell Paul about this? What would he do to Tim when he heard?

"We confiscated all his copies. Tim is suspended for three days, and I'm recommending expulsion. He's lucky I don't bring charges against him for that libelous piece of trash!"

"It's freedom of the press," Tim said. "And no more than everyone in the student body already knows about what you keep in your bottom drawer."

Principal Kalish's face turned beet red. "Who else was involved in your little enterprise?"

Tim crossed his arms and slouched. "I refuse to divulge my sources."

"I want *names*!"

The meeting went from bad to worse.

On the way home, Eunice dissolved in tears. "Help me to understand, Tim." *Help me understand, God.* She felt powerless. "Why did you do this?"

"Because I'm sick of games." He glared out the front windshield. "I'm sick of everyone telling me to live one way while they live another. I'm sick of the whole—" he used a vile word—"system."

Eunice blushed. "You don't have to talk that way to get your point across."

"If you think I'm bad, you ought to stand in our school corridor for five minutes. You'll hear a lot worse!"

"You're not supposed to talk like everyone else, Tim. You're a Christian."

"Yeah? Well, what I've seen of Christians lately doesn't make me want to be anything like one."

She pulled into the garage. "Does that include me?"

"You most of all."

Stunned into hurt silence, she could only look at him. He got out of the car and slammed the door. She got out, afraid he might try to leave. What would she do if he did? "We need to talk about all this, Tim."

"I don't want to talk about it. Okay? Go ahead and call Dad. Tell him whatever you want. You think I care? He won't listen anyway. And all you ever do is try and fix everything. You can't! Don't you get it?" He stormed into the house.

She fought the urge to follow him and scream at him for getting her into this mess. What was she going to tell his father? What would the congregation think when they heard about it? A story like this would spread like wildfire with LaVonne and Jessie and Shirl fanning the flames. One of the students would say something to one of the parents who would say something to a friend who'd call another friend until the entire congregation was involved.

Weeping in frustration, Eunice tried to figure out what to do. She couldn't think straight. Maybe a cup of tea would help.

The phone rang as it did countless times during the day. Someone always wanted to talk with her about something, ask her advice, complain, or cry on her shoulder, until she wanted to press her hands over her ears and scream. The answering machine picked up and she heard her own voice. "This is the Hudsons'. We're sorry we can't answer right now. Please leave your name, number, and a short message after the beep. We'll get back to you as soon as we can." So sweet. So calm. So phony.

"Euny, this is Mom."

Eunice clenched and unclenched her hands, took a deep breath, and picked up the phone. "Hi, Mom."

"Screening your calls?"

"I just walked in the door with Tim."

"What's wrong?"

"Nothing." She pressed a hand over her mouth and shut her eyes tightly. Sitting, she rocked back and forth on the chair. *Nothing is wrong. Everything is fine.* How many times had she uttered that lie over the past few years?

"All right," Lois said slowly. "If everything is all right, then there's nothing to stop you and Tim from coming down for a few days, is there?"

What was the use of lying? "After what happened today, I think Paul will ground Tim until he's eighteen and can leave home."

"That bad?"

"Worse than bad. Tim thinks all Christians are hypocrites. Including me. And you know what?" She started to cry. "I'm beginning to think he's right."

"What'd he do? Burn down the church?"

Eunice gave a weak laugh. "Nothing that drastic. He wrote a zine."

"A what?"

"An underground newspaper. He seems to have a talent for satire and expressing teen angst."

"What will Paul do about it?"

She was afraid to think. "Ground him." Lacerate her.

"Tim and I have always gotten along, you know."

"I know." There were only two people in the world Tim seemed to listen to these days: Samuel Mason and his grandmother. She wished it didn't hurt so much that he couldn't trust her anymore.

"I could certainly use his help, Eunice. The house sold this morning. That's what I called to tell you. I've put an offer on a three-bedroom condo. I have a lot of packing and discarding to do. He wouldn't be coming down here for a vacation. I'd put him to work. It would give him something to do and time for us to talk. Sometimes a grandmother can reach in where a mother can't."

"I can't seem to do anything right these days."

"Don't blame yourself for everything, honey. You think about my offer. Talk it over with Paul. If he has qualms, tell him to call me."

Eunice was shaking when she called Paul. "I know, Eunice. I just got off the phone with Don Kalish." She was relieved at the gentle sound of his voice. Maybe he would be reasonable this time. Maybe they could talk things over and try to figure out what they could do to help Tim through this hard time. "Hang on a second," he said. She could hear Paul speak to Reka. "Thanks. I'll get to it as soon as I'm off the phone. Just close the door on the way out, would you? Thanks again. You're a real peach." He came back on the line. "As I was saying . . ." His voice was different. Rippling over dark water.

Nothing was going to change. She stood in the kitchen, body rigid, eyes closed, while he read her the riot act. He told her what the principal had to say about their son. He managed to keep his voice quiet enough that Reka wouldn't hear, but it was a scream of rage in her ear. Everything was her fault. She was a lousy mother. He dredged up every misdeed Tim had committed since he'd been "old enough to know better" and laid the blame for all of it at her feet. He didn't give her a chance to say anything in her own defense or in defense of *her* son.

"I don't want to see his face when I come home this evening. You tell him to stay in his room, or I won't be held responsible for what I say or do to him."

She could hear his other phone line ring. "Hang on, Eunice. We're not done talking."

We?

He put her on hold.

She stood, shell-shocked and wounded. She waited two minutes. Feeling came back—deep, turbulent, rising. She waited another minute before Paul came back on the line. "Now, where was I?"

Did he really expect her to remind him? Was she supposed to take her position as target, hand him the ammunition to reload? He was a trained sniper. He never missed.

"I'm taking Tim to your mother's."

"No, you're not. You can't dump Tim on her and expect Mom to solve your problems. She has enough problems of her own."

"Tim isn't a problem, Paul. He's a person. He's our son."

"Now, look—"

"No. *You* listen. Your mother sold her house. She called a few minutes ago. She knows the situation. She invited me and Tim to come down. She said she could use Tim's help. And I'm taking him."

"You listen to me, Eunice."

"I've listened, Paul. I've listened and listened. One of these days, *you're* going to have to try it." She hung up. How was it possible to love someone so much and dislike him so intensely? The telephone rang again. Ignoring it, she went upstairs. She tapped on Tim's door and walked in. He was sprawled on his bed, his arm flung above his head as he stared morosely at the ceiling.

"I don't feel like talking."

"Get packed. We're going to Grandma's. We're leaving in half an hour."

"How long am I staying?"

"We'll figure that out when we get there."

Eunice drove south on Highway 99, praying with every mile that she was doing the right thing. When her cell phone rang, she turned it off and tossed it into the backseat. Time enough to face the music when she reached North Hollywood.

Tim sat in the passenger seat, earphones on, eyes closed, pretending to be asleep. She didn't presume to know what he was thinking. She tried not to allow her imagination to create scenarios. Her heart was breaking because she knew she needed to relinquish her son into Lois's hands, even knowing that she had not always been successful with her parenting either. If she had, would Paul be so far from the Lord, so blind to his own insensitivity toward others, especially in his own household?

Oh, Father, forgive me for failing this child of Yours. Forgive me for all my mistakes in rearing him. All I have ever wanted is for my son to love You more than anyone or anything else. And now he says he doesn't think he wants to be a Christian.

She gripped the steering wheel tighter.

Lord, Tim sees my submission to his father as weakness and cowardice. Is he right? Have I used submission as a means of avoiding my responsibility? Is Paul right? Am I too permissive and too blind to see what Tim needs? I don't know anymore. I don't know anything except that time is running out. My son is going to be sixteen soon. In two years, he'll be old enough to leave. And then what, Father?

She had never known how to fight Paul's ambition. In the beginning, she had seen his zeal as evidence of his vibrant relationship with Jesus. It was only later that she wondered if he was more interested in proving himself to his father than the Father. Whenever she had tried to draw him out of the tide sweeping him along, he had resisted and lashed out against her. Finally, she had watched him pour his passion and energy and time into building something he said would glorify God. And all the time she watched, she felt less and less peace about his work, less and less peace about him. Sometimes she resented the church because it seemed the very thing destroying her family. She couldn't get away from it. It invaded her life.

It had been so different growing up. She had never felt abandoned by her father. She had never doubted his love. She had seen him at work with his congregation. He had taught with conviction and by example. She had seen his peace, experienced it in his presence. She could not remember a time when he had lost his temper and used his knowledge of God's Word to beat her down, to crush her beneath his heel. She had been able to rest in God's love in those days. But she had been a child with little life experience.

Oh, Daddy, I miss you so much.

I'm here.

She felt goose bumps.

The Grapevine loomed ahead, the long, narrow stretch of freeway going up into the mountains. She took the off-ramp and pulled into a gas station. Tim took off his earphones and looked at her. "Can I have some money so I can get something to eat?"

She gave him enough money to buy sandwiches, chips, and sodas while she pumped gas, checked the oil and water, and washed the windshield. She went in to freshen up. She washed her face and pulled a paper towel from the dispenser.

Tim was swallowing the last of his sandwich when she got back in the car. She unwrapped her sandwich and popped the top of her soda before starting the car.

"You okay, Mom?"

"I'm going to be." She smiled at him. "Everything is going to be all right, Tim."

"Sure, Mom."

"It is. I know it is. God has a plan." *You do, don't You, God?*

When they arrived, Lois came outside to meet them. "I didn't expect you until late this evening."

"Mom's in a hurry to unload me." Tim swung his duffel bag onto his back and headed for the front door.

"There's homemade beef soup on the stove, Tim. Help yourself. I'll put the garlic bread in the oven in a minute." She put her arm around Eunice's waist. "How was the trip?"

"Quiet."

"You didn't bring much."

"I'm going home tomorrow."

"Paul called. I told him the house sold and I could use Tim for a while. He was amenable to the idea."

Eunice smiled wryly. "I'm sure he was."

"I think this is all God's timing, Euny. And His mercy, too. Tim and I have a lot to talk about."

Lois did most of the talking during dinner. "I want you to help me go through all of your grandfather's files, Tim. I'm taking the pictures down and putting them into one album. . . ."

Tim's surly, bored demeanor was gone. He hadn't been in the house ten minutes before he had begun to relax. Eunice watched and listened. When they finished eating, she waved Lois into her seat and cleared the dishes. Tears pricked as she listened to the change in Tim's voice. Lois had always been able to make him laugh. Eunice started the dishwasher. "I'm going to hit the sack," she said.

"The blue bedroom is ready for you, honey. I put fresh towels out on the counter."

"Thanks." She kissed Lois's cheek. Tim turned his face away when she tried to kiss him. Her heart felt as though it would burst with pain. *Oh, Lord, reach into my son and draw out the hurt. Turn him back to You. And me. Please.*

"I hope I'll see you in the morning, Tim."

Eunice didn't sleep well that night. She rose as the sun came up, tiptoed into the spare bedroom where her son was sleeping. He looked like a little boy, all the angst and strain gone as he slept. She brushed a few strands of sandy-blond hair back from his forehead. It was still soft and silky. He was still her baby. He always would be no matter how old he was. "I love you, Timmy. I love you very much." *Enough to let you go.* She leaned down and kissed him softly. He didn't stir. She closed the door quietly behind her.

She showered, dressed, brushed her teeth and hair, packed her few toiletries in her overnight case, and headed downstairs. Lois was in the kitchen, coffee ready. They had sat together at this table many times before. Lois stretched her hands out to her. Eunice took them. "God won't let us down, Euny. Hang on to that."

Eunice squeezed Lois's hands and let go. "I'd better be on my way."

"You should have breakfast first."

"I'm not hungry."

"Coffee, at least."

"I'll stop somewhere along the way."

Lois's eyes were tear-filled. "I'll take good care of him, Euny. I promise."

Eunice nodded. She couldn't trust herself to speak.

As she drove down the hill and headed for the freeway, she started to cry.

My son, Lord, my son, my son . . .

Only He could understand.

CHAPTER 14

STEPHEN WASTED NO TIME in getting to work on his property. With the money he was paid from a conceptual design of an office building in Vacaville, he brought in a crew and jacked up the Rockville building. He drove down to a corner market and hired Mexican day laborers to remove the old foundation stones, chisel off the old mortar, and then wash and stack the stones behind the building. Stephen had them excavate four feet of earth. He made the rebar grate for the basement floor and set up the frame for a block wall.

Once the concrete was poured, two masons set the blocks up to ground level. Stephen laid the old foundation stones himself, setting in lines of black and white stone to create a pattern in the three-foot aboveground base. It was two months before the old store was lowered into place and secured.

Next, he raised the sagging roof two feet, removed and replaced damaged beams, shingled the roof, and reconstructed the false front. He hired an electrical engineer to remove the old wiring and upgrade to surpass code, and a plumbing engineer to remove the archaic pipes. He removed the old water closet for restoration and ordered replicas of antique bathroom tubs, sinks, and fixtures. The back door and main-floor bathroom would have handicap access.

With the foundation finished, the wiring and plumbing redone, he moved into the downstairs and started work on the upstairs apartment. It had been a long time since he'd been on the labor end of a project, but he was enjoying himself despite a smashed thumb, various cuts, bruises, and slivers, and aching muscles when he fell into bed each night.

The town drunk peered in the windows every few days. He had an awkward way of walking, which Stephen figured had more to do with his disability than the amount of alcohol he was drinking. Other citizens of Rockville stopped in to see how the work was progressing. Most thought Stephen was eccentric for wasting so much money on a building in the middle of a run-down town like Rockville. Even the mayor. "I'd move if I could afford to. I've had my house on the market for three years without an offer," he'd told Stephen.

"Times are changing. People are commuting farther and farther to work."

"So I hear. So I've been saying. Why don't you run for mayor?"

Stephen had shaken his head. "I'm not a politician."

"Neither am I."

Stephen had spotted the town drunk across the street and raised his hand in greeting. The man turned his back and pretended to stare in a store window.

"That's Jack Bodene." The mayor shook his head. "Sad case, like a lot of other sad cases in this town. He lives in the trailer park at the end of town. First eyesore people see when they drive into Rockville. He lives on disability."

The next time Jack peered in the front window, Stephen opened the front door. "Come on in and take a look around."

Jack backed off. "Sorry. Didn't mean any harm."

"Everyone else in town has had a look-see. You might as well." He extended his hand and introduced himself. Now that he got a closer look, he realized Jack couldn't be more than thirty.

Edgy, Jack entered. "You're making a pretty big mess."

Stephen laughed. "You could say that."

"I used to do this kind of work." Jack scratched his shaggy beard as he looked around.

"Carpentry?"

"Restored houses."

"I used to do what you're doing. I had a real taste for scotch."

"I can't afford scotch."

"Poison is poison, no matter the cost."

"You don't look the type."

"What type would that be?"

"Loser." It was clear he'd heard the word often.

"Lost my wife. Lost my daughter. Almost lost my business. Hit rock bottom and stayed there for a long time. Went through six months of rehab at a Salvation Army facility. I've been living one day at a time ever since." He set a board on two sawhorses.

"How long has that been?"

"Twelve years." He pushed the plane along the edge of the board, leaning on it deliberately. "It's helped to have friends to keep me accountable." Samuel Mason had been a godsend.

Jack winced. "You're gouging that wood."

Stephen straightened. "Be my guest."

"It's been a long time."

"Can't do worse than I am." He watched Jack closely. Not bad. "How long since you had a job?"

"Year and a half. Didn't finish my last project."

"Why not?"

"Fell. Broke both legs. Spent six months in the hospital. Got addicted to pain medications. Went bankrupt." He made a long smooth run with the plane, and a perfect curl of wood came up. "Then things got really bad."

A drunk with a sense of humor. Stephen liked him. Jack looked like he'd been down and out for too long. He was thin, his hair long and shaggy. He needed a bath, a shave, some clean clothes, a new pair of boots. "Booze won't help you get back on your feet. Take it from someone who knows."

"No, but it helps me forget."

"Forget what?"

Jack gave him a tired, cynical smile. "What are you? A shrink playing weekend warrior?"

"I'm an architect and contractor." Stephen grinned. "It's just been a while since I've done any real work."

"Better stick to your drawing board or you'll waste a lot of good wood."

"I could use a good man."

"Better keep looking." Jack looked around the room again, slowly, sadly. "I'm an alcoholic. Ask anyone in town. I'm not sure I could do it."

Stephen had the feeling Jack was talking about more than carpentry. "You just took your first step toward sobriety, my friend. The bottom line is you can't. My sponsor at rehab taught me something that's stuck with me and taken me through those days when my mouth is dry and I think I'm dying for a drink. 'I can't; God can; I turn my will over to God.'"

"Helps if you believe in God."

"Give Him a try. He'll surprise you every time."

"I don't know. Is that going to be a condition of employment?"

"No. But I'm a Christian, and Jesus is the center of who I am now and who I want to be from here forward. He gives me the strength to get through the day without a drink. So if you take on this project, you'll be hearing a lot about Him while you work."

Jack looked around again. "Beats talking politics."

Stephen chuckled. "What do you say we break for lunch first? I have a couple of subs in the fridge. Usually stock up on Friday before coming back from a job site in Sacramento." He opened the refrigerator, took out a white paper–wrapped sandwich, and handed it to Jack before looking back in the fridge. "I've got sodas, fruit juice, milk, or water. Or strong coffee."

"Coffee." Jack tore the paper off the sandwich and took a big bite.

"Where are you living, Jack?"

He swallowed. "Trailer park." He took another big bite.

Stephen poured coffee into a thermal cup with a lid.

Jack's hands shook as he took it. "You got some plans to this madness?"

"Take a look." Stephen rolled out the blueprints and tacked them down.

Nursing his coffee, Jack looked them over. "You would've saved yourself a lot of money demolishing this place and starting from scratch."

"I know, but I needed the challenge."

"Some challenge. What're you hoping to make of this building? You got a split personality going here. Renovation, restoration, modernization."

"I'm trying to keep the old touches."

"Like the foundation you laid. Nice job, by the way."

"And some of the old fixtures, the style. This floor will be my office and work area; upstairs will be my living area. Basement for game room, guest quarters, whatever. I don't know yet. I'm replacing boards upstairs right now. Come and take a look."

Jack followed, hitching his right leg up each step. He looked at the metal braces holding the roof in place. "Well, that's a modern touch, all right. You planning on leaving it like that?"

"I've been debating the high rounded ceilings, but I've never done that kind of work, and I'm not sure I want to tackle plastering. What do you think of redwood beams?"

"Oh, sure. No problem." He snorted. "If you're related to Rockefeller. Why don't you just plate those pipes in gold? It'd be cheaper and you'd have a whole new look."

"Okay. What do you suggest?"

Jack drank some more coffee, still eyeing the ceiling. "You've raised the roof enough to have an attic. Close it off, put in insulation, add subflooring, and you can have your storage area up there. I can build you a slat frame if you can install it. I can't work on a ladder anymore."

"And the plastering?"

"I know a guy who does first-rate plastering. Crown molding would look good in here. You going to have central air?"

"Not sure."

"It'll cost you a fortune to put into this place. An insulated attic will help with that, and you can wire it for ceiling fans. Otherwise, you're going to bake like a Thanksgiving turkey come summer." He looked around. "What about the rest?"

"Open space. Strictly functional. Over there will be a kitchenette with built-in stove, microwave, double sinks, dishwasher, wall refrigerator-freezer above the counter space, breakfast bar. Bookshelves, entertainment center on that wall."

"You might think about a Murphy bed. It'll keep with your schizophrenic design, and keep your open space open."

"Good idea. When do you want to start work?"

"You're kidding."

"Nope. As a matter of fact, I could use a hand right now."

———— ❧ ————

Paul hung up the phone and sank back in his office chair. It was the ninth complaint in four days about the music Eunice was choosing for Sunday morning worship services. Her recent solo had sent ripples of discomfort and disgust through the congregation. Had she discussed her selection with him, he would have told her to choose something else. Now he was the one fielding complaints and trying to smooth the ruffled feathers and outraged sensibilities of several primary donors to the church.

Even Sheila had remarked about Eunice's choice when she had come for her counseling session. "The whole idea of blood is rather repulsive to me."

The problem was how to tell Eunice. He felt uncomfortable with the idea of telling his wife she was causing trouble for him. Music had always been one of the most important aspects of her life and her part of the ministry.

"Eunice has a beautiful voice, Pastor Paul," Ralph Henson had said the other day. "It's what she's singing that has so many people upset. If we want to appeal to the younger generation, we need to keep the services upbeat." The new associate, John Deerman, didn't agree, but he hadn't been around long enough to get with the program. Paul would have to set him straight on a few things.

Eunice was in the kitchen when he got home, a bowl of tossed green salad on the counter with a carafe of homemade salad dressing. She was taking chicken breasts from a marinade and arranging them on the broiler pan. "How was your day?"

"Busy." He loosened his tie. "Looks good." When she glanced at him, he felt a sharp twinge of guilt. "I'm going to get into sweats." He needed to buy more time before he talked to her about the complaints.

She slid the chicken onto the top rack in the oven. "What's the problem, Paul?" She spoke evenly. Leaning against the counter, she looked into his eyes. Hers were clear, guileless.

She was the problem. "We'll talk about it after I change."

Tossing his suit jacket into the wing chair near the windows, he went into their closet. He shouldn't make such a big deal of this. All he had to do was explain. She'd listen to reason. She always had. Why this uneasy feeling in the pit of his stomach that things would never be the same between them after tonight? All he was going to do was ask her to select music compatible with his seeker-friendly services. She'd understand.

When he saw lit candles on the dining room table, he felt sick. Taking his seat at the head of the table, he prayed, emphasizing their call to draw others to Christ.

"What's bothering you, Paul?"

"Let's eat first." He cut a bite of chicken breast and jammed it into his mouth. He took a sip of ice water and swallowed.

"Is the chicken too dry?"

"No. It's great. As always."

She took a white linen napkin off the table and laid it in her lap. "You have a meeting tonight, don't you?"

"Not until eight."

"I'll be leaving at seven fifteen."

"Where are you going?"

"It's Wednesday."

"So?"

"I've been attending Samuel's Bible study."

Irritated, Paul looked at her across the table. "I thought we had an agreement. People might get the wrong idea about why you're going."

"The people attending the study don't attend our church anymore."

His irritation deepened into anger. "What's that supposed to mean?"

"It's the way things are, Paul." She took a small bite of chicken.

He put down his fork. "What's going on, Eunice? What's with you, anyway?"

She stared at him in surprise. "What do you mean?"

"Why are you really going to Samuel's?"

She searched his eyes. "To study the Bible and spend time with believers who are also friends. And it's the one place I can be myself."

"It couldn't have anything to do with Stephen Decker, could it? He goes to that Bible study, doesn't he?"

Her lips parted. "Not anymore. Why?" She stared at him. "What are you implying?"

"Stay away from him."

She put her fork down. "Stephen stopped attending shortly after

I started. He moved to Rockville. I love *you*, Paul. Surely you don't doubt that."

Her perusal made him nervous. "I don't doubt it." He took another bite of chicken.

"Then what did you mean by what you just said?"

He thought of Sheila and gulped down his bite of chicken. "Never mind. It's not important. Forget it."

"What's really going on, Paul?"

It wasn't like he was having an affair with Rob Atherton's wife. One kiss, that's all that had happened. "Nothing." He drank half a glass of water and could still feel the heat rising up his neck. He concentrated on his dinner. "Let's just leave it alone. Okay?"

"Why is your face all red?"

He put his knife and fork down loudly. "Because I'm mad! All right?"

She flinched, eyes widening.

Why did she have to look at him like that? She knew how to push all his buttons. "Maybe I do doubt your loyalty. Do you have any idea how much trouble you've caused me this week?" Was she doing it on purpose?

She left her meal untouched. Cocking her head, she searched his eyes again. "You might as well tell me. If you don't spit it out soon, it's going to choke you."

"Okay. You offended several very important people with the songs you've selected the last few Sundays."

"By very important people, whom do you mean? Those with money?"

Heat surged into his face again. His heart hammered. Clenching his fists, he glared at her. "Maybe you have the luxury of being impartial, Eunice, but I don't. People get offended. The church bills don't get paid. Everything comes to a screeching halt. Is that what you want?"

"Is everything we do in ministry now based on how much money comes in?"

"Are you trying to pick a fight? Ever since Tim moved in with my mother, you've been sulking."

"Not sulking, Paul. Grieving."

She was pushing again. "I miss him, too, you know. I'm his father." He kept looking at her, staring hard. "Just don't do it again, Eunice. I don't want another day like today."

"I have to follow my conscience, Paul."

He couldn't believe she was defying him. "And I don't? That's what you're saying, isn't it?" She bowed her head. Her silence was answer enough. "I think you need to take a break from the music ministry. Until you're back on an even keel." His appetite was gone. He couldn't even pretend. "Look. I don't want to hurt your feelings, Eunice, but you've betrayed my trust in you. You've set yourself against my ministry."

She folded her napkin and put it back on the table. "You can't please everyone all the time. You have to make choices. *I've* had to make choices."

He shifted in his chair. "A number of people have found the hymns you've chosen *depressing*."

"How could they be depressing? They were about salvation."

"You know what I mean. Why do you have to make this difficult for me?"

"Am I going to have a right to defend myself? Or has some kind of decision already been made? Tell me who and how I offended."

"You chose two hymns the week before last about the blood of Christ. Do you remember?"

"Two out of six."

"And then you sang a solo about the Crucifixion. There are a number of people—including one of our elders, not to mention others—who find the subject . . . less than appealing, for lack of a better word. Do you understand now?"

He regretted his harshness, but she had pressed him. She had changed over the past few months. She used to do anything just to please him. Now, he felt as though they were locked in mortal combat. He longed for the tranquility of the old days. All he had to do was hint, and she would bend. She never questioned him. She never interfered.

"There was a time when you listened to me, Paul."

"I still listen."

Her expression softened. "Then I hope you will take this as it's intended, with love behind it." She took a deep breath. "If our people are not going to hear about Jesus shedding His blood for them in the sermons, they need to hear about it in the music."

For all the quiet sweetness of her voice, the words came like a hard slap in his face. "I'm sorry you think so little of my ministry."

"I think a great deal of *you*," she said gently. "I *love* you."

"Then you might try showing it. Love means loyalty."

"Love also means telling you when you're wrong."

"Maybe you need to remember your place. *I'm* the pastor, not you."

"What is my place, Paul, if not to be honest with my husband?"

He stared at her for a moment. "You're not going to compromise, are you?"

"No. I'm afraid I've compromised too much already."

"Okay, Eunice. Have it your way. LaVonne Lockford will be selecting the music from now on."

Her eyes filled with tears. "Do you think LaVonne cares as much about your ministry as I do?"

"I think you're a little confused about what part you play in my life. You're supposed to be my helpmate. Instead, you've become a hindrance."

"I'm not fighting *you*, Paul."

"Oh yes, you are!"

"There is a battle going on, Paul, but it's spiritual, not physical."

He was shaking. "And you think you're more spiritual than I am? You think you're a better Christian? You know what I think this is all about? I think you've been against me since Tim moved in with my mother. I think this is all about your resentment, you feeling sorry for yourself, and you trying to get back at me for whatever you think I did wrong as a father! Try denying it! Just try it!"

The tears spilled down her cheeks. "How little you really know me."

"Whether you realize it or not, Satan is using you against me." He watched her face go white. Satisfied, he stabbed again. "I'll talk with Ralph in the morning and see if there isn't another area where we can use you."

Her eyes flickered. "Please don't."

"Don't what? Expect you to behave like my wife?"

"Try to *use* me anymore. I think it's best if I step back for a while."

He felt as though she'd punched him. "What am I supposed to tell people?"

"Tell them I'm sick."

"Are you?"

"Yes, Paul. Sick at heart at what I've witnessed in our church."

Paul threw his napkin on top of his half-eaten dinner and shoved his chair back. "I'm going out for a run."

But even after a mile, he couldn't get away from the guilt that chased him.

———— ❧ ————

Samuel finished waxing his DeSoto and decided it was a good day for a drive. It had been a few weeks since Stephen Decker had knocked on his door. Samuel figured it wouldn't do any harm to go to Rockville and see how his new project was coming along. He hadn't been down that way in a month of Sundays. Not since Bjorn Svenson had gone into convalescent care.

Avoiding the freeway, he took a quiet country road. Windows down, he enjoyed the hot breeze over his bare arm. He could smell the hot sand and almond trees ready for harvesting. As he entered Rockville, he couldn't help but wonder why Stephen had decided to pull up stakes in Centerville and move to a town with its best days long gone. He had no trouble finding Stephen's building. In fact, it drew a laugh. Did Stephen know? Or did God have a sense of irony? He parked on the street. As he got out of his car, he heard the high-pitched scream of a saber saw sinking its teeth into wood. The front door was open, the smell of sawdust strong. Someone was hammering below.

A giant carpenter shoved his goggles up. "You looking for someone?" Samuel guessed him at six feet nine.

"Stephen Decker."

"Hey, boss! You got a visitor!"

"Ask what he's selling!" Stephen called.

The giant eyed him. "You a salesman?"

"Nope. My name's Samuel Mason. I'm a friend—"

"Oh, hey! I know who you are." He yanked off his glove and extended his hand. "You're the Bible teacher he's been yapping about. My name's Carl, but everyone calls me Tree House." He hollered to Stephen. "Hey, boss! It's Samuel!"

"Well, show him some hospitality, you oaf! Offer him a soda! Send him down to the basement. Ask him to bring a couple more with him."

"Okay! Okay! Like you're paying me!" Grinning at Samuel, he nodded. "Ice chest is over there. Help yourself. Stairs at the back."

Samuel took out three cans of soda. The stifling heat on the main
floor gave way to the coolness of stone block and cement. Stephen had
his foot up on a box as he leaned over a drawing board, studying plans
with a young man with a ponytail. Straightening, Stephen grinned.
"Samuel! Good to see you." He handed a soda to his company and
popped the lid off the other. "I'd like you to meet Jack Bodene. Jack,
this is Samuel Mason, my Bible study mentor."

They shook hands. "Nice to meet you, Samuel."

"Likewise." The young man had old eyes.

"So what did you think of the place when you drove up?" Stephen
lifted his soda. "Think I'm out of my mind like the rest of the population?"

"Nope."

"Wasting my money and my time?"

"Depends."

"On what?"

"What the Lord wants."

Stephen laughed. "I haven't got a clue on that score. Come on.
I'll show you around." Samuel met Hector Mendoza and Cal Davies
upstairs.

The building was going to be a jewel in the middle of a rock pile,
and smack-dab in the center of town, no less. Nothing happened by
chance. Samuel couldn't help but smile. He had needed a good reminder
that God was sovereign. And here it was. Solid as the Rock of faith
Stephen was still standing on. Thank God. Man plans, but it's God's
will that prevails.

Stephen suggested they all take a break. Tree House, Jack, Hector,
and Cal joined them in the basement. They all sat on folding chairs,
enjoying the coolness of the block walls.

"You know, I've been thinking." Stephen sported a sly grin.

"Look out, *amigos. El hombre* has got another harebrained idea."

"Duck for cover!"

Stephen grinned. "Any chance of getting you to come over to
Rockville once a week and teach a Bible study?"

"I'm too old to be on the road at night."

"Small problem. You can stay over. I'll give you the best room in the
house."

"If he gives you a choice, pick the basement," Tree House said.

Samuel realized Stephen was serious. "Why don't you teach?"

"I've been trying, but these guys have more questions than I have answers."

Samuel looked around at the small gathering of men. It would be nice to step in and start another class, but he felt the Lord nudging him in another direction. "Let's talk about it."

Stephen nodded and let it go.

Samuel stayed another half hour. "I'd better go so these men can get back to work." Stephen walked outside with him and asked him again about leading the Bible study.

"You know, my young friend, the Lord will equip you for whatever job He's given you to do."

"You have years of experience and a lifetime of studying behind you."

"You've got to start sometime, Stephen. This is as good a time as any."

"I miss Wednesday nights. That group was my church family."

"We miss you, too."

"Is everyone still coming?"

"Sally and Charlie are still coming. And Eunice . . ." *Oh.*

Stephen laughed softly. "Don't give me that look, Samuel. It's better if I keep a distance. Abby knew."

"Yes. Abby knew. We both knew. I just forgot."

"Good. Do me a favor and forget again, will you?"

He saw it was more than Eunice keeping Stephen away. "What else is bothering you?"

"Paul is what's bothering me. He's been given enough rope to hang himself."

"What do you mean?"

"Nothing. Never mind." Stephen smiled wryly. "As you can tell, I still have a long way to go before I can learn how to love my enemy."

Samuel hadn't realized Stephen's feelings ran so hot. "I've had my struggles where Paul is concerned."

"Yeah. I guess you have at that."

"Paul isn't the enemy, Stephen. Our battle isn't against flesh and blood."

"I know."

They shook hands at the DeSoto. Samuel got in and cranked the window down. "Pray for him."

"Easier said than done."

"I've been doing it for years. Make it an act of obedience. Which it will be for a while. But I'll tell you something, Stephen. You won't be able to keep hating Paul if you pray for him. God will give you another vision of what Paul can be if he surrenders himself again." He started the car. "Remember, Christ died for us *while* we were yet sinners."

"Paul's going to have a lot to answer for one of these days." Stephen didn't look like he relished the thought.

Samuel felt the gentle nudging again. God had something more for him to say. "You need to know, Stephen. Be ready."

"Ready for what?"

"I don't know that yet. What I do know is one of these days, Paul Hudson is going to need us. When that day comes—and I don't think it's far off—we need to be ready to do whatever Jesus asks of us."

Raising his hand, Samuel pulled away from the curb.

Nothing was by accident. Impulses were often nothing of the sort. The hot wind swirled inside the car, bringing with it the scents of the Central Valley. Peace settled over Samuel as he headed home. Inexplicable, precious peace.

The message God had sent him to give had been received.

Paul listened to the members of the building committee and felt a growing despair and disgust in the pit of his stomach. Everything seemed to be going wrong. Rather than working together, they were all going off on their own pet projects. Gerald Boham had spent a weekend up on Nob Hill in San Francisco and gone to services at Grace Cathedral. Now, he was all hot on the idea of a labyrinth. "We could have it in the new multipurpose room."

"What's it for?" Marvin poured himself another glass of water.

"Well, the idea is for people to walk a spiritual path. There are stations on the labyrinth."

Another snorted in contempt. "You mean like the Stations of the Cross?"

"I didn't see it in a Catholic church."

"But what's the point?" another wanted to know. "Isn't a labyrinth something that brings confusion?"

"No. That's not the idea as I saw it. By the time you get to the end of the thing, you've reached enlightenment."

"Just because you walked along some tiles in a floor?"

"You stop and read instructions every few feet and meditate on whatever it says. Then move on and so on."

"It sounds like New Age religion," Paul said.

"Well, maybe, but aren't we trying to bring in the New Agers? We'd be the ones writing the messages."

"How much would a thing like that cost?" Marvin was always concerned about the bottom line: money. It was his job as church treasurer.

"A couple of thousand, I'd guess. Not that much."

"Not that much?" Marvin snorted. "We're barely scraping by as it is. We need every penny coming in to pay the bills we have now."

Sweat broke out on the back of Paul's neck. "I thought giving was up this month."

Marvin flushed. "It's up. Sure it's up. I'm not saying we don't have enough. It's just that we don't have surplus to spend on new projects."

"So what are you saying?" Gerald's face darkened. "That my idea is stupid?"

"Did I say stupid? Expensive. It'll be expensive."

"Okay," Paul said quickly. "Okay! It's an idea to think about, Gerald. And you're right, Marvin. We need to keep to the budget. Maybe we could put it on the list of things to consider next year." It took a few minutes to settle them down again, and by that time, his stomach was churning. Tempers were running high tonight. No one seemed to agree on anything anymore, other than that a lot needed to be done.

"Maybe you could come up with another one of your bright fund-raising ideas, Gerry," Marvin said in a tone that could have been serious or seriously combative.

"Marvin—" Paul gave him a quelling stare—"we do not need another fund-raiser right now."

"Easter is coming," Gerald said. "Giving is always up at Easter."

"And what if it isn't?" Marvin was always the doomsayer. "We can't wait around until the Christmas pageant to make money, Paul."

"So what's the problem?" Gerald, on the attack. "Seems to me, last meeting, you were telling us we had enough money to sail through the quarter."

"Well, I thought we did. But we had some unexpected expenses."

"What unexpected expenses?" someone asked.

"That guy who fell off the ladder. Tibbitson. Remember him? The medical bills are heavy."

"What about the insurance?"

"I'm working on them. But now Tibbitson is saying he needs physical therapy."

Everyone started talking at once.

Paul was beginning to feel like a fireman trying to stomp out sparks blowing into a field of wheat. When it was clear no one was listening to anyone, he slammed his fist on the table. A shocked silence followed. He tried a soft laugh. "Let's take a breath, shall we? Why don't each of you give me your reports, and I'll go over everything? Right now, let's just calm down and enjoy the rest of the meal."

"Sounds like a good idea to me." Marvin took another bite of dessert. Others agreed.

"So," Paul said, eager to change the subject to more pleasant things, "I heard your daughter received a college acceptance letter, Hal. Congratulations are in order."

"She's not going if I have anything to say about it."

"What do you mean?"

"She's got some quixotic notion about being a missionary. I told her I'll send her to USC, but I'm not about to waste twenty-five thousand dollars a year so she can go to some no-name Christian college to prepare for a job that'll pay less than a postal worker. Not on your life!"

Paul had a splitting headache by the time the meeting was over. On the way out to the parking lot, the men were talking about their wives attending a candle party that evening.

"Aromatherapy is the new rage. Kristin has been raking in the money ever since she became a rep."

"Yeah, she's got my wife burning those candles all the time. I can tell what mood she's in when I walk in the door. If it's lavender, she's trying to calm down about something."

"And if it's cinnamon, romance is in the air, eh, Don?"

They all laughed.

"Is Eunice feeling any better, Paul?"

"A little. She's taking it easy."

"Jessie said she looks like she's lost weight." Gerald talked about Jessie's job as the high school nurse and how many girls were coming in looking like starving Ethiopians because they wanted to look like some movie star.

Larry slapped Paul on the back. "I'll have Kristin bring a couple of candles over. Eunice will be feeling better in no time. Kristin's got some herbal blends that are guaranteed to enhance good health."

Paul didn't want to think about what Eunice might say if Kristin came over with aromatherapy candles. "She's been doing a lot of meditating on Scripture since giving up the choir."

"Oh, well, that's good. Kristin meditates, too. She's got one room all set up for it. She bought a fountain last week. She says the sound of running water is soothing to the soul. She lights up a whole table of candles, turns off the lights, and listens to Yanni. She says it helps her feel centered. Maybe that's what Eunice needs. Centering."

Centering on what? Paul wanted to ask, but didn't. Gerald might be offended. Paul bid them all good night and headed for his new Lexus parked on the far side of the lot. He could hear them talking as they headed for their cars.

"My wife has a dozen of those Celtic CDs. She's playing them all the time."

"That's better than the rock music my kid's playing. . . ."

Paul clicked the remote, opened the car door, and slid in. Letting out his breath, he popped open the glove compartment and took out the medicine his doctor had prescribed. His stomach was killing him again. His cell phone vibrated in his jacket pocket. He took it out and tossed it onto the leather passenger seat, where it buzzed like a rattlesnake. Stomach churning, he gripped the steering wheel until it stopped. Then he picked it up and pressed a button. He recognized the number. *Sheila.* The dash clock said 10:18.

Temptation gripped him. He could feel it sinking its fangs into him and sending hot currents through his body. The fangs turned to teeth gnawing at him.

He could call Eunice and tell her there was an emergency.

Or he could ignore the call.

Rob Atherton was on another one of his business trips. He knew because Sheila had mentioned it on Sunday morning when she gave

Eunice a hug. "You should come over for a swim, Eunice. I get lonely all by myself. Rob's going to be gone all this week. He's going to Florida again." Sheila kissed Eunice's cheek. "You're so pale, honey. A little sun would do you a world of good." She had smiled at him as though he was an afterthought. "Oh, and you're invited, too, of course, Pastor Paul." He'd laughed about it, made the expected remark about being the poor forgotten husband. He couldn't look at Eunice, afraid she might see guilt in his eyes.

He'd had only one lapse. That's all. What Eunice didn't know wouldn't hurt her. And he wouldn't let it happen again. Gripping the wheel tightly with one hand, he started the car.

The house was quiet when he entered. He saw the light was on in the family room. Eunice was sitting with her head back, her eyes closed, her Bible open in her lap. For a second, he had the sensation of déjà vu, only it was his mother. Maybe it was just that Eunice had so much in common with her. She was always reading her Bible, more now than she had when they were first married. She opened her eyes and found him looking at her.

"You look tired. Was it a rough meeting?"

A fiasco! He felt as though he had been in a mud pit with professional wrestlers. But he wasn't about to say any of that to Eunice. "It went well. We got some work done." He had managed to rein them in again and keep things under control.

She closed her Bible and put it on the side table. "Do you want to talk?"

"Not really." The last thing he wanted was a heart-to-heart talk with his wife. Most of what was going on inside him lately didn't bear discussing with his wife. He was falling in love with Sheila Atherton and was afraid there was nothing he could do about it. "I think I'll hit the sack. I'm beat."

"I've been praying for you, Paul."

He raised his head.

She smiled self-consciously. "Not that I haven't always prayed for you." Her smile waned as she searched his eyes. "I just had the feeling you needed extra prayer tonight."

He was glad of the dim light that hid his blush. "Any particular reason?"

"I don't know. Can you think of anything?"

He thought of Sheila again and shame filled him. "Nope. Everything's fine." He gave her a weak smile. His conscience writhed. "But don't stop."

She got up and turned out the lamp on the side table. The streetlight illumined the family room enough that he could see her come toward him. She touched his face tenderly. "I love you."

"I know." His throat closed. "I love you, too." He did. Just not as much as he once had. He pulled her close and heard her soft intake of breath. "I know it doesn't seem that way at times, but I do." *I want to love her, God.* Lifting her chin, he kissed her. Gently. At first. Until he thought of Sheila.

He thought everything was fine until he awakened later and found himself alone in bed, the sheets cool where Eunice should have been. A line of light shone beneath the door to the master bathroom. He rose. He was about to tap when he heard Eunice's muffled crying. Not soft, but anguished sobs stifled against something soft. A towel? An image of Christ washing His disciples' feet came to him. Paul shut his eyes for a long moment and went back to bed, careful not to make a sound.

She came back to bed an hour later and curled beneath the covers away from him. He could feel her warmth.

Paul lay awake in the dark. He tried to pray, but his mind kept wandering. When had his life gotten so out of control? Why couldn't he seem to manage anything anymore?

It was probably just something he ate at the club. Maybe he was getting the flu. He needed to stop worrying all the time. God said he wasn't supposed to worry. It was a sin. Everything was under control.

Paul drifted, his mind wandering back and forth like waves on a shoreline. He was swimming in the ocean and the water was cold. No matter how hard he swam, the current kept pushing him closer to the rocks. He could see the violent splash, the white foam. Helpless against the power of the sea, he hit the rocks. He couldn't get a handhold. Each time he grabbed on to something, the current yanked him away. He was swept into a forest of seaweed. His legs became entangled, and still the waves beat him, pushing him, pounding him, covering him with a crushing weight. He couldn't get to the surface for air. He fought, clawing to be free, the light shining through the thick, slippery fronds of seaweed above him. Air! He needed air! His lungs were bursting, his heart exploding! A hand reached down to him, but he was more afraid of taking it than drowning.

He awakened abruptly. It was still dark and his heart was pounding. He reached out and found Eunice gone. The clock said 5:30. She was up, probably making the morning coffee.

Shaking, gulping, he tried to relax. He tried to tell himself it was just a nightmare. It didn't mean anything.

But he couldn't get away from the feeling that God had been trying to tell him something for a long time, and he couldn't hear what He was saying.

CHAPTER 15

STEPHEN WAS WORKING late on the conceptual design for an office building in Roseville when he heard a soft tap at the front door. It was eleven. Maybe it was Jack. Those first months of sobriety were rough. Stephen left his stool and headed for the door.

The front windows were covered with wooden venetian blinds now, so people couldn't peer in anymore. And the beveled glass of the new front door gave some semblance of privacy and elegance. He could see through the glass that it was someone smaller than Jack.

Turning the dead bolt, he opened the door and found a stranger wearing a multicolored knit cap, an Army jacket, ragged, dirty jeans, and black military boots. Dumped on the sidewalk was a grimy canvas bag. The stranger didn't say a word, but stood head down, shoulders slumped.

Though he couldn't see a face, Stephen had a gut feeling. "Brittany?"

"I didn't know where else to go."

"Oh, God! Oh, Jesus, thank You." He pulled her into his arms and felt her stiffen. "I've been worried sick about you." She was shaking, probably from the cold night air. He loosened his hold. "Come on inside." He picked up her bag. It weighed no more than a couple of pounds.

"Rockville," she said dryly as she walked into his workroom and looked around. "I thought maybe you moved back to Sacramento."

He set her canvas bag on the leather couch. "You went to Centerville?"

"Yeah. Then I called Mom." She wouldn't look at him. "Her husband answered, said he thought you'd moved to Rocklin or Rock Hill or Rockville. He couldn't remember for sure. He said to try the yellow pages under Decker Construction."

He was getting a piece of the picture. "You didn't talk to your mother?"

"Jeff said she wasn't home." She shrugged. "No big deal."

If Kathryn had gotten the message, she hadn't passed the information along to him. He heard Brittany's stomach growl. "Come on upstairs. You can take a look around while I fix you some dinner." He walked ahead of her, but when he glanced back, she kept her head down. He left the lamp on and pushed the dimmer for the stairs. The strip of carpet up the center muffled the sound of her military boots. Were they steel toed?

"Can I get you something to drink?"

"Yeah." She gave a grim laugh. "How about a martini?"

It was more a wisecrack than a question. He wasn't sure of her motivation, and decided to be straight with her. "I don't drink anymore, Brittany, and I don't keep booze in the house."

"Afraid you might fall off the wagon?"

Again, the edge. "I take things one day at a time, and I don't pretend it's not an ongoing battle."

She lifted her head enough for him to see her black eye, cut and swollen lip, and scraped cheek. Everything inside him went wild. He wanted to pull his little girl onto his lap and rock her and ask her who'd hurt her, but he didn't move. He didn't say anything either. Her posture, her silence, her clenched fists told him to keep away, to rein in the questions pounding through his head.

Opening the refrigerator, he ducked his head so she wouldn't see his face. "I've got milk, orange juice, club soda." He was glad he had grilled two rib-eye steaks earlier. One was left. He had a bag of tossed salad, plenty of dressing. It'd take two minutes to microwave a potato, dab on some butter and sour cream.

"Milk," she said. "Please."

He poured a tall glass. Her fingers trembled as they brushed his. She didn't meet his eyes as she thanked him. He returned to the kitchenette, washed a potato, punched holes in it, and put it in the microwave. As the machine hummed, he dumped a portion of salad into a bowl and set it on the small table overlooking Main Street. He put out silverware, a napkin, blue cheese dressing, salt and pepper. The microwave pinged. He forked the steak onto the plate and set the timer again. Brittany had finished the milk and was holding the glass in both hands. "Dinner'll be ready in thirty seconds, honey. Take a seat."

She moved as though she were so tired she could hardly stand. Slouching into a chair, she put the empty glass on the table. He set the carton of milk on the table. "You've only got one place set," she said.

"I ate earlier." He stood near the microwave. "How'd you get here? Bus?"

"I hitched a ride."

He wished he hadn't asked. "Did your ride give you the black eye and split lip?"

"No." She didn't elaborate.

The microwave pinged again. Swallowing down a hundred other questions, he took the plate out and set it in front of her. She lifted her head. The look in her hazel eyes brought a memory surging through his mind: Brittany, age three, standing in the living room between him and Kathryn as they had a screaming fight. His little daughter staring in fear and confusion, tears streaming down her white face as she yowled like a wounded animal. He shut his eyes tightly.

"Can I wash my hands first, Daddy?"

He looked at her again, grief rising up and bringing a heavy burden of guilt with it. "Sure. Sorry I didn't think of it." His voice was gruff. "The bathroom's back there, through that door. Take your time."

His chest heaved as soon as the door was closed. Turning away, he braced himself on the kitchen counter. *How much of what's happened to her is because of my sins, God?* Shaking himself, he turned on the tap and rinsed his face in cold water. Brittany was here, alive, safe. For the time being, at least. He needed to keep his head or she might run again.

When she came out of the bathroom, her hair was wet. It was short-cropped, bleached white-blonde with dark roots, and smelled of his bar soap. He noticed the tattoo on the back of her hand as she set the knit cap on the table beside her place setting. Her ears and nose were pierced with small silver hoops. She picked up her fork and knife, hesitated, and rested her wrists on the edge of the table. "Are you going to stare at me the whole time?"

"It's just so good to see you." He stood. "I'm going to put some things away downstairs. I'll be back up in a few minutes."

He flicked the lamp on as he settled onto his work stool. He tried to check over his work, but couldn't concentrate. He put his notes into a file cabinet and slid the drawer closed. Turning the goosenecked lamp off, he headed back upstairs.

Brittany was still sitting at the table. She was asleep, her head resting on her crossed arms, the empty plate pushed away. She'd eaten everything, even the skin of the potato. Stephen stood beside her, crying silently as he lightly touched her hair. It was still baby fine. What had happened to her over the last six months while she lived on the streets or wherever she'd been all this time? How had she managed to survive? Did he really want to know?

As he leaned down to lift her, she struggled and made a sound that broke his heart. "It's okay, honey. It's Daddy." Brittany relaxed as he carried her. He gently laid her on his bed, removed her camouflage jacket and military boots. Her socks had holes and bloodstains. He removed them and brought a pan of warm water. He washed her feet tenderly. Then he covered her with his blanket, leaned down, and kissed her forehead. "Sleep well, honey. You're safe."

It was after midnight, but he called Kathryn anyway. If he were in her shoes, he'd want to hear Brittany was safe, no matter what the time. She answered on the fourth ring, her voice bleary.

"Sorry to wake you, Kathryn."

"I wasn't asleep. If it's more bad news, I don't want to hear it."

He knew it was booze and not sleep that made her sound befuddled. "It's good news, Kat. Brittany is here. She's safe."

She started to cry. "Thank God," she sobbed. "I wanna come see her. I wanna see my baby."

That was the last thing Kathryn should do. "She's asleep. Worn-out. Get a good night's sleep, Kat, and come tomorrow."

"Tomorrow I have to go to my lawyer."

"Your lawyer?"

"Divorce lawyer. Tell Brittany I'm divorcing Jeff. She'll be happy about that."

Was she casting blame again? He was in no position to judge.

"Jeff's in Soho with his new girlfriend. Probably taking her to a Broadway play."

"Ouch," he whispered.

"Yeah." She cried again. "You could say that."

"Are you going to be okay tonight?"

"What do you care? What does anyone care?"

He found he did care, but knew telling her would do no good. He didn't want to probe her pain or hypothesize. Instead, he held the telephone and prayed for her silently.

"You still there, Stephen?"

"Yeah. I'm here." He heard the clink of a bottle against glass.

"You're the one who started me drinking. Did you know that?"

It wasn't true, but he wasn't going to argue with her.

"Just makes things worse," she added.

"Yeah. I know."

"I wish I knew what went wrong. And when it went wrong. I keep thinking. I keep looking back. Way back. My life's been a mess so long I can't even remember if it was ever right. Know what I mean?"

"I know." She needed Jesus, but this wasn't the time to tell her.

"Brittany's there?"

"Asleep. Safe." Battered and bruised, wounded deeper than either of her parents could fix. They had done enough "fixing" over the years.

"She might not wanna see me."

He wanted to ask why not, but didn't.

"Ask her. Okay? I don't wanna drive up and have her run away again. You know?"

"Yeah, Kat. I know."

"Gotta go," she said in a little-girl-hurting voice. She fumbled the telephone as she hung up.

It was the first time Stephen had grieved for his ex-wife rather than over her.

———— ❧ ————

Eunice was sitting in her mother-in-law's living room having tea when Timothy walked in the front door with his friends. He looked different, wonderfully different.

"Hey, Mom!" He came to her and embraced her tightly. "You look great!"

She put her cup down, her throat closing. "So do you."

He was tan, eyes bright and clear. He seemed to have grown an inch in the last month and was filling out with muscle. His friends were all talking at once, greeting Lois. They were clearly at home in the condo.

One of the boys punched Tim on the shoulder. "Whoa, dude. You never told us your mother was such a fox!"

Eunice's face went hot.

Another leaned close to Tim and said in a stage whisper all could hear, "Why don't you ask her to come along and be a chaperone?"

"Enough, you guys. You're embarrassing her." Tim laughed easily. "Don't let them bother you. They're just kidding."

"All right, boys and girls." Lois stood. "Into the kitchen. I made cookies this morning." They all followed like oversize chicks after a tiny mother hen.

Eunice touched Tim's hair. It was down to his shoulders. He shrugged as he searched her eyes. "I know," he drawled. "Dad would have my head if he could see it."

"Jesus had long hair."

He grinned. "Yeah. As far as we know, anyway." He sat beside her. "Did you come down to check on me?"

"I miss you." She couldn't say more. She was proud of the young man he was becoming, thankful and grieving that it was her mother-in-law's wisdom and love that was guiding him toward Christ.

"I'm heading for Mexico day after tomorrow."

"So your grandmother told me. Building houses, she said."

"We've got a crew together and a carpenter who's willing to tell us what to do and how to do it. Young guy who can take the heat." He detailed the venture, the preparatory work, the early-morning meetings, the goal to serve the poor and bring the light of the gospel message.

She could hear the others talking and laughing in the kitchen. "Are they going?"

"Every one of them."

He had good friends to lift him up instead of pull him down.

"Do you think you'll come home after your trip to Mexico?"

His eyes shadowed. "I don't think so, Mom."

"Not even to visit?"

"I think I'd better stay here."

Her heart sank. She looked down so he wouldn't see the tears coming. She knew he was right, but it hurt all the same. She wanted to say Paul had asked him to come home, but he hadn't. He told others he missed Tim. He told her, too. But he never talked about changing the arrangement with Lois. He talked to Tim on the phone, but not often and not long. He had too many other people on his mind. But she was Tim's mother, after all. She had nursed him. She had helped him take his first steps, taught him his first prayer, taught him how to ride a bike. Not once in those early years had she thought there would come a day when she would willingly give up her son to someone else to raise, even Lois whom she loved like her own mother.

"I pray for Dad all the time, Mom." She saw the hurt in his eyes, still alive, fresh whenever she came to see him and his father stayed home. Why should he want to come back to Centerville? "And you."

"I pray for him, too, honey." *Constantly.* "He loves you, Tim."

"As long as he can have it his way."

He didn't say it with any bitterness. It was just a simple, painful, hard-learned fact. She was the slow learner.

The others laughed loudly in the kitchen. Tim turned toward the sound, leaned toward it. She relinquished him again. "Why don't we join them?" Though she longed for time alone with Tim, life intruded.

She sat on a stool at the breakfast bar and listened to the rush of conversation. Four boys and two girls excited about serving the Lord. It was heaven to hear. She soaked it in like dry earth after a long drought.

Lois smiled at her and poured more tea. "You look a little more relaxed than when you arrived."

"It's good to be here."

"Sometimes the condo feels a little small."

"I used to dream my home would be like this. Packed from floor to ceiling with children."

A strange look came into her mother-in-law's eyes. "You can stay as long as you like, Euny. You're always welcome. Anytime."

Lois didn't ask questions or press her regarding her feelings. Eunice was thankful. She didn't really know what she was feeling. There was no foundation for the depression that hung like a dark cloud over her, or the feeling that her life was falling apart around her and she didn't know why. She didn't know the what or the how, either.

Sunday morning, she attended the neighborhood church. Tim sat on one side of her, Lois on the other. She was close to tears during the entire service. The aging pastor reminded her of her father: gray haired, thin, eyes bright and alive with passion for Christ, every word out of his mouth concerning the gospel, love for his flock spilling over. Paul would've hated the music. The congregants sang with thanksgiving about Christ's blood. They sang about Jesus' suffering and death on the cross with sorrow and His resurrection with joyful abandon. They didn't care if the hymns were politically incorrect and might offend someone visiting. *Let it be heard! Let us rejoice in Christ our Savior! Sing to the Lord a new song of celebration!*

When the service was over, they filed down the aisle. The pastor was at the door to greet them before they left. His handshake was firm, his eyes kind. No need for introductions. "It's good to see you again, Eunice." He didn't mention Paul Hudson. She thanked God for that. She had her own identity here. She was a sister in Christ. No more, no less.

They went out to lunch at a hamburger joint owned by Christians. Everyone knew Lois and Tim, and they were pleased to meet her. Eunice wasn't hungry. For all the bad reputation of Los Angeles, she felt more at home here today than she had felt anywhere in years. Even in her own house with her own husband.

What's wrong with me, God? What's happening?

"You okay, Mom?"

"I'm fine, honey. Just fine." When had she become such a good liar?

They talked for more than an hour over lunch. Lois said they would come up for a visit at the end of summer. Tim had a summer job lined up, but he would be able to take a little time off by then.

Friends came by the booth. Tim leaned over and kissed her. "I love you, Mom. Don't stay away too long." And then he was gone, the chick flying from the nest and joining the flock heading south to the beach.

Lois and Eunice walked out to the car. "Are you angry with me, Euny?"

"No, Mom. Don't ever think that." She felt left out, left behind, alone, and lonely. But how did she dare admit to those feelings without sounding as though she were wallowing in self-pity? "I'm thankful,

Mom, but it hurts." Tim was where he belonged. He was growing in Christ here. In Centerville, he had been under a microscope. All eyes on him, and none too kindly. Especially the eyes of his own father.

As soon as they arrived at the condo, Eunice packed her things and set the overnight case by the front door. Lois looked worried. "Something's wrong. What is it?"

"I wish I knew." Then again, maybe she didn't.

"Why don't you stay for another day, Euny? We haven't really had a chance to talk."

"I can't."

"Can't . . . or won't?"

"Can't."

If she stayed one more day, she might never go home at all.

Samuel rose slowly at the sound of the doorbell. He wasn't eager to talk with the Realtor, but knew he needed to think over all his options. Selling the house was one of them. He opened the door and faced an attractive young woman wearing a yellow spring dress that reminded him of something Abby had worn years ago. Swallowing the lump in his throat, he looked past her and saw the car parked in front of the house. A Cadillac. Apparently Mrs. Lydikson was a successful Realtor.

"May I come in, Mr. Mason?"

"Oh. I'm sorry." He unlatched the screen and opened the door. He had called her, after all. The least he could do was let her look around and give him a ballpark figure of what his little bungalow was worth. "Would you like some coffee, Mrs. Lydikson?"

"You needn't go to any trouble."

"It's already made."

"Then, yes." She smiled. "That would be nice."

He ushered her into the kitchen. "Have a seat."

She looked out the windows. "You have a lovely backyard, Mr. Mason. And a large lot."

"Abby and I bought this place right after the war." He set a cup and saucer on the table and poured. "Cream or sugar?"

"Black, thanks."

A businesswoman. Abby had always poured in a dollop of cream and two spoonfuls of sugar. He took a seat and rested his hands on the Formica table.

Mrs. Lydikson lifted her cup. Her brows rose slightly. "This is great coffee."

"My wife taught me how to make it."

"Will she be joining us?"

"She passed away several years ago."

"Oh." She put her cup down. "I'm so sorry."

"You had no way of knowing." He was having second thoughts about selling. Every nook and cranny of this house reminded him of Abby.

Mrs. Lydikson seemed to read his mind. "Are you sure you want to sell, Mr. Mason? I mean, when we talked, you seemed to have made up your mind."

"I'm checking over my options. Selling my home is one of them."

"It's a hot market."

"So I've heard." Several of his neighbors had sold and moved. One had gone to Nebraska to live close to his daughter. Another couple had moved into a pricey retirement community that wouldn't allow anyone under fifty-five to move in and had rules about yards, cars, and guests. Not to mention the homeowners' association dues. But the couple liked golf, and they would have easy access to a course as long as they had strength to climb in a cart and swing a club.

Samuel wasn't interested in golf. "Why don't you look around the house? Tell me what you think."

"All right." She set her cup down and rose.

Samuel stayed at the kitchen table, staring out at his backyard. Abby had helped him put in the red Blaze climbing roses that were spilling over the back fence. She'd picked out the crepe myrtle and the Washington thorn tree. The last time he'd mowed the lawn, he'd been so tired he couldn't get out of bed the next day. And there didn't seem to be any teenagers around anymore who were willing to make a few dollars to mow a lawn and do a little weeding. They wouldn't even talk to him when he told them what he could afford. He had a nice little pension and Social Security, but it didn't stretch far enough to pay for weekly services like gardening and housekeeping.

Still, he always looked forward to Wednesday evening Bible study. He loved the people who came. He loved their eagerness to learn the Word. He loved the way they had melded together like a family. And he enjoyed being spoiled by Charlie and Sally Wentworth, who had gotten into the habit of bringing him a nice hot meal. Whatever the diner special was— meat loaf, roast beef, fried chicken. It was the best meal he had all week, except for Sunday dinner at Millie Bruester's. The rest of the time, he lived off TV dinners. Sometimes all he felt like eating was a bowl of cereal.

The Bible study was what worried him most. If he sold his home, would the group disband? Would their zeal diminish? Half of those attending were fairly new Christians. The other half had been sitting in church pews for years, but they didn't know anything about the Bible. They were all like his children. He felt a paternal affection for each and every one of them.

He had to remind himself repeatedly that God loved each of them even more than he did, and God would make certain that the work He had started in them would be completed. Samuel wasn't the Holy Spirit. He wasn't irreplaceable.

But sometimes it was nice to think he would be missed.

He had been praying about his situation for months, and the answer seemed to be to sell and move. But it was hard to pull up roots that had sunk so deep. He was eyebrow deep in good memories here.

Mrs. Lydikson returned from her tour of the house. "Do you mind if I go outside?"

"Please. Be my guest."

He watched her walk to the edge of the patio and look around. She looked back at the house. Checking on the condition of the roof, most likely. He saw her smile and give a slight nod before she walked briskly to the back door. "You have a lovely home, Mr. Mason. It's a real charmer."

"Thank you."

She had come prepared with comps, and laid out several other houses that were on the market, in escrow, or had sold. When she told him what the house was worth, he couldn't believe it. "*That* much?"

She laughed. "Yes, sir."

"It's just a three-bedroom bungalow."

"A very charming, beautifully maintained American bungalow in an established neighborhood in a small town with good schools."

"Abby and I bought this place for forty-eight hundred dollars." That had seemed like a fortune to them at the time, a mortgage that would keep them working hard for years to come.

Her eyes were sparkling. "Things have gone up a little since that time."

"I guess so." How did young couples manage to survive when they had to pay so much for a house? If he sold, he would have enough money to live at the Vine Hill Residential Apartments until he was over a hundred. Of course, the money wouldn't go that far if he ended up in a convalescent hospital. Always a possibility when you reached his age.

Poor old King Solomon knew what he was talking about in Ecclesiastes. Samuel's limbs trembled after an hour of working in the garden. Unlike Solomon, he had the blessing of modern conveniences. He could chew with dentures. He could see with bifocals. He could hear with his hearing aid, provided he remembered to have the pharmacist replace the battery. He had a cane, but one of these days in the not-too-distant future, he'd be needing a walker.

As for sleeping, he hadn't made it through a night in a month of Sundays. If chirping crickets didn't awaken him, his bladder did, and the bird brigades started their wars at dawn. Lack of nighttime sleep wasn't a problem. He slept like a baby every afternoon in his recliner, lulled by the drone of his television. He was white haired and withering, toothless and dragging along slower every day. He'd gotten to the point where he sat on the porch watching for the mailman so that he wouldn't have to make the trip down the steps. It might be only three feet down, but at his age, he might as well fall out a three-story window.

No one but the Lord knew what the future held. All Samuel wanted was to be a good steward with the resources God had given him, and he prayed fervently that his body wouldn't outlive his mind.

Mrs. Lydikson talked about the market, how she would get the word out, what advertising she would do. "I've learned from experience that few buyers come from newspaper advertisements." A sign would be out front with leaflets. "If people come to your door, don't let them in unless they're accompanied by a Realtor." She felt it was most productive to spread word through the Realtors in the area. They met every week, and she would push his house every time. "We can film the inside and outside of the house for our website. People can log on and take a virtual tour."

The world was changing too fast for him. Mrs. Lydikson was full of enthusiasm and energy. He was worn-out just listening to her. She had no doubt his home would sell. In fact, she'd be surprised if it lasted on the market for longer than a week.

A week? Panic gripped him. What would he do if his home sold in a week? Was there an apartment available at Vine Hill? What was he going to do with all his furniture and knickknacks and pictures? What about the lawn chairs and glass table with the umbrella?

Mrs. Lydikson kept talking. It would help if he had a pest inspector come and do a report. "That would save time and trouble, and it gives a buyer a feeling of confidence." She asked if he thought the house might have termites. He said no. The house was built with northern California redwood. And he'd always checked over the house for dry rot. Then she told him about disclosure statements. People didn't trust anyone anymore.

He couldn't think of anything that was wrong with the house other than that the appliances were all old. "Not as old as I am, but they've been around for a long time. Except for the microwave."

Having dispensed and received all the information she needed, she thanked him for the coffee and rose to leave. "I'll have the paperwork ready for you to sign tomorrow." That gave him twenty-four hours to think about it some more. He had her business card. He could call her if he changed his mind. He knew he wouldn't. If he did, it would only mean a short delay before the inevitable.

As soon as she left, Samuel sank into his easy chair, exhausted and depressed.

He awakened to the doorbell. Surprised, he realized it was dusk and he had slept three solid hours. Charlie and Sally Wentworth were at the door with a boxed dinner. "Are you okay, Sam?"

He felt rumpled and ancient. "I will be as soon as I freshen up. Come on in and make yourselves to home."

"We'll wait for you in the kitchen."

Sally had washed the cups and saucers and was putting them away when he came in. She'd set out silverware and a napkin and put the dinner they'd brought on one of Abby's favorite Blue Willow plates. Ham, mashed potatoes, and peas, with peach cobbler for dessert. "You two spoil me."

Sally grinned. "It's entirely our pleasure. Take a load off your feet." She poured him a cup of coffee. "It's decaf. New brand. Customers like it."

She and Charlie kept up a running commentary of Centerville residents. They never said a bad word about anyone, and Samuel soaked up the news. When he finished the sumptuous supper, he thanked them and rose to clear his dishes. "Sit. Sit." Sally picked up his plate. "It'll take me thirty seconds to wash, dry, and put it away."

He told them about Mrs. Lydikson.

Charlie folded his hands on the table. "Well, I can't say I'm surprised. That's a lot of yard to keep up out there, Samuel. I couldn't do it, and I'm thirty years younger than you."

"What I'm most concerned about is the Bible study." He looked between Sally and Charlie. "I don't want to see it end."

Charlie shrugged. "No reason it has to."

"Who's going to teach it, Charlie? You?"

"Not me! You're not saying you're going to leave the area, Samuel. Are you?"

"I've got an application in at Vine Hill." One lady was going to be moving into the convalescent hospital within the month. And they never knew from one week to the next if someone else might die and leave an apartment available.

"Well, Monday nights, we're closed. What do you say we switch the class to that night and move the study to the diner?"

Sally laughed. "You're a genius, honey! Why didn't I think of it? If we offered dessert, we could really pack them in. Thirty instead of twelve. Are you giving up your driver's license, Samuel?"

"I hadn't thought about it."

"Well, if you do, Charlie can pick you up and take you home afterward."

Charlie was watching closely. "You okay with this, Samuel? It was just a thought. Don't let Sally go over you like a Mack truck."

Samuel felt good, real good. "Sounds fine to me. For the time being. But I'm not going to live forever, you know." One of these days he was going to leave this tired, worn-out body and go to be with the Lord and Abby.

"Yeah," Charlie said, "but let's cross that bridge when we come to it, shall we?"

Everyone at the Bible study thought the idea of moving the study group to the diner on Monday nights was a good one. "I know four people who have been wanting to come to the study, but knew there wasn't enough room."

"So it's settled. We can give it a dry run next week, if you'd like."

Everyone was gung ho. "When the house sells, we'll help you pack and move, Samuel." Everyone agreed to that as well.

When the For Sale sign was posted on the white picket fence out front, Samuel sat in his recliner and cried. He dozed after a while and dreamed of Abby as he often did. "So what do you say about all this, Abby?"

"I say it's about time, you old coot." She was needling him as always, her blue eyes as alive as they'd ever been.

"Well, I wasn't sure. It's a big decision, you know."

"You're up to it. Who knows what the Lord will do, Samuel? You've got time to serve yet, you know."

In his dreams, he could still talk with Abby in the garden. He could sip her homemade lemonade and hold her hand or watch her bustle about the kitchen and hear her laugh. In his dreams, he took long walks with her. Once they had flown high on wings like eagles. In his dreams, his body didn't hold him down. There was no such thing as gravity. Anything was possible. Sometimes he even had a glimpse, the faintest glimmer, of heaven.

"Where are you going?"

"You know where."

"I want to come along."

"Not yet, Samuel. Thy will, not mine, be done. Remember?"

"But, Abby . . ."

"All in God's time, my love."

"Abby!"

It was the awakening that always brought back his frailty. And sorrow with it.

---— ❦ —---

Eunice saw the sign for Rockville and thought of Stephen Decker. How long had it been since she'd seen him? It was even longer since they'd talked. She debated stopping by to see how he was doing. Samuel had told the Bible study group that Stephen was leading his own group now. That pleased her very much. She had seen him grow as a Christian over the years. It was a pity he and Paul weren't still friends. Considering the character assassination Paul had allowed, she doubted they could ever be friends again.

The exit came up and she pulled off the highway. Paul wouldn't miss her. He always played golf with one of the board members after Sunday services. Unless he had another call for emergency counseling. That had happened more often lately. Even though VNLC now had two psychologists on staff, Paul had a hard time letting go of anything.

Rockville was a quaint little town with a wide main street, high-false-front, Western-style buildings, tree-lined streets. She had no difficulty finding Stephen Decker's place. She'd looked up his address once, but changed her mind about stopping by then.

The front door was wide open. Her heart quickened when she saw Stephen. She hadn't expected that, and debated turning around, getting back in her car, and driving away before he noticed her. Instead, she stood rooted, her heart in her throat. He was at a table, several books spread out around him, his Bible open. He was jotting down notes. When he lifted his head, her stomach dropped at the look on his face.

"Eunice?"

"I'm sorry if I interrupted. I just thought I'd drop by on my way home and see how you're doing." She knew it was a mistake, but didn't know how to turn around now and walk away without adding insult to injury.

"Centerville is north."

"I was in Los Angeles visiting Tim."

He rose slowly from his stool. "You're thinner."

She felt a slight fluttering in her stomach. "Older, too." Her laugh came out flat. Why had she come here? What impulse had driven her? "I was here once before. A long time ago." She looked around. "Of course, I didn't come inside the building. I just looked through the window." She looked at him, and the warmth in his eyes stirred her. "When it was first given to the church."

He frowned, perplexed. "Given to the church?"

"You didn't know?" She was relieved. "This was the property bequeathed to Centerville Christian. It belonged to one of the founding members. I never met the gentleman. He lived in a convalescent hospital north of Sacramento. We didn't even know about him until Paul received word that Bjorn Svenson had left his property to the church."

He understood. "And Paul sold it and put the money down on the property where VNLC is now."

"Yes. That's right."

He looked shaken. "I didn't know."

"I was hoping you didn't."

"Why?"

She shrugged. "Some notion of getting back at Paul, I guess."

He lowered his chin, eyes challenging. "That wouldn't make me much of a Christian, would it?"

She was making a mess of things. "I'm sorry. I didn't mean to bring up past differences." That seemed to annoy him further.

"Why are you sorry, Eunice? It wasn't your fault things fell apart."

"VNLC is still standing, Stephen. It's magnificent. A testimony to your love of Christ."

"Yeah, well, that's one way of looking at it."

"You don't see it that way?"

"Time will tell if VNLC will stand or not."

He had reason to be cynical. Paul had ill-used him. Worse, Paul had allowed gossip to cast shadows over Stephen's reputation. Not that they had lasted long. People couldn't be around Stephen for long without knowing he was a consummate professional. She hadn't come with the intent of rousing old animosities, but to open the doorway for healing. She was naive—stupid and naive. "I shouldn't have come."

"I'm glad you did."

His tone had softened. So had his expression. Her heart thumped heavily.

"Dad?"

Stephen turned. "Brit. Come here. I'd like you to meet an old friend of mine."

Eunice watched the girl saunter forward. Brittany tucked her thumbs into the pockets of her faded blue Levi's and studied her disdainfully. Despite the punk clothes and haircut, the piercings and tattoos, Eunice thought she was beautiful. She had Stephen's eyes. "Your father often talked about you." Eunice extended her hand to the girl she had prayed for since hearing she was missing.

"Nothing good, I'll bet." Brittany shook her hand limply and let go. Eunice glanced at Stephen. She could read nothing in his expression, nothing that gave her any indication of what kind of response was needed. She looked at Brittany again, looked deep. "I always had the impression your father adored you and couldn't get enough time with you. He went to Sacramento every week to see you. Sometimes he mentioned plans he'd made." Why did the girl's eyes flicker? Eunice decided to take another track. "We prayed for you, Brittany. Your father, me, Samuel. Have you met Samuel Mason yet?"

"No."

"Well, I hope you will. You'll like him. Anyway, we were all praying for your safety and that you would call or come home or the private investigator would have good news—"

"Private investigator?"

"Your father hired him right after you left home. Didn't he tell you?" She looked at Stephen, who still stood silent. "You went down to San Francisco, didn't you, Stephen? I heard you stayed there for a week looking for Brittany."

Brittany looked at him. "You did?"

"Yes, I did." It was a flat statement, no hint of what he was feeling.

"I didn't think you cared."

"I *care* a great deal."

The girl's face changed. She looked young and uncertain, even a bit frightened. "I wasn't in San Francisco for more than a few days before I went down to Santa Cruz and then to Los Angeles eventually. I . . ." She grimaced, bowed her head, and then tipped a look at Eunice. "I didn't mean to interrupt anything. Sorry."

Eunice blushed. "You didn't interrupt anything, Brittany. I just stopped by on my way home. I have a son close to your age. He's living with his grandmother in Los Angeles."

"Why isn't your son living with you?"

It was a rude question, faintly challenging, but Eunice felt compelled to answer. "Timothy felt as though he were living under a magnifying glass. It's not easy being a pastor's son." *Or wife.* She tried to change the subject. "I heard about your father's latest project, and thought I'd take a look. He built the Valley New Life Center, where my husband is serving as pastor. Did you know that?"

"He's always building something."

Stephen's mouth tightened. "How's Tim doing, Eunice?"

"Fantastic. He has a nice group of friends, and he and Lois get along very well." She spoke brightly past her pain. "He's on his way to Mexico with a youth group this week. They're building houses south of Tijuana. And he's talking about going to college in the Midwest."

"Any chance of him coming home?"

Afraid to trust her voice, she shook her head.

"Why not?"

Eunice faced Brittany. The girl had no way of knowing she was probing her pain. Or did she? "Because he's better off where he is. He can be himself. He's free to spread his wings and fly anywhere God directs him."

"In other words, he's old enough to make up his mind where he wants to be and he'd rather be with his grandmother than his own parents."

"That's enough, Brittany."

Eunice tried not to show how much the girl's words had hurt. "Everyone wants to choose how they live and with whom, Brittany. As much as I want my son home with me, I see how he thrives with his grandmother. So I won't ask and I won't pressure him to come home." She had Brittany's full attention. "That's a question you need to answer now. Where will you be able to grow into the woman God intended you to be? Where will you thrive?"

Brittany frowned, but she had no comeback.

The three of them stood in uneasy silence.

Eunice spoke first. "Well, it was good to see you, Stephen."

"Don't go. You haven't even seen the place yet." He reached out.

Brittany looked at her father and back at Eunice. There was something troubling in that look, something all too knowing. "You want me to make some coffee?"

"Great idea, Brit. The coffee is in the right cabinet and—"

"I can find what I need."

Stephen gave Eunice the grand tour from basement to second-story apartment. When they came upstairs, Brittany picked up an Army coat. "I think I'll go out for a walk."

Eunice felt Stephen's tension as he watched his daughter head for the stairs.

Stephen poured coffee into two mugs. Eunice heard the front door downstairs close firmly. "When did you find her?"

"I didn't. She found me. Brittany showed up on my doorstep out of the blue." He took a chair and leaned back. "Every time she walks out the front door, I wonder if she's going to disappear again. But I know if I try to hang on to her, that'll send her running faster than anything." He lifted his gaze, his eyes dark with pain. "It's been awful the past few years."

She had a feeling he wasn't just talking about his runaway daughter. "That's part of the reason I came by. I wanted to say how sorry I am that things didn't work out better between you and Paul."

"Why are *you* apologizing?"

"Well, I . . ." She couldn't very well say that Paul had no intention of doing so, as badly as it was needed. "I don't like to see brothers at odds."

"Nice thought, Eunice, but you can't make someone else's apology and have it mean anything."

"I guess not. I keep hoping Paul will . . ." *Come to his senses?* She couldn't say such a thing aloud, not about her own husband. It was disloyal.

"Don't worry about it." He lifted his mug and looked at her over the rim as he drank. "I wasn't mortally wounded."

"Sometimes Paul rides roughshod over people when he's doing the Lord's work."

"The Lord's work? Is that what you call it?"

She blinked. He was angry, more angry than she had ever seen him. "You and Paul aren't getting along too well right now, are you?"

Confused, she stammered. "W-we're getting along as well as we always did."

"Oh. That good, huh?"

"I beg your pardon?"

He put his cup down. "You can't possibly know what a temptation I'm facing right now." He looked at her. "On several fronts."

Her heart started pounding. It wasn't what he said. It was the way he looked at her. He seemed closer, even with the table between them.

"I used to put it off as a stupid, childish crush, something that would pass with time. But it didn't. It grew and went deeper. Remember that day at the hospital when you followed me out to the parking lot?"

She wanted to deny it and couldn't. "Yes."

"The fact that you remember tells me more than you might like me to know."

She felt her cheeks heating up. How long had it been since Paul had looked at her as though he wanted more from her than her abilities as a pianist or church volunteer? Was this the reason she had come?

"You avoided me for months, Eunice."

"I thought it was best."

"You could hardly look me in the eye."

"I . . ."

"You don't have to explain. We were both treading the straight and narrow. It hurt. At other times, it made me mad because . . ." He shook his head. "But you were right." She clasped her hands around her mug. He leaned forward slowly and her breath caught. "When I saw you in the doorway a while ago, I realized something." His fingers brushed her hands and she felt a wild rush of sensation. "Nothing's changed. For me, at least."

"Or me, Stephen."

"Careful how you say that."

She drew her hands away from his touch. "I mean . . ." She swallowed hard, her breath jittery. "I'm married."

He leaned back. "I know." His eyes gently mocked her. "Married and unhappy. And there's the rub. I'd like to be the one to make you happy. Not just for a couple of hours up here in my apartment, but for the rest of our lives."

She'd felt the sparks fly between them before, but the blaze of fire now frightened her. "I didn't come to start anything."

"I know that, too, Eunice. I know *you*. A pity Paul doesn't."

Wincing, she stood and went to the windows overlooking the street. She didn't know what to say. She didn't know how to leave gracefully. Why had she come? She and Stephen had never been able to make casual conversation. Too many currents moved beneath the surface. Riptides. Undertows. It would be so easy to be swept out to sea. What would Paul say if he knew she had come to Rockville to see Stephen Decker? She knew she shouldn't be alone with this man. What had she been thinking? As a pastor's wife, she shouldn't be alone with any man in his home. It bred gossip. She stepped away from the window, turned, and found him standing right behind her. She had been so caught up in her own struggle she hadn't heard him move. And now she would have to step around him to leave.

"You know what I think, Eunice? I think God moved me to Rockville to protect us both. And I think God brought Brittany home to make sure nothing happened between us now."

She looked up and saw the pulse hammering in his neck. She was afraid to look into his eyes, afraid of seeing her own needs mirrored there. *Oh, Lord. Lord, help me!* She was trembling.

Stephen stepped back. "I'll walk you down."

She let out her breath softly.

He gave her a tender, all-too-knowing look. He opened the door for her, but held it so that she couldn't pass through it. The intensity was back in his eyes, the fire banked but still burning. "If I ever hear Paul's out of your life, expect to find me on your doorstep."

"That's not likely to happen, is it?" She hadn't meant to sound disappointed.

His expression changed. He avoided looking into her eyes as he let go of the door.

What was he thinking? She waited a few seconds before stepping over the threshold. "It was good to see you again, Stephen. You've done wonders with this building. Samuel said you're teaching a Bible study. He's very proud of you."

"Samuel's a straight guy."

"None better. Everyone misses you at the Bible study."

His gaze held hers. "You can tell them hello for me."

She knew then why he wasn't attending anymore. "I'm sorry, Stephen."

"Eunice, you're the best thing Paul has going for him."

She felt safer in the sunshine, less out of her depth. "He has the Lord."

"Let's hope so."

Stephen watched Eunice drive away. One glimpse of her and the attraction was resurrected. With a vengeance. He'd sensed an open door, a small opportunity to step through it. And what if he had? What ramifications? What consequences? What repercussions? He didn't even want to imagine what it would have done to Eunice if he'd given in to his impulse to take her into his arms and kiss her. What if she'd responded?

"So what's her deal, anyway?"

Startled, he turned and saw Brittany lounging on the bench Jack Bodene used to inhabit. Had she been sitting there the whole time? "She's an old friend."

She stood and came toward him, head cocked, eyes searching. "Did you two have a thing going or what?"

"No." He stared her down. "Never. Get that straight in your head."

She paled, but tilted her chin. "Why so defensive?"

"Because Eunice is a pastor's wife, and the mere hint of scandal could do her a lot of harm."

"So, why did she come here to see you?"

"For the reasons she said." *And others she didn't mention.* He could see Eunice was deeply troubled. Why *had* she come? Would she have explained if Brittany hadn't been here? He stopped his thoughts from going down that path.

"I'm a big girl, Daddy. I have two eyes in my head. You love her, don't you? More than you ever loved Mom."

"If you're asking if I've ever had or would ever want an affair with her, the answer is no. I admire Eunice Hudson. I care deeply about her. How can you not love someone who consistently puts other people's needs ahead of her own wants? Her son is a prime example of the sacrifices she's willing to make."

"Why did he really leave?"

"Because he couldn't live up to his father's expectations."

"You mean his father is like Mom? Well, no wonder."

"What do you mean?"

"You know what I mean. You lived with her. You know what she's like. No matter what you do, it's never enough to please her. And anything that goes wrong is your fault. That's why you left us, isn't it? Because all she ever did was scream at you for being a drunk. Like she screams at me for not getting straight A's, or having the right kind of friends, or a hundred other reasons she can think of. 'You could stand to lose a few pounds, Brittany.' 'When're you going to stop chewing your nails, Brittany?' 'You're just like your father. . . .' You have to be drunk or high to live with her. You have to be so out of it you can't hear her anymore."

He tried to calm her. "Easy, honey." He put his hand gently on her shoulder. "Your mother isn't the only one with a problem, Brit."

She shook him off. "So now you're going to get down on me, too. Right? You're going to tell me what's wrong with my life. You're gonna lay down the law."

She was coming down off something. Pills, grass, speed—he didn't know what, but he could read the signs. "I was talking about myself, Brittany. I'm an alcoholic. I made a habit of casting blame on your mother and rationalizing my behavior. But the truth is, I don't have to go any further than my own mirror to see who was responsible."

"But you're not drinking anymore, Daddy. You haven't got so much as a bottle of wine in your house. I looked. And she still blames you for everything."

"I'm still an alcoholic. Just because I don't drink, it doesn't mean I'm cured of that. Thank God, Jesus has taken away my thirst for it. But I'm still living one day at a time. I'm not taking anything for granted." Watching Eunice drive out of sight had made him thirst for a bottle of scotch. The first drink was the killer. "Why don't we go back upstairs? I may not have wine, but I have plenty of soda."

Brittany followed him and slumped in a chair near the window. "What'd the private eye cost you?"

"I would have paid more if it would've gotten you home sooner." He made bologna sandwiches while she stared out the front window, silent, troubled. He wasn't about to start an interrogation.

"I'll have to go grocery shopping later." He set her sandwich on the table. "I'm low on everything."

"I don't want to put you out anymore or cost you anything. I don't have to stay here, you know."

"I'd like it if you lived with me."

"You would? For real?"

Why should it surprise her? "I've missed you, Brittany. From the time your mother took you away. You didn't have any way of knowing that or understanding how much I loved you then. You're my flesh and blood." He could see her struggling harder with each word he said. "You're my daughter. I've always loved you. I always will. Nothing's going to change that."

"You say so now, but you don't know anything about me or what I've done." Her mouth trembled. Her eyes welled, hot and bright. "You haven't got a clue!"

"I can imagine." It was what he had imagined happening to her that had driven him mad at times—and made him thirst for scotch and oblivion.

She drew her legs up into the chair. Covering her head with her hands, she sobbed.

Stephen squelched the urge to tell her everything was all right. It wasn't. And it wouldn't be. Not right away. Some wounds took longer to heal. And trust didn't come overnight. He went to her. Crouching, he took her hands from her head. "Look at me, honey."

"I can't."

"You don't have to be afraid of what you're going to see in my eyes, Brittany. I'm not going to throw stones at you, or look down at you. God knows how many times I've sinned. Or how many times I still fall short of what I should be. I wake up each morning and thank God for another day, and I ask Him for the strength to make it a clean and sober one. And then at night, I thank Jesus again for getting me through."

She looked at him then. "Is every day that hard?"

"Some days are harder than others. But I've got tools now, and good friends. More important, I have a relationship with Jesus Christ." He recognized the look that came into her eyes, but didn't let it stop him from saying what needed to be said. "I know I can go to Him whenever I'm in trouble, and He'll show me the way to walk away from it." As He had with Eunice. "God shows me what I can change, and what I can't change, and He gives me the wisdom to know the difference."

"That's a prayer, isn't it? I saw something like it written on a wall in the Tenderloin."

He didn't want to think about what she was doing in that area of San Francisco. "Yep. Anytime you talk to God, you're praying. The hard part is learning to listen." He had been practicing for a long time. But he still had a long way to go. He thumbed a tear from his daughter's cheek.

"You're so different, Daddy. I hardly know you."

"We have all the time in the world."

PART 4

And the SHOFAR BLEW

CHAPTER 16

❦

Britany 24 yrs old

7 yrs.   Tim is 19 yrs old
Samuel 70 yrs old

2003

Samuel opened his apartment door and faced a tall young man wearing a blue shirt, black leather jacket, and Levi's. "Timothy Hudson! It's good to see you." He embraced him. Choked up, Samuel drew back and gestured for Tim to come in. He fought tears. The doctor said the tears came so easily because of a mild stroke.

"Man, it's good to see you, Samuel. I've missed you."

"You look good, Tim." The disheveled, hard-eyed rebel who had left Centerville had come back much taller, filled out in the shoulders, and exuding an air of confidence. The only remaining touch of nonconformity was the shoulder-length sandy-blond hair.

"I missed you at church, Samuel."

"I stopped driving after my stroke. I've missed services for some time now." He didn't tell Timothy he'd never set foot in Valley New Life Center. It wouldn't do to tell Tim that the only member of CCC who came to call was his mother. When Samuel had left the church, no one had bothered to ask why, not that he would have felt free to explain. Those who knew just didn't care. It had hurt and troubled him that he was so little missed after so many years of service. "I meet with a group

331

here in the rec room. We have our own service. We study the Bible together, sing hymns, and pray."

When Samuel had moved in, he'd been surprised to find there were no Sunday services conducted at Vine Hill, and only a few clergymen bothered to come by. The only regular visitor was Father James O'Malley, a Catholic priest almost as old as his parishioners at the residential-care facility.

"I don't mind ye teaching members of my congregation," James had said in his Irish brogue the first time Samuel met him. "You're teaching them from God's Word, and I've nothing against that. Just so ye don't go filling their heads with any rebellious ideas."

James O'Malley dropped by every Thursday for a long visit. Though they didn't always agree on theological matters, the priest loved Jesus and the people God had entrusted to him. And it was good to have friends.

"Do you like it here, Samuel?" Timothy looked dubious.

Was the boy feeling sorry for him? Samuel would have none of that. "I couldn't keep up with the house. And the yard work was too much for me. Here, I can relax and enjoy life. There's someone to cook for me, wash my sheets, take care of my laundry." He had plenty of time to pray and teach those whose hearts were open to Jesus. "Sit and make yourself at home."

Timothy sat in the old wing chair facing the windows, the one James often sat in. Vine Hill was built so that all the apartments looked out into the courtyard. It gave the old folks a pleasant view of a marble statue of a young peasant woman pouring water from a pitcher tipped into a lily-covered fishpond. Samuel slid the window open so that Timothy would hear the birds that gathered at the feeders in the courtyard garden. "I can enjoy the gardens without a care in the world. Tomas Gomez keeps everything tidy and plants new flowers every season."

"You have a nice place here, Samuel."

A temporary home until he joined Abby. "I saw your mother last week. She didn't tell me you were coming home."

"She didn't know. It was a surprise. Grandma and I thought a trip to Centerville was in order."

"Any particular reason?"

"I guess you could say I just wanted to see how everything was shaping up at Dad's church."

A guarded answer. "And?"

"It's a beautiful facility."

"Yes. It is." Samuel settled into his easy chair and put his cane aside. "I should've offered you something. Would you like a soda? Some cookies? Make yourself at home." The kitchenette had a mini fridge, a microwave, and a few cabinets.

Timothy fixed two glasses of iced tea. Smiling, Samuel took the glass, stirred the tea, and sipped. Tim had even remembered to add lemon. "Perfect. Just the way I like it. Now, you were saying?"

"Do you listen to Dad's sermons?"

"Uh-huh."

"And?"

"Your father is a powerful speaker."

"Yeah, I know that, *but* . . ." Tim's expression was watchful, waiting, testing.

Samuel had no intention of gossiping about Timothy's father, or sharing his thoughts on the matter of Paul Hudson's preaching. He'd talked about all that with the Lord. Many times. "Now that you're through high school, what do you intend to do?"

Timothy rested his head against the back of the chair. "I'm not sure yet. It was good to take a year off to work and think about my options. I've received four college acceptances."

"That's good. Which ones?"

"UCLA, UC Berkeley, California State in Sacramento, and Mom and Dad's alma mater, Midwest Christian."

Samuel smiled. "I guess you've changed your mind about being a cowboy."

Timothy gave him a lopsided grin. "Might be easier if I went back to that idea. Move to Montana. Live somewhere far away from everyone who wants a say in my life. I'm not certain what God wants yet, Samuel. I've been asking Him for the last two years. You could say I'm covering as many bases as I can."

Timothy spoke of the Lord like a young man who now knew Him intimately. "Any idea of what you want to major in?"

"I'm not even certain I'm going, Samuel."

"Is money a problem?"

"Not one that'll keep me away. Mom and Dad set aside savings for me from the day I was born. Not enough, but I'm not against working my way through school. Dad's been pushing for Midwest. Third-generation legacy, he says, as though it's a done deal." The young man's sardonic smile reminded Samuel of Paul Hudson. "First time I can remember doing anything that made my father proud of me." He shook his head and looked away. "The problem is, I'm pretty sure Midwest is *not* where God wants me."

"How do you know?"

"I don't have any peace about it. I applied to please Dad. Now I wish I hadn't." He stood and leaned against the windowframe, looking out at the courtyard. "It's complicated."

"You'll know where God wants you when the time comes."

"I hope so. If I go anywhere other than Midwest now, Dad will be disappointed. I'm not sure what I should do."

"Depends on whom you want to please."

Tim looked at him with complete understanding. "What about the command to honor your father and mother?"

"The greatest commandment is that you love the Lord your God with all your heart, and with all your soul, and with all your mind, Timothy. The second is to love your neighbor as yourself. On these two commandments depend the whole Law and the prophets of the Old Testament, and both were lived out in Christ's life, death, and resurrection. We are to follow Jesus, not others, no matter how much we love them."

"That's clear and simple in theory, Samuel. It's just not that easy to do in life."

"No one ever said it would be easy. That's where the battle has been from the beginning. Even Jesus faced it in the garden. Remember? 'Thy will, not mine, be done.' Life is ever thus. The mind and heart are Satan's battleground. Jesus and God's Word are your strength and shield."

Timothy took his seat again. Leaning forward, he rested his forearms on his knees. "I'm worried about Mom." He cocked his head. "Has she ever talked to you about anything?"

"She talks to me about all kinds of things."

"Anything I should know about?"

"Not unless she wants to tell you." Abby had always been Eunice's confidante. Eunice had come to him a few times, deeply troubled, but never said what was bothering her. Her mere reticence told him her worries centered on Paul, but Samuel had never felt the right to ask or press her for more information.

Tim shrugged. "Mom and Dad are different with each other. I don't know what it is. He's edgy, secretive. They talk like they're strangers. Surface stuff."

"Marriage is hard work, Timothy."

"So I've heard, but shouldn't they be getting better at it? I don't see either one of them working on anything but church stuff. Mom seems tense. She's never been like that." Timothy shrugged and looked out the window. "She seems intent on keeping busy. Keeping up appearances. She insists everything is fine, but I get the feeling nothing is. I don't know if she believes it or is just hoping it's true. Maybe all the pretense is more for herself than others. I don't know, Samuel. I can't get a fix on what's wrong. She goes through all the motions, but . . . something's missing."

"By getting a fix, you mean you'd like to fix things, don't you?"

"Sure. If I can."

Samuel thought about the sacrifices Eunice Hudson had made, and wondered if her son was up to it. "Why did your mother take you down to Los Angeles, Timothy?"

His expression became guarded. "Things weren't going well between me and my dad."

"Why did she leave you there?"

"She told me she knew I needed the space to find out who I am other than Paul Hudson's son."

"Do you think that was easy for her?"

"I know it wasn't." He grimaced. "It still isn't. She cries every time before she leaves."

"You want my advice?"

"Yeah. That's part of the reason I'm here."

"Okay. Listen up. Follow your mother's example. Let go. Step back. Pray. And see what the Lord does."

"I thought maybe if I talked to Dad . . ."

Samuel saw Paul Hudson in the boy. "Oh." He smiled gently. "You know how to make things better. Is that it? You figure you can tell your father how to live his life and make your mother happy." Samuel shook his head. "Ah. Impetuous, prideful youth."

Timothy blushed crimson. "I've got a gut feeling their marriage is disintegrating, and I don't want to stand around and watch it happen without saying something."

"Is either one of them asking for your advice?"

"No."

"Then don't give it. Let God do the molding and shaping—and the breaking, if necessary. Keep your focus, Timothy. What we believe about God determines how we serve Him. Often, that means keeping our noses out of God's business." He couldn't say it any clearer than that.

"Wait on the Lord, you mean."

"That's about it."

"I have a hard time with waiting."

Samuel chuckled. "Don't feel like the Lone Ranger." People created their own little gods when the Lord didn't work according to their timetable. A program. A plan. A schedule. All with the illusion of control. Until disaster hit.

As Samuel had hoped, Timothy changed the subject. He asked about Samuel's health. Samuel told him about the stroke. Minor though it was, it'd caused definite changes in his life. "I miss driving, but I don't want to take a chance on wiping someone out on the highway. It's one thing to kill yourself, quite another to take someone out with you." He still had his license and his DeSoto, though neither was in use these days.

Samuel invited Timothy to join him for lunch in the dining room downstairs. He called the desk and informed the manager, Gladys Townsend, that he would have a guest. "Almost everyone comes down for meals," he told Timothy. For some, meals were the only social activity they had, unless they joined in the myriad of recreational activities planned for them each week—everything from putting puzzles together to tai chi. Samuel attended oil-painting classes once a week, not that he cared to show anything he'd painted to anyone with good eyesight.

Samuel introduced Timothy to his tablemates: Bessie Enright, Tom Orion, Foley Huddleston, Loraine Cramer, and Charlotte Witcomb. As soon as introductions were made, all but one tried to make Timothy feel welcome.

"Another long-haired hippie." Tom Orion leaned forward, chin jutting. "At least it isn't dyed blue like my grandson's. You have any tattoos?"

"No, sir."

"Well, I do."

Charlotte looked horrified. "Nobody wants to see it, Tom."

Bessie patted Timothy's hand. "He's too young to be a hippie."

"He's got long hair, hasn't he?"

"Long hair is the style, Tom," Loraine said. "My favorite actor has long hair."

"Soap-opera drivel! No wonder your brain is mush."

Loraine pulled her glasses down and glared at Tom over the top of the rims. "Better soap operas than hanging around in the front lobby and railing at the staff."

"I don't rail."

"You bleat like an old goat," Charlotte said, joining Loraine in the attack.

"Orion," Timothy said. "There was a Coach Orion at Centerville High School."

"My son."

"The football team started winning when he took over."

Apparently, Timothy had inherited his mother's winsome ways. Tom Orion was diverted from his complaining. Charlotte, Loraine, and Bessie were more impressed with Timothy's manners and good looks. After ten minutes of listening to football game recaps, Charlotte interrupted Tom and asked Timothy if he'd found a girlfriend yet.

"No, ma'am. Nothing serious, at least."

"I have a nice granddaughter. She's very pretty."

"He's not staying in Centerville, Charlotte," Loraine said. "He's just visiting."

"What a pity. They'd make such a nice couple."

Loraine patted Charlotte's hand. "Your granddaughter is forty-four."

Charlotte wasn't willing to give up. "How old are you, Timothy?"

"I just turned nineteen."

Samuel enjoyed his meal and the scene playing out around him. Timothy seemed perfectly at ease with everyone. Even Tom mellowed and talked about the good old days of Centerville, days when there were more almond orchards and vineyards than subdivisions. They were having such a good time, one of the staff had to ask them to vacate the dining room so the cleanup crew could finish. Timothy helped the ladies from their chairs and shook hands with Foley Huddleston and Tom Orion.

Tom turned to Samuel before leaving. "He's all right." High praise from the cantankerous old butcher.

Bessie Enright stayed with them all the way to the elevator. "You have such a nice grandson, Samuel."

Samuel made no attempt to correct her about his relationship to Timothy. In ten minutes, she wouldn't remember Timothy had even been here.

Samuel stepped into the elevator with Timothy. "Did you enjoy your meal?"

"Good food. Nice people."

"Lonely people. Some forgotten. Bessie Enright hasn't had a family visitor since I moved in. Her children and grandchildren live back East." He'd mentioned that to Eunice once when she came by for a visit. The next time she came, she stopped by Bessie's apartment as well, and brought her an African violet to add to the collection on the windowsill.

"Are you staying with your folks while you decide which college to attend?"

"Nope." Timothy shook his head. "I'm taking the bus home late tonight. I've got a job lined up the beginning of next week. Construction."

"Construction?"

"I'm going to be a hod carrier." He grinned. "I've been told it's a good way to build muscle." He flexed his arm.

"Is your mother picking you up?"

"No."

"Your grandmother?"

"She left for home yesterday."

He couldn't imagine Paul Hudson taking time out of his busy schedule to pick up his son. "How're you getting home, Timothy?"

"Same way I got here. Walk."

Three miles in ninety-degree heat! Samuel was touched that Timothy had gone to such efforts to see him.

They talked about sports, college, Timothy's mission trips to Mexico, his mom's busy schedule, politics. Neither mentioned anything about Valley New Life Center or its pastor. "I'd better get going." As Timothy stood, Samuel felt a pang of regret. He might not see the boy again this side of heaven. Pushing himself up from his easy chair, he walked Timothy to the door.

"Can I ask you to do something for me, Samuel?"

"Anything. Anytime."

"Would you pray for my father?"

"God forbid that I ever stop." He'd started praying for Paul Hudson before he even knew his name. He could still remember the first conversation he'd had with Paul years ago, the certainty that he was the one being called to Centerville.

Again, the troubled look came into Timothy's eyes. He was carrying a burden and was hesitant to set it down.

"What's bothering you, Son?"

"I have a feeling things are going to come down hot and heavy on my father one of these days."

Samuel didn't have to ask for reasons.

"It's been great seeing you, Samuel." Eyes moist, Timothy extended his hand. His grip was firm, like a man's. Samuel saw a hint of the little boy before Timothy embraced him. "I've missed you." His voice roughened. "Of all the people in Centerville, I've missed you and Mom most. And Abby . . ." He drew back, embarrassed. "Anyway." He shook Samuel's hand again, and his grip tightened for a few seconds before he let go. "Thanks for everything."

"I'm not dead yet, you know."

His grin was sheepish. "Yeah, I know, but when I was learning to drive, you told me not to take life for granted. Some things ought to be said when there's the opportunity. I love you, Samuel. You were more of a grandfather to me than my own grandfather."

Samuel was too full of emotion to speak. Timothy had healed the ache in his heart for the son who'd been killed in Vietnam. Standing in the open doorway, Samuel felt the gentle nudging of the Holy Spirit. Over seventy years of walking with the Lord, he had learned not to resist Him. "Wait a minute, son. I have something for you." He limped to the secretary, opened a drawer, and leafed through the papers till he found what he was looking for. Pulling down the desktop, he wrote a brief note and signed his name. He slipped it into an envelope. He picked up the keys in the desk organizer and came back to Timothy, who was still standing at the open door. "A little something to help you on your way." He held out the keys to the DeSoto.

"You're kidding!"

"I'd never kid about that baby. Believe me." He handed over the envelope. "That's the title, signed over to you. All you have to do is stop by the DMV and she's all yours."

"I can't take your car, Samuel. I know how much you love it."

"I don't love it, Timothy. I've enjoyed it. I love *you*. Besides, I ask you—what am I going to do with a car I can no longer drive?" He pointed down the corridor. "Go out that door, down the back stairs, and outside to the garage. She's all yours with one stipulation: that you remember there are no strings attached. If she doesn't suit you, sell her and use the money for college."

Timothy stood undecided. "I don't know what to say."

"Don't say anything. Just go and have your first spin with her. Call me in a few weeks and tell me how she runs."

Timothy hugged him and headed down the corridor. Samuel watched him swing the DeSoto keys around his finger. Tim paused at the door. Grinning, he waved. "Thanks, Samuel!"

Samuel raised his hand and resisted the urge to call out driving advice. The door banged behind Timothy.

Samuel closed his apartment door. He'd given away most of what was in his home before he moved into Vine Hill, but he hadn't been able to give up his car. Over the past few months, he'd gone down to the garage and spent a couple of hours each week polishing and checking everything over. He'd even gotten into the driver's seat and started the engine just to make sure she was in good running order, all the while wondering why he bothered.

"Now I know, Lord." Chuckling, he eased into his recliner and pushed back.

There is an appointed time for everything. And there is a time for every event under heaven.

Smiling, Samuel savored the pleasure of shedding another trapping of this life. He could almost see Timothy driving down Highway 99 to the intersection with Interstate 5, window open, arm resting on the door.

Oh, it feels good, Lord, real good to give a young man wheels.

Especially knowing it would be God who did the driving.

Paul struggled with mixed feelings about his son. He was proud of him, and felt curiously bereft. He hadn't expected Timothy to make it through high school, let alone excel and have good enough grades to be considered by UCLA. Timothy was already planning ahead, looking into his options. Had Tim listened to him at all? Then again, why should he? Paul hardly knew his son anymore. He'd talked with him on the phone every week or two, but the conversations were brief and stilted. It wasn't his fault or Timothy's that they couldn't seem to talk. Their personalities didn't mesh. Eunice had been the bridge, but lately she had a guardrail up.

Had she heard rumors? Paul had been careful to time Sheila's appointments when there weren't people in the church. Neither one of them wanted to end their marriages, even though those marriages weren't what they should be. And both of them had a lot to lose if rumors started. She was a parishioner, and she needed comfort. She needed to know at least one other man in the world saw her as a desirable woman, and she made him feel more of a man than Eunice ever did.

But he'd been worrying lately. Sheila was taking risks he didn't like. A kiss on his cheek as she headed out of church, a telephone call at home, a note on his desk. Timothy had given him an eagle-eyed stare this morning when Sheila talked to him. His son had paid no attention to the teenage girls whispering and watching him. If Timothy said anything to Eunice about Sheila, Paul would just tell the truth. He was counseling her. Eunice would believe him. She always did. Even if Eunice questioned him, he would ask what sort of pastor he'd be if he refused help to the wife of one of the church's major donors?

He needed to call his pharmacist and get some more pills. His stomach was killing him again. He didn't like the way Sheila had taken to playing little games with him. He knew it was just another sign of her low self-esteem. Rob didn't show her any attention, so she sought his. He would call her and talk with her about it again. Rob was away again. Maybe he'd go up and see her at her house. They wouldn't have to worry about anyone seeing them there or overhearing their conversation.

Eunice's car was already parked in the garage. She and Timothy had gone for hamburgers at Charlie's Diner, but he'd made an excuse. He didn't want to sit across the table from Timothy and have a staring contest, and worse, have to answer any questions Eunice might bring up. Even if he was suspicious, Tim wouldn't say anything about Sheila. Why risk hurting his mother?

Paul remembered being in Tim's position once, and was glad he hadn't said anything. Shrugging out of his coat, he went through the kitchen. Maybe he should've called Sheila before leaving the church.

Guilt gripped him, anger following. Why should he feel guilty? It was part of a pastor's duty to counsel people. It wasn't as though he were arranging meetings with Sheila or making clandestine arrangements for a private getaway. If he were doing that, he'd be making reservations at some out-of-the-way bed-and-breakfast. Maybe at that nice place in Mariposa. Someplace where no one would know them. They could have dinner together, a nice walk, a long talk, and . . .

He halted his thoughts. All he'd done was comfort a lonely woman whose husband was too stupid to know what he was missing. He loosened his tie and unbuttoned his collar. Edgy and irritated, he almost ran into Eunice on her way out of their bedroom.

"Oh, sorry." She laughed and looped her purse over her shoulder.

"Where are you going?"

"Shopping." She stepped around him.

He followed her into the hallway. "It's Sunday night."

"I know, but you said we're out of coffee and you need more shaving cream. I've got a list of things."

"Where's Timothy?"

"He took a walk. He said he'd be back in plenty of time to catch his bus."

"How long do you think you'll be gone?"

"An hour at the most."

An hour would be perfect. He could talk to Sheila without any worries.

She frowned. "I can wait until tomorrow, if you'd like." She slipped her purse from her shoulder. "Maybe I should wait. It is kind of late."

"No. Go ahead. I've got plenty to do."

Paul waited until he heard the garage door open and close. He drew aside the bedroom drapes just enough to watch Eunice head down the hill for Centerville. He looked at the phone on the bedside table. Somehow it didn't feel right to make the call in the master bedroom. He tossed his jacket over the chair and went down the corridor to his home office. Closing the door, he locked it and sat at his desk. He would talk to Sheila about her behavior this morning. He wondered how long Rob would be gone. Sheila always needed him more when Rob was away.

Paul didn't have to look up her number.

Stephen saw a silver Lexus pull up in front. It was barely nine in the morning and his client wasn't due until eleven.

Kathryn got out of the car.

"Oh, Lord, help!" He put his pencil on the drawing board. He didn't wait for her to knock. "Hi."

"Hi." Her tone was curt. She barely glanced at him as she walked into his office. She'd let her blonde hair grow out again, and was wearing it soft and loose around her shoulders. He'd told her in their courtship days that he liked her hair long. Maybe that was why she cut it after a few years. She only took two inches off the first time. By the end of their marriage, she'd cropped it short and used gel. It had galled him. As she well knew.

She was still in good shape. Probably worked out at some gym every other day. Probably had a personal trainer, too. Catching the drift of his thoughts, Stephen halted them. She hadn't even opened her mouth other than to say hi, and here he was tearing her down in his mind, looking for faults and failures, looking for weaknesses. God knew he had plenty of all three.

"Why on earth did you buy this building, Stephen? Why didn't you renovate or remodel something in Sacramento? Or Roseville? Why *Rockville?*"

She wasn't going to make things easy. "It appealed to me." He wasn't about to go into how the Lord had led him here, or that he was conducting a Bible study in his basement. She wasn't ready to listen, and she was on a roll.

"How much money have you dumped into this building? I've never known you to be foolish with investments. This is a dead-end town with dead-end people. Most of the houses I saw don't even have foundations. And that trailer park! What an eyesore with all those Mexicans loitering in front."

"Day laborers. Most of them get picked up before nine." Two were attending his Wednesday evening Bible study. Nice guys, lonely, families south of the border.

"No one in their right mind would want to live in Rockville if they had the money to live anywhere else. Even Centerville is better than this. I don't think Brittany should be living here."

Stephen blinked. After four years, Kathryn suddenly had an opinion on where their daughter should live? He opened his mouth to tell her Brittany had lived in worse places than Rockville, or anything she could imagine, but caught himself in time. *Keep your head, Decker. Don't jump back on the merry-go-round.*

Kathryn looked toward the stairs at the back. "Brittany must've seen me drive up. Would you make her come down?"

"She left early."

She lifted her head, but he couldn't see her eyes through her sunglasses. "Did you tell her I was coming over?"

"I didn't know you were coming, Kathryn. I haven't heard from you in ages." He was careful to keep his tone neutral, but he could see her trying to read something more into it.

"I didn't know when I was going to be able to get over here. Okay?"

He ignored the sarcasm. "Brit usually leaves in the morning and comes back midafternoon. It wasn't personal."

"Where does she go?"

"I don't know."

"And you don't ask?"

"I made some promises to Brit when I invited her to stay here, Kathryn. One of them was that I wouldn't pry into her personal affairs if she didn't want to tell me about them. I wasn't exactly actively involved in her life before she showed up here." Brittany left early every morning, never volunteering any information about where she was going or what she planned to do. He was thankful she came back, even more thankful when she wasn't drunk or high. Sure, he wondered where she went all day. Sure, he wanted to ask her. But he held his silence and waited. He didn't want to do to Brittany what Kathryn used to do to him: put her through the third degree every time she walked in the front door. He had the feeling Brittany had already been down that much-traveled road to nowhere.

Kathryn walked to his drawing board and looked at his drawings.

Stephen squelched the urge to step over and roll them up. Kathryn sighed heavily. "It probably wouldn't take much to send Brittany on the run again." She gave a short, bleak laugh. "The sight of my car out front might do it."

He reined in the urge to ask Kathryn why, but he wanted to tear down walls, not build them. Right now, his ex-wife was walking her battlements and making sure her cannons were loaded. She studied his conceptual drawings for an office building. Buying time?

"Why don't I make us a pot of coffee?"

She glanced up, surprised. "Coffee?"

"I could use a break. I've been at those drawings since seven."

"They're good."

He hadn't expected a compliment and stood dumbfounded.

"Where's the site?"

"Northeast of the arena in Sacramento." He headed for the stairs. "Come on up. Look around." She followed.

As he took coffee and filters out of the cabinet, Kathryn took in her surroundings. He looked her over. She was thinner, paler, and less kempt than he'd ever seen her. Even when they were heading for divorce, she'd been meticulous about her appearance. Now her designer jeans were loose, her salon tan faded. She still had long, red-lacquered nails. She took off her sunglasses, folded them, and tucked them into her jacket pocket. The skin beneath her bloodshot hazel eyes was puffy. Whatever makeup she'd applied didn't disguise her age or the shadows of late nights, booze, and disillusionment.

Stephen knew the signs of a hangover. He'd suffered from them often enough in the past. "Have you eaten, Kat?"

"No." She turned her back to him, and stared out the window, arms crossed.

"Neither have I. What do you say I fix some eggs?"

She glanced over her shoulder, one brow raised. "You cook now?"

He let her mockery slide. "Nothing fancy." Brittany told him once that Kathryn was taking gourmet-cooking classes so that she could put on fancy dinner parties to impress Jeff and his rich friends. "I can manage an omelet. What do you say?"

"This I've got to see." She took Brittany's chair and watched while he prepared the eggs and grated cheese. He knew she was trying to irritate him. He poured the whipped eggs into a hot pan, sprinkled grated cheese, put the lid on, and lowered the heat. While the omelet cooked, he set the table for two. She smirked. "Wonders never cease."

"You'd better hold off with the compliments until you've tasted the food." He saw the start of a smile, but she squelched it. He poured her a cup of steaming coffee. "Sorry, I don't have cream. Would you like a little milk instead?"

Her gaze was questioning, wary. "Black is fine."

He divided the omelet and served her portion first. He took the seat across from her and said a quick, silent prayer of thanks for the food, topping it off with a plea for presence of mind and patience. Kathryn didn't have to do or say anything to get his hackles up.

"Why are you being so nice to me, Stephen? Are you going to ask for custody again?"

Was she serious? "Brittany just turned twenty-one, Kat. She's a little old for custody."

Kathryn blinked, a shadow flickering across her face. "Oh. I guess so." She looked ready to cry. She turned her head away and swallowed. She was fighting tears. How much drinking had she been doing over the past few years? "So much time . . ." She shook her head and faced him again. Her eyes hardened in challenge. "What're you staring at?"

"Sorry."

"You still haven't told me why you're being so nice."

How much of what she had become was his fault? "I thought it was about time we stopped trying to find ways to hurt each other."

She looked pointedly at the omelet and then at him, her expression wry. "Is this a twist on the Trojan horse?"

Chuckling, he reached over the table, took a forkful of her omelet, and ate it. "Not enough salt. Absolutely no arsenic."

A smile did come this time. Brief, halfhearted, sardonic—but still a smile. She took a tentative bite. "Not bad, either."

They ate in silence. He took the empty plates and set them in the sink to wash later. "More coffee?"

"Please." He poured and then set the coffeepot on a hot plate between them. She held her cup between her hands. "I thought you'd gloat."

"Over what?"

She gave him a droll look. "Over Jeff leaving me. Over another failed marriage."

"I find no pleasure in your unhappiness, Kat." He knew some things needed to be cleared up. "I did at one time. Not anymore."

"What brought the change of heart?"

"I accepted Christ as my Savior in rehab. And I've been learning to give Him lordship over my life ever since. Without Him, I wouldn't make it through a day without a drink."

"You used to say I drove you to drink."

"I was looking for someone to blame."

"So, you walked into a church and everything's all better. Is that it?"

"I'm not talking about a building. I'm talking about a relationship."

"Must be nice to have personal rapport with God Himself."

She was pushing hard. So had he, just before surrendering. "I needed Jesus in my life. It was as simple as that. I didn't have the strength to say no to alcohol."

"I remember that all too well."

He resisted the urge to catalog *her* sins. "There's a saying in rehab: 'I can't. God can. I turn my will over to God.' I've been doing that on a daily basis ever since. And—by the grace of God—I've stayed sober."

She looked at him, really looked this time. Her eyes clouded. "Is it hard?"

"Some days are harder than others."

She stood and went to the window again. Crossing her arms, she stared out. "I used to blame you for everything. I blamed you when I was unhappy. I blamed you when our marriage started to fall apart. I blamed you when I got pregnant and couldn't work anymore. I blamed you when I couldn't make the child-support checks stretch enough to live the way I wanted to live." She raised her head. "And then I met Jeff and thought everything was going to be wonderful." Her shoulders shook. "And it wasn't. So I blamed Brittany."

That hadn't been hard to guess, but he was surprised she could admit it. He saw hope in her confession, and a small opportunity. "We like the illusion of having control of our lives, that the sins we commit have nothing to do with anyone else. We close our eyes to the consequences and point our finger at someone else. Don't feel alone, Kat. I did more than my share of blaming."

He remembered telling Kathryn she was the reason he drank, that a man had to stay drunk to stand living in the same house with her. He'd rationalized and justified his lousy behavior. Was it any wonder she fought back? What did it matter how the war started or who was ahead? He wanted peace between them. For Brittany's sake as much as their own. The only thing that stood in the way was pride.

"It's not your fault I'm an alcoholic, Kat. It never was." He rose and went to her, standing behind her. "I'm sorry." When he put his hand on her shoulder, he felt her stiffen. He let his hand fall to his side.

They stood silent, staring out at the street.

"So am I." She gave him a wry look. "Especially now that you've turned into a decent human being again."

He'd once found her acerbic wit appealing. "Your mascara is running." He took his handkerchief from his pocket and handed it to her. "Don't worry. It's clean."

They sat at the table again. Kathryn took a compact from her purse, opened it, looked at her face as she dabbed briefly. With a heavy sigh, she snapped the compact shut and dropped it back into her purse. "I'm sick of keeping up appearances and trying to live up to others' expectations. I don't even know who I am anymore. I just know I don't want to go on like this." Her mascara was running again.

She turned her coffee cup around in the saucer. "Brittany didn't like Jeff from the beginning. I thought she would warm up to him, but she didn't. So I kept her out of the way with ballet lessons and piano lessons, soccer and summer camp. I told her I was doing it for her own good, but she knew why I was doing it. She wanted to live with you. Did she tell you that?"

"Yeah." He could guess the rest. The thought that Brittany would choose her alcoholic father over her mother must have eaten at Kathryn's self-confidence and roused her jealous anger.

She closed her eyes. "When did she tell you?"

"When she first came here. You told her I didn't want her."

She raised her head. "Maybe it wasn't right."

"Maybe?"

"Okay." She looked away. "The more you wanted her, the less inclined I was to give her to you. I wanted to hurt you the way you hurt me."

"You did."

"I thought I'd be happy about it."

He studied her. "It's to your credit that you aren't."

Her shoulders loosened. "I never thought I could talk to you about all this, Stephen. Not in a million years."

He'd never tried to make it easy for her to talk about anything. He'd been like a football player sitting on the bench, watching the opposing team and waiting for his chance to control the ball.

Poor Brittany. No wonder their daughter was such a mess.

She sipped her coffee. "I know why she ran away, Stephen. Brittany and I had a terrible fight. She told me she saw Jeff with another woman. I slapped her face and told her she was just trying to ruin my marriage. She said it wasn't the first time she'd seen them together. She said he was a jerk and I was a fool to listen to his lame excuses about why he was late all the time and why he had to go away so often on business trips." Her mouth jerked. "I slapped her again and said she was a drunk, just—"

"Just like her father?"

Kathryn looked sick. "And I said more, a lot more. Cruel things I can't even remember now, but I know she'll never forget." Her hand shook as she wiped tears from her cheek. "I was so angry. I told her I was sick to death of her and wished she'd grow up and leave. And she just stood there, taking it and looking at me as though she hated me. I said I was sick of the sight of her with her blue hair and her nose ring. I said . . . I don't even remember what all I said. And she just turned her back on me and walked down the hall to her room. She slammed the door and locked it. The next morning, she was gone. I thought she'd just gone out as usual. She was always going out. Sometimes she'd stay away for a day or two, but she always came back. After three days and nights, I knew she was really gone. And I was glad. For a week, I was glad."

She buried her face in the handkerchief and sobbed. "That's what a great mother I've been. Then after two weeks, I was so scared. I was afraid to call you. I didn't know what to do. And then, a few weeks later, I found out for myself that everything she said about Jeff was true."

"That's when you called and wanted me to tell her you were divorcing Jeff."

She blew her nose and said a watery yes.

He prayed his confession wouldn't bring an end to this conversation.

"I didn't tell her, Kathryn. I'm sorry. I wish I had now. But I was afraid you might be blaming her for the breakup of your marriage."

At least she wasn't screaming at him. At least she was still sitting in her chair and not flying at his throat.

She released her breath slowly. Closing her eyes, she blew her nose again, then crumpled his handkerchief in her hand. "I'm glad you didn't. I want to be the one to tell her she was right." Her mouth jerked. "Maybe then she'll be able to forgive me."

Given time, maybe Brittany would be able to forgive both of them for their faults as people and their failures as parents.

"Thanks." Kathryn barely whispered it.

"For what?"

"For listening."

He should've started the practice a long time ago. "Anytime." It was a habit worth cultivating.

"Well, well, this is something new." Brittany stood at the top of the stairwell, watching them. She hooked her thumbs under the straps of her backpack and looked from him to her mother. "I've never known the two of you to be in the same room longer than five seconds without having a fight."

Stephen leaned back in his chair and smiled at his daughter. "Your mother and I had breakfast together."

"You don't say."

"Your father cooked."

"Was it up to your standards, Mother?"

When Kathryn didn't answer, Brittany looked at him. "She complains about everything. Don't let her get to you, Dad."

"She said it was good."

"Miracle of miracles. Another first." Brittany stared hard at her mother. Stephen had the feeling that one wrong word would send her back down those stairs and out of their lives.

Kathryn broke the silence. "You were right about Jeff, Brittany."

"Tell me something I don't already know."

"I divorced him."

"Do you think I care?" Brittany tilted her head in the same manner Kathryn often did. "I've learned a few things since coming here. Dad *did* want me. You told me he didn't."

"I lied."

Brittany looked momentarily surprised by Kathryn's confession before her young face hardened. "Is there any reason I shouldn't hate you for the rest of my life?"

"No. But I hope you won't."

"Don't hold your breath."

Stephen pitied Kathryn. He knew how hard it was to confess.

Kathryn took the strap of her purse and looped it over her shoulder. "I'd better go."

Stephen stood. "I'll walk you down."

Brittany shrugged off her backpack and held it tightly in one hand. Stephen had the feeling she'd use it as a weapon if Kathryn tried to get too close. Kathryn didn't. Mother and daughter looked at one another. Brittany turned her back before Kathryn could say anything.

Stephen walked down the stairs behind Kathryn. He opened the front door for her. "Are you going to be all right?"

"I guess I'll have to be."

"I want to know for sure."

She looked at him, pale and sad. "You have changed." Her lips curved sardonically. "Relax, Stephen. We all know I'm too selfish to do anything to hurt myself." The smile died. She put her sunglasses back on and gave a flippant wave. "At least I know Brittany is safe and doing well. That's enough to keep me going right now."

Stephen watched Kathryn walk out to her car, open the door, and slide in. She started the engine, sat for a moment, head down, and then pulled away from the curb.

———— ❦ ————

Eunice was buying a box of pills reputed to ease migraine headaches when she saw Rob Atherton talking with the pharmacist.

"I know; I know." Rob's impatience came through clearly. "I have an appointment in two weeks." Again the pharmacist talked low, his expression grim. Eunice stood back, not wanting to eavesdrop. "How long a wait are you talking about?" The pharmacist said he would call Rob's doctor, confirm that a refill was in order, and have the prescription ready in a few minutes. "Fine. Go ahead."

Rob turned and spotted her. Why would he give her such a pained look?

The clerk called her attention, asking if she needed help. Eunice handed over the box of pills. The lady chattered pleasantly as she rang it up, took Eunice's money, made change, tucked the small box into a white bag, and stapled the receipt to it. She handed Eunice's purchase back. "Have a nice day, Mrs. Hudson."

She noticed Rob loitering in one of the aisles. "Is everything all right, Rob?"

He glanced up. "Not really. I need a refill on my nitroglycerin tablets, and he's insisting I should've had a checkup with my doctor. He's right, of course, but my schedule hasn't allowed for it."

"Isn't nitroglycerin for a heart condition?"

"Angina."

"I didn't know—"

"No reason you should, unless Sheila mentioned it to your husband during one of their . . . counseling appointments."

He said it in such an odd way, she was left wondering what he meant. Was he concerned that Paul was talking about things he shouldn't? "I can assure you," she said gently, "Paul never tells me anything that's said during any of his counseling sessions."

His eyes narrowed slightly. "I guess I shouldn't be surprised."

Again, the undercurrent of something unpleasant. What was wrong here? Paul would never break a confidence. It was a matter of ethics. She wasn't sure what to say other than what she'd already said. "I feel remiss for not knowing you've been having health issues, Rob. I'm sorry."

"Well, to be frank, I could use a little sisterly advice." The pharmacist called his attention. "Would you mind giving me a few minutes, Eunice? I'd like to ask your opinion about something."

She had an uneasy feeling in the pit of her stomach, but agreed to wait. He paid for his prescription, and listened to the pharmacist caution him on the side effects of the medication and explain proper usage. Rob joined her again in the aisle lined with headache and stomachache medications. "Is there someplace we can talk?"

She suggested the coffee shop at the end of the block. "They put tables out on the sidewalk a few days ago. It's nice and sunny, and there shouldn't be many customers this time of the morning."

Rob picked a table farthest from the front door. The umbrella hadn't been put up yet. "I'm not sure how to begin. I don't know how much you know."

"Know about what?"

"Sheila's counseling."

"Well, nothing, of course. Paul never talks about his counseling appointments to anyone."

His mouth turned down slightly as he studied her. He opened his mouth to say something, then closed it when he saw the waitress approaching. He asked Eunice what she wanted. "A latte, please." He ordered a decaf coffee for himself.

He leaned back in his chair and studied her. "How much do you know about me and Sheila?"

"I know you've both been very generous to the church." She wasn't certain how much to say or how to say it. "Sheila seems to be far more interested in being involved in the church than you are."

He gave a short laugh. "I guess that's one way of putting it."

"I've heard you travel a great deal."

"As often as possible."

His dry tone disturbed her. "On business, as I understand it."

He nodded. "On business. And sometimes, personal." He put his hands on the table and tapped his fingertips together. "I go to Florida every other month. My ex-wife lives there. It's all pretty messy, Eunice. I'm just going to lay it all out for you and then ask your advice. Is that all right?" He leaned back again as the waitress delivered their order.

Eunice thanked him for the latte before taking a sip. She almost hoped he would resist the impulse to tell her any more about his private life, but he moved his chair closer to the table, apparently intent on doing so.

"Molly, my first wife, put me through college. She helped me get started in business. She's the mother of my two children. About the time they were entering high school and giving us some problems, I hired a new secretary. Smart, young, beautiful. As you can guess, it was Sheila, and it wasn't very long before I was having an affair with her. My wife seemed boring compared to her. Molly never went to college. She never had the opportunity." He leaned back again, his eyes distant.

"I guess, in some ways, Molly embarrassed me. Here I was with a master's degree, making more money than I ever dreamed I'd make, and involved in a lot of social functions, and Molly didn't seem to fit in. Worse, she didn't seem to want to fit in. I started taking Sheila to business dinners, and it went from there. I asked Molly for a divorce. Of course, it devastated her and the kids, but by that time, I was so besotted by Sheila, I didn't care what I did to my family. I had friends who'd gone through similar things and given me advice. Bad advice. They told me to get as much money out of the joint accounts as I could and put it all in my name. So I did. I justified it to myself that I'd been the one making the money all through the marriage, except for the first four years when Molly was working and putting me through school."

He shook his head and looked away. "I got a high-powered attorney to make sure I retained most of the assets. Molly didn't fight me. She said she hoped I'd come to my senses and come home. So it was easy to take advantage of her. She agreed to everything my attorney proposed. Child support. Alimony for ten years. Half the house. She never stopped to think how she'd pay me for my half on what little I was going to give her."

Leaning forward, he held the tall cup for a moment. He sipped, winced, and started again. "Molly didn't put the house on the market until the week after I married Sheila. It was in an exclusive neighborhood and sold the first week. She didn't have the money to buy another house like it. So she rented a cheaper house in the same school district. She wanted to make sure the kids could finish school with their friends. Which they did. I saw Molly a couple of times. She lost a lot of weight. She was taking computer classes at the local junior college so that she could find a job. The alimony wasn't enough, you see. Not that she ever asked me for more. My son told me, the last time he spoke to me."

Eunice could see his pain. When he studied her, she had the feeling he was checking to see if she was judging him harshly. She was trying hard not to judge him at all.

His shoulders relaxed. "The thing is, I still love Molly. I still love my children." He gave a bleak laugh. "Neither one of them will have much to do with me. Not that Molly ever poisoned them against me. They saw right through everything. I got myself a trophy wife. Someone younger and prettier than their mother who didn't care what methods she used to get herself a rich husband. Sheila still sneers about Molly, still resents every dime I send to my children. The truth is, Sheila doesn't even care about me."

"I'm sure that's not true, Rob."

He looked at her with a strange mingling of pity and impatience. "You haven't got a mean bone in your body, have you? You haven't got a clue how a woman like Sheila works. How devious and deceptive she can be. How ambitious. She's probably—" He stopped. Pressing his lips together, he shook his head again. He took another sip of coffee. "Just take it from someone who knows her. Sheila bores easily, and she was bored with me after the first few years. It bothered me in the beginning, and I did everything I could to hold her interest. After a while, I looked the other way and immersed myself in business."

"Sheila's still with you, Rob. Surely that says something."

"Yes. I believe it says *something*." What he thought it meant clearly gave him no comfort.

Eunice felt out of her depth. "Maybe you should talk to Paul . . ."

He gave her a droll look. "I don't think I'd get a fair hearing."

"Paul has counseled couples before. He—"

"It's too late, Eunice."

"It's never too late."

He shook his head. "Sheila isn't my problem. My feelings for Molly are. I used to be eaten up by guilt. Now I realize it's more than that. I still love her. I've made a point of going back to Florida every other month. To see my children. That's what I tell Sheila, anyway. But the truth is, I go back there to see Molly."

His smile was pained. "She's really something. It took her ten years, but she put herself through college. She turned fifty-six last month and she looks better than ever. She's done things I never even knew she wanted to do. She took up hiking a few years ago. My daughter told me Molly trained with weights and packs for months because she wanted to come to California and climb Mount Whitney. I thought she was nuts and she'd give up the idea. But she did it last year. I couldn't believe it. Now she's planning to go to Europe with some friends and walk through Spain. She's even been taking Spanish lessons." He shook his head. "And I thought she was boring."

The waitress asked if they wanted anything else. He asked for another decaf. Eunice had hardly touched her latte. Her stomach was churning. Why was she so tense? Countless people had come to her over the years wanting her advice. Why was she so uneasy now?

Rob leaned back. "I went back for my son's wedding last month. I didn't even tell Sheila about it because I knew my son wouldn't want her there. Molly and I were seated together at the reception. We talked all afternoon. When my son left with his bride for their honeymoon, Molly and I went out to dinner and talked some more. The bottom line is I still love her. I never really stopped. What I felt for Sheila was lust, and that died a long time ago. I love Molly a little more every time I go back there and see her."

"Did you tell her that?"

"Yes, I told her. She cried. She's built a life without me. And she reminded me I'm married to Sheila now. If you can call it a marriage." He swore under his breath. "I can't stand to be in the same house with Sheila. She harps about everything. Nothing satisfies her. If I gave her the moon, she'd want Mars. She saps my strength. Our marriage is a disaster. I feel like I'm living in a nightmare!" He couldn't hide his despair.

"You loved Sheila once, Rob."

"It wasn't love, Eunice. That's what I'm saying." His eyes were filled with anguish. "I want my wife back. I want to come home at night to Molly. I want a relationship with my kids. I want restoration. Doesn't God talk about restoration?"

Eunice's eyes burned with tears. What could she say that would be any comfort to this tormented man? He didn't understand the restoration of which he spoke. "Rob, if you turn to the Lord, He'll give you peace in this. He'll help you build—"

"I don't need to hear about the Lord! What I want to know from you is if a woman can forgive a man for betraying her the way I betrayed Molly. Would you?"

"That's not a fair question."

"It's fair. I need to know! Molly says she's forgiven me, but she won't even talk about us getting back together. She loved me once. I remember how much she loved me. She sacrificed her own dreams to get me through school. Don't you think some of that love could still be there? That it could be revived?"

Eunice felt torn. However the marriage between Rob and Sheila had come about, it was a marriage, nonetheless, and not to be tossed aside heedlessly. "Rob, if you're asking me to give you approval to leave Sheila so you can try to win Molly back, I can't give it."

He surveyed her. "Why not?"

Her heart thumped. She thought of what Paul would say if he knew what she was about to say to a man who had given so much money to the church. "Because it's self-centered." She said it as gently as she could. "You're not considering the life Molly has built, but what you threw away."

"I wonder if you'd feel the same way if you really knew Sheila."

She reached out and put her hands over his. "Rob, *you* made the decision to leave Molly. Isn't that what you've said?"

"Yes."

"Then is it fair to cast all the blame on Sheila for the trouble you're having? Or to put the responsibility for your future happiness on Molly? These are things you need to take to the Lord. Seek His will for your life. He can heal, if you're willing to let Him."

His eyes narrowed. "What if I told you Sheila isn't faithful to me?"

She took her hands away and drew back, heart pounding strangely. "Do you have any reason to believe she isn't?"

His expression was cynical, his tone bitter. "You mean other than the adulterous affair I had with her?"

"Yes."

"Oh yeah. Enough." He held her gaze.

The Spirit moved within her, but she didn't want to listen. She didn't want to pursue what Rob meant. And she didn't want to ask herself why.

Rob sighed heavily. "I guess it comes down to the old tried-and-true saying: 'When you make your bed, you have to sleep in it.'" He finished his coffee. "I'd better get to work." He stood.

She felt she had failed him. "I'm sorry, Rob."

When he extended his hand, she took it. "Not half as sorry as I am." He put his other hand over hers and squeezed her hand gently, his expression oddly tender and sad. "You remind me of Molly."

Eunice remained at the table in front of the coffee shop for another half hour, her latte cold and untouched.

CHAPTER 17

PAUL ENTERED THE CHURCH OFFICE. "Hi, Reka. How are you? Good to see you." He held out his hand and took the mail from her as he passed by her desk. "Clear my calendar this morning, would you?" He sorted his mail. "I have some work I need to do. And hold my calls."

He closed the door of his private office and tossed half a dozen letters into the trash can. There was always someone on the mission field with a hand out. Since the board had agreed to cut the missions budget in half, he hadn't even bothered to pass on the newsletters from Korea, South Africa, and Mexico. Valley New Life Center needed the money. They had their own mission field to harvest.

He pulled out a letter from Dennis Morgan. Thank God. The budget needed an injection right now, and Morgan always sent a sizable check. He slit the envelope open and looked at the check first. Two thousand dollars? Was that all? The note read, *Designated gift—scholarships to the Promise Keepers seminar. D. M.*

Annoyed, Paul crumpled the note and tossed it into the wastebasket. Now he had a contract plumber telling him what to do! Morgan didn't have a clue where the money was most needed. The board would decide what to do with the measly two thousand dollars.

His intercom buzzed. Irritated, he pushed the button. "Reka, I told you to hold my calls."

"That's what I was just telling Mrs. Atherton, Pastor, but she insists she has to talk with you."

His pulse rocketed. "All right." He hoped he sounded cooler than he felt.

"Mrs. Talbot called a few minutes ago. Her husband passed away last night."

"I'm sorry to hear that. I'll call her later." He released the button, came around his desk, and opened the door. "Sheila." He was satisfied with the cool sound of his voice. "How can I help you?" She was wearing the pretty yellow summer dress he liked.

"I'm sorry to be such a bother, Pastor Paul." Ignoring Reka, Sheila walked into his office. "I know you're busy, but I had to talk with you about something important."

Paul made eye contact with his secretary. "Is the church newsletter done yet, Reka?"

"I have it right here, all ready."

"Why don't you take your lunch break now and drop it off at the printer?"

"I usually drop it off on my way home."

"And it was late last time. I want it in the printer's hands by ten. That gives you half an hour to get it over there."

She blushed. "Yes, sir."

She had never called him sir before. He glanced back at her, but she'd bent over the bottom drawer of her desk, taking out her purse. "I didn't mean to be abrupt, Reka. You're doing your best. Take your time. I'm leaving shortly for an appointment and won't be back until two this afternoon." He closed the door.

Sheila smiled and ran her hand down his arm. "I know you don't want me coming to your office anymore, Paul, but I had to see you. I couldn't help myself. Do you really have an appointment?"

He caught her hand. "Reka's still right outside the door."

Sheila tossed her purse on the couch. "Reka was rude to me. She looks down on me."

Did his secretary have suspicions about his relationship with Sheila? He hoped not.

"You should've seen her face when I walked in. She took one look at my dress and looked like she'd swallowed a mouthful of vinegar."

"You weren't dressing to please Reka."

"No, I wasn't." Smiling, she moved closer. "You like it, don't you?"

Too much. She'd worn it to a church picnic, and he'd had trouble keeping his eyes off her. He was having a hard time concentrating now. "Reka is just doing her job." Sheila's skin was golden brown. He wanted to run his hands over her bare shoulders. He wanted to do far more than that, but this wasn't the place. She knew that as well as he did.

"You know, it's not a secretary's job to run her boss's life."

"Reka doesn't run my life. She helps me keep to my schedule."

"She's overstepping herself, and you know it." She toyed with a button on his shirt. "You should fire her—and hire me."

"Then we'd really have a problem."

"Meaning what?" She took her hands away. "I couldn't do the job? It's what I used to do for a living before I married Rob."

She wasn't herself today. "I'm sure you have the skills, Sheila, but I'd have a hard time keeping my mind on my work."

Her demeanor changed. "You might enjoy coming to the office a lot more."

"I was going to call you, Sheila."

"Were you?"

She was so close he could smell her perfume. Something exotic that went to his head. Nervous, perspiring, he stepped past her. "Reka should've left by now." He looked through the sheer drapes to the parking lot below. She was just going out to her car. She had her cell phone to her ear. She stood beside her Toyota as she talked.

"Is Reka gone yet?"

"She's getting into her car."

"So we're alone now. You can relax." Sheila sat and crossed her elegant legs.

His heart hammered. "We need to talk first."

Her expression became guarded. "About what?"

"You have to stop calling the house, for one thing."

"I never leave a message."

"And you kissed me on the way out of church again. You have to stop that."

"Why?" She smiled. "It was only a little kiss between friends." She swung one sandaled foot back and forth. "No one thought anything about it, Paul." She lifted her brow. "Eunice didn't even notice."

"Eunice isn't the one who starts gossip." Sometimes he wondered why he was taking such chances. Was he in love with Sheila? She made him feel more of a man than Eunice did.

"What's really bothering you, Paul?"

Things were getting out of control. "I think we're getting in over our heads, Sheila." He never should have allowed things to go this far. He couldn't even think straight where she was concerned. He'd catch himself daydreaming about her while he was sitting across the dinner table from Eunice.

She started to cry. "I thought you cared about me."

"I do care." He sat beside her.

"I'm sorry I was careless on Sunday, but it'd been four days since we'd talked. I couldn't wait any longer. You've been my savior, Paul. You're the kindest, most thoughtful man I've ever known. I'd dry up and die inside without you."

He felt himself weakening. She needed him. He couldn't turn his back on her. "You have to promise not to come to my office, except for your appointments. We have to be careful." He took her hand and kissed it. "Gossip could destroy both of us."

"Rob doesn't care what I do. And Eunice doesn't make you happy, not the way I do."

His stomach tightened. "The church cares what I do. We don't want to hurt anyone, do we?"

"No, of course not." She drew back reluctantly. "It's just so hard to stay away from you. Nobody has ever made me feel the way you do. You only have to look at me and I melt inside. I wish you cared about me the way I care about you."

He gave her a soft kiss on the mouth. "Does that tell you?"

She leaned toward him, lips parted. "Oh, Paul."

The door was closed. Reka was gone. Why was he so worried? He kissed her again. When he raised his head, her eyes were like dark water. "Is that better?"

"Much." She toyed with his collar. "Rob left this morning. I looked at his airline tickets last night while he was in the shower. He won't be back until Wednesday next week. You could come over to my house when the board meeting is over tonight. It'd be so wonderful, Paul. Just the two of us. No phones ringing. No secretaries camped outside the door. You could park in the garage. Nobody would see your car. Nobody would know. Nobody would get hurt."

"And what do I tell Eunice?"

"Tell her there's a crisis and you're needed. You called her the last time, and she didn't question you when you got home after two in the morning."

Eunice believed everything he told her. "I don't think it's a good idea."

"Eunice won't even miss you. You said all she ever does is read her Bible."

He couldn't think straight when she touched him.

"We can do anything we want, Paul. No one will know. Besides, Eunice doesn't love you the way I do. And it's not fair the way Rob leaves me alone all the time. Eunice is always busy helping other people, and all Rob ever thinks about is money. You could come up and go into the spa with me."

Eunice no longer fulfilled him. She hadn't in a long time. She was too innocent to understand a man like him. Sheila did. It would be good to relax and be himself.

"We'll be careful, Paul, so careful not even a little birdie will peep about us." She drew his head down. "Nobody's going to find out."

And Paul was too pressed by his desire to consider that someone already knew.

———— ❦ ————

Eunice heard the phone ringing as she was heading for the back door. Groaning, she glanced at her watch. She'd been looking forward to her date with Samuel for a cup of tea at Vine Hill. She still had time. "Hudson residence. Eunice speaking."

"Eunice, it's Reka. You need to come down to the church office right away."

"Why? What's wrong?"

"Everything. I won't be in the office when you get here. I'm going to the printer, and then I'm going home. And I'm not coming back. I'm sorry, Eunice. I can't work for him anymore. I just can't. I'm sorry. I'm so sorry to do this to you." She hung up, crying.

Oh, Lord, what's happened? Eunice hung up the telephone and went out the back door. Sliding into the front seat of her car, she took her cell phone out of her purse, and plugged it in. Slipping on her headset, she punched in Samuel's number and started the car. "Samuel! It's Euny. I'm not going to be able to make it today." She backed out of the garage and pressed the remote to close the door.

"You sound upset."

She changed gears and headed down the street. "Reka just called. I think she just quit. She said Paul needs me at the church right away. I don't know what's happened, but I have to find out."

"How can I help?"

"Pray, Samuel. Pray real hard."

"Been doing that for years."

"I know. Thanks." She didn't want to sound any alarms. "I'm sure everything will be all right. I'll call you later. Say hello to Bessie for me, would you? Tell her I'll come over to see her soon."

"Will do. Drive safe."

She punched the Off button, tossed her headset onto the passenger seat, and turned onto the main road. When she turned in to the church parking lot, she saw a dozen cars scattered in what shade was available. She remembered there was a wedding rehearsal at eleven. One of the associates was performing the ceremony. She parked her old Buick next to Paul's new Mercedes. Grabbing her purse, she headed for the main entrance of Valley New Life Center.

The phone was ringing on Reka's desk, but before Eunice could pick up, the answering machine clicked on, identified the church, and went through the schedule of services, finally asking the caller to leave a message and promising that someone would get back to them as soon as possible. "God bless you!"

As the message ended, Eunice heard other sounds. Her heart stopped. "Paul?" When she pushed the door open, she caught her breath and stared, too hurt and horrified to speak.

"*Eunice!*"

She thought her heart would burst and she would die right there in the open doorway. "Oh, God, oh, God . . ."

"Eunice." It seemed the only word Paul could say as he tried to straighten his clothes. There was no doubt what they had been doing. "Eunice."

She'd never seen such a look on her husband's face before. Horror. Shame. Fear. Anger.

Eunice stepped back out the door and closed it. Gasping for breath, she let go of the knob as though it had burned her hand. Then she turned and fled.

"Eunice, wait!" Paul was cold with shock.

Sheila scrambled up. "What was she doing here?"

In the heat of the moment he'd forgotten to lock the door. Regret gripped him. "Eunice, honey, wait!" He went after her, but by the time he reached the exit, she was backing out of her parking space, her tires squealing. Sick with fear, he watched her head for the street. Luckily, no one was in the parking lot. He strode back to the office, his heart bouncing around in his chest like a frightened rabbit.

Sheila was white-faced and pacing. "What am I going to do? Why didn't you lock the door?"

"You distracted me."

"I distracted you? You couldn't wait to have me! Don't blame me for this mess, Paul!"

He should've locked the door, but it was too late now to think about that. At least Reka hadn't been in the office. At least he'd had the forethought to send his secretary away before anything got started. He wiped the sweat from the back of his neck. He could reason with Eunice. She'd never say anything to hurt the church.

Sheila's eyes were wild. Paul had never heard her utter a swearword, let alone the string of them that came out of her mouth now. "What am I going to do?"

Paul was asking himself the same question. Why had Eunice picked today to visit him at his office? She'd never interfered before. "We'll work it out." How was he going to work it out? Why had Eunice come walking in on him without waiting until he gave her permission to enter? At least he and Sheila could've straightened themselves up enough to make it look like an emotional counseling session had been going on and nothing more. She could have at least warned them before barging in. "Calm down, Sheila. It'll be all right. I'll talk to her."

"Are you kidding? You don't get it, do you? Rob would love to divorce me. If he finds out about this, he'll file for divorce."

"I thought that's what you wanted."

"No, it's *not* what I want."

She was so adamant, he was hurt. "I'll talk to him then." He hoped Rob didn't have a gun.

"Oh, great. Just great. And say what? You couldn't help yourself? He'll know what's been going on. He'll *know*."

What had been going on? He'd never seen Sheila like this before. "I'll figure out something, Sheila. I'll—"

"Shut up, would you? Just let me think! All you can do is make things worse." The face Paul had thought so beautiful was now twisted and ugly. She glared at him. "What are you staring at?"

"You. I've never seen you like this before."

"Like what?"

Raging, foulmouthed, black-eyed with malice. Contemptuous. He had the feeling he was seeing the real Sheila for the first time. "It's all been a game to you, hasn't it?"

Her eyes flickered. "No. Of course not."

Anger came up from a deep well inside him. "You're lying."

"I've never lied to you about anything!"

He saw the bigger truth she tried to hide.

"All right, but all I ever wanted was to have a little fun. Rob is so boring." She gathered her things. "Don't look at me like that. You were willing to play along. Don't pretend otherwise. You've been having a good time."

"You harlot!" He was so mad he could have used his fists on her. "A pastor, was that it? I was a challenge to you. That's all."

Her eyes flashed. "A challenge? Don't flatter yourself." She snatched her purse from the floor. "Your guilty conscience was beginning to bore me anyway."

"Get out of here." Whatever he had felt for her was gone, burned away with the firestorm of discovery. "If you say anything about this to anyone, I'll tell them my part of the story."

She turned on him, the innocent, wounded facade she'd worn for months gone. "Oh, you mean the part where you seduced me?" Her sarcasm ripped into his confidence.

"I did not!"

"I came to you for *help*, Pastor Paul. Remember? And you *used* me."

"That's a lie!"

"So what?" She laughed at him. "Do you think people won't believe me? People always want to believe the worst. Don't you know anything?"

"They know me."

"Not as well as I do, and I'd only have to convince a few."

How could he ever have thought he loved this woman? What had he ever seen in her? She was conniving, vicious. He felt compassion for Rob Atherton for the first time since he'd begun counseling Sheila. "Do you think you could convince your husband?"

She paled, her eyes darting. "I don't want a divorce any more than you do." She looked toward the door, then at him. "Look, I'm sorry, Paul. I never meant to hurt you." Her eyes narrowed. "All you have to do is convince little Goody Two-shoes you've repented, and swear you'll never look at another woman again. She'll forgive you. Women like her always do." She hurried out.

Paul felt his life crumbling. He couldn't go tearing out of here after his wife without having people talk. What was he going to do? He needed to give Sheila time to drive away before he could leave. He had to make everything look normal before he went down the corridor and out the door. If anyone saw him, they'd know something was wrong.

He could feel the sweat beading. He yanked the curtains open. What an idiot he'd been! What a stupid, gullible fool! He took his wallet, car keys, and cell phone from the top desk drawer. He'd talk to Eunice. He'd make her understand it was all a mistake. He'd lost his head. He'd say he was sorry. She wouldn't do anything to hurt his ministry. Anything she did to hurt him would hurt her, too. She was his wife, after all. People might want to know why he'd had to turn to another woman for love.

Thank God, Reka had been on her way to the printer's when Eunice walked in.

He'd make it up to Eunice. He'd tell her he loved her. He'd tell her it had all been a mistake, that it would never happen again. He'd always been able to make her listen. And with so much at stake, she surely would listen this time as well.

Eunice dumped her empty suitcase on the bed and flung it open. She wouldn't take everything. Just enough to get by for a week. Or two. She had to get away. She had to think. Sobbing, she fumbled through her clothing. Wherever she was going, she'd need a dress for church. *Which one? Which one?* She picked a pale-green one and snatched it out. The hanger fell to the floor. Eunice stooped and picked it up. Abby had crocheted the covering for this hanger. She fingered the pretty rosebuds around the base of the metal hook, her eyes tearing up. How many hours had her dear friend spent making this gift? Every Christmas, Abby had given her two more.

Jamming it under her arm, Eunice yanked out dress after dress, letting them drop to the floor as she tucked hangers under her arm. She didn't stop until she had every one that Abby had made for her. With shaking hands, she arranged them carefully in her suitcase, folding one dress over the top. She packed Timothy's picture inside a sweater. Pulling a dresser drawer open, she dug for the small jewelry box that had belonged to her mother. Opening it, she took out the small heart locket Paul had given her on their fifth anniversary. Inside was a picture of her handsome husband, smiling, looking so young and confident. With a cry, she flung it across the room and packed her mother's jewelry box.

"What are you doing?" Paul said from the doorway.

She jumped at the sound of his voice. "What does it look like I'm doing?" Her heart began pounding. "I'm leaving."

"Don't leave me, Eunice. Please. I love you."

He loved her? Did he think she was stupid?

"Please, Eunice. Listen to me."

"I need to get away. I need to think."

"You can think here. Let's sit down and talk this over."

"Don't use your counselor's voice on me! Save it for Sheila!" She started to cry again, great heaving sobs of anguish and fury.

"Honey . . ." He tried to approach her, but she backed away. She hated him. She could smell Sheila's perfume in her bedroom. "Sheila's out of my life. Let me explain what happened."

"I don't want to hear—"

"Okay. Okay. Not right now. But we'll work things out."

"You work things out." She yanked another drawer open and reached for her nightgown. She'd slept with Paul in that nightgown. He'd touched her when she was wearing it. She left the nightgown where it was and shut the drawer. She spotted an embroidered Twenty-third Psalm in a glass frame. Her mother had given it to her on her sixteenth birthday. She took it off the wall.

"It wasn't as bad as it looked, Eunice."

She glared at him through tears, then turned back to the suitcase she had tossed on the bed. What was his definition of *bad*? What could be any worse than finding him in the arms of another woman? It hadn't been a friendly peck on the cheek this time. She remembered a time when he'd kissed her the way he was kissing Sheila Atherton. Not that she would ever let him kiss her that way again. *Oh, Father, shut it off!*

Paul caught her arm. "Will you please stop packing long enough to hear me out?"

"Let go of me, Paul."

His fingers loosened enough for her to pull free. "Doesn't our marriage mean enough to you to hear me out, Euny?"

"If our marriage meant anything to you, I wouldn't've found you on the floor with another man's wife!"

His face turned red. He should be embarrassed. He should look ashamed. She brushed past him and took a few more garments out of the dresser.

"You could at least give me a hearing before you play judge and jury. It wasn't entirely my fault. Sheila came to me for marriage counseling. She was miserable. She said her marriage was disintegrating. Rob was too busy with other things. He was distant, consumed with his work, traveling a lot."

"So it's Rob's fault you're having an affair with his wife."

"No. I'm not having an affair. Not exactly."

"What would you call it?"

"None of this would've happened if Rob had bothered to be some kind of husband to her. Rob didn't even bother to show up after the first appointment!"

She could tell him what Rob had told her. She could tell him a lot of things she'd heard and not put together until today. She turned away, fighting the impulse to spill others' secrets.

Paul came around to the other side of the bed. He stared at her. His beseeching look. She'd seen it before. "I knew Sheila was getting too attached, so I encouraged her to see one of the other pastors. She refused. She said she didn't trust anyone but me. I guess I was flattered. It was nice to have a woman need me for a change."

"I needed you."

"You never showed it. You always had places to go and people to see."

"And you always had a counseling appointment."

He blushed again. "You were distant, Eunice. You can't deny it. I'd come home in the evenings and you'd hardly say anything to me. Ever since Timothy moved in with my mother, you've been punishing me. If you'd been any kind of wife to me, none of this would have happened!"

His attack hurt unbearably. Was that true?

Paul came around the bed. "You know things haven't been right between us. And I've been under pressure you can't even imagine."

Think! I've got to think! "You have three associates, a wonderful secretary, and a legion of volunteers."

"But I'm the one in charge."

"I thought God was in charge."

"You know what I mean!" He was angry, defensive. "Ever since I removed you from the music ministry, you've had something negative to say about every one of the programs I've laid out. How do you think that's made me feel? As a man? As your husband?"

Hot tears burned. Her throat ached. She could see where he was going with this. Where he always went. "You're telling me it's my fault you had an affair."

"I never slept with her."

She saw the way his eyes shifted when he said it and knew it was all semantics. *Sleep* was the operative word. "No, that's true. You weren't *sleeping* with her in your office today, were you?" She remembered the night he came home after two in the morning. She remembered other evenings. How long had he fought the temptation before giving in? Had he fought at all? She remembered phone calls he had to take in his office. "'I tell you that anyone who looks at a woman lustfully has already committed adultery with her in his heart.'"

"Don't quote Scripture at me!" His face was red, with anger this time. "I know Scripture better than you do!"

"You know it. You just don't live it."

His face hardened. "I'm trying to tell you I'm sorry."

"Sorry you were caught." She knew what was really worrying him, even if he didn't.

"What do you want me to do? Grovel?"

His sarcasm made her shrivel inside. She closed and locked her suitcase with trembling hands. "I want you to speak from your heart, not your head. I want you to understand that lame excuses and a halfhearted apology aren't enough." As she hauled her suitcase off the bed with two hands, she looked at him through her tears. "I want you to understand that I need to get away from you. I need time to think about what I should do."

He blocked her way. Oh, he was afraid now. But not of losing her. "I'm not going to let you leave me, Eunice. Please. Think what you're doing! Stay here and think. I'll leave you alone. I swear it. I'll sleep in the guest room. I'll tell everyone you're not feeling well on Sunday."

So there it was—what really worried him, and it wasn't the disintegration of their marriage. "I don't want to be in the same house with you."

Paul swore at her and wouldn't let her pass. "You're not just any man's wife! You're my wife. And I'm the pastor of a big church! I'm responsible for the lives of three thousand people. If you leave, everyone will want to know why. You know how little it takes to start gossip. You'll destroy my ministry! You leave me and you'll tear down everything it's taken me years to build! Is that what you want?"

"At this moment, yes."

He paled. "And what about all the people you love? What about them? What do you suppose will happen if you start talking about me and Sheila? Do you want to be the one to tell Rob Atherton his wife's been cheating on him?"

"Stop it!" She dropped her suitcase and covered her face. *"Stop it!"*

"It's all in your hands what happens to Valley New Life!"

Did this man know her at all? "I've never been the one to start gossip, and you know it." Neither had Reka. *Oh, Lord. Poor Reka.*

"Sheila isn't going to say anything. She doesn't want a divorce. She'll do everything she can to stay married to Rob."

"I don't think everything will be enough."

Paul gripped her shoulders tightly. "You can't say anything, Eunice. You can't do anything. We have to stay together. I know I've hurt you. I know you're angry with me. I understand. Don't you think I've disappointed myself? I never thought I could be taken in by some little hussy."

Everything was always about him. She jerked away and reached for her suitcase.

"I love you."

"No, you don't." She choked on a sob. "I wonder if you ever did." She tried to step around him.

He yanked the suitcase from her. "I'm sorry, but I'm not going to step aside and let you destroy the church. You're in no state to think rationally. If you run out on me now, you'll regret it tomorrow. I know you. You'll be eaten up with guilt over the trouble you'll have caused. And it'll be too late. The damage will be done. And there won't be anything either one of us can do to fix it."

"You aren't protecting the church, Paul. You're protecting yourself!"

"I am the church, Euny, and you know it. People come to hear me preach. They come to be part of what I'm building." His tone softened. "I know you want to hurt me right now. You'd like to annihilate me."

He didn't know her at all.

"But I want you to stop feeling sorry for yourself and think of the people you'd hurt. Think about the people who've supported us through the years, and how they'll feel if you say anything. Think of all the people who've believed in us." Setting the suitcase down, he cupped her face and forced her to look at him. "You want to know the first thing that will come into their minds? Why I had to turn to another woman for love."

If he'd had a knife, he couldn't have stabbed her more deeply.

The phone rang. She watched him struggle. The battle was over in seconds, and she lost.

"I'm sorry, Marvin. I forgot. I'll be there in about twenty minutes. Have Reka make you some coffee. Oh. She isn't?" He hung up and glanced at his watch. "Reka's late getting back. And I forgot I had a meeting with Marvin."

Eunice didn't know whether to believe him or not. For all she knew, Sheila was calling and telling him to hurry back to church so they could pick up where they left off.

"Something's not right with the budget. And Reka's not back yet. She must have a dentist appointment or something. I've got to go."

Paul leaned down to kiss her. She turned her face away. He caressed her cheek. "I love you more than you know."

But not enough to do any good.

Paul crossed the room, took her purse, and dumped the contents on the dresser.

"What're you doing?"

"Taking your car keys. You're in no state to drive."

That wasn't the reason and both of them knew it.

He came back and picked up her suitcase. "I'll give it back to you this evening. I won't be gone long. We'll talk some more when I get back." He closed the door behind him. Fortunately for her, the lock was on the inside.

Eunice knew if she stayed, nothing would ever change.

CHAPTER 18

SAMUEL WAITED UNTIL SEVEN in the evening before he called the Hudson residence. The moment Paul answered, Samuel knew something was wrong.

"She's not in this evening, Samuel. Sorry. I think she had a meeting. Do you want me to check her calendar?"

If everything was all right, Eunice would've called him. She would never have left him hanging after telling him there was an emergency involving Paul. It wasn't like her. "Was everything all right at the church this morning?"

"This morning? What do you mean?"

He'd never heard Paul sound so nervous. "Reka called Eunice and said you needed her at the church."

"Reka called her?"

Samuel wished he hadn't mentioned names. "Eunice was planning to stop by for tea this morning."

"Yes, I know."

And clearly wasn't happy about it. Samuel let the hurt go. "Euny called and said you needed her. She was going to let me know that everything was okay." He waited. Silence. "Is everything all right, Paul?"

"Sure. Why wouldn't it be?" Anger had replaced impatience.

"I don't know. You could tell me."

"Everything's fine, Samuel. Take my word for it. Our numbers are way up. Have you heard?"

Samuel knew something was wrong—very wrong. Paul's bravado was forced, his confidence shaken. "Numbers aren't everything, Paul. How are *you?*"

"I've never been better."

"If you say so." Samuel was too old for a dogfight, and backing Paul into a corner wouldn't help Eunice.

"I don't know what Reka meant about this morning, but nothing was going on that I can remember."

He was lying, but Samuel had other concerns now. Would Paul target Reka for church discipline? Samuel hoped he hadn't gotten that sweet woman into trouble. "It might not have been Reka. I could be mistaken. My hearing isn't what it used to be."

"Now that you mention it, Eunice did come by the church, but she didn't say anything to me about a call. Probably realized it was a mistake or somebody's idea of a practical joke. You know how people are."

"Yes, I do." Samuel wished he didn't.

"Good talking to you, Samuel. I'll tell Eunice you called."

Samuel had no illusions. His imagination created a dozen scenarios of what might've happened or what was happening inside the walls of the church and the Hudson household. *Enough of this.* He knew better. Oh, how easily the enemy put his foot on the accelerator and sent Samuel's mind into overdrive. Only faith could put the brakes on.

Oh, Lord, I don't know what's happened over there, but You know. You see into men's hearts, and their plans are laid bare before You. Nothing is hidden. Jesus, please strengthen me. I'm an old man and tired of the battle. Renew me. Give me the strength to keep running the race.

I have this awful feeling in the pit of my stomach, the same kind of feeling I had when I sat across the street from Centerville Christian and saw the cross smash on the sidewalk. Oh, Father, don't let that happen again. And if it has to happen, take me home so I won't see it. Lord, turn us around. Please, Father, whatever Paul's done, don't let it destroy Your church. Don't let it shake Eunice's faith. Don't let it crush her spirit. You know Satan does his best work in a church. If Satan can get to the shepherd, he can prey on the flock. Whatever's happened down there, Lord, take hold of those responsible and discipline them so they will repent. Lord, Lord . . .

When would men learn they couldn't go against the Lord without facing the consequences? They thought they could go about their lives and do whatever they thought right in their own eyes, and then have the unmitigated audacity to call it "serving the Lord."

"Our numbers are way up. Have you heard?"

Paul's heart hadn't changed since the last time Samuel had talked with him. He still dwelt in the shadow of his earthly father, still ran ahead of the Lord, still let fear and pride reign.

Oh, Jesus, when will the boy learn? What will it take to bring him to his knees?

Samuel wept because he knew the Day of the Lord was at hand, and it was Eunice who was in the olive press being crushed.

Fat hissed on red-hot charcoal as Stephen flipped hamburgers. Leaning back from the smoke, he took a look around. Over forty people had come to the midweek evening picnic. He hoped the Lord would multiply the hamburger patties because he'd only planned for the twenty-five members of his Bible study. And it seemed their gathering was attracting others to Rockville's little park south of the center of town. The only facilities were the two Porta-Potty units Stephen had rented for the day.

Blankets were laid out, umbrellas set up, and a line of card tables arranged to display bowls of potato and macaroni salad, baked beans, casseroles, and rolls. Brittany helped Jack Bodene man the larger barbecue. He talked while she listened, both turning foil-wrapped ears of sweet corn. Something was going on between those two. There was enough heat between them to cook the corn without the barbecue. Stephen just hoped they wouldn't set each other ablaze and end up in ashes again. Even though Jack had been sober for four years now, Stephen knew how long it took to really get your life in order. Brittany didn't have that great a track record, either.

He spotted Kathryn's car pulling up. She waved as she got out.

Brittany saw, too. "What's she doing here?"

Stephen looked his daughter in the eye. "I invited her."

"What for? She's a pain in the—"

"She could use some good friends."

Brittany gave a derisive laugh. "You were married to her. Do you think she'll approve of anyone here? You know what she's like."

"People can change."

"Not her."

"She needs Jesus, Brit," Jack said from his post.

"You're on her side, too?" She seethed resentment.

"It's not a matter of sides. Good grief, Brit. Like your mother is the only major screwup at this gathering. You and I haven't exactly had it all together either."

"It's her fault I didn't have it together."

Jack said one foul word that summed up his opinion of that excuse. "And you know it. Why don't you give her a chance?"

Her eyes glistened. "You don't understand. Neither one of you understands."

"Understands what?" Jack wasn't backing down. "That you want your pound of flesh?"

"You expect me to forgive her!"

"Yeah. I do."

"Well, what if I told you I wasn't ready? What if I said I wasn't going to stick around if she stays? What would you say then, Jack?"

Stephen saw Brittany had all of Kathryn's angst, sarcasm, and controlling instincts down pat.

Jack shrugged. When he told her exactly what he'd say, mincing no words, her mouth fell open. He wasn't finished with her. "I guess you'll go on feeling sorry for yourself. You'll justify and rationalize your lousy behavior and blame her for everything you ever did wrong. Convenient, isn't it, to have a scapegoat?"

"Are you finished?"

"Too bad you're gonna take another one of your long walks and miss out on a good picnic."

"Well, it's nice to know how you really feel about me, Jack."

Jack lifted his head and looked at her. "You know how I feel. No games. Remember? Whatever your mother did wrong or didn't do right, give it to God and let it go. If you can't walk the walk with me, you and I aren't taking another step forward."

Brittany spat out a curse at him and stalked off.

Jack winced. "Sorry, man."

"Nothing I haven't heard before." Stephen gave a sardonic laugh. He noticed Jack didn't take his eyes off Brittany as he tonged an ear of corn and slammed it on its other side.

Kathryn approached with a tray of cupcakes. She was wearing Levi's, a white tank top, and a straw hat with a silk scarf tied around the crown. Stephen couldn't see her eyes behind her sunglasses, but he knew she was watching their daughter stalk across the last grassy patch on the edge of the park. Her shoulders drooped slightly. "Maybe I should just leave these cupcakes and go."

"Nothing doing. Stick around and enjoy yourself. The fireworks are just getting started."

"In case it slipped your notice, the Fourth of July was two months ago."

"Brit might come back this time."

"Wishful thinking, but I'll stay. For a little while, at least."

Stephen introduced Kathryn to Jack Bodene. They exchanged pleasant greetings, and she went off with her cupcakes. Stephen kept his eye on her as he cooked the hamburgers. Did she feel as ill at ease as she looked? She stood at the table, fiddling with the platters, pretending to be busy while she watched the small groups laughing and talking together. Shouts came from the pickup baseball game at the far end of the grass. Hector Mendoza was hauling toward home plate while his wife and kids jumped up and down screaming.

Kathryn was heading for her car.

"Hey, Sal, take over for a while, would you?" Stephen handed over the spatula and intercepted Kathryn. "You know, Kat, you and Brit are going to have to stop running away from each other."

"What makes you think she'll come back if I'm here?"

He grinned. "Jack Bodene. He's got more sway with our daughter than the two of us put together, and he just read Brit the riot act. If she feels about him the way I think she does, she'll be back." He put his hand beneath her elbow. "Give it another two hours. If she isn't back by then, and you're bored out of your mind, you can split. I won't try to stop you." He steered her back to the gathering. "In the meantime, why don't I introduce you to the people I know?"

He left Kathryn with Lucinda Mendoza and half a dozen other

women watching and laughing over the baseball game and returned to the barbecue pit. A newcomer had dropped in and brought a grocery bag full of packaged hot dogs.

When the call went out that the hamburgers and hot dogs were ready, everyone lined up. Stephen saw Brittany standing under a sycamore tree, her forehead against Jack's chest. He held her shoulders as he bent to say something to her. She slipped her arms around his waist, her face turned away from the gathering.

Kathryn was on the other side of the food table, serving herself baked beans. He knew she'd spotted Brittany with Jack. "Why don't we sit together?"

Her gaze lifted to his in surprise. "Sure. Thanks."

His plate laden, he headed for a shady patch of green on the edge of the softball field, where half a dozen other families had laid down blankets to stake out their territory. Brittany and Jack moved to the end of the food line. Kathryn sat down and lifted her head, watching them briefly before she took a small bite of baked beans. "Lucinda says you're a very good teacher. I didn't know you knew anything about the Bible—let alone, how to teach it."

She wasn't baiting him. "I never cracked the cover of a Bible until I was in rehab. Then I met Samuel Mason, and he lit a fire in me to learn more. Now I'm hooked on it." She looked troubled. "Try not to worry about Brittany, Kat. If it doesn't happen today, it'll happen next time. Keep trying." He took a big bite of his hamburger.

"I wasn't thinking about Brittany." She looked at him and shook her head. "I just don't get it, Stephen."

"Get what?"

"The way you talk about Jesus, as though He's someone you know. Personally." She grimaced. "I'm not trying to start a fight. I just want to know what happened to make you this way."

He told her, and for once, she listened without interrupting or making wisecracks. She heard him out while she ate her meal. Her silence depressed him. He figured he'd done as bad a job as anyone could in sharing his faith, but he'd told her the truth without frills. She could do with it whatever she wanted. Within reason.

"Would you mind if I sit in on your class sometime?"

He coughed. "You want to come to the Bible study?"

"You don't have to choke on it. I won't come if it—"

"No, no." He waved and coughed again. "Sure. Yeah. Please. Come."

She laughed. "You should see your face!"

He hadn't seen her really laugh in a long, long time. It changed everything about her.

As the sun set, people started roasting marshmallows. Some sang songs. Hector surprised everyone with his melodious tenor. The laughter died down and the talk turned serious.

"We have enough people to start a church, Stephen."

The suggestion raised the hackles on the back of Stephen's neck. "No way, Tree House. Why spoil everything?"

"You're running out of room," Tree House said. "If the fire department ever finds out how many people you've got down in your basement every Wednesday night, they'll shut you down."

"What's the big deal?" Brittany said. "I've been in crack houses where there were more people than my dad has in his basement."

Nice going, Brittany. Great way to tell your mother what sort of life you were living before you came home. Stephen rubbed his temples. He was getting the twinge of an oncoming tension headache.

"There's a church on Third Street that's dying on the vine," one of the men said. "Why not talk to the pastor there and see if we can't rent their building for one night a week? We could get something going here in Rockville."

"They might even be willing to sell. I've been to services there. They haven't got more than a handful of people."

"Maybe we could pool some money and buy the place."

"Needs renovation."

"That's Stephen's bailiwick."

"We've got six guys here right now who've been on your work crews. We could fix that church up in no time."

"Whoa!" Stephen held up his hands. "If you're going to start talking about buying, renovating, or building a church, you can count me out. Been there, done that, don't want any part of it again."

"You're running out of room, boss."

Stephen reined in his emotions. "We don't need more churches, Hector. We need more teachers."

"Good teachers," another said.

"I've spent my whole life in church, *hombre*, and I've learned more about what the Bible says in the last six weeks from you than I did in all my catechism classes put together."

That was depressing news, considering how little Stephen felt he knew. "I don't want to get in the business of raiding churches. Or into church business, period. You start planning building programs and the focus shifts. Pretty soon, all eyes are on the budget and what it's going to take to put up a structure. You've got permits, meetings with the building committee, ad nauseam. Then someone wants a gymnasium to go with the sanctuary and a fountain out front. You start forming committees and fund-raisers and more energy goes into the building than the people sitting in the pews. No way. Besides, you don't even have a pastor."

"You could be our pastor," Jack said.

Stephen laughed. He couldn't help it. "I'm no pastor. I couldn't be a pastor in a million years."

"Why not?"

Jack was serious! "I'm divorced. I'm a recovering alcoholic. I was a lousy father. I don't have a degree in theology. You need any more reasons?"

"I doubt the apostle Peter had a degree in theology."

"He was trained, and he was ordained by Jesus."

"Aren't we all? Or, at least, that's what you've been telling us. Anyone who accepts Jesus as Savior and Lord receives the Holy Spirit, who becomes our personal instructor. Isn't that what the Bible says?"

"Right!" Half a dozen more spoke up, some amused at Stephen's predicament.

"Look, folks—"

"It's not like you'd be shouldering the load alone, Dad."

"Where's your faith, Brother Stephen?"

He looked around the group, but couldn't see the one who said it. Probably just one of the crashers, inciting trouble for the fun of watching. He had to make it clear. "I'm not qualified."

"God will equip you."

Stephen felt a bubble of panic. "You're looking for a contractor, and the church isn't a building, people. It's the body of Christ. It's not about ritual. It's about relationship."

"Assuming we all agree on that," Jack said into the silence, "where do we go from here?"

"What do you mean?"

"We still have the same problem. Your basement can't hold everyone who wants to hear the gospel."

Stephen saw where they were heading and didn't know how to divert them. Everyone was looking at him.

Tree House was grinning like an idiot. "Looks like you're elected, whether you wanted to run for office or not."

"Don't bother coming to work on Monday morning. You're fired." Tree House laughed at him. The big lug knew him too well. "Listen to me," Stephen said. "You don't elect a pastor. God calls one."

"You've been called, *hombre*. You're just too chicken to step into the pulpit."

Stephen opened his hands. "The only thing I want to build in each of you is an understanding of who and what you are in Christ. You don't need four walls around you for that."

"Four walls and a ceiling will keep the rain off our heads while we're learning."

"And the sand out of our eyes."

Samuel, where are you when I need you? He'd have answers for this group. He'd know where to go from here. Just the thought of starting a church made Stephen want to run for the hills. But when he looked into the faces of these friends, he saw the hope in their eyes, the expectation. It humbled him. And the responsibility made him want to run.

Tree House leaned back on his elbows and chuckled.

Stephen glowered. "You want to be a deacon? We'll put you on the moving committee."

The others laughed.

Stephen let his breath out slowly. Resting his forearms on his raised knees, he bowed his head. *Lord, where do we go from here?* When he looked up, he saw all of them had bowed their heads. Except Kathryn, who was looking at him and waiting. For what, he wasn't sure. He shut his eyes again and bowed his head. His heart drummed. He didn't say a word, but inside he was screaming, *Oh, Lord, help me. I'm not fit for the job. Look at the mess I've made of my life.*

Look at Me.

One by one, others began to pray. As Stephen listened to their words of faith, their assurance, their pleas for guidance, their praise and gratitude for all Jesus had done and was doing in their lives, he felt small and cowardly. *Jesus, I have so little faith, less faith than those sitting around me now.* He couldn't squeeze any more people into his basement and more were asking to join. These people wanted a place to gather together and pray and worship the Lord. *Strengthen me, God. Show me what to do.*

Let go and let God. One day at a time. Easy does it. Think. All the slogans he'd learned in AA flooded in at once. If it was God's will, it would be done.

His shoulders relaxed. His stomach stopped churning. He stopped measuring everything by past failures and hurts. How was he any different from his ex-wife and daughter, looking back instead of forward? His heart stopped pounding hard and heavy. Fear and pride dissolved. Everything around him was still and quiet. Was it only his imagination, or did he feel the Spirit moving, hear Him whispering? *I am the Way—yes, and the Truth and the Life. I am the Bread of Life, the Living Water. I AM.*

Gooseflesh rose on his arms and the back of his neck. *Oh, Lord, Lord, You changed the heart of Moses. Please change me. Make me whatever suits Your purposes here.*

Stephen knew what God wanted. Obedience. As to building a church, what came to him wasn't a new vision, but an old one. He wasn't to look ahead, but to look back to a small group of men and women who met in an upper room for a prayer meeting.

———— ❦ ————

It was close to midnight when Eunice reached Reseda and the condominium complex where Lois and Timothy lived. She pulled into a space marked for guest parking, her fuel gauge in the red. She hadn't even noticed how close she was to running out of gas. All she could think about was Paul in the arms of Rob Atherton's wife. She'd cried for two hundred miles. Her head was pounding. Shaking with exhaustion, she turned off the engine and pushed the keys into her purse.

Making her way along the illuminated walkway, Eunice debated going back to the car and looking for a motel for the night. It was late.

Lois and Timothy would be in bed. She wiped tears from her cheeks as she reached their section of the complex. A light was on in the living room window.

What if it's Timothy? What do I say to him, Lord? How do I explain why I've come in the middle of the night?

She stood outside in the cool of the night, crying, undecided. She should have thought of all these things before driving over two hundred miles. Now she was too tired to drive another block to a gas station, let alone go searching the main drags of the San Fernando Valley for a decent hotel she could afford.

Standing on the stoop, she tapped lightly. The porch light went on and she knew whoever was up was looking through the peephole at her. She forced a smile. A chain jingled, the door opened, and Lois appeared in her pink chenille bathrobe, her hair in curlers. "Eunice! For heaven's sake! What're you doing here at this hour of the night?"

When Lois opened the door wide and reached out to her, Eunice went into her arms. She'd thought she had cried herself out for the night, but more tears came like a flood as the pain of betrayal welled up, spilled over, choking her with grief and confusion.

"Paul," Lois said, her voice choked. "Something's happened to Paul."

Eunice drew back. Lois was Paul's mother, after all. Why hadn't she thought about that before racing to Lois for comfort? "He's well. There's been no accident, no bad news from the doctor, or anything like that." Should she leave?

"Sit down, honey. You look ready to collapse."

Eunice sank onto the sofa and covered her face. "I'm sorry. I shouldn't have come here. I don't even know what I was thinking to come here."

Lois sat slowly in her easy chair. She looked as though she were bracing herself for the worst kind of news. Eunice kept her hands over her mouth as she looked at her mother-in-law. "I'll make us some tea." Lois stood and took the afghan off the back of her chair and draped it around Eunice's shoulders before she headed for the kitchen.

"Timothy."

"Don't worry, honey. He's away for a few weeks. Tad has an apartment closer to the work site in Anaheim. We're alone."

Thank You, Lord.

She tried to batten down her emotions, to stop the burn of tears and get some control over herself before Lois came back. She kneaded her temples. Her stomach was churning. How long had it been since she had eaten? Just the thought of food made her nauseated. Sleep. Maybe she could sleep for the night, and talk to Lois in the morning. Did Lois use sleeping pills? How many would it take to stop the rush of adrenaline in her blood now? How many to quiet the chorus of voices screaming at her from all sides about what she should or shouldn't do?

Rob Atherton knew. He had been trying to tell her that day at the coffee shop. Did Sheila make a habit of going after other women's husbands? Just for fun?

It wasn't all Sheila's fault. She had seen with her own eyes how willing a participant Paul was in this moral fiasco.

Forgive, You say. Forgive.

"Euny." Lois held out a cup of tea.

"Thanks, Mom." Eunice took it. The cup rattled in the saucer. She put it on the coffee table with meticulous care, not wanting a drop of it to spill on Lois's nice beige carpet. Hadn't she been talking about redecorating? Eunice hadn't even looked around. "Everything looks nice. French country?"

"More like shabby chic."

Eunice sipped her tea. "It looks nice. You have a knack, Mom."

"I'm glad you like it."

Eunice stared at the magazines spread out on the coffee table. She fingered one. Anything to distract herself. Christian magazines mixed with home decorating and travel. It was like being in a doctor's office, picking up anything to keep from thinking about what was to come. A consultation about major surgery. An amputation. No. Open-heart surgery without anesthetic. Or some kind of incurable cancer. "I'm sorry, Lois. I shouldn't've come." *Why am I here, God?* "I should've gone somewhere else." *Lord, where do I go?*

"You're like my own daughter, Euny. I love you. Where better than here?"

"I don't know." Emotions balled up inside her chest. Too many to make sense of what she was feeling. She clutched her sweater together and rocked back and forth against the pain. How could she open her mouth and tell Lois what she'd seen? Paul, Lois's only child. Paul, the apple of Lois's eye.

"Oh, honey, just say—" Lois's voice broke—"just spit it out before it chokes you to death."

"He's having an affair."

"Is it someone you know?"

"Yes."

"Someone in the church?"

"Yes."

"Is it just beginning, or is it almost over?"

What difference did that make? "I think it's been going on for a long time." She'd answered the phone dozens of times to Sheila Atherton in some crisis or another. "He's been giving her marriage counseling." She laughed bleakly. "Her husband knows." *You remind me of Molly.* "I didn't understand." *"Sheila bores easily, and she was bored with me after the first few years."* "I didn't want to understand. And Reka called this morning." *"I'm sorry, Eunice."* "Reka said Paul needed me at the church." *"I'm so sorry to do this to you."* "She said I should hurry." Reka had wanted her to walk in on them!

"Paul came home while I was packing. He made all kinds of excuses." Her mind raced back over everything. She couldn't shut it off. *"Rob didn't even bother to show up after the first appointment." "You know things haven't been right between us."*

So many things made sense now. Heart-ripping, soul-shattering sense.

Oh, Lord, forgive me for missing all the signs. I felt Your Spirit move in warning and ignored You because I didn't want to confront Paul. I didn't want to hear the lies. I didn't want to feel the pain. I kept telling myself that love always believes the best. But love doesn't ignore what's wrong. Love doesn't sweep sin under a carpet and pretend it isn't there. I was ashamed of my suspicions. I didn't want to believe Paul could be unfaithful. But I saw, Lord. Oh, Lord, I saw his unfaithfulness to You. Oh, God, forgive my arrogance. How foolish to think my husband could cheat on You and still remain faithful to me.

"Excuse me." She fled to the bathroom. Gagging, she sank to her knees. How soon after Sheila came for counseling had the affair started? A few weeks? A month? Two? Had Paul gone back to church to comfort Sheila? Was he at Sheila's house now, trying to figure out a way to get a divorce without ruining his ministry? She vomited what little was left in her stomach from breakfast. Choking on sobs, she continued retching.

She flushed the toilet and turned on the faucet. Panting, she cupped cold water and washed her face. Dampening a washcloth, she closed the lid of the toilet and sat with the cloth over her eyes. If things weren't bad enough, now she had the hiccups. She gave a broken laugh.

Lois tapped at the door. "Are you all right?"

"I'll be out—" she hiccupped—"in a minute."

"Can I help you, Euny?"

"No. I'll be fine." *Fine!* Would she ever be fine again? She pressed the cloth to her eyes, trying to press away the memory of Paul and Sheila.

"I'll be in the kitchen."

"Okay." Eunice held her breath, but it did no good. Hiccup. She splashed more cold water and pressed her face into a soft towel. She had to get control of herself. She had to think. She couldn't just blurt out everything. What would it do to Lois's opinion of her son?

Why should I care what anyone thinks of him? Why should I protect him?

She leaned on the sink, chest heaving. *Because. Because! More lives are at stake than his. Or mine. What will it do to all those precious souls sitting in the pews of Valley New Life Center if word gets out?* Hands shaking, she tried to straighten her hair. She looked awful. Maybe if she dabbed a little lipstick on, she'd look less like a cadaver. Her purse was on the floor in the living room. *Help me, Jesus. Oh, Jesus, help me.*

Lois was standing at the stove when Eunice entered the kitchen. "Chicken soup."

Eunice sat at the nook table. Food, the great restorative. As if chicken soup could restore her soul. "I don't know if I can hold anything down, Mom." First she had to get rid of the pictures playing over and over in her mind. The sounds. The smells.

"I know what you're feeling, Eunice. I've been through it."

Her eyes welled. "I know." Maybe that was why she had made a beeline for Lois. She had known a little of what was wrong with her in-laws' marriage. Who better to comfort her and give her some kind of understanding than a woman who had fought to keep her husband and still managed to keep her faith? Eunice wasn't sure she had any fight in her, or if Paul was even worth it. He had changed. He had been changing for a long time. First he'd turned away from the Lord. Then he'd turned away from her.

"I'm sorry, Euny." Lois ladled soup into a bowl and set it in front of

Eunice. "I thought I raised Paul better." Her eyes were dark with anger and pain as she took the chair opposite Eunice.

Eunice stirred the soup slowly. "I couldn't stay. He said he had to go back to the church for a meeting, but he might've been lying and going back to her."

"It won't last. It never does."

"What doesn't last?" Her agony? Her marriage?

"The affair. It's probably already over. There is nothing like the shock of exposure to bring the quick kiss of death to something like that."

"Maybe." It had certainly been the kiss of death to every sense of security she'd ever felt with Paul. Their marriage had been founded on faith, and now, she saw he was faithless.

"If nothing else, it will make Paul think about what's important."

"His church."

"No, Euny. You. He loves you. I know he does."

A mother-in-law's wishful thinking. Empty words. *Love.* Did Paul even know the meaning of the word? He'd always had time for everyone except his own son and wife. And plenty of time for Sheila Atherton.

"Oh, Euny. Think back. I remember the way Paul looked at you on your wedding day. When you came down the aisle, he couldn't take his eyes off you. He looked as though he would melt. I thanked God my son fell in love with a young woman of faith who would stand by him through every storm life brings. I knew the moment I met you that you weren't just another beautiful girl. You were special. God's blessing upon my son. You still are." She reached over and touched her hand. "Give him time. He'll come to his senses. Be patient with him."

"Is that what you did?"

"Yes." Her eyes shadowed. "After I swallowed my pride. It hurts when the man you love turns to another woman. It's humiliating. You feel as though you weren't enough of a woman to hold on to your husband, that something was lacking in you, that you were somehow to blame." She shook her head. "That's not true. Some men are just weak in regard to other women. They're in a position of authority and power. Women come to them and fancy themselves in love. It's a boost to a man's ego. One thing leads to another. It's just an innocent little flirtation at first, nothing serious. And then they get caught up in it. The headiness of having a woman other than their wife adoring them removes restraints. Of course, it doesn't last."

"Usually." Eunice put the spoon down. Was flirtation ever innocent? "We've both heard about pastors who have left their wives for another woman."

"David never even considered that. Neither will Paul." She smiled bleakly. "Paul will try to make it up to you, Euny. David did. At least Paul has told you he's sorry. David never said it in so many words. But he treated me better after it was over. He gave me a beautiful diamond tennis bracelet once."

"I've never seen you wear it."

"How could I? Every time I took it out, I was reminded." She shook her head. "Men are so foolish." She rose and poured two fresh cups of tea. "When did you eat last?"

"Breakfast."

"You need to eat something, Eunice. Try. One bite. You'll feel better for it."

She managed a few spoonfuls.

"It would be better if you didn't say anything to Timothy." Lois put a buttered piece of toast in front of Eunice. "It can only do damage to Tim's relationship with his father, and you don't want that. There's been enough hurt already." She sat again. "I never told Paul anything about his father's misdeeds. Remember. Love covers a multitude of sins."

Misdeeds? How many times had David Hudson committed adultery? Was covering up such sin love? Was it right to hide the truth from others? Let people go on believing an angel was in the pulpit while a devil was in the home? Eunice didn't know what to say. She didn't know what to do. Should she go before the elders, tell them the truth, and ask their help in making Paul accountable? The thought made her sick. How could she expect fair and righteous treatment from Gerry Boham, Marvin Lockford, and the rest of Paul's sycophants? More likely she would be reprimanded and told to keep silent, to plaster a smile on her face and pretend everything was fine.

Lord, help me. The seed of bitterness has grown in me. I don't want to feel anything.

"Do you have someone like Joseph to stand with you when you speak with Paul?"

Joseph, the able, faithful elder who had taken over David Hudson's ministry.

"Samuel." She thought of Stephen Decker also, but said nothing about him.

Lois smiled. "Samuel is a good man. But far too old."

"And he no longer attends our church."

"Why not?"

"He and Paul couldn't see eye-to-eye. When Abby became sick, Samuel stepped down. Paul was glad when he did."

Lois put her hands around her teacup and bowed her head. "A pity. Pastors need good men around them, men who can see trouble brewing and confront it before it gets a foothold."

The pastor had to be willing to listen. Paul used to listen to her. Until he had gotten caught up in "building a church for the Lord." If he wasn't held accountable now, would he ever straighten out? What would happen when he faced the Lord? He would have to answer for the way he was leading God's people. Had he forgotten that?

Eunice felt numb. Should she convince herself that it was all a mistake? How could she? She couldn't pretend it had been a bad dream. And she didn't know if she had the strength to shove it into a shadowed compartment in her mind, close the door, and lock it in.

No. No, she couldn't let it go. Not yet. She had to remind herself that the meeting with Marvin Lockford had been more important to Paul than talking with her.

"You look so exhausted, honey. You can't work it all out when you're this tired. We can talk everything over in the morning. Is your suitcase in your car?"

"I don't have a suitcase. Paul took it away from me. Along with my keys. I had to use the spare set."

"I have an extra nightie you can use, and I buy toothbrushes by the bushel load at Costco. They're in the hall cabinet, along with packages of toothpaste."

Eunice pushed herself up. She started to clear her dishes, but Lois put her hand over hers. "Just leave them. I can take care of them. You go to bed. You look dead on your feet. Try to get a good night's rest. Everything will wait until morning."

"Thanks for letting me stay."

"Did you think I'd throw you out because my son's behaving like an idiot?" Her smile was shaky.

Eunice realized how tired she was. She could hardly put one foot in front of the other. Was it emotion that had sapped her? She braced her hand on the doorframe and looked back at her mother-in-law. "How did you do it, Mom? How did you get through it?"

Lois looked every day of her seventy-eight years. "When you live with a faithless man, you learn to lean on a faithful God."

It was past ten when Stephen packed the last of the leftover charcoal and his Coleman cooler into his truck. A few stragglers remained to stargaze. Brittany and Jack were standing with Kathryn. Jack appeared to be doing all the talking. Kathryn reached out and shook his hand. She said something to Brittany and headed for her car. At least they weren't running from each other this time. Kathryn swung her jacket around her shoulders and appeared in no hurry as Stephen walked over to her car.

"Take it easy on the way home, Kat."

"I don't plan to stop at a liquor store."

Touchy. "Okay."

"Brittany says I'm a bigger drunk than you ever were. What do you think about that?"

He wasn't going to step into a minefield. He stayed silent.

"Okay. Okay. I know I have a problem. I was planning to cut down anyway. Alcohol isn't good for the skin."

"Or anything else."

"Though it does help you forget."

"Until you wake up in the morning and have to face the music for what you did the night before."

"The voice of experience." She winced. "Sorry. I wasn't going to do that. You've been nice through the whole thing, Stephen. A pity you weren't this understanding when we were married."

A few cordial meetings didn't mean she would change. How many years had it taken him to see the Light and then decide to follow Him?

"Brittany just told me I should check into a treatment center like you went to, but I have to support myself. I don't have the luxury of taking six months off work."

She was trying hard to start a fight. Let her take her punches. He wasn't going to hit back this time.

She looked at him. "Jack suggested I come to your Bible study. I told him I'd already asked if you'd mind if I sat in on it. Brittany wasn't too keen on the idea."

"She's talking to you again. That's good."

"Every word out of her mouth is a barb."

He smiled at that. *Like mother, like daughter.*

She slipped her arms into her jacket. "I had a good time today, Stephen, despite everything that's happened. Largely because you introduced me to your friends."

"What'd you expect me to do? Leave you out in the cold?"

"I've felt like I was out in the cold most of my life. Just when I think I know the rules of the game, the players change. I'm tired of trying." She shrugged. "Anyway. Thanks for the invitation. I enjoyed the day, despite our daughter's attempt to slay me with that remark about the crack house. It wasn't true, was it?"

"You'll have to talk to her about it."

"I don't think I want to know. At least she came back this afternoon. Largely because of you, I'm sure."

"Don't forget Jack."

"How could I forget Jack?" She glanced back. "Where on earth did you find him?"

"He used to come by and see how the work was going."

"Brittany said he's a craftsman."

"He's a carpenter. Actually, he's a talented artist. He's putting together a mural with bits and pieces of scrap lumber, everything from pine to mahogany. Pretty remarkable. He calls it therapy. Keeps his mind occupied and his hands busy."

"What does he plan to do with it when he's finished?"

"I haven't got a clue."

"If it's any good, I might be interested."

"I thought your taste ran to original oils."

She gave him one of her looks. "Since I no longer have a rich husband, and not enough alimony to keep my head above water, let alone purchase art, I'm working again. For an interior decorator. High-end. She likes unusual pieces."

"You landed on your feet."

"Kats always do." She took her keys out of her purse and pressed the remote to unlock her car.

Brittany came over and stood next to him as Kathryn headed down the main street of Rockville. "She's a royal pain."

"So are you, Brit. So am I, for that matter."

"After all these years, it's strange hearing you defend her."

He smiled at her. "Where's Jack?"

"He went home. He said he was tired of listening to me whine about my mother's faults."

"Do you want a ride the six blocks home, or would you rather walk?" Stephen knew better than to take anything for granted.

"I'd like a ride, if you promise not to lecture."

"Wouldn't think of it."

───── ✿ ─────

Eunice had a bad night. Exhausted, she slept two solid hours and then awakened from a bad dream at three in the morning. What day was it? Thursday? She slept fitfully, awakening at every little sound in the condo complex. She could hear the freeway noise from six blocks away. A low roar of an ocean of cars. A tide of traffic to and fro. Never ending. Where were all those people going in the wee hours of the morning? She was lulled back to sleep for a while, but she awakened again, the digital clock glowing *4:00*.

What should she do about Timothy? Should she call him and let him know she was in town for a few days? Or a few weeks? One look at her and he would know something was wrong. She'd never been good at hiding things. Should she tell him the truth about his father? Mending had begun between them. What would happen to their relationship now? She could stay a few days without letting Timothy know. But she would have to leave soon. Where would she go? She couldn't bear the thought of going back to Paul and listening to his excuses, or being told again she was to blame. She wondered what he was doing right now. Rob Atherton was in Florida. Paul and Sheila were both free to do whatever they pleased with their spouses out of town.

She wept into her pillow. She felt as though he had ripped her heart out and stomped on it. She hated him, but she loved him, too. How was that possible? Could she go back and forget what happened for the sake of their marriage? Assuming he sincerely wanted to rebuild. Or was he merely worried about his position? She was afraid she knew the truth—that all he cared about was what other people would say and what could happen to his position in the church. But if she returned, what could she expect from him in the future but more betrayal? How could she ever trust him again? Every time he went out the door, she would wonder where he was going and if the meeting was just a pretense to have another clandestine affair. If Sheila moved away, other beautiful, needy women would come to their pastor and fancy themselves in love with him. *She needed me.* If he was deaf, blind, and dumb about his sins now, what would stop him from falling into sin later?

At six, she gave up trying to sleep. She felt as though her head were full of cotton. Thinking a cup of tea might help, she put on the robe Lois had loaned her. Lois was talking to someone in the kitchen. Eunice's heart began to pound. Had Timothy come home? What could she say to him? What was Lois saying?

"She knocked on my door a little after midnight. Yes. I know all about it. Oh, what a mess! Of course, I'm disappointed in you." A long silence, then Lois's weary voice. "No. I don't think she's said anything to anyone else. I told her she could stay with me as long as she feels she needs to stay." Another pause, and then Lois's anger. "Yes. Yes. I know it makes things difficult for you. You should've thought about that before you started having an affair with . . ." Teary. "Have you stopped to think about how difficult you've made it for your wife? You should come down here . . ." A harsh breath. "Oh, don't use that excuse." A pause. "You could tell everyone there's been a family emergency." Silence. "Yes, she needs time to calm down." Silence. "Tonight would be better. Monday may be too late." Another sigh. "You know exactly what I mean. Don't pretend you don't. Well, of course, I'll do everything I can." Tear-choked. "I always have. I love you both. I can't believe you let this happen. I never thought you, of all people, would do such a thing. I know. I know. These things happen all the time."

Eunice stood in the doorway. Her mother-in-law glanced up, blushed to the roots of her gray hair. She turned away and dropped her voice.

"I've got to hang up now. You know what you should do. I hope you'll do it." She hung up and stood. "Good morning, honey. I hope you slept well last night. Would you like some tea? I have Earl Grey. You like that, don't you?" Her smile was forced.

"Was that Paul?" Her anger wasn't cold anymore; it was raging hot. She had never felt such wrath before. It came up inside her like hot lava. Lois turned the stove knob until it clicked and a flame came on. "Yes."

"I didn't hear the phone ring."

"I thought he should know you arrived safely."

"Did it occur to you that he *should* worry? That he *should* think about someone besides himself for a change? I didn't want him to know where I was! I wanted a safe place to think."

Lois looked crestfallen. "I'm sorry, Eunice. I was trying to help. You weren't yourself last night. You looked ready for a nervous breakdown."

"You're probably right, but I have good reason, don't you think?"

"There's no good reason for leaving Paul in the dark about your well-being. That's cruel and unchristian, and not at all like you."

"No. It's not like me. It's more like me to let him walk all over me again!"

"He's not. He's sorry. We're to love one another the way Jesus loved us. And Paul was worried sick. I thought—"

"I heard how worried he was." Eunice gave a bleak laugh. "He's scared to death at what might happen if word gets out in his church. That's what he's most concerned about. Himself. 'Tonight would be better,' you said. 'Monday might be too late.' What did you mean by that, Lois?"

Lois looked at the table. "He's going to have one of the associates cover for him so that he can come down here. The two of you can talk things over, straighten things out."

Eunice could feel the tears mounting again. "I can't even trust you, can I?"

Lois looked up, crying. "How can you say that to me? Of course you can trust me. I'm trying to do what's best for both of you."

"The same way you've been trying to do what's best for years. By covering up! By pretending everything is fine. By looking the other way and hoping the problem will evaporate. Isn't that the truth, Lois? How many times did Paul's father cheat on you?"

Her eyes filled with hurt. "That's none of your business."

"I don't care if you think it's my business or not. It was his pattern, wasn't it? To lie and cheat? And you allowed yourself to be drawn into it. And now, here's Paul, following in his father's footsteps. The father's sins are being visited upon the son because we sweep everything under the carpet and pretend everything is fine when it's not! God forbid that anyone should find out a pastor is weak. God forbid anyone should know he's fallible. Isn't that the truth? How many times, Lois? How many times did you cover up for David Hudson?"

"You have no right—"

"And you did it all in the name of love. You convinced yourself of that. Did you ever tell Paul the truth about why his father retired so unexpectedly?"

"No."

"Why not?"

"How could I? It would have destroyed David in Paul's eyes."

"So you allowed Paul to go on thinking his father was perfect, his father was a man to be emulated. You helped him make an idol of David Hudson." And she had helped Lois do it.

"I never said David was perfect. Paul knew—"

"Paul forgot. If he ever knew anything, he learned sin didn't matter if the man was powerful enough to keep his family quiet."

Lois paled. "You're not being fair. I tried to train up Paul in the way he should go, without turning him against his father."

"You brought him up with a mixed message, Lois. But God doesn't compromise. What about discipline? What about accountability? David Hudson never experienced any of that."

"I did what I thought was right!"

"You did what your husband told you to do, even when it was wrong! You did what was easiest. You were in anguish when you came to Centerville and told me about the retirement banquet. And now I know why. *Misdeeds*, you said yesterday. It wasn't the first time your husband was unfaithful to you. It was just the last time while he was serving in his church." She dashed tears from her cheek. "You told me part of the truth and then swore me to secrecy. You made me a part of your sin."

"No."

"I should've taken it as a warning. I'm as much to blame as you. I've had those stirrings inside me. The Holy Spirit has been trying to tell me something has been wrong for a long time, and I've ignored that quiet voice the same way you have. Did you tell me about David so that I could see what Paul was becoming?"

"Paul isn't like his father."

"Why else would you burden me with the truth about your marriage?"

Lois wept harshly. "Paul isn't like David."

"Oh yes, he is. Like father, like son!"

"He's repentant."

"He's not repentant, Lois. He's remorseful. He's sorry he was caught. And now, he's scared to death everything he's built for himself will come tumbling down. If he were repentant, his first thought wouldn't have been to rush back to the church for his meeting with Marvin Lockford! He would've been on his knees begging for forgiveness." And his mother wouldn't have had to pressure him into coming down right away instead of putting off his trip until Monday.

"Is that what you want, Eunice? For Paul to be on his knees? Crushed and destroyed? Publicly humiliated? His church in ashes?"

Yes! Eunice wanted to scream. Where better to be than on his knees before God? Hadn't Jesus been publicly humiliated? And He had been innocent. He had been pure and holy. If the Lord could humble Himself to such a degree before all mankind, couldn't one man humble himself before almighty God? The Lord had knowingly taken every sin ever committed, ever to be committed, upon Himself. No one but God could turn Paul's life around. No one but God could heal the wounds Paul had inflicted. And no one but the Lord could change the course of what Paul had set in motion!

Oh, Lord of mercy and strength, I am powerless.

A calm settled over Eunice. The eye of the storm. "There's no talking to you, Lois. You're as big a liar as David Hudson ever was." She saw the shock come into Lois's face. Eunice walked out of the kitchen.

I can't stay here, Lord. Where do I go? What am I to do now?

She went into the bedroom and closed the door. She quickly changed into her clothes, made the bed, folded the nightgown and robe, and went out into the living room. She picked up her purse.

Lois stood in the doorway to the kitchen, face pale, tears streaming down her cheeks. Eunice was filled with compassion. Maybe her mother-in-law's eyes were finally open, too. "I love you, Lois. I always have. I always will. But I don't intend to follow your example. Not anymore."

"Where will you go?"

It came to Eunice in that instant where she needed to go. "Home."

The tension wilted from Lois. "Thank God. Do you want me to call Paul and tell him you're on your way?"

"Centerville isn't my home." She opened the door and walked out.

CHAPTER 19

———— ❦ ————

STEPHEN COULDN'T GET AWAY from the idea of starting another church. Was he holding back because of the disillusionment in building VNLC and missing the needs of those now coming to his Bible study? He prayed that if the Lord was calling him to ministry, He would make Stephen's motives pure. Stephen didn't want a competition with Paul Hudson. To make sure, Stephen went to the one man he knew he could trust to be completely honest with him—and to back up his views with Scripture.

"Mr. Mason is in the courtyard, Mr. Decker," the receptionist said.

And, as he often did, Samuel had company. Florence Nightingale was sitting with him in the shade of a canvas umbrella. Stephen knew the moment she spotted him. She stiffened, leaned forward, said something to Samuel, picked up her purse, and rose. She pushed the lawn chair into place at the round glass table and stepped back.

"Don't leave on my account."

She always bolted when he came within twenty feet of her, no doubt due to the embarrassment he'd caused her when Eunice had tried to set them up. How long ago had that been?

"I didn't know you were coming today."

"I'm sure you didn't."

Samuel looked up. "You haven't even finished your tea, Karen."

"I'm sorry, Samuel. I'll stay longer next time."

"I'm sure Stephen wouldn't mind if you—"

"I wouldn't at all." How much of a jerk had he been that day to put this good woman to flight every time she spotted him? "Are you still heading up the singles club at VNLC?"

"I haven't attended VNLC in over a year."

Oops. "Really?" He raised his brows. "Any particular reason why not?"

"None that I should discuss with you."

"That answer makes me want to ask more questions."

"Not my intention, I assure you."

He was getting nowhere fast in his attempt to make amends. Maybe the direct approach would work better. "Look, Karen, I know I was a jerk that day at the hospital. I'm sorry. Can we call a truce?"

She blushed. "I just don't want any misunderstandings between us."

That she was *not* trying to get his attention. Oh yeah, he got the point. "There were no misunderstandings the first time we met. My reaction had nothing to do with you."

She looked him squarely in the eyes. "I know that."

He could see she did and felt the heat rush into his face. "That obvious, huh?"

"Not obvious enough to cause anyone worry."

A careful answer much appreciated. But it left him wondering how many other people at VNLC had noticed his attraction to Pastor Paul's wife. When Karen edged back another step, he drew her chair out and gestured for her to sit. "If I ask nicely, will you finish your tea? I growl, but I don't bite."

She relaxed with a soft laugh. "All right. I'll risk it this time." Shrugging the purse strap off her shoulder, she took her seat again.

"Karen's attending a big church in Sacramento now." Samuel sipped his tea. "She enjoys the services, but isn't sure she wants to continue going there."

Stephen looked at her. "Trouble with the preaching?"

"No. The pastor is right on base with the gospel, but it's too far a drive for me to be any real part of the church. The singles club meets on Tuesday evenings, the choir on Thursdays. I tried both a few times and didn't get home until after ten. I don't like to be out that late at night by myself, and no one else comes from my area."

"Where's your area?"

When she seemed reticent to answer, Samuel did so for her. "Your neck of the woods."

"You live in Rockville?"

Karen's expression was pained. "Not in Rockville, but a mile north on Gelson Road. I put an offer in on a small place about six years ago, and I've been there ever since."

Six years. She was still making sure he understood she wasn't chasing him. She must think him the most conceited man on the face of the earth. "I'm a newcomer to the town." He wanted to make sure she knew he understood. She had a nice smile. "I'll ask you the same question everyone asks me. Why Rockville?"

"I grew up in San Francisco and thought it would be romantic to live on a farm. I didn't have a clue how much work it would be."

She had a nice laugh, too. "Do you farm?"

"I have a vegetable garden and a few fruit trees. Enough that I don't have to buy produce at the grocery store."

"No animals?"

"No time. I had a dog, but I had to put him down last year. Cancer. I miss Brutus, but I'm not home enough to give an animal the proper amount of attention. My schedule at the hospital keeps me busy."

Samuel said nothing, but Stephen knew why his old friend had opened the subject of Karen's dilemma. He might as well get it said, though he expected she would shoot him down. "I hold a Bible study at my house every Wednesday evening. You're welcome to come. Mix of men and women. Blue-collar and a couple of migrant workers. My daughter. My *ex*-wife. You never know what someone's going to say or do."

"Are you trying to talk me into it or out of it?"

"I'll engrave you an invitation."

Karen looked at Samuel. "Is he a good teacher?"

"Yes. And he works at it."

She gave Stephen a sidelong look. "What can I bring?"

"Your Bible and an open mind."

Samuel looked pleased. "How did the barbecue go?"

Stephen leaned back in his chair. "Fine, until someone brought up the subject of starting a church."

Karen's brows shot up. "You're going to start a church?"

"Not if I can help it."

Samuel looked intrigued. "Why not?"

"You want one reason or twenty? The last thing I want to do is get into another church-building project."

"You can build a church without building a building, you know."

"A nice little Bible study is all I ever bargained for, Samuel."

"Well, that's a pretty pathetic attitude."

Stephen pulled his sunglasses down and stared at Karen over the rims. "Careful. You aren't part of the group yet."

"Too late. Invitation extended and accepted."

"You might think about holding off on any opinions."

"And you might try taking your own advice and opening your mind."

Samuel chuckled. "So, what did you tell them?"

"I didn't say anything." Stephen pulled his gaze from Karen. "We prayed about it."

"And?"

"I'm still praying." He scratched his head. "The thing is, I had this feeling that I'm supposed to move forward in a backward sort of way." Samuel and Karen were both looking at him, waiting. "The church started with a hundred and twenty people praying together in an upper room in Jerusalem. Right?"

Samuel nodded. "Yes, but it didn't stay hidden in an upper room, Stephen."

Or a basement, he might as well have said.

"Nor did the church stay small," Karen said. "They were a handful for about forty days, and then Pentecost happened. As soon as the Holy Spirit came upon those few, they rushed out with the Good News and the Lord added another three thousand to the body of Christ."

"Yeah, but they still met in homes after that."

Samuel smiled faintly. "They also met in the corridors of the Temple."

"In Solomon's portico."

Stephen glowered at Karen. "Maybe *you* should be teaching."

She held up her hands. "I thought you said you didn't bite."

Disgruntled, Stephen persisted. "The point I'm *trying* to make is the first order of business in the church wasn't to go out and put up a building for meetings. It was to win souls, teach, have fellowship, break bread together, and pray. If I'm going to be part of building a church, I'd like to find a way to build a church without walls. Isn't that what Jesus meant? It's not the building that matters or the programs or the numbers. It's not the music or the ritual. It's about our relationship with *Jesus Christ*. Believers make up the temple. They are the church. Christ's resurrection power is revealed through our new lives."

"Are you planning to keep everyone hostage in your basement?"

Stephen faced Karen. "I can see I'm going to have nothing but trouble with you."

"No. I'm just asking. I want to know where you stand before I walk in the door. I fled one man's kingdom. I don't want to fall down the stairs and into the basement of another."

He went hot. "Are you comparing me with Paul Hudson?"

"Not unless you think you have all the answers." She spoke softly, eyes gentle.

He let his breath out slowly. "No, I don't have all the answers. I just don't want to make the same mistakes over again. As soon as Centerville Christian decided to build, the focus changed. It was all about bringing in more people so there'd be money to continue the project. It wasn't a sanctuary anymore. It was a gymnasium. It was about events. It wasn't about building a relationship with Christ. It was about a head count and the take on Sunday morning. How many times did the Lord have to destroy the Temple? And we're still trying to rebuild it."

Karen seemed to be considering what he was saying. "Why do you think we do that?"

"I'm not sure. Maybe it's easier to pour our efforts into building a house for God rather than building a relationship with Him. One requires a few years of hard work, but the other asks for a lifetime of commitment. The problem is, the building becomes the idol we worship. The programs are the sacred cows. Numbers are our means of evaluating our success. And it's all about vanity. Vanity, vanity. My church is bigger than your church. My pastor draws a bigger crowd on Sunday morning. Hey, haven't you heard? He's on television and does a radio show that's on who knows how many stations across the country. And man, now they're going to have a Bible with his name on it. Can you beat that?"

"He really hurt you, didn't he?" Karen said quietly, all eyes.

"Who?"

"Paul Hudson."

"This isn't about Paul Hudson."

"Oooo-kay." She drew out the word quietly and looked at Samuel.

Stephen sighed. Was he holding a grudge? He hoped not. He bore the scars of standing against Paul, but that didn't mean he was going to buy into his philosophy of what a church was. He didn't have to know Karen well to see her wheels turning. "You have something to say. Go ahead."

"Just because Paul Hudson's motivation was wrong doesn't mean yours wasn't right."

"Oh yeah. I'm such a great guy. Everyone thought I was making a bundle off that project. Lining my pockets with dough."

"Not everyone."

Maybe he was falling into hyperbole. He studied her expression. He'd never told anyone how far into the hole he had gone to do what was right, but he had a feeling she knew. He wasn't about to complain. God had provided work to keep his head above water and his name out of a bankruptcy hearing. "Fact is, my motivation didn't make any difference to the outcome for the church."

"Not that we can see with our human eyes," Samuel said. "But don't think for a minute God isn't at work. He has been from the beginning, and He's not finished."

"No." Stephen gave a wry grin. "I think I'm pretty clear about that." He could feel the Lord chiseling away his armor. It left him feeling vulnerable and uncertain.

Samuel's look was full of clarity. "Just don't let what happened in Centerville get in the way of what the Lord may want to happen in Rockville."

Stephen took a long pull from his glass of tea. "God seems to be getting His way on that score. Eunice told me the property I bought was the same piece donated to the church and that Paul sold for seed money on the new facility."

Karen tilted her head. "Did you know that before you bought it?"

Did she think he'd done it to take some kind of revenge? The same thought had occurred to Eunice. Stephen shook his head. "No." Was she wondering when he'd talked to Eunice and under what circumstances? "I didn't have a clue. I only wanted to know there were no liens on the property and there was plenty of work to do. I needed something to keep my mind and hands occupied." Just to make things clear. "I didn't want to end up back in another alcohol-rehab center."

Karen raised her brows. "Not everyone wears their confession on their sleeve."

He laughed. "I wasn't waiting for your confession, just a comment."

"Such as?"

"Such as you'd already heard that I was an alcoholic." One of the rumors he knew had circulated during the time Paul was pushing him out of the church.

"I don't listen to gossip and I don't hang around people who do."

No wonder Eunice liked this woman.

Samuel cleared his throat, and Stephen realized he'd been studying Karen for longer than was polite. She wasn't wearing a ring.

She glanced at her wristwatch. "I need to run. I'm on duty tonight." She shouldered her bag and rose. Samuel leaned on his cane and stood. Stephen shoved his chair back and rose. How long since he had stood for a woman? Karen glanced at him with amusement. Did he look as uncomfortable as he felt? She took Samuel's hand between hers, thanked him for the pleasant afternoon, and said she'd come back soon. As she turned, she gave him a cordial smile. "It was nice to see you, too, Stephen."

"Likewise." He thought it might be nice to get to know her a little better. Maybe take her out for coffee. Or dinner. "I should have your phone number. In case I have to call off the Bible study at the last minute." He hoped the excuse didn't sound as lame to her as it did to him.

"I'm in the book." She walked away without a backward glance.

It would help if he could remember her last name.

Stephen took his seat when Samuel did. "I think God has wanted a church in Rockville for a long time, Stephen. The fields are ripe and the workers are few."

"I agree. I'm just not sure I'm the one to do it. I don't want to go in with the wrong motives."

"God put you there for a reason."

"Leading a Bible study is a far cry from pastoring a church."

"Take it one day at a time. Stay focused on the Word. Get on your knees and pray. Then stand up and do the work God gives you. Don't try to cross any bridges until you reach them."

"I have to work for a living."

Samuel shifted in his chair. His face tightened with pain as he stretched out one leg. "The apostle Paul was a tentmaker." He eased back into his chair again. "More than half of the people attending your Bible study met you on the job or met someone who works with you. The Lord knows the job is too big to be shouldered by any one man. He equips you so that you can equip others. You don't have to have a degree in theology or stand in a pulpit to do that."

Stephen saw the new lines in Samuel's face. How was it possible for someone to age so much in a few days? They were silent for a long moment. Stephen finished the last of his tea. "Would you like me to walk you to your apartment before I leave?"

"Sorry. I'm sure poor company today."

"You're worrying about something. Should I ask?"

"Better if you don't."

"Okay." *Eunice?* "Anything I can do?"

"Just what you're doing. Keep your focus on Jesus. Be obedient to His call on your life. Whatever it is, however difficult it's going to be."

Stephen searched his face. The old man was distracted, his mind occupied in some inner battle.

Samuel stared out at the garden. "I think I'll stay out here awhile longer."

"Okay." Stephen rose. "I'll come back tomorrow."

"Wait a minute, Stephen." Samuel felt his shirt pocket. "Do you have a pen handy?"

Stephen handed him his ballpoint.

Samuel took a paper napkin from the dispenser and wrote something on it. He handed the napkin and pen back to Stephen with a smile.

Karen Kessler. And her phone number.

———— ❦ ————

Paul looked for Eunice's car as he pulled into the visitors' section of the condominium complex. He was tired from the drive, exhausted from lack of sleep. He'd expected better of Eunice than running off to tell his mother everything. She should've stayed home like he told her. They could've talked it out and reached an understanding without involving anyone else. No one should be privy to their problems, especially his mother! Eunice had reason to be upset, but that didn't give her the right to be disloyal. She was a minister's wife. She should know better than to say anything against him to anyone!

Pulling the key out of the ignition, he shoved the car door open, got out, and slammed it shut. He had a vague memory of his father laying down the law a few times. Maybe that's what he'd have to do. Be a little less apologetic and a little more firm for the sake of his ministry. There was too much at stake to allow feelings to run rampant.

He found his mother's condo and rang the bell. He shifted his feet when no one answered right away. He'd told her he was coming. She would've told Eunice. Was his wife sulking inside while making him stand on the porch? He jabbed the button again and held his finger on it.

It was his mother who opened the door and stood looking at him. Her face was splotched and puffy, her eyes red-rimmed from crying.

"Mom, it isn't as bad as it seems."

"Isn't it?"

"What did Eunice say to you?"

"What do you think she said?"

He cursed Eunice for causing his mother such pain. "Where is she? She had no right to come down here and dump our problems on your doorstep. Eunice!"

"She's gone."

"What do you mean, she's gone? Gone where?"

"She said she was going home."

His temper erupted. "Great! Just great! I wasted the drive down here. What kind of game is she playing with me? What's she planning to do now? Go back to the church and announce we're having some problems?"

"*Some* problems? Is that the way you see adultery?"

He felt heat rush into his face. "It's not all my fault, you know. She wouldn't have walked in on anything if Reka hadn't set the whole thing up. And I wouldn't have even looked at Sheila if Eunice had been any kind of wife to me over the past few years. She's been sulking ever since Tim moved down here with you."

"So it's everybody's fault except yours, is that right? Even I'm to blame."

"I didn't say that. That's not what I meant."

"You have no excuse, Paul. Not one that will get you out of this mess."

"Okay." He held up his hands. "Okay! Could we have this conversation inside so the whole neighborhood doesn't hear about it?"

She stepped back and stared at him as he walked around her. He flung his Windbreaker onto the couch and rubbed the back of his neck in frustration. "If Eunice had bothered to answer her cell phone, I could've waited at the house for her."

"She's not going to Centerville."

"You just told me she was going home." He'd had a long sleepless night and then a long drive on top of it. He was in no mood for double-talk.

"Don't use that tone with me, Paul Hudson."

He'd never seen that look on his mother's face before. As though she hated him. It shook him.

"She said Centerville isn't her home. And no wonder."

He could thank Eunice for his mother's attitude. Why couldn't she have kept her mouth shut and their problems private? If she had to tell someone, why couldn't she have picked someone other than his mother? A good thing Eunice wasn't in the condo or he'd say things he would regret. As it was, he was going to have to chase after her again. How far this time? How long before she'd sit down and listen to reason? "So where is she going?" He tried to sound patient.

"You tell me, Paul. Where is home for Eunice?" Her eyes glittered through the tears. "Heaven?"

He felt a coldness seep into the pit of his stomach. "She wouldn't do that. You know Eunice as well as I do, and she wouldn't even think it."

"How well do you know me? I thought about suicide the first time your father cheated on me."

First time? He rocked back. "What are you talking about?"

She shook her head. "He never had much time for you, did he, Paul? Or for me. But he had plenty of time for others."

He swallowed hard. What was she saying?

She wept bitterly. "Eunice was right. I have been wrong. All these years, I've been so wrong."

"Mom." He'd seen her cry, but not like this. "Mom." He took her shoulders, but she jerked free.

"I should've talked to you about all this long ago. I should've warned you when I saw what was happening. I could see you changing. I could see the way your ambition played you like a fiddle. But I hoped you'd remember what I taught you. I hoped I wouldn't have to spell it all out for you." She sat in the wing chair and blew her nose. "You'd better sit. I'm going to tell you the truth about your father now, whether you want to hear it or not."

He slowly sat, tense, stomach churning.

"From the time you were a little boy, I've tried to protect you. And myself." She glared at him. "I can't tell you how much it hurts to live with a man who cheats and lies and thinks he has a right to live however he pleases without answering to anyone, even God. I prayed for him. Oh, how I prayed for him. Year after year. Even after he'd destroyed every bit of love between us, I prayed for his salvation."

"Salvation? If anyone was saved, Dad was."

"I'd like to believe that. I really would like to believe God reached him. But I don't think so. I never saw evidence in his life that he was really a Christian."

He couldn't believe she would say such a thing about one of the best-known evangelists in the country. "He brought thousands to Christ, Mother. He had a congregation of thousands. He had a television show and a radio ministry. He wrote a bestselling book!"

"And you think all that is a sign of God's approval? Your father never brought a single soul to salvation. I thought you understood. Salvation is a work of the *Holy Spirit*, Paul. It's *God* who saves. It's *Jesus*. No man can or should take credit for anyone's salvation. I tried to teach you the truth. I tried to teach you the proper way to walk. Without compromise. To strive to live a holy life. I tried to tell you the Christian life isn't a sprint. It's a grueling marathon. And you used to believe. Your heart was tender toward God. And your faith earned your father's disdain. Do you remember?"

"He was a little tough on me, I guess."

"You *guess*? May God help you to remember the way it really was. You wanted your father's attention, Paul. You craved his approval. I didn't know how much until I heard you preach. I said you were more like your father than I realized. You took it as a compliment. I didn't mean it that way. I should have made it clear."

He stood. "I'm not sure I want to hear my own mother rip my father's reputation apart when he's dead and can't even defend himself."

"There was a time when you didn't run away from the truth."

"I had an affair. I admit it. It's over. I'm sorry. It'll never happen again."

"That's what he said—in the same unrepentant, unconscionable tone. Did you also tell Eunice it was her fault? That she wasn't enough of a wife to keep you happy? Did you lay the blame for your sins at her feet the same way your father laid his at mine? I can see by your face you did. *Sit down!*"

He sat. Shocked. His mother had never spoken to him like this before.

"Your father didn't *choose* to retire, Paul. He was *forced* to retire. One of the elders found out your father was having an affair with a woman he was counseling. And it wasn't his first, I can tell you.

"The elder confronted your father. He wouldn't listen. Then two elders went to talk with him. He put an end to the affair and thought that was the end of the trouble. But he'd grown careless. He was involved with more than one woman at a time. One found out about the other and came to the elders.

"They told him if he didn't tender his resignation, they would expose him before the congregation. If he agreed to step down, nothing would be said about it. The women would be asked to leave the church. His reputation would remain intact. He agreed; they kept their word. Nothing was ever said. We all swept the sordid episode under the carpet along with all the other sordid little episodes he'd conducted over the years. We all thought we were protecting the church."

She paused, tears filling her eyes again. "But we were just adding to the corruption . . . because here you are, his son, following in his footsteps."

"I've only had one affair."

"You lie to me as easily as you lie to yourself."

"Sheila's the only one, I swear, Mom. It's over. It was a mistake. The biggest of my life." He was shaking. He felt cold inside.

"Oh, Paul, you're so blind! You've been cheating on God for years.

I've been in your church. I've seen how you work people, how you charm and manipulate them. You've become just like your father. He used people up and threw them away. I was the first one of a long line of people who loved him and prayed for him. He used my love to control me, to keep me silent. And you've done the same thing to Eunice. You used her talents, too. Until she refused to compromise. And then you set her aside because you were more interested in pleasing people than doing what was right in God's eyes."

He felt a shiver up his spine, hair standing on end. He rubbed his neck, trying to rub the feeling away.

She leaned forward, hands clasped. "Do you think God doesn't see what you do? Do you think the Lord doesn't know what you think about Him? You use His name to get your way. You water down His Word in order to entertain your people. You've been spitting in the face of the One who saved you and loved you as your father never did!"

Her words cut into him. Never in his life had he faced her condemnation. Clenching his fists, he fought tears. "I've worked hard to build that church. It was dying when I came to Centerville. I have over three thousand people in my congregation now!"

"And you think that makes you a success?" She leaned back, hands resting on the arms of the chair. "And what does your church stand for but your own pride of accomplishment?"

He drew back. "It stands for Christ."

"No, it doesn't. A visitor doesn't have a clue what kind of doctrine they'll hear when they walk through the doors. They don't even know what doctrine is. What do they hear, Paul? What truth? The gospel? *No.* All they get is an hour of entertainment. Exciting music. Special effects. A titillating speech to rouse their emotions. You care more about the number of people sitting in your pews than who they are—lost souls in need of a Savior. People can't be healed and made whole by Christ until their hearts are broken over their sin, and you've made them comfortable with it—and yourself right along with them."

He couldn't look her in the eyes.

His mother wilted. She covered her face. "I was wrong to protect your father. I was wrong to cover for him. I tried to convince myself that I was protecting the church by protecting him." She looked up, face ravaged. "God, forgive me. Eunice was right. I lived a lie. I was protecting myself from the humiliation and the shame." Her smile was self-deprecating. "I didn't want people to know I wasn't enough of a woman to hold my man." She gave a bleak laugh. "The truth is, no woman could've held him. It was a game he played. Maybe if he'd been held accountable, some things would have changed. The discipline would've put the fear of God into others. Like you. You wouldn't have thought you could do things your own way. You would've learned that God is merciful, but He doesn't compromise."

"Dad was a good man. I can't believe you're saying all this." He didn't want to hear. He didn't want to feel the conviction.

Lois shuddered. "The Lord gave your father opportunities to repent, Paul. He gave him chance after chance. Instead, your father's heart grew harder and more proud. Sometimes I think the Lord struck him down on that airplane. God took his life before he could do any more damage."

"He built a church, Mom."

"He drew a crowd." She leaned forward again, hands outstretched. "Listen to me, Paul. Listen carefully. Your father was never a shepherd. He was a cattleman driving his herd to market. He tried to drive you. Don't you remember? He belittled and mocked you. He pushed and prodded. He did everything he could to mold you and make you into what he was. And you resisted him. I saw how tender your heart was. You were more like your grandfather Ezra than your father."

"My grandfather was a failure."

"You couldn't be more wrong. All Ezra ever wanted to do was serve the Lord, to spread the good news of salvation in Jesus Christ. And he did! If you go back to the places where he preached, you'll find churches, Paul. Small but living churches, centered on Christ and the Bible. Your grandfather served the Lord more faithfully than your father ever did."

"But Dad said—"

"Your father only saw there was never enough money for the things he wanted. Your father hated him for that. He wanted no part of the kind of life your grandfather led, a life of self-sacrifice. He wanted a big house and a fancy car. He wanted fame. So he used the talents God gave him for his own aggrandizement. He used preaching to live exactly as he pleased. And God gave him over to his sin."

"I thought you loved him."

"I loved the man I thought I married. And when I knew who and what he really was, I loved him out of obedience to Christ. I didn't always succeed. Divorce was never an option for me. But there came a time . . ." She shook her head and stared down at her hands. "I stopped sleeping with your father after the fourth affair." She raised her head. "Eunice knew. Not everything I've told you. Not how many times your father cheated, but she knew enough of what I was suffering and why. She never broke trust with me, Paul. And I've been wondering since she left this morning. Did I tell her about your father because I hoped she would do my dirty work and tell you? What a terrible burden she's carried for me all these years."

Paul held his head. He couldn't shut out the ring of truth, nor the flood of memories. "I don't know what to do. I don't know what to think."

"Yes, you do."

"I need to sleep on it. I need to think things over."

"You can do all that somewhere else." His mother stood. "I love you, Paul, but it's time for you to go."

He raised his head and stared at her. "You're kicking me out? Mom, I hardly slept last night. I drove five hours to get here. It's not my fault Eunice isn't here. I'm too tired to—"

"I, I, I!" She looked at him in disgust. "You got yourself into this mess, and it's going to take more than whining and excuses and self-pity to get you out of it."

"I understand. It's just that—"

"You haven't even considered what you've put Eunice through, have you? Not really."

"Of course I have."

"God help you. You're a liar just like your father. I made things easy for him. And now look at the trouble it's brought upon all of us." She went to the door and opened it. "I'm not going to offer a safe haven to the one who sent Eunice out into the night."

"I don't know where she is, Mom. I haven't a clue."

"Then you'd better find out." Her voice broke. "That poor girl. What you've done to her. What I helped you do." She drew herself up and spoke firmly. "You're not welcome in my house until you make things right with your wife." Tears spilled over her cheeks as she made a cutting gesture toward the open doorway.

Paul picked up his jacket and went out the door. When he turned and looked into his mother's eyes, his heart plunged. She'd always been there for him, always his ally. No one loved a son like his own mother. She looked at him as though he were a stranger she didn't want to know.

"Wait just a minute." She disappeared for only a moment. "Take this." She thrust his wedding picture into his hand. "It might make you think about what you stand to lose." She closed the door and turned the dead bolt.

The first flight to Philadelphia was full. There was no choice but to wait. Eunice took a seat by the windows, looking out over the runways. She was so tired, she thought about stretching out on the floor and tucking her purse under her head. But it wasn't to be done. What would people think? A Starbucks was just down the concourse. Maybe a caramel latte would give her a boost, and maybe the courage she'd need for her first airplane flight.

It didn't.

She tried not to think about anything, especially Paul's possible reaction when he arrived in Reseda and found her gone. She could guess. What would he say to the congregation about her absence? Assuming anyone bothered to ask. *Family emergency? A cousin died? Thank you for your condolences.* Of course, there were no cousins.

Bitter thoughts ran through her head. She prayed God would stop them. She prayed for help to get through the racking pain, prayed to know what to do, prayed the Lord would just swoop down like an eagle and rescue her.

Her cell phone rang. She took it out of her purse and looked at the caller's number. Paul. She tossed the cell phone back into her purse.

Four hours crawled by before she boarded the plane with nothing but her purse.

"Would you like a pillow and blanket?"

"Please." She smiled her thanks at the attendant. Scrunching up the pillow, she tucked it into the curve of her shoulder and leaned against the window.

She awakened once as an in-flight meal was being served. As soon as she finished the lasagna, she went back to sleep, and didn't awaken until the flight attendant tapped her on the shoulder. "You'll have to put your seat into the full upright position. Is your seat belt fastened?" She nodded, dozing again as the plane landed.

Everyone was out of their seats and pulling luggage out of overhead compartments and from under seats. People stood in the aisle, loaded down and eager to depart the aircraft. Eunice watched their faces as they passed. As the line of passengers trickled, she stood, looped the strap of her purse over her shoulder, and stepped out into the aisle. She was the last one to leave the airplane.

"Thank you," she said as she passed the pilot and senior flight attendant, "for the smooth flight." A pity she had slept through the experience and missed looking out the window at the tapestry of America below. She'd been too tired to keep her eyes open. She had been lulled to sleep by the hum of the engine.

She found the line of rental car agencies and went from one to the next. But the prices were higher than she had imagined. She didn't want to buy the car, just rent it. Finally, she gave in and handed over her credit card for a small compact that was doable and came with unlimited mileage. An agency bus picked her up and dropped her off next to the car. She sat in the driver's seat for a long while, looking through the owner's manual to learn how to turn on the headlights and windshield wipers, and how to release the brake. It was the first time she'd driven a new car, and she didn't want to put a dent into it before she drove off the lot.

It was late. Most travelers were probably checking into hotels, but she had slept all the way across the country and knew that renting a room would be a waste of money. She found her way onto the main highway.

She missed Tim. Her throat closed up thinking about him. Perhaps she should have called and told him she was in Southern California. But if she had done that, he would have come over, and he would have known immediately something was wrong.

Jesus, in Your mercy, let it be Paul who tells him. Or Lois. I can't do it. Don't let me be the one to see the disappointment come into Tim's eyes, the realization that everything he said was true. "This church is full of hypocrites, and Dad's the biggest one of all." Her son had seen more clearly than she had.

Headlights flashed by, one pair after another, passing her in the night.

Had Paul ever really loved her? She'd wondered why he even looked twice at her in college. A little backwoods girl. Unsophisticated.

What now, Lord? Didn't You say infidelity is reason for divorce?

She unclenched her hands on the wheel and changed positions. A friend had told her once that the horror of divorce was never over. Especially when children were involved. But Tim wasn't a child anymore. He was a young man, ready to embark upon whatever adventures the Lord had in store for him.

Give my son a faithful, loving wife, God—a girl who will cherish him and fight for their marriage. Someone he will love and hold dear all the days of his life. Let him be a man who keeps his promises.

------ ❦ ------

Paul spent a restless night in a Hilton off Interstate 5 near Santa Clarita. It hadn't occurred to him when he headed south that he would need a change of clothing, his razor, and toothbrush. He'd purchased the necessities last night before he checked in. He'd watched a movie to stop thinking about what his mother had said.

It didn't help.

He had to get back to the church. He had to see if anything had been said, any questions raised. He needed to write a sermon for Sunday. No matter what disaster had befallen his life, he still had to stand up in that pulpit and give some kind of message to the people filling the pews. He sat up and fought the nausea of exhaustion and emotional upheaval.

Maybe a shower would help clear his head.

He turned the water all the way up and stood in the hard, hot stream. It didn't make him feel any better. Nor did he feel clean. He couldn't shut out the memory of Sheila's contempt or Eunice's eyes so full of pain.

The photograph his mother had given him was still in the car. He hadn't wanted to bring it into the hotel room with him, to wake up to it this morning.

He nicked himself shaving. Cursing, he finished more carefully, then threw the toiletries into the wastebasket, dressed, and went down to the lobby restaurant to have a continental breakfast. They wouldn't be serving until six. He wasn't willing to wait. He checked out. He could always stop on the other side of the Grapevine and have breakfast.

Samuel listened. He heard birds, the soft hum of bees in the honey-suckle, the trickle of the water fountain in the center of the courtyard, the metallic glide of a window opening, and the muted sound of a television game show.

In the midst of such peaceful surroundings, he imagined the sound of the shofar. The Lord was calling, and the sound resonated in his heart. It carried. Stephen had heard it, too. God no longer needed men to blast the ram's horn to hear His Word. He was writing on men's hearts through the indwelling of the Holy Spirit. But few listened. Few leaned in and sought out God's will for their lives.

Once, on Mount Sinai, the Lord Himself had blasted the shofar as He was giving the law to Moses. It must have been a sound so intense and beckoning, it made the human heart tremble.

Oh, God, how I long for You to sound the shofar again! Let deaf men hear You so that they will never doubt again that there is a God in heaven. You are Creator, Father, almighty God, and Son. Oh, Lord, I know You speak to us through the Holy Spirit now, but You blew the shofar once. Please blow it again so that Paul—and indeed, all men—will turn back from destruction. How long must I listen to the hollow words of a man who claims he speaks for You and yet lives in the shadow of judgment and death? I hear Your quiet voice, but his ears are shut. Blast him out of his compla-cency before it's too late, Lord. Shake him up. I see the evidence of You in every dawn and sunset . . . and his eyes are closed.

The sun was rising at her back as Eunice approached the bridge half a mile outside of her hometown. She used to sit on this bridge when she was a girl and drop pebbles into the water. Coal Ridge seemed deserted except for two old men sitting in rocking chairs outside the general store. They watched her drive past. She turned up Colton Avenue and slowed almost to a stop as she drove by the home in which she had been raised. It was boarded up, weeds overgrown in the yard, an old For Sale sign posted on the white picket fence. She parked in front.

The gate was broken. She remembered how many people had come through it each week to visit her father and mother. The front steps were rotting. She picked her way cautiously. She looked through the window. The house was vacant, dust on the floors, cobwebs in the windows.

Someone had said you could never go home again. She hadn't understood until this moment. This broken-down shell wasn't her home. The people who had made it a place of warmth and love and safety were gone.

Eunice wished she hadn't come. Leaning her forehead against the glass, she closed her eyes, feeling a sense of loss so deep she felt she was drowning in it. Turning away, she went down the steps and closed the gate behind her. She walked along Colton Avenue, looking at the houses where friends had once lived. Tullys, O'Malleys, Fritzpatricks, Danvers. Where were they now? Where had they all gone when the mines closed?

The street came to a dead end. She walked back on the other side and got into her rental car. She sat for a long time, her mind numb with disappointment and confusion. Where now? She turned the key, made a U-turn, and headed up to the main street. Turning right, she headed for the south end of town and then turned left and drove up the hill.

Paul turned the wedding photo his mother had given him facedown on the passenger seat. He wasn't going to think about what his mother had said. Not now. Not when he was so tired he couldn't think straight. He found the on-ramp to I-5.

Bone-weary and groggy, he turned on the radio. He needed something to get his mind off depressing matters and worries about the future. Patsy Cline was belting out "Your Cheatin' Heart." He punched the Select button and heard Carly Simon singing, "You're so vain, I'll bet you think this song is about you, don't you—" Swearing, he tried again and heard the first strains of a song he'd once told Eunice reminded him of her: Jim Croce's "Time in a Bottle." He punched the Off button.

He felt sick to his stomach.

The steep Grapevine was ahead of him, winding down from the mountains, the Central Valley stretching out like a patchwork quilt in front of him. Trucks moved at a snail's pace in the far right lane, gears tortured, brakes at the ready. He stopped at the foot of the mountains for gas and a cup of coffee to go. At this rate, he'd be back in Centerville by ten. He'd have time to swing by the house, change his clothes, and be in the church office by noon. He could straighten it up, put it to rights before anyone came in. Nobody would even know he'd been gone. And if anyone did ask about Eunice, he'd just say she was visiting Tim again.

Was it only because of his Scripture reading that morning that Samuel could not stop thinking about the ram's horn? The only place the shofar was still used was in Jewish ceremonies, and even many Jews didn't understand. All men were accountable for their sin, and the penalty was still death. The shofar sounded to announce the coming of the Lord. When it sounded, the people were to assemble, confess, and repent. When it sounded, the people were to worship. The shofar announced the Day of Atonement and Jubilee. It sounded in the midst of battle.

A call to gather God's people, a call to repentance, a call to enter into battle. God's voice came to the multitude through the prophets in the days of old, but now the Lord spoke to each believer through the Holy Spirit.

Oh, Lord, I know I am in battle. How long must I fight this war? I'm weary of it. Heartsick. Despairing. Only You can save him, and yet he turns away and turns away and turns away. How do You bear it? What kind of power-love did it take for You to hang on that cross and listen to them mock You when You were making a way for them to have redemption and eternal life? What keeps You from wiping the world clean by fire?

He bowed his head, wishing he could give up his soul as Jesus had done, and enter his rest. But God was the one who counted his days. God gave him breath for a reason. Samuel had been at war for years now—one voice weeping before the Lord, pleading for the softening of a single human heart that grew harder with each year that passed.

Eunice hadn't been back to this cemetery since her mother passed away. She parked the car and entered beneath the rusted iron arch. The first funeral she'd attended here was for a boy she knew who drowned in the river when he was eight. The last funeral was for her mother, two years after her father had been carried up the hill by six pallbearers. She and her mother had planted forget-me-nots around the grave after her father's service, and Eunice had planted more of them when she returned to bury her mother. Then she put the house up for sale.

When she found their resting place and knelt, she plucked weeds and smoothed the grass as though it were a blanket over them. She missed her father and mother even more now. Alone and far away from a place she should have been able to consider home, away from a man she had pledged to love until death parted them, she longed for connection to those who'd love her unconditionally.

Oh, God. Oh, Abba, I want to come home. Couldn't You take me now? Let this grief stop my heart from beating.

Wishful thinking. God had already counted her days and was not likely to take her life just because living was so painful. Jesus knew better than anyone the pain of life on this earth. Jesus knew what it felt like to be betrayed.

Weary, she stretched herself out upon the graves, arms spread wide as though to embrace them both. The earth was cold beneath her.

Oh, her parents were the fortunate ones. They no longer had to suffer disappointment. And they would have suffered with her if they'd lived long enough to know Paul was not a man of his word. She longed for their wisdom. She ached at the loss, knowing she could've told them anything and everything and it wouldn't have changed their opinion or their love for her or Paul. They would've wept with her and advised her. But would she have listened?

She knew already what her father would've said, and her mother would have agreed. *Forgive. No matter what Paul's done, you're still his wife.* No matter what she had seen when she walked into the church office, her responsibility was unchanged. Jesus was Lord. What had He seen as He looked down from the cross but a crowd gathered to mock Him? Yet He died for them.

Her mother and father would have told her to forgive, but what about going back to Paul? Would they have told her to go on living with a man who excused his sin and continued to walk in the ways of his father rather than obey God?

God said to do what was right.

Oh, God, what is right in this situation?

———— ❧ ————

Paul wondered how many times Eunice had driven this route to see Timothy. How many times had she stopped somewhere and had a meal alone because he'd been too busy to go south with her?

He didn't want to think about that now. He had to consider sermon ideas. Every one that came to him made him uncomfortable. He could always pull out notes from a past sermon, make a few changes, and go with that. Was there a holiday approaching? Some civic activity that needed a boost?

When the freeway branched, he took Highway 99 north. He reached for his coffee. He took his eyes off the road for only a couple of seconds, but when he looked up again, a jackrabbit was running across the road in front of him.

———— ❧ ————

Samuel remembered the evening three elders came together in the old church and decided not to close the doors.

We gave it one last try, Lord. Were we wrong? Oh, Father, it's as though I stood on the shores of the Jordan and saw the Promised Land. And I'm still looking at it, from the valley of death this time, hoping and praying I'll see the day when Paul leaves the wilderness of sin behind him and crosses over into the realm of faith.

Eunice. Sweet Eunice. *Don't let her slip away from us. Lord, help her. Protect her heart, for from it has come springs of living water. Keep her on the Rock, Lord. Keep her in the palms of Your scarred hands.*

———— ❧ ————

"Daddy." Eunice sobbed. "Daddy." *What do I do?*

"Miss?"

A man stood nearby, holding a shovel. Startled, Eunice clambered up, dashing the tears from her eyes. He was a few years older than she, dressed in soiled jeans and a checked wool shirt, his boots clumped with earth. A grave digger? The groundskeeper? He looked concerned.

"Can I help you, miss?"

Embarrassed, she brushed the grass from her blouse and slacks.

"I was just . . ." Just what? Confiding her problems to her dead parents? She looked at his shovel uneasily. She didn't know who this man was or if he was a threat.

He set the shovel aside. "Would you like to talk about it?" His face was so kind, his eyes so gentle.

"My husband . . ." Her throat closed. Her mouth worked. She looked away. The man sat on the grass as though he had all the time in the world. She felt calm in his presence. He seemed so ordinary, just a man taking a break from whatever work he had been doing. She told him everything.

"I don't know whether to go back. He's a pastor, you see."

The man said nothing.

She looked into his eyes. "It's not just about his infidelity to me."

"No, it isn't."

She ran her hand over the grass that covered her parents' graves. "My father was a pastor, too. He worked at being a good one."

"What advice would your father give you?"

"Forgive." She smiled wryly through her tears. "It would be so much easier if my husband were repentant." Her smile died.

"Were those at the cross repentant?"

She bowed her head, aching at the thought of what Jesus must have felt. What she was suffering now was merely a drop of the sorrow Jesus had drunk on the day of His crucifixion.

"Let the Lord's strength sustain you, Eunice."

"I know that in my head. But my heart . . . even if Paul were repentant, I don't know if I could ever really trust him again. And if I can't trust him, what sort of wife would I be? It could never be the way it was."

"Are you looking for a way out?"

"Maybe. Out of the pain, at least."

He smiled tenderly. "There's no getting around that. It comes with life in this world, and following the One you do."

"I don't know what kind of future we can have together after what he's done."

"One day's trouble is enough. Face tomorrow when it comes."

"I'd like to run away from it all and never look back."

"You'll carry it with you everywhere you go."

She knew that already. She'd come all the way across the country and escaped none of the anguish. "So what's your advice?"

His eyes filled with compassion. "Trust in the Lord. Do what's right. And rest." He rose, took his shovel, and walked away.

Rest, she thought. *In Him. I need to be still and stop running. I can't trust my husband or mother-in-law or friends, but I can trust God. And I can believe that the Lord is working, even now. I can trust that Christ will turn all this pain to His good purpose.*

Someday.

In the meantime, she needed to find a place to eat and then a place to sleep.

Alone in the courtyard, Samuel continued to plead before the throne of heaven. *How long, O Lord, how long must I bear this sorrow? I have known and done Your will for over seventy years, but I know men, too, and it will take the blasting of a shofar to make Paul stop and listen. Lord, please. Make him aware of the pain he's caused. Bring him to account for it. Turn him, Lord, turn him so profoundly, there will be no turning back for him. So profoundly that the change in him will bring light to others.*

Paul cried in pain as hot coffee splashed over his right leg. Jamming on the brakes, he gripped the wheel with both hands and turned sharply to avoid running over the jackrabbit in the road ahead of him. Horns blasted. He heard a loud screech, felt the car swing into a hard circle. Terrified, he tried to compensate and screamed as a semi barely missed plowing into his door.

The sound of the horn was in back of him, in front, bearing down on him long and loud. He was going to die! He was going to die!

I don't understand, Lord, Samuel prayed. *How could I have been so wrong about a man? I thought I was doing Your will in calling Paul Hudson to Centerville Christian. But I have watched him go in like a wolf among Your sheep, leading them astray, filling them with false teaching and groundless hope. Or is he the lost lamb? Oh, God, I don't know anymore. How I wish*

Your voice was as loud as that ancient shofar so that I could hear and know what You want me to do.

You know.

Tears rolled down his cheeks.

Paul skidded off the road. Enveloped in a cloud of dust, he came to a dead stop, heart pounding so hard he thought he'd pass out. Still gripping the wheel, he shook, adrenaline roaring in his veins. He got his breath back, shoved the gearshift into park, and put his head against the steering wheel.

Someone tapped on the window. "Mister! You okay?"

No, he wasn't. He was anything but okay. He raised his hand and nodded without looking at the stranger.

"Do you need a tow truck?"

How many others had been hurt in his attempt to miss hitting a jackrabbit?

He pressed a button and lowered the window enough to ask if anyone was hurt.

The man looked back. "No one that I can see. But cars are stacking up. My truck's blocking one lane. I'd better get rolling. Are you sure you're okay? I can call in for help."

"Yeah, I'm okay."

"Man, someone's watching out for you. That's all I can say. Another split second and I would've hit you head-on with my semi. What made you swerve like that?"

"Instinct, I guess. Something ran across the road."

The trucker said a couple of choice words and ran back to his vehicle. He jumped up, slammed the door. The truck roared to life, ground into gear. The air horn blasted. The truck was so close Paul felt he was being melted by the noise. The driver brought the truck around and back onto the highway, heading north. A dozen cars followed, all slowing as each driver took a good long look at Paul.

He was too shaken to get back on the road yet. So he sat, waiting for his heart to slow down. He saw his wedding picture shattered on the floor below the passenger seat. Eunice gazed up at him—adoring, trusting—through broken glass. And it hit him then like a blow in his stomach what he had done to her, what he had done to their marriage.

Oh, God . . .

He'd almost killed himself in the effort to miss a jackrabbit running across the road, but he'd been running over Eunice for years.

Every word Paul's mother had said sank in and took hold, shaking the foundations of his lifework. *I've lost her. I've lost Euny.*

All his life, Paul had wanted to be like his father. And now he had succeeded, realizing much too late that his earthly father was not a man to be emulated. He had become like his father, all right—cheating on his wife, cheating on his Lord and Savior, Jesus Christ. He'd become good at using the church to fan his pride and build his own empire. He'd served the same idols his father had: ambition and arrogance. Oh, he'd made sacrifices—plenty of them. His dreams, his integrity, his restraint, his moral fiber and character. Those he should've been protecting, he'd abandoned—faithful friends like Samuel and Abby Mason, Stephen Decker, and a dozen others before he cast away his own son and wife. Or had he cast them off first?

They'd all tried to reach him. They'd all tried to warn him. But he'd been too full of pride, too full of himself to listen. Oh, he knew what he was doing, he thought. He was building a church, wasn't he? He was working for the Lord, wasn't he? And that justified everything, didn't it?

Oh, God, oh, Jesus . . .

How dare he even utter the name?

———— ✺ ————

When Paul arrived home, there were fifteen messages waiting for him. He prayed as he listened to each, but there wasn't a call from Eunice. All had to do with church business, including a reminder that he didn't have to worry about Sunday. He had scheduled a well-known ecumenical speaker. Well, that was a relief, anyway.

The last message was from Sheila. "I think Reka is the one who told Eunice to come to the office." She called her a foul name. "If you don't fire her, you're an idiot. I'm sorry about what I said to you in the office. I think you can understand I was upset. I do love you, but I think we both know it's over. I'm calling from Palm Springs. Rob is going to fly here on the way home from Florida. I haven't told him anything. I have no intention of telling him. I just thought this was a good idea for damage control. If any rumors arise, they'll die quick enough when I come home with a nice tan and my hubby on my arm. You just have to deal with Eunice—"

He punched the Delete button. *Deal with Eunice.* Wasn't that what he'd been doing for the last ten years? He looked at the notes, schedules, and programs on his desk, a dozen neatly laid out. He picked up the class schedule and read down the list: Power Praying: How to Get God to Answer; Embracing the Imposter Within: Making Friends with Your Past; Improving Your Self-Image; Alternate Lifestyles: A Course in Loving Your Neighbor; Yoga: Exercise to Inspire Meditation. One of the deacons' wives was holding a party on finding peace in the midst of storms through aromatherapy. He felt the hair stand up on the back of his neck. Sheila wasn't the problem. She was just the most recent in a long line of sins he'd been committing over the years. The mountainous weight of them pressed down on him until he could hardly breathe.

How do I get out from under this? How do I get back on the road? Oh, Jesus, help me! How did I ever get so far off track in the first place?

Who do you say that I am?

Paul held his head and wept. He'd been behaving worse than an unbeliever.

He got up from his chair and went down on his knees. He hadn't prayed like this since his first years serving the Lord at Mountain High.

Oh, Lord my God, Jesus, Savior and Redeemer, be kind to me according to Your mercy and grace. Cancel out my sins. Jesus, let the blood You shed for me wash me clean again.

What one believes about God determines what one does. Who had said that to him? Eunice? Samuel? His mother? *Oh, Lord, I've sinned against You.*

He lay flat, face to the floor. *I've done what is evil in Your sight, all the while convincing myself I was serving You. Lord, have mercy on me! Let me hear Your Word in joy again. Wipe away my sins. Give me a new heart and mind, a new spirit and steadfast faith. Oh, God, don't cast me out into the darkness, but restore my soul.* He sobbed. *Let me be like a child again. Let me be Your child.*

It was over an hour before he rose to his feet, weary, depressed. He used to feel God's presence when he prayed. Now, he felt alone and lost. He wanted to talk with his mother about it, but she wanted nothing to do with him until he made things right with Eunice.

He didn't want to think about Eunice. He didn't want to think about the pain he'd caused her or what she must be feeling right now. But he was remembering Scripture. It was filling his mind, bringing him up short, taking him back, pointing the way.

He needed to make amends with Eunice before he could even hope God would turn an ear to his prayers. *A good wife is a gift from God.* And what had he done with his gift? He'd already asked God's forgiveness and knew the Lord kept His Word, kept His promises. But he needed to find his wife and beg for her forgiveness now, too.

Where would she go? Did she have money to eat or rent a room? He winced as he remembered how he'd taken away her suitcase and keys, thinking that would be enough to keep her in the house, silent and waiting like a little mouse for the cat to come home. She'd fled. Could he blame her? What had she learned to expect from him but rationalization and justification for his behavior? Worse, he had made her the scapegoat.

Did she have any money other than what had been in her purse? How was she going to get by?

She would've had to use a credit card!

Paul took out his wallet and looked through his cards. He only carried two and used them strictly for business, luncheons at the club, new suits, and books. Eunice carried a different card. Which one? He wasn't sure. She paid their monthly bills, except for the ones he hadn't wanted her to see. He went into the master bedroom and opened her desk drawer. In front were bills, neatly organized by due date. He took out two and picked up the phone.

It took him almost an hour to find out the most recent transactions on both credit cards. An airline ticket to Philadelphia. A rental car, gasoline, and a motel. *Thank You, blessed Jesus. Oh, Father, protect her!*

He took her suitcase out of the trunk of his car. Returning to the bedroom, he dumped everything out on the bed. He looked at the hangers and pictures, the small jewelry box, every item representing someone who'd loved her, someone she'd been able to trust. Heart in his throat, he hung up her clothes, put the picture back on the wall, and tucked the jewelry box back into her drawer. Then he packed—for both of them.

On his way to the Sacramento airport, he used his cell phone to call one of the newer associates. He'd been in conflict with John Deerman since he hired him. Paul understood why now. John had clung to the gospel. He taught Scripture. His classes had been small, too small in Paul's opinion. So he had tried to use John elsewhere, but John had held his ground. One of the things on Paul's personal agenda had been to have Deerman dismissed. Now he saw him as a man like Joseph Wheeler, the man who had taken over his father's pulpit.

Paul told John he wouldn't be in church on Sunday. He needed to make a trip. He didn't give his reasons. "Pray for me, would you, John? Pray hard."

"What's happened to you, Paul?"

"I'm on the Damascus road. Do you understand what I'm saying?"

"Yes, Paul. Praise the Lord!"

CHAPTER 20

——— ❦ ———

EUNICE SLEPT DEEPLY, so deeply that when she awakened in the morning, she couldn't remember her dreams. She'd driven to Somerset to buy a few things: a brush, toothbrush and toothpaste, a nightgown, two cheap polyester dresses, and a washable cardigan sweater. Enough to tide her over until she knew what she was going to do.

She ate breakfast at a local diner, ordering an egg and a piece of toast, a small glass of juice, and a cup of coffee, but she couldn't finish. As her mind wandered to Paul and Sheila, her throat closed up. She took out the small Bible she always carried in her purse and opened it to Psalms. Her emotions were too raw to take much comfort. She prayed as she sipped coffee. But her prayer seemed to turn into a long-winded, one-sided conversation, and she was doing all the talking.

Another woman would have understood what Rob Atherton had been trying to say to her. Another woman might have grabbed Sheila Atherton by the hair and poked her eyes out. Another woman might have stayed and fought to keep her man. Another woman might have known what was going on before the church secretary had to call her and tip her off. But she'd just been a coward. She hadn't wanted to look too closely at what was happening, because if she did, she would have to make a stand and risk losing her husband. And now, as it turned out, she had lost him anyway.

She paid for her breakfast and went out for a long walk, ending up at the cemetery again. She looked for the groundskeeper. The hut at the back looked deserted. The door had a rusted padlock on it. She looked back over the grounds and didn't see any fresh graves. In fact, there was no evidence that she could see that anything had been done in years. The grass was high, weeds growing everywhere other than under the trees, where they wouldn't have received enough sunlight to propagate.

"Hello!"

The birds stopped singing. She waited, but the man didn't answer. She wandered through the cemetery. She recognized many of the names on the headstones. Returning to her parents' graves, she sat for a while, chin on her raised knees. As peaceful as it was here, she knew she wouldn't come back for another visit. Her parents weren't here. They were with the Lord now, all the pain of this world gone. Only their shells remained here. What comfort she had been given by her visit hadn't come from their resting place, but from the things they had taught her in life. And from the listening ear of a stranger who told her simply to pray, do what's right, and rest in the Lord.

If she could find the courage.

She stood and looked around again. "Thank you!" The birds stopped singing at the sound of her voice. She closed her eyes. "Thank you," she whispered. Turning away, she walked back to the motel.

She drove along country roads in her rental car. She stopped at the Country Store in Shanksville and bought a soda and fixings for a sandwich. She stopped at the memorial marking the spot where Flight 93 had crashed on September 11, 2001. It seemed strange to see a beautiful field of green grass marking a place of such carnage and tragedy. How many more lives would have been lost had those brave souls not fought and overcome the terrorists who wanted to turn their airplane into a flying bomb aimed at the White House? By the grace of God, the crash had occurred short of the Shanksville-Stonycreek School with five hundred students and teachers inside.

Eunice remembered how visitors had poured into VNLC, seeking answers during the first weeks after 9/11. On some level, they knew they needed God. They needed protection. What they really needed was truth and hope. Instead, Paul had fed them morsels without nourishment. White bread and soda pop instead of the Bread of Life and the Living Water. Some had stayed for the entertainment. Others had gone away, still starving.

Was the word *sin* even in the dictionary anymore? Did people understand that the God they cried out to for help was holy and uncompromising? "I am the way, the truth, and the life," Jesus said. "No one comes to the Father except through Me." What used to be called self-indulgence was now called self-fulfillment. What was once called moral irresponsibility was now considered freedom to find oneself. What was once considered disgusting and obscene was now tolerated—and even taught in schools as "alternate lifestyles." Temporary fixes. Feel-good religion. Discipline was considered repression; depravity, creative self-expression; murder, a matter of choice; and adultery, sex between consenting adults. What was wrong was called right, and what was right was called wrong!

Oh, Lord, I've been fighting against worldly thinking for years, and what good has it done me? Even Paul, who should've known better, has fallen for the lie.

Depressed, Eunice drove back the long way to Coal Ridge and found another white rental car parked at the motel. The door to the room next to hers was open. With all the other empty rooms, why had the proprietor seen fit to put another guest right next to her? She got out of her car.

A man appeared in the open doorway. Her heart jumped. It was a few seconds before she could speak. "What are you doing here, Paul?"

"I came to talk with you."

Talk? Or ask for a divorce? She fought the flash flood of emotions threatening to drown her again. Her throat was so tight she felt she was strangling. "Why?"

"Because I love you. Because I've sinned against God and I want to make things right."

She searched his face. She was desperate to believe him, but she knew he could sound so convincing, so passionately concerned when it suited his purposes. "I came all this way to get away from you." And what she had witnessed.

"Do you want me to leave?" He looked crushed, grieving. Was it all an act?

"You do what you have to do." She went into her room, closed the door, and put the chain on. Sitting on the edge of her bed, she wept.

She cried for more than an hour, took a long hot shower, dressed again, and peered out the window. His car was still there. Well, it was a long trip. He would need a good night's sleep before he headed back to California. Her head was pounding. She stretched out on the bed and tried not to think about the fact that her estranged husband was in the next room. What was he doing? Why should it matter to her? She started at a soft tap on the door. Shaking, she waited. Another soft tap. She rolled over, presenting her back to the door. She heard the door to the room next to hers open and close again. Would he try calling her?

The telephone didn't ring. She didn't hear any sound coming from next door. The tension kept building inside her. Tomorrow was Sunday. She flung herself from the bed, marched to the door, and threw it open. She stepped next door and knocked, loudly. Paul answered immediately, his expression beyond anything she could decipher. She didn't try. "Tomorrow is Sunday. You're supposed to be preaching."

"You're more important."

"Oh, don't expect me to believe that, Paul. Not now. Not after so many years."

"I don't expect you to believe me. I've been behaving like a fool for years." His shoulders didn't seem as straight, but his eyes were clear and he was looking straight into hers. "Don't worry about the church, Euny. I called John Deerman. He'll stand in for me wherever necessary. I came about us."

Euny. How long since he'd said her name in that tone? "John? You can't stand John." She didn't want to think about the rest. She didn't give in to her impulse to say, "What us? There is no us." God would say otherwise.

Paul shoved his hands into his pockets. "I thought John was the best man for the job."

Part of her wanted to stay and scream at him. Another part wanted to get in the car and drive away. Neither prospect was good. Neither would accomplish anything. She had run as far as she dared go and was right back where she started. "I'm not ready to talk to you, Paul."

"I'll wait."

"It might be a long, long time."

"I'll wait. Whatever it takes, Euny, however long it takes, I'll be here."

Shaken, she went back into her room and sat on the edge of the bed again. Resting her elbows on her knees, she covered her face. *Oh, God, help me. Should I believe him? How can I believe him? I don't want to believe him. I don't want to be hurt over and over again. I don't want to be set up and used. You know who he is, Lord. You know how he's been. You know what I saw. I'll stay married to him if I have to, but please don't ask me to live with him. Oh, God, please.*

She didn't talk to Paul again that day. She fixed herself a sandwich for dinner and turned on the television in an attempt to keep her mind off him. White noise didn't help.

She slept fitfully, then went to church the next morning. The old pastor gave a good sermon. He didn't deviate once from the pure message of the gospel. The choir was small and sang off-key, but it was a joyful noise that made tears spring into Eunice's eyes. There was no question in her mind as to whether the Lord was present in this house. She had felt His presence with every word said, every song sung. When the service was over and she got up to leave, she was greeted by half a dozen people.

She spotted Paul in the back row. He wasn't looking at her. His head was bowed low. As she passed by him, she saw his hands clasped between his knees. She flashed back to years ago when she was still in college. She'd walked into the chapel and seen Paul sitting just that way.

The ache in her heart warned her of more hurt to come. . . .

Had he followed her to church, too? Or had he come all by himself? She didn't stop to ask.

Several people approached her outside the church, greeting her and asking if she was visiting or moving to the area. She said she wasn't sure yet. She talked with them while keeping an eye on the door of the church. Everyone but Paul had come out. The pastor went back in. As the gathering dispersed, Eunice walked back to the motel, thinking it would be a nice day for a drive in the country. Restless, she sat in her motel room, the curtain ajar just enough that she could see out.

It was more than an hour before Paul returned. And he didn't head for his room. He came to hers and tapped on her door. She felt that tap inside her heart. *Tap, tap.* Was she willing to let him in again? Was she willing to take the risk? *Thy will, Lord, not mine, be done.* Smoothing her skirt, she went to the door and opened it. Her heart did a small flip and landed in a pool of sorrow. How could she still love this man after all the years of abuse crowned by a final blow of betrayal?

"There's a nice little café just down the street. May I take you to lunch?"

She was more nervous now than she had been the first time he asked her out. But she was hungry. "All right." There was no reason to sound pleased with the idea. "I'll get my purse." And her armor.

They walked side by side. A bell rang as they entered the front door. The waitress cleaning the counter said they could pick whatever table was open. The café was almost full. Paul let her lead the way to a booth toward the back. They sat facing one another. He looked at her until she picked up the menu and hid behind it. Her heart was pounding like a locomotive racing down the tracks. Toward what? More disaster? More heartache? If she let go, the tears would come and never stop.

How can I trust him, Lord?

The silence stretched. The waitress came for their order. "Eggs over easy, toast, orange juice, and coffee, please."

Paul ordered chicken-fried steak, eggs, grits, and coffee. He gave Eunice a faint smile. "I haven't eaten since yesterday."

Was she supposed to feel sorry for him? How long since she had eaten a full meal? Chances were she wouldn't be able to take a bite of this one, but at least he was paying. *Oh, God, make him pay. Oh, Lord, forgive me. I don't mean that.* She rubbed her forehead, wishing she could rub out the confusion of images flashing. Maybe this wasn't such a good idea. Maybe she should excuse herself, cancel her order, and go back to the motel and cry herself out. Could she? How long would it take?

"I know you're uncomfortable with me, Euny. I can tell you're thinking about leaving, but I hope you'll stay."

His voice was so soft, so tender. He sounded broken, but hopeful. She looked at him through her tears and saw his eyes were awash with them, too. Speechless, she pressed her lips together, her throat aching.

"Mom and I had a talk." He smiled wryly. "Or I should say, Mom talked and I listened. Halfheartedly. Then, on the drive home, something happened that woke me up." He told her about a jackrabbit and a near-death experience, and their wedding picture smashed on the floor of the car.

Anger rushed up inside her, hot and heavy. *Oh, sure. Tell me another good story, Paul.* Now he'd have her believe he was just like the apostle Paul on the road to Damascus! The scales fell from his eyes. Hallelujah! He'd been blind and now he saw the truth! Glory be! And everything was going to be right with the world.

Did he really think she was so naive? Maybe once. Not anymore. Thanks to him.

She felt smashed to pieces, the fragments of her life scattered at his feet.

"How nice for you," she said blandly, not looking at him, not wanting to get sucked into the vortex of his charm. His story was a little too clichéd for her to swallow hook, line, and sinker.

Her husband had always been too good at taking stories and turning them this way and that in order to pull at people's heartstrings. She wasn't going to be Paul's puppet any longer. She wasn't going to dance to his music.

Paul hung his head.

And she felt ashamed. She wished she hadn't said anything because her words showed more of a change in her than in him. Better to have kept silent and let him hang himself. She winced inwardly. She didn't like the thoughts coming unbidden into her mind.

The waitress poured their coffee. Eunice put her hands around the warm cup and tried to capture her rebellious thoughts and focus them on Jesus. What would Jesus have her do? *Oh, God, I know.* She didn't even need to ask that question! It was the other one that reared its ugly head. Did she *want* to forgive Paul? And the avalanche of other questions flowing over her. Could Paul be trusted? What guarantees did she have that her husband wasn't the same selfish, ambitious manipulator he'd been for so many years? And even if Paul was sincere now, did that mean he wouldn't fall right back into the old ways the moment she softened toward him and he felt safe to be himself again? If she walked away right now, no one would blame her. One foot in front of the other. Out the door. And don't look back.

Where do you want to go, beloved?

The age-old question. Was her decision going to be based on the temporal things of this world, or on the eternal things of God?

Our lives are like the grass that withers. Short. Oh, but sometimes life seems to go on forever.

Would running away get her where she really wanted to go?

She sipped her coffee, mind racing with questions. And Paul wasn't trying to talk his way out of the mess he'd made this time. That was the most surprising. It wasn't like him to let the silence go for so long. He knew she was skeptical, and it wasn't like him not to defend himself and his position, making her feel small and somehow to blame.

The waitress brought their plates. She came back with more coffee. Other than to say thank you to her, Paul was silent. Was this a new strategy?

"I talked with your mother, too. Did she tell you?"

He met her gaze. "Yes."

"And?"

"She said you were right."

"Then you know I'm not going to follow her example. I'm not going to go back to VNLC and sit in the front row and pretend everything is all right with our marriage and your ministry. I'm not going to let your sweet talk put a veil over my eyes or keep me from using my brain. Not anymore. I'm not going to sweep anything under the carpet. I'm not going to cover for you."

"I know." He said it so simply, eyes clear, looking back at her without the faintest hint of cunning, anger, or fear.

Her armor began to come unhinged. She tried to make repairs. "Tell me, Paul. How's Sheila?"

"She's in Palm Springs awaiting the arrival of her husband. She's not going to tell him, and it's not my right to do so."

"He knows already. He tried to tell me." Paul looked surprised, but not frightened at the prospect.

"I'll make amends any way I can."

She wasn't about to tell him Rob Atherton would probably thank him for providing grounds for divorce.

When left to our own devices, what a mess we make of our lives.

"Sheila wasn't the problem, Eunice. And despite what I said to you at home, you were *not* in any way to blame for what happened. You've always been a true, loving, and faithful wife." His voice broke. He cleared his throat. "I'm responsible for the bad decisions I made, starting with rejecting Christ. I filled the void any way I could. Pride. Plans. Projects. That was only the beginning of a long downward spiral into all manner of sin, not the least of which was rationalizing and justifying my affair with another man's wife. It's over."

"Well, I guess so, if Sheila dumped you and went off to Palm Springs to wait for Rob." She couldn't believe she had said anything so blunt or cruel. She'd always taken such care. What sort of Christian was she? Had she always harbored such hateful feelings? Had they been lurking just below the surface, waiting to rise up and spew out like venom?

"I'm not just talking about the affair." He spoke quietly, no edge of self-defense in his tone. "I'm talking about the way I was living, my walk with Christ."

Is this what you do, Eunice? Beat a repentant man when he's down? Her hand trembled as she covered her mouth.

"It's all right, Euny."

She shook her head, trying to blink away the onrush of hot tears. No, it wasn't. It wasn't right at all. He hadn't retaliated. That told her, more than anything, that he had changed.

But how long would that change last?

"One day's troubles are enough," the stranger had said in the cemetery. Jesus had said the same thing to His people on a hillside beside Galilee.

And they crucified Him.

"Say what you need to say, Euny. Try not to worry about how it comes out. I love you."

She looked at him. "I've tried to talk to you before."

"But now I'm listening."

God help her, she looked into Paul's eyes and still loved him. How was it possible after what he'd done? *God, don't do this to me. Please. How much more hurt do I have to take from this man before You'll allow me to be free of him?* She wanted to squash the tiny seed of hope growing inside her. She wanted to cling to the memory of his betrayal, the anguish of discovery, the battering waves of disillusionment over the years, the aching wave of sorrow now. Paul Hudson wasn't her knight in shining armor. He hadn't been for a long, long time.

No, beloved. He's just a man fooled by a common enemy. The same enemy who is trying to fool you now into believing Jesus hasn't the power to restore the stolen years.

She could say what he needed to hear and see where that would take him. "I forgive you, Paul." *In obedience to You, Lord, I forgive him. As I've forgiven him over the years, so I forgive him again now. Because of You, only because of You, and only in Your power can I forgive.* She let out her breath slowly, her muscles relaxing.

Paul put his hand over hers.

Her heart fluttered like a trapped bird. Repulsed, she snatched her hand away and shook her head. It had only been a few days ago that she had seen his hands caressing the body of another woman. God could put sin as far away as the east is from the west, but she was only human. And Paul was moving too fast.

He searched her eyes, his expression gravely concerned. "Forgiveness is a start."

What was he waiting for her to say? What assurances did he want? Oh, she knew. "If you're worried I'll go back and call the *Centerville Gazette*, you can relax."

He shook his head. "I wasn't. It's not your style. But I am worried how you're going to feel about my decision. I'm going to resign from the pastorate."

"Resign?" That was the last thing she expected him to do.

"I have to get my own life in order again before I can stand at a pulpit and tell other people how to live."

"You're going to run away." Just like she had done, and her problems had chased after her.

"No. I'm going back. I'll call the board together and talk with them first. Then, if they allow it, I'll give one last sermon so the congregation will understand why it's necessary for me to leave."

"Sheila—"

"Sheila's name won't be mentioned. I'll be confessing my sins, not hers."

"When did you decide all this?"

"This morning. I talked with the pastor after the service. He didn't mince words."

All the years of trying to reach him, and it was a stranger who got through his thick skull. Everything she and his mother and Samuel and even Stephen had said had rolled off Paul like water off a duck's back. It should be enough that her husband wasn't blind anymore. It shouldn't hurt so much that he was hearing the truth and taking it to heart. Even if he'd been willing to listen to a stranger rather than those who knew and loved him through all the years of watching him wander in the wilderness. It shouldn't have bothered her, but it did.

Oh, Lord, why couldn't he have listened to me? And now it's too late. No matter what he does, the consequences will come down upon him like a rain of hot coals. And he won't be the only one to suffer from his actions. All those people who love him, all those who hung on his every word as though it were gospel, all those who have worked so hard to build something.

Build what? A pedestal for Paul Hudson to stand upon? How many had come to worship Christ? How many times had she overheard conversations in the narthex about Paul's catchy phrases, the elocution that imprinted his titillating message on the brain? Like a bad joke passed on and on. It should've been God's Word that was remembered!

Those poor people had made him into an idol, and now they would learn from his own lips he had feet of clay. They would sit in their comfortable cushioned pews and watch him topple.

They wouldn't be happy about it.

Assuming they cared at all about God's call for purity. Assuming they would be offended by his adulterous affair. She knew many of them wouldn't. They were so worldly; they might be willing to pass it off with "everyone does it."

And then what?

Another temptation for Paul to face. Was he up to it? Had he the strength to do what was right after so many years of habitually doing what was evil in the sight of God?

She rubbed her forehead, wishing that were all it took to wipe away a splitting headache.

At least he was making his peace with God through Christ. She should rejoice with him. His sins were covered by Christ's blood. His debts canceled. *"Rejoice in the Lord always. I will say it again: Rejoice!"*

You ask too much, Lord. My joy is crushed beneath the weight of hurt. I failed. I tried and I failed. Wasn't it a wife's duty to safeguard her marriage and her husband? Apparently she hadn't said the right words or done the right thing when it was needed.

"Each is responsible for his or her own sins," her father had told her. "Everything in God's time," he used to say. "The Lord is sovereign."

Couldn't You have gotten through Paul's thick skull a little earlier, Lord?

Before he crushed Samuel? Before he ran all those precious old people out of the church? Before he did his best to destroy Stephen Decker's reputation and life because Stephen dared confront him? Before I found him in the arms of another man's wife?

"Will you come home with me, Eunice?"

She raised her head. She wanted to scream at him. How could she sit in the front pew of the church and listen to him preach again? How could she face all those people he'd lied to over the years? How could she bear the whispers, the smirks, and the firestorm he was going to set? "I don't know if I can, Paul."

"Then we'll stay here. I'll wait awhile."

"No. You go. You have to go." Now, before he changed his mind. If he waited, he might weaken. "It's more important that you make things right with God than try to piece our marriage back together." Confession would bring with it accountability. No more secrets. No more closed doors. No more Sheilas. She could hope, anyway. If she chose to do so.

"You know," he said, head down, "I almost decided against going into the ministry once. Just after I graduated."

"You never told me that."

"No. I wouldn't have told you. I was afraid you wouldn't marry me." He looked sheepish. "Your mother told me you went to college to marry a pastor like your father. I was in love with you. The first thing that attracted me to you was your depth of faith. Most of the girls on campus were just looking for husbands. You were different."

"Unsophisticated. Simple. From the backwoods of nowhere." She mocked herself.

"No. That's not what I saw in you. I saw someone who sought God's will in everything. You didn't try to fit in or pretend to be anyone but yourself. You walked the walk, eyes on Jesus. I'd watch you sitting on the bench outside your dorm, the sunlight streaming down on you while you read your Bible. You looked like an angel. You were so solid in your faith, so uncompromising. The last thing I wanted to do was admit any doubts about my calling to be a pastor."

And she was called to obedience. The Lord said to love one another, not just when it was easy, not only when you felt the stirrings of passion, but always, despite circumstances. Hadn't Jesus been thinking of others even as He hung on the cross, racked with pain and carrying the sins of the whole world upon Him? Hadn't He been making provision for His mother and looking out for His young friend John? *"Love is patient, love is kind."* Oh, she remembered the passages as though the Lord were speaking them into her heart now. And wasn't He? He was branded with His own suffering, His abounding love, His inexplicable mercy, and His incomparable grace.

"Love always protects, always trusts, always hopes, always perseveres." Her father would have said the whole thirteenth chapter of 1 Corinthians by heart if he had performed their marriage ceremony. No compromise? She'd given in to Paul because, after all, how could the heir to David Hudson's church get married in a poor coal miner's living room?

Tears slipped down her cheeks. She, too, was a sinner saved by grace. And by His grace, and through it, she was to extend grace to others. For wasn't that what grace was all about? Extending love to someone who trashed what you held so dear? If Jesus had done that for the unrepentant, couldn't she bring herself to do likewise for a man with a broken and contrite heart?

Or so it seemed.

Human love ebbs and flows, blows hot and cold. God's love never fails. *God. God, help me.*

You know what I want of you, beloved.

Heart torn, she surrendered. She belonged to Him, after all. He was her first husband, faithful—always faithful—through time and beyond it. He'd died for her. And risen so that she might know she would never be separated from Him. What strength she needed would come from Him and not through her own measly efforts.

All right, Lord. So be it. However long, whatever pain may come. Before You I vowed that it would be so, though I was young then and full of dreams and didn't know.

I know.

And because of her love for Jesus, she could say what needed to be said—not later when she felt like it, but now when Paul needed to hear it.

"I wasn't called to be a pastor's wife, Paul. I was called to be *your* wife."

And so she would remain until God told her otherwise.

Paul felt an urgency to leave, but he didn't want to rush Eunice. He'd been rushing her for years, pushing her, prodding her in the hope of getting her to do what he wanted. *Help me break that habit, God.* She was still pale, still skeptical, though she was doing what she'd always done before, stepping out in faith, trusting that God would catch her in the free fall.

So he was surprised when she suggested they should go back to Centerville together and as soon as possible.

He wanted to give her a way out of what he knew he would be facing. Why should she have to stand with him before the lions? He stopped on the sidewalk and faced her. "I want you to do what you need to do, Eunice. If you need to stay and rest and think things through some more, I'll come back."

She didn't answer quickly. "We're paying for two rental cars and two motel rooms. Where's the sense in that?"

He didn't suggest they stay in the same room together. Her body language told him very clearly that she wasn't ready for him to touch her hand, let alone sleep in the same bed. They didn't talk about it, not yet, but he wondered if it would ever be the same between them. She would need time, maybe a long time. And he would wait. He intended to woo her, not just in the ways he had in the early days of their courtship, with flowers and love letters, soft music and dimmed lights, but with the right decisions. Walking the walk, one step at a time. Keeping faith with her, safeguarding their marriage.

"You're sure you want to go back with me?"

"As sure as I'll ever be."

Paul prayed that with time and tender care, Eunice would feel more confident of his repentance.

———— ❧ ————

Samuel looked up from the newspaper he was reading and saw Paul Hudson walking across the Vine Hill courtyard toward him. Samuel's heart started to pound with dread. Why would Paul come here unless there was bad news about Eunice? He folded the newspaper with shaking hands, placing it on the table. Gripping his cane, he tried to rise. "Eunice. What's happened to . . . ?"

Paul's face softened. "Eunice is at home, Samuel. She said to tell you she would be by later this afternoon for a long visit."

Samuel sank into his chair. "Thank God." Still, it wasn't like her to stay away. Something was wrong. He'd called Reka Wilson, but she'd cried, said she didn't know anything, and hung up. He could see now by the grim expression on Paul's face that he had something to say. Paul didn't take the seat on the opposite side of the glass table, but the one closest to Samuel. He looked more ill at ease than Samuel had ever seen him.

"I've come to ask for your forgiveness, Samuel."

Samuel couldn't have been more surprised had Publishers Clearing House arrived with a check for a million dollars. But a wave of warmth spread through him, like life coming back into his old dead limbs.

Paul looked up into Samuel's eyes for the first time in years. "I've wronged you more times than I can count. You called me to pastor Centerville, and I came thinking I had all the answers. You offered me friendship and I gave you grief. You tried to mentor me, and I fought every attempt you made to bring me back on the path." Paul sat like a man strapped in an electric chair, but he was willingly dying to self. "I was so blind with arrogance and ambition, I didn't care what methods I used to get my way." He bowed his head. "I'm sorry." His voice hoarsened. "More sorry than words can say. From day one, I've had my own agenda, Samuel. I thought I was building a church for the Lord." His voice became raspy. "But I ended up building my own self-esteem and leading my followers straight to the gates of hell."

Samuel never expected to hear such a speech from Paul Hudson. All he had ever hoped for was the boy's repentance before the Lord. He had figured it would be too much to hope for that to happen in his lifetime. He was just an old man who had been a thorn in Paul's side. "How did the Lord get ahold of you?"

Paul told him everything.

Samuel chuckled. "Leave it to the Lord to use a jackrabbit." And then the humor left him as insight came. Paul Hudson had been like that poor jackrabbit making a dash for safety. He had been running for most his life, trying to get out of the way of the drivers bearing down on him with expectations and demands. Some were just looking for a chance to run him down and crush him beneath the wheels of "progress."

Oh, Jesus, precious Savior, I never thought You'd turn him around in my lifetime. Forgive me. Thank You! Oh, God, thank You! Here he is. The boy has come out of the wilderness and crossed over the divide to faith in You. He's finally listening to Your Holy Spirit.

Samuel wept.

Paul wept, too. "I'm so sorry for the pain I've caused you, Samuel."

The tears kept coming, streaming down Samuel's withered cheeks. Tears of joy, tears of hope fulfilled.

Paul's shoulders sagged. He clasped his hands over his bowed head and continued to weep. "I've used every blessing God gave me for my own purposes. I have no right to ask you to forgive me, not after the way I've treated you all these years."

"I forgave you, Paul, a long, long time ago. So did Abby. She told me to keep praying for you the day she died."

Paul raised his head and stared at him.

Samuel smiled. "Just see to it that you treat me better in the future!"

Nodding, Paul closed his eyes and released his breath. "I promise." A man reprieved and pardoned. When Paul opened his eyes again, Samuel was struck by the tenderness in them. He wasn't looking through Samuel to the appointment beyond, but was here, in the moment, unhurried and thankful.

Oh, Abby, I wish you were here to see Paul Hudson now. We weren't wrong about him after all. The boy sits, humbled and repentant. Only God could manage this miracle. Only the Holy Spirit.

Samuel leaned back in his chair, absently rubbing the ache in his hip. "What will you do about Valley New Life Center?"

"I'm going to confess my sins to the congregation Sunday morning and step down from leadership."

Oh. Paul meant to waste no time. "Maybe they'll listen to you. The world seems less safe these days. Some are awakening to the fact that they aren't in control of their lives." He considered. "But don't be too quick to walk away, Paul. Who will guide them in the days ahead?"

"I'm unfit for the pastorate."

"Peter denied Christ three times, and yet, the Lord used him mightily."

"Peter didn't manipulate people to get where he wanted to go. He didn't commit adultery with another man's wife."

It was a few seconds before Samuel got his breath back.

"I'm going to need prayer, Samuel. All I can get. If you're willing. It'll help me knowing you're praying for me." He smiled. "'The prayer of a righteous man is powerful and effective.'"

"What specifically are you asking for?"

"That fear won't get the upper hand. That I won't weaken. That I'll hear and speak the words the Lord wants me to speak. I've been a people pleaser all my life. Now, I want to be a God pleaser."

Samuel nodded. "I have prayed for you for years, Paul." He leaned forward and held out his hand. "The only difference now is I will be praying *with* you."

———— ❧ ————

Paul spent another hour with Samuel. Samuel told him about Stephen Decker's home group, and Paul didn't have to wonder why. He felt convicted. He'd done his best to destroy Decker's reputation when the contractor refused to compromise his principles. They'd been friends in the beginning, then adversaries, later enemies. Maybe he could make amends, with Samuel as mediator. Maybe.

On the way home, Paul stopped by Reka Wilson's house. Her car was parked in the driveway. He rang the doorbell and waited. He heard someone approaching, then silence. He wondered if Reka was looking out at him through the peephole. He wouldn't blame her if she didn't answer her door. He rang the bell again and waited. No answer. He walked slowly back to his car and wrote a brief, heartfelt note.

I'm ashamed for the position I put you in, Reka. You played a part in bringing me to my senses. You've always been a true and loyal friend. I hope you'll be able to forgive me someday. May God bless you for all your years of faithful service to Him. And to me.

Paul Hudson

He tucked it into her door.

On the way home, he wondered if he'd live long enough to make amends to all the people he'd hurt.

Samuel Mason's old DeSoto was parked in front of the house. Timothy was home.

Cold with fear and shame, Paul pulled into the garage. He closed the door and sat for a long time in silence, hands still gripping the wheel. He could imagine what his son would have to say. Paul felt sick—deep-down, gutter-soul sick—over what he'd done to his son. He'd followed in his father's footsteps, pushing, bullying, expecting more and more. Instead of running away as Paul had, Timothy had rebelled. He'd stood up and called his father a hypocrite. And been exiled for it. Paul had been relieved, even thankful that Timothy wasn't around to embarrass him anymore. Worse, Timothy had sensed something was wrong with his parents' marriage the last time he was home.

Whatever Timothy had to say, he'd listen. He'd let his son vent. If Timothy wanted to take a punch, so be it.

After a brief prayer, Paul got out of his car and went into the house. He heard voices in the family room. Timothy hadn't come alone. He'd brought his grandmother with him. His mother glanced up when he entered the room. Eunice looked away and wiped her cheeks.

Timothy stood. "Dad." He said the word respectfully, as though acknowledging his authority. And then he held out his hand. It struck Paul that his son knew more about grace at nineteen than he did at forty-four. He took Timothy's hand and gripped it tightly. His throat was too tight to speak.

His son wasn't a boy anymore. He had a look of maturity about him despite the jeans and T-shirt and shoulder-length hair. It wasn't the broader shoulders and arms or the deeply tanned skin that hard work in the sun had brought on. It was in his carriage, his expression.

Eunice looked up, her eyes glassy with tears, her cheeks pale. "Your son has something to tell you." She made a soft choking sound and fled the room.

"Why don't you go and see if she's okay, Grams?"

Paul's mother rose without a word and left them alone in the room.

"Can we sit?" Timothy said.

"Sure. Of course."

They sat facing one another like strangers.

Paul waited. All the years he'd cajoled, managed, and manipulated people and he didn't have a clue how to talk with his own son. His own father had never been able to talk with him unless he was giving orders. Even during those last years when Paul had thought they were close, Paul realized his father had been working him, pointing him down a path Paul had never intended to go. Still, he couldn't blame his father. Paul knew he was accountable for his own sins and would be paying for them on Judgment Day if Jesus hadn't already paid the price on the cross. He was redeemed. It was time to live a redeemed life.

His stomach was tight with tension. What was it his son had to say to him?

"Did your grandmother tell you about . . . ?" He didn't know how to say it—or if he should.

"I know, Dad. It was the blonde, wasn't it? The one who kissed you on the way out of church."

Paul felt the heat fill his cheeks. "Yes."

"She was a piece of work. I had to leave. I knew if I didn't, I'd cause trouble. It was all I could do not to beat your head in." Tim gave a sardonic smile. "I didn't dare because I knew Mom would want to know why. She didn't have a clue what was going on, and if I told her, she still wouldn't have approved of patricide."

"Your mother's always believed the best about people."

"She's not naive anymore."

Paul winced, knowing the fault of her lost innocence could be laid at his feet. He had used her sweetness against her, talking his way around every question she'd ever raised. "You wouldn't have gotten through to me if you'd used a baseball bat, Tim. I was running with a head full of pride."

Tim tilted his head and studied him. "Mom said you flew back East and tracked her down. I guess that means you're going to try to patch things up."

"I'm going to give it everything I've got, Tim. I love your mother."

"How could anyone not love her?" He shook his head, his expression full of pity and disappointment.

The silence stretched again.

"I didn't come to throw stones, Dad. I came to tell you and Mom I've enlisted. I thought it might be better to tell you in person than over a telephone." He grimaced, glancing toward the hallway where Euny had gone. "Now, I'm not so sure."

Paul couldn't have been more shocked if a terrorist armed with a machine gun had walked into his living room. "Enlisted?" The war hit home.

"In the Marines."

Paul shut his eyes.

"Ever since 9/11, I've been thinking about our country and what freedom costs. And I've been thinking about times in history when people have turned their backs on evil and the consequences that came from that. Where would we be if men hadn't enlisted to fight Hitler? I've been praying over this for a long time, Dad. And I've had others praying for me as well. It hasn't been an easy decision."

Shaken, Paul looked at his son. "You don't know what you're getting yourself into."

"Not completely. I don't have to know everything. I just have to move forward in the direction I believe God is leading me."

Into war?

"I know America isn't doing everything right, but we have Christian foundations and the freedom to speak and worship as we choose. Maybe God is showing mercy because we still do. Every time there's a disaster, Americans are the first to pitch in and help. God has allowed us to prosper, and we've tried to help other countries. And not always for political reasons or oil. The kindness we've shown other nations might be the only reason God hasn't taken action against us for all the things we're doing wrong."

Timothy stood and paced. "You've got to know, Dad. There are a lot of kids my age who don't have any idea who Jesus Christ is. My room-mate's a good example. He grew up believing Christmas was all about Santa Claus, a pile of presents under a decorated tree, and a January vacation in Vail, Colorado. He'd never set foot in a church until I took him. God was ousted from the schools back in the sixties, and now we've got a generation that's never heard the gospel. Where better to spread it than among the men going out to fight for our country?"

Help him, God. "They won't let you preach in the Marines, Son. You're not going to end up a chaplain. You'll end up a grunt carrying a rifle."

"I'm not talking about preaching, Dad. I'm talking about sharing my faith. I'll use words if I have to." He gave a lopsided grin. "Although I asked for language school. My high school counselor said I have an aptitude for it."

Oh, the naiveté of youth. Or was Paul's own faith so weak he couldn't trust the Lord to work through a nineteen-year-old boy in a war zone? Would he be cannon fodder? "Did you sign any papers?" Maybe there was still a way out.

"Yes. I gave my boss two weeks' notice. I'll have a week after that before I'm to go to the induction center in Los Angeles. I wanted it settled before I came here to talk to you and Mom. For obvious reasons."

There would be no way to talk him out of it. Or get him out of it. Timothy's next stop would be boot camp, then specialized training and orders.

Oh, Lord, You gave me nineteen years of opportunity, and I let them pass me by. And now Tim may never come home.

"This kind of war isn't going to be won just with guns, Dad. It's going to be won with truth. Where better to minister truth than in the military ranks? Maybe I'll even be able to witness to those who've swallowed the lie that murdering people will get them the reward of seventy virgins!"

A military missionary? Was there such a thing?

"You're disappointed in me, aren't you? You think I'm being stupid."

Paul realized his silence had given Timothy the wrong impression. And no wonder, considering their relationship over the years. Paul knew he had been a lousy father. Despite all his good intentions and promises to himself, he had followed his father's example in more ways than one. Unreasonable demands for perfection. Bouts of verbal abuse followed by long periods of indifference. Did Timothy hunger for his acceptance and approval the same way he had craved them from his father?

Paul wanted to make his feelings clear before it was too late. "No. I'm proud of you for living your convictions. And if anyone's been stupid, it's been me for all the years I've wasted avoiding my son. And now, there's so little time." His voice broke. A week. Seven short days. After all the wasted years.

"You say that as though I'm going off to get myself killed."

Paul's eyes burned. "I hope not."

Timothy smiled gently. "It's okay, Dad. Whatever happens, I'll be all right. It's not like we're saying good-bye forever, you know."

Paul didn't want to let another opportunity slip away. "Would you mind if your mother and I came down and spent some time with you before you have to report?"

Tim looked pleased. "Sure. I'd like that." He stood. "I was going to go over and see Samuel. I want him to know about my decision before he hears about it from someone else. And then there's the car. I'm hoping he'll keep it in storage for me."

"If he can't, we will."

"Thanks." He took his keys out of his pocket. Pausing in the doorway, he looked back, troubled. "You think we can get Mom to promise she won't cry the whole week?"

"I'll try, Son. I can't promise." He was perilously close to tears himself.

The front door opened and closed. Paul heard the DeSoto start up.

Poor Eunice. What must she be feeling? In the last few days, she'd walked in on her unfaithful husband, and now she'd come home to receive the news that her only son was going off to war.

His mother came down the hallway. She barely grazed him with a look. "I'm going out for a long walk." She opened the door. "Eunice said you're preaching on Sunday."

"Yes."

She closed the door firmly behind her.

He couldn't expect his mother to believe he'd suddenly changed overnight. She'd probably heard plenty of empty promises from his father.

He went down the hall and opened the door to the guest room. His mother's suitcase was open on the bed he'd been sleeping in. He closed it and put it on the couch, stripped the bed, and changed the sheets. Then he moved the few things he would need over the next few days into his office. He'd sleep on the couch.

Timothy's room was as it had always been. Eunice had seen to that. She had always hoped their son would come home. Paul realized now the only way Timothy would've done that was by personal invitation from his father. Paul put his hands over his face. How much pain had he caused his wife over the years? She'd weathered his neglect and endured his persecution. She'd even given up her son. Adultery was her crown of thorns.

The door of the master bedroom was closed. Paul tapped on the door. "Eunice? May I come in?"

"The door's unlocked."

She was sitting in her reading chair near the windows, the drapes open so the sun filtered through the lace curtains. She looked like an angel, even with eyes puffy from crying.

"Are you okay?"

She didn't look at him. "I just called Samuel to tell him I didn't feel up to coming by today."

"Tim's headed over there."

"I saw him go." Her voice was choked.

Paul came into the room and shoved his hands into his pockets. "How're you feeling?"

"Like a truck ran over me. Twice."

He'd driven the first one. "I'm sorry." He wondered if she was asking herself the same questions he was asking himself. "Do you think Tim did it to get my attention?"

Her face crumpled. "I don't know." She bent over, sobbing. "I don't know."

The sight of her grief filled him to overflowing with sorrow. He took his hands from his pockets and went to her, hunkering and putting his hands on the arms of the chair. "I'd take his place if I could."

Her weeping softened. She studied him. Then she drew in a shaky breath and leaned back. "You're too old." She pulled another tissue angrily from the box in her lap. "I've cried enough for a lifetime over the past few days. I'm sick of crying. Just when I think I'm dry, the sea rises." She blew her nose noisily, glaring at him. She wadded up the tissue in a tight fist. Did she want to hit him? He would let her. "Get up, Paul."

At least she didn't say, "Get out."

He straightened and moved away, standing near the windows, hands in his pockets again.

She sniffed and took a shaky breath. "Knowing Tim, I think he did just as he said. I think he heard the news, got down on his knees and prayed, then got up and did exactly what he believed God was telling him to do." Her voice wobbled. She pressed her lips together, her chin trembling. She didn't say anything for a long moment. "I just have to hope and pray . . ." She gave up and cried again.

Paul sat on the edge of their bed, staring at his loafers. He wasn't going to offer any platitudes or pretend he knew what God was thinking.

"God is faithful," she said softly. "Even when we're not." She dropped the damp tissue into the wastebasket and yanked out a fresh one.

Paul could think of nothing to say that would bring her comfort. His heart ached for her. If she would have allowed, he would've held her.

"Reka called. She said you left her a note. She said she was sorry she didn't open the door, but she just didn't feel up to talking to you. She said she hoped you and I would be able to work things out. She'll be praying for us."

The silence stretched, but he didn't try to fill it. The mantle of regret was heavy.

"I know you're feeling guilty now, Paul. Timothy isn't a little boy anymore. He makes his own decisions." She looked at him. She pressed her fingertips against her lips for a moment, then folded her hands in her lap. "Samuel told me you came by earlier. He said you asked for his forgiveness. He said you two talked for almost two hours." Her blue eyes were so soft and luminous. "Your visit meant a lot to him."

"He could've been the best friend I ever had."

"He *is* your friend." She looked down, toying nervously with the tissue she held. "There's someone else you should see. Someone you hurt deeply. I don't think he's over it yet."

Paul knew who she meant. "Stephen Decker."

Eunice lifted her head only a little, but enough that he saw a faint flush in her cheeks. "Stephen could have done us both great harm, Paul. But he didn't. Even when the opportunity was presented, he let it go."

Paul's heart sank. He didn't want to ask what opportunity she meant. He had a feeling he knew already.

Stephen was rolling up a blueprint when he saw Paul's Mercedes pull up in front. What did Hudson want? Shoving the blueprint into its cubby, Stephen leaned back on his stool and watched Pastor Paul get out of his car, look up at the building, and come around to the sidewalk.

Hudson came to the door and walked in. One of the drawbacks to living in your place of business was having to leave the front door unlocked.

"May I talk to you, Stephen?"

"I gave at the office." Hudson had better not be coming to him about some problem with the building. Stephen had used the best men and materials. Anything that was wrong now was someone else's fault and Hudson's responsibility. Stephen was out of it and glad.

"You tried to warn me I was getting off track," Paul said. "You said once I wasn't building a church; I was building a monument for myself. You were right."

What ploy was this? "What are you after, Hudson?"

"Forgiveness."

Stephen gave a cynical laugh. "Well, you know where to go for that."

"I've taken my sins to Jesus, but I want to try to make amends with the people I've hurt."

"Eunice should be your first stop."

"We flew back from Pennsylvania together."

Stephen raised his brows. He hadn't heard Eunice was out of town, let alone across the country. Samuel had probably kept that news to himself—if he had known. "You should talk to Samuel."

"I visited him yesterday. He forgave me. I'm here to ask if you'll do the same."

"A lot of rough water has gone under the bridge since you and I went our separate ways, Hudson." Paul had been the one to wash their friendship right out to the open sea.

"I'd like to make it up to you."

Stephen gave a derisive laugh. "How? You got another building project in mind?"

"No. An invitation to church on Sunday."

"You've got to be kidding!"

"No. I'm not. I know my apology isn't worth much, Stephen. I set out to ruin you."

He spread his hands. "As you can see, you didn't succeed."

"I spoke against you. A friend who tried to warn me."

The guy was dogged. He was determined to confess whether Stephen wanted to listen or not. Angry, Stephen had no choice but to stand there. *Oh, Lord, I know what You want from me, but I haven't got Samuel's strength.*

Paul kept on with his confession. Finally, he stopped, let out his breath slowly, and said, "I've tendered my resignation."

Walking away from VNLC? Giving up his empire? Stephen was stunned.

"I'm giving my confession on Sunday. I thought you might want to be there to hear it."

Stephen saw no bid for pity, but he was suddenly filled with compassion for Paul Hudson. He wasn't sure he could trust him, but he wasn't going to beat a man when he was down. Stephen remembered when he'd called Paul his closest friend and a brother in Christ. Paul had been the one to extend his hand during the hard, tough early days of recovery, and it had been Paul who'd encouraged his faith.

Now, Stephen was facing some of the same temptations Paul had, and running away because he wasn't sure he could handle them. He would have to keep his focus so that he didn't give in to the temptations leadership brought. He'd learned by watching Paul's mistakes to have a good mentor. Every pastor needed a Samuel in his life. A couple would be even better.

Stephen had seen in the last few weeks how leadership brought power with it. It was heady having people look at you as though you had all the answers and the personal ear of God besides. Heady, and terrifying. He didn't want to lead people down the wrong path.

"Come on upstairs, Paul. I'll fix us some coffee."

Stephen set up the coffeemaker.

Hands in his pockets, Paul looked around. "You've always been a craftsman." He spotted some of Brittany's things. "Are you married?" He sounded relieved.

"That's my daughter's stuff. She finally came home." Had Paul even known she was missing? Had Paul cared about the months of agony he'd suffered, worrying about his runaway daughter? Probably not. If he even knew. Stephen let it go. "She lives here now. I'm living in the basement."

"Samuel said that's where you hold services."

Stephen glanced at him. "I'm not holding services. Just teaching one class."

"And doing a good job from what Samuel says."

"Yeah, well, you know Samuel. He's full of hope."

"From what he told me, I think you're going to turn out to be a fine pastor."

Flattery? Stephen put two mugs on the table. He wanted to change the subject. Better to hear about Paul's wake-up call. "What brought your change of heart?"

"The look on Eunice's face when she walked in on me with another woman. A long talk with my mother. And a close call on Highway 99."

"That's all it took, huh?" *Poor Eunice.*

"I made my peace with God, but it's going to be a long time before I can make the amends I need to or repair the damage I've done. If I ever can."

"Did the board ask for your resignation?"

"No. They want me to stay. But I don't belong in a pulpit or in any leadership position until I'm back on track. Even if the Lord calls me back to ministry, I'm going to need men to hold me accountable."

Stephen raised his fist and grinned wolfishly. "I'd like to hold you accountable." Odd, that all the sting was gone.

Paul smiled. "You'd be the second one I'd count on. Samuel has the lead."

"You've really made a mess of things, haven't you?"

"Yes."

"And hurt a lot of people along the way."

"I know."

He looked as though he *did* know. Stephen had never seen such a look of misery on Paul Hudson's face. Who was he to throw stones? "I guess we do still have some things in common. We're both major screwups. You know, we ought to start our own AA support group. Autocrats Anonymous. What do you think?"

Paul laughed.

Stephen was only half-joking. "I've been faced with some of the same temptations you've dealt with over the years. It's not easy making people understand that you're just another human being like they are, struggling to live by faith."

"It's when you stop struggling that you're in trouble," Paul said. "When you start thinking you know what you're doing. I thought I had all the answers. I saw anyone who questioned my methods as a threat.

My mother put it better. I've been a cattleman driving a herd instead of a shepherd leading a flock."

The coffee was finished. Stephen poured. "Who's your replacement?"

"I've recommended John Deerman."

"I don't know him."

"He's a solid man of faith. I've kept him busy in the background."

"Ah. Another man who questioned you."

"John has strong faith and a sound knowledge of the Bible to go with it. If the board gives him the pulpit, the congregation will be hearing the straight gospel from here on."

Stephen wondered if the membership of VNLC was ready to listen to the truth.

You've performed miracles before, Lord. One's sitting across the table. But it's going to take a great big one to pull that church out of the fire.

"Timothy enlisted in the Marines."

"Oh, man! I didn't know he was old enough."

"He's nineteen."

"How'd Eunice take the news?"

"She's crying."

Two heavy blows. Stephen hoped they hadn't rocked her faith.

"I drove by the church on the way here," Paul said. "You really built something to last, Stephen. It's a beautiful facility. I wish there were some way . . ."

Stephen recognized the temptation of hanging on to things. "See it for what it is, Paul. A building. A monument to one man's endeavor. Let it go." He lifted his mug in faint salute. "If I walked away from it, so can you."

They made small talk, then dug a little deeper. Paul asked about Kathryn. Stephen was surprised he remembered her name. Paul did remember Brittany. Stephen told him she was doing okay. She was getting her GED and hoping to go to junior college. When Paul asked for a tour, Stephen showed him the rest of the place.

They talked cautiously, around the edges of past hurts and failures, feeling their way. Maybe they could be friends again, but it wouldn't happen overnight. They'd have to pick their way through the debris. Forgiveness was a decision; trust took time.

"I'd better get back." When Paul extended his hand at the front door, Stephen hesitated.

"Before we shake hands, there are a few things I need to confess, Paul." Color ebbed from Paul's cheeks even as Stephen felt heat coming up into his own. "You're already aware that I've harbored bitterness against you since I left Centerville, but beyond that . . ." *Get it said. Get it out in the open.* "I've been in love with your wife for ten years. There have been a lot of times when I wished your marriage would fold so I could ride in like Prince Charming and sweep Eunice off her feet."

"Euny told me this afternoon that you could've done serious harm. I knew what she meant."

The attraction had been mutual. He hadn't intended to mention that. "Nothing happened, Paul."

"Because you and Eunice were wise enough to make sure it didn't."

It hadn't been easy to show her the door the last time he saw her. Having his feelings out in the open would keep him accountable. "She's something special."

"In the words of my son, how could anyone not love her?"

It was good Paul understood what wasn't being said. Sometimes Stephen wondered if he'd ever get over Eunice Hudson. There weren't many women like her, and she should be treated like a treasure straight from heaven. But at least the Lord was building hedges. If Paul cherished Eunice the way he should, Stephen would never again have to face the temptation of finding her alone on his doorstep. Stephen had the feeling Paul would be more careful with the treasure God had given him. "Another thing. You didn't give the name of the woman."

"No."

"It was Sheila Atherton, wasn't it?"

"It doesn't matter who it was. It was wrong."

"It does matter because I knew her. She tried her games with me while I was building the house in Quail Hollow. I knew what she was up to the minute I saw her in your office. I kept quiet for all the wrong reasons. I was angry and nursing a grudge. I wanted you to fall off your high horse. Or get knocked off it. I should've warned you. I'm sorry I didn't."

"At that point, I doubt I would've listened to you, but apology accepted."

"You weren't the first, Paul. I doubt you'll be the last."

"That doesn't make me feel any better. Whatever Sheila is, I'm without excuse." Paul extended his hand again. "But thanks for telling me. Especially about Eunice." He smiled sadly. "I'll be treating my wife a lot better in the future."

Stephen closed the door and asked God's blessing on Eunice and Paul's marriage and protection for it as well. Then he sat at his drawing board, where he had been studying and preparing for the days ahead.

Paul spent hours working on his confession, writing out what he needed to say, going over it to make certain he hadn't left anything out. When Sunday morning rolled around, he was exhausted. He spent an hour on his knees praying before he took his shower. His hand shook when he shaved. He nicked himself. If he wasn't careful, he'd slit his own throat. He washed his face, used a styptic pencil to stop the bleeding, and dressed carefully. His tie felt like a noose.

The house was quiet when he came out of his office. The master bedroom door was closed. So was the guest room door. Timothy's door was open, but he wasn't there. Paul knew he had no right to expect his family to attend church with him, especially today of all days.

He arrived an hour early and alone, his carefully organized notes in a folder on the front seat. He wanted to be prepared. He needed to get it right this time.

The church was unlocked, the choir members practicing. They sounded great, but the words had nothing to do with the message Paul was going to give that morning, and nothing to do with the blood of Jesus Christ who'd saved them from eternal damnation.

Paul went into his office. The last time he'd been in here was the morning Eunice walked in on him and Sheila Atherton. His face burned as he straightened the cushions on the couch, put the chair back where it belonged, and sat at his desk. He removed Sheila's number from the speed dial. He took Eunice's picture out of his desk drawer and looked at it. He set the picture on his desk. He thought about Jesus in the garden of Gethsemane, sweating blood because of what He knew He had to do.

He wept.

Help me do what's right, God. For once, let me get it right. Oh, Lord,

You've seen my wandering. You watched me as I led these people astray. You were a witness to every sin I've committed. I've been so busy making my way in the world that I lost the way. Against You and You only have I sinned, and in doing so brought immeasurable harm to others.

Cars were filling the parking lot. Ushers collected the bulletins in the outer office. He could hear them talking. He hadn't even titled his sermon this time.

It was quieter now. Everyone would be finding their seats. He could hear the music playing, the kind that made everyone comfortable. A medley of songs. Not a hymn among them. He cringed as he remembered telling Eunice she would no longer be a part of the music ministry because she had dared to sing a song about the cleansing blood of Jesus.

He took a last look at his typed notes, tucked them into his Bible, and left his office. His heart pounded harder with each step. His stomach clenched. His palms were sweating. He entered the inner corridor to a small waiting area. Like a theater's greenroom, he realized. The choir was singing.

"There you are!" One of the associates approached with a nervous laugh. "I was beginning to wonder if I should run downstairs to my office and pull out one of my old sermons."

John Deerman met him at the side entrance to the stage and shook his hand. "I'll be praying for you, brother."

Everything was ready for Paul Hudson. The audience had been primed. It was time for the headliner to come onstage and wow them.

Everywhere he looked, Paul came face-to-face with what he had done over the last fourteen years. The congregation applauded as the choir members—dressed in red satin, white-trimmed robes—filed out in orderly fashion. "Glad to have you back, Pastor Paul," several said as they passed.

One leaned close. "Boy, did we miss you last Sunday. It's just not the same when we have a guest speaker!"

Paul crossed the stage and put his Bible on the podium. He opened it, took his notes out, and laid them out so he could glance down. It was the most important sermon of his life. He didn't want to botch it.

It was suddenly so quiet, he felt the hair rise on the back of his neck. He raised his head and saw the sea of faces.

Eunice was sitting in the front row, head bowed. Timothy sat to her right, looking up at him the way he must have looked at his own father. His mother sat to Eunice's left, her expression guarded. Was she preparing herself for another disappointment?

Row by row, he recognized the faces of people who had come to hear him talk over the years. Talk, not preach. Entertain, not enlighten.

He was surprised to see Reka sitting in the eighth pew. She clasped her hands and pressed them to her heart. Forgiveness and fellowship offered. His throat closed.

Two men stood in the open doorway of the sanctuary. Samuel Mason leaned heavily on his cane as he stepped into the last pew, moved down enough to make room for Stephen Decker, and sat.

Paul heard the soft rumbling of the crowd. They were uncomfortable with his long silence. They were used to him striding out onto the stage and letting out a booming "Good morning!" People looked at one another and whispered. He saw a few who prayed.

Was he going to speak to please the crowd? Or was he going to speak to the audience of One? Was he going to walk by fear or by faith? It all came down to that. Fear had made him focus on his problems. Fear had made him rebel and run the wide road his father had laid out for him, a road to prestige, popularity, prosperity—the road of pride and perdition.

What was it going to be? Half turns and half-truths? Or an about-face?

Paul didn't look at his notes. He didn't need them. He needed Jesus. He prayed silently that the Lord would give him the words, and then he said, "I have given my resignation to the board, and I am removing myself from any leadership position in any church for the foreseeable future." He saw their faces, heard the rush of whispers, and continued. "It is necessary that I do this because I have sinned grievously against the Lord."

Broken and contrite, Paul Hudson bared his soul before his congregation, and as he did, the fear left him. He spoke openly of his struggle with truth, his surrender to pride, his headlong fall into sin, and the devastating costs to those he loved the most: his wife, his son, his friends, his brothers and sisters in Christ. After all he had done, even now, they were faithful and praying for him.

And then he talked about his Redeemer, Jesus Christ. He talked about the love of God, who gave His only begotten Son so that all who believed in Him would have eternal life. Even men like him, who had failed on all fronts—as husband, father, friend, and pastor. As Jesus hung on the cross, dying, He said, "It is finished." And so it was. Victory would not come through the efforts of men, but had already been achieved by Christ Jesus when He proved He had power over death, that only in Him would there be life.

"In this world you have tribulation, but in Christ, you have life. When you give yourself to Jesus Christ, nothing can separate you from the love of God. He will never let you go."

Paul didn't know what awaited him at the end of this service. He didn't know what would come in the days ahead. What happened to him didn't matter. These people did. He spoke without looking at the wall clock or trying to keep his presentation to fifteen minutes exactly because he might lose their attention. He said what had to be said, and prayed God would do something with it.

Whatever comes, Lord, whatever happens, keep me faithful.

"You have looked to me for answers over the years, and I led you astray. Today, for the first time in years, I have preached the true gospel of Jesus Christ, God the Son of almighty God. And now I must warn you. When I leave this position, another man will come and speak to you. And I tell you in all truth now, you will be held responsible for what you believe. Ignorance will be no excuse. And this is the truth: It is Jesus Christ you must follow! Jesus is the one who died for you. Jesus is the one with power over sin and death. Jesus is your Savior and Lord. There is no other way to salvation than through faith in Him."

He had said everything God called him to say, and said no more. Not a soul whispered in the church. No one moved. There was no sound in the sanctuary.

Paul took one long, last look at his congregation and felt an overwhelming love for them. So many lost sheep. Tears filled his eyes. "Beloved, hear the truth. Take it into your hearts and be at peace. In Christ, you have nothing to fear. Without Him, you have no hope."

Paul Hudson picked up his Bible and left the stage.

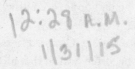

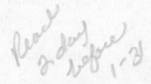

THE BOARD OF VALLEY NEW LIFE CENTER followed Paul's recommendation and replaced him with John Deerman. Letters of complaint began pouring in within a few months. The membership was no longer willing to listen to the gospel from John. The board fired Deerman.

With no one in command, the leadership quarreled, created factions, and fought over control. Guest speakers were invited in; films were shown. Attendance dipped. Offerings fell. Bills piled up. In desperation, the board unified long enough to hire a new pastor, one experienced in multimedia presentations and gifted in public speaking. Offerings increased, but the money problems didn't go away. Creditors were threatening action against the church.

The board hired an auditor.

Marvin Lockford disappeared. Sheila Atherton was also missing. The auditors informed the board that over three million dollars had been skimmed during the ten previous years. The ten years that Marvin Lockford had been church treasurer.

Rob Atherton filed for divorce on grounds of desertion and put his Quail Hollow house up for sale. The market was hot for luxury properties and it sold within days, the contents at auction. He moved to Florida, hoping to reconcile with his first wife.

VNLC crumbled like a house of cards. Parishioners scattered like stampeding cattle. Some showed up grazing in churches offering a wide variety of programs to entice them. Others, devastated and disgusted, swore never to set foot in a church again. A small group remained and struggled to resurrect VNLC. But unable to raise the money for the mortgage payments, they put the property on the market. It was purchased by a conglomerate. Renovation started soon after a sign was posted: *Future Home of the Valley Performing Arts Center.*

Stephen Decker continued to teach Bible studies in Rockville. The group outgrew his basement, so they began renting the fellowship hall of a church whose membership was declining. He started dating Karen Kessler.

Kathryn Decker checked herself into a drug and alcohol treatment center.

Brittany Decker passed the test for her GED and enrolled at a junior college in Sacramento. Jack Bodene kept busy doing custom cabinets for a contractor building homes in Granite Bay and Gold River. He organized a Christian twelve-step recovery program at a local church. He and Brittany announced their engagement a few months later.

Lois Hudson remained in Reseda and attended a small neighborhood church where she taught a high school class.

Timothy Hudson finished boot camp, and was deployed to the Middle East. He communicated with his parents by e-mail. Within a few weeks, he had six guys attending his barracks Bible study.

Samuel passed away quietly in his sleep a month after Timothy left. The memorial service was held in Rockville.

Paul Hudson found work as a substitute teacher in area high schools. Eunice got a job as a checker in Walmart. She was often asked to sing at weddings and funerals. She's writing music again. When they heard Millie Bruester had decided to move, they made an offer for her modest American bungalow. Millie accepted. Paul and Eunice helped her move into Samuel's apartment at Vine Hill Residential Apartments.

A remnant of Centerville Christian's membership came to Paul and asked if he would teach a Bible study. After praying about it for some time, and discussing it with Eunice and Stephen and Karen, Paul suggested John Deerman. The group began meeting every Monday night at Charlie's Diner, but it soon outgrew the small restaurant.

Paul and Stephen started meeting for lunch every week. They shared their struggles and prayed for one another. Tuesday and Thursday evenings, Paul went to Vine Hill Convalescent Hospital for a Bible study and to visit residents.

Paul and Eunice Hudson were often seen walking together and having coffee at the small sidewalk café on Main Street. Many said it took a lot of courage for Paul Hudson to stay in Centerville after what he did. Perhaps it's the only place in the world where Paul Hudson couldn't hide, and where he would be held accountable for the way he walks in the days ahead. For people were watching him as he stood in faith and allowed the Lord to rebuild His temple on the firm foundation of Christ Jesus.

Maybe it's the one place where Paul Hudson could still be a shepherd in a church without walls.

Discussion Questions

Dear Reader,

We hope you enjoyed this timely novel by Francine Rivers about relationships, the church, and God's call on people's lives. As always, Francine's desire is for you, the reader, to get into God's Word and discover His life-changing truths for yourself. We hope the following questions will help you to do that.

The shofar is a trumpet. It is usually a ram's horn. In the Old Testament, Joshua, Gideon, and Joab, to name a few, used the shofar to lead the children of Israel. It was used to announce, to alert or warn of danger, to call to battle, or to call to action. It is still used in Judaism to call the people to accountability on the Day of Atonement (Yom Kippur). We read in Zechariah 9:14 that the Lord Himself will blow the shofar to call His people. In the New Testament, we read that angels will use the trumpet to announce the warnings for the "end times" and, ultimately, Christ's return.

Today, the Holy Spirit and God's Word, the Bible, call out to us in much the same way as the shofar: God's voice warns us, alerts us to danger, calls us to action or to times of rest, and, most important, calls us to accountability. In *And the Shofar Blew*, we read about different ways people think they are hearing God's voice—sometimes authentic, sometimes counterfeit—as well as different responses to Him. Sometimes He speaks in a "still, small voice"; other times, in a resounding blast. The questions begging to be asked are: Are we listening? Are we attentive to God's voice? How will we respond?

May God bless you as you seek Him for the answers. For surely, the shofar will blow!

Peggy Lynch

1. Choose two of the characters from the story and compare or contrast the ways in which they heard God's voice.

2. Discuss a counterfeit call from the story—a time someone believed he was hearing God's voice but was mistaken. How did the person respond? What were the results?

3. 1 John 4:1 says, "Dear friends, do not believe everyone who claims to speak by the Spirit. You must test them to see if the spirit they have comes from God. For there are many false prophets in the world." What do you learn from this passage, and how might you apply it to the story?

4. God often speaks to us through His Word, the Bible, or through the prompting of the Holy Spirit. Share such a time from your own experience. How did you hear God's voice? What were the circumstances? What was your response or actions, and what were the results?

5. Romans 8:28-29 says, "And we know that God causes everything to work together for the good of those who love God and are called according to his purpose for them. For God knew his people in advance, and he chose them to become like his Son." For what purpose does God call us? How does He choose to work this out?

6. Examine your heart, mind, and life. What evidence do you see that God is speaking to you?

7. Discuss the different views of church building held by Samuel, Paul's father, Paul, and Stephen.

8. How did Paul's view change? What prompted the changes? What actions confirmed the change? In what ways did Stephen change?

9. How do you develop relationships? How do you view church growth?

10. Psalm 127:1 says, "Unless the Lord builds a house, the work of the builders is useless." What does this verse imply about building—both relationships and churches?

11. Acts 2:41, 47 says, "Those who believed . . . were baptized and added to the church—about three thousand in all. . . . And each day the Lord added to their group those who were being saved." According to this passage, how did the early church grow numerically? What were the requirements?

12. 1 Corinthians 12:4-7, 27 says, "Now there are different kinds of spiritual gifts, but it is the same Holy Spirit who is the source of them all. There are different kinds of service in the church . . . there are different ways God works in our lives, but it is the same God who does the work through all of us. A spiritual gift is given to each of us as a means of helping the entire church. . . . Now all of you together are Christ's body, and each one of you is a separate and necessary part of it." For what purpose are spiritual gifts given? What role are you and your gifts to play in the church, the body of Christ?

About the Author

New York Times bestselling author FRANCINE RIVERS began her literary career at the University of Nevada, Reno, where she graduated with a bachelor of arts degree in English and journalism. From 1976 to 1985, she had a successful writing career in the general market, and her books were highly acclaimed by readers and reviewers. Although raised in a religious home, Francine did not truly encounter Christ until later in life, when she was already a wife, a mother of three, and an established romance novelist.

Shortly after becoming a born-again Christian in 1986, Francine wrote *Redeeming Love* as her statement of faith. First published by Bantam Books, and then rereleased by Multnomah Publishers in the mid-1990s, this retelling of the biblical story of Gomer and Hosea, set during the time of the California Gold Rush, is now considered by many to be a classic work of Christian fiction. *Redeeming Love* continues to be one of CBA's top-selling titles, and it has held a spot on the Christian bestseller list for nearly a decade.

Since *Redeeming Love*, Francine has published numerous novels with Christian themes—all bestsellers—and she has continued to win both industry acclaim and reader loyalty around the globe. Her Christian novels have been awarded or nominated for numerous honors, including the RITA Award, the Christy Award, the ECPA Gold Medallion, and the Holt Medallion in Honor of Outstanding Literary Talent. In 1997, after winning her third RITA Award for inspirational fiction,

Francine was inducted into the Romance Writers of America Hall of Fame. Francine's novels have been translated into more than twenty different languages, and she enjoys bestseller status in many countries, including Germany, the Netherlands, and South Africa.

Francine and her husband, Rick, live in northern California and enjoy time spent with their three grown children and taking every opportunity to spoil their grandchildren. Francine uses her writing to draw closer to the Lord, and she desires that through her work she might worship and praise Jesus for all He has done and is doing in her life.

Visit her website at www.francinerivers.com.

BOOKS BY BELOVED AUTHOR
FRANCINE RIVERS

The Mark of the Lion series
(available individually or in a collection)
A Voice in the Wind
An Echo in the Darkness
As Sure as the Dawn

A Lineage of Grace series
(available individually or in an anthology)
Unveiled
Unashamed
Unshaken
Unspoken
Unafraid

Sons of Encouragement series
(available individually or in an anthology)
The Priest
The Warrior
The Prince
The Prophet
The Scribe

Marta's Legacy series
(available individually or in a collection)
Her Mother's Hope
Her Daughter's Dream

Children's Titles
Bible Stories for Growing Kids
  (coauthored with Shannon
  Rivers Coibion)

Stand-alone Titles
Redeeming Love
The Atonement Child
The Scarlet Thread
The Last Sin Eater
Leota's Garden
And the Shofar Blew
The Shoe Box (a Christmas novella)

www.francinerivers.com

CP0098

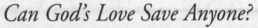